The
BACHELOR BETRAYAL

THE SECRETS, SCANDALS, AND SPIES SERIES

The
BACHELOR
BETRAYAL

<svg>◦◦</svg> THE SECRETS, SCANDALS, AND SPIES SERIES <svg>◦◦</svg>

RUBY® AWARD–WINNING AUTHOR
MADDISON MICHAELS

Entangled Publishing, LLC
10940 S Parker Rd
Suite 327
Parker, CO 80134
rights@entangledpublishing.com

Amara is an imprint of Entangled Publishing, LLC.

Edited by Alethea Spiridon and Stacy Abrams
Cover design by Bree Archer
Cover images from Chris Cocozza
fotoVoyager/Getty Images

ISBN 978-1-64937-322-9

Manufactured in the United States of America

First Edition February 2022

I dedicate this book to my amazing sister, Jordanha, who is not only a remarkable woman and super talented photographer, but is also the very best sister a girl could ever have! I love you sis, and I'm truly so blessed and grateful to have you in my life xox

Chapter One

The shrill hiss of steam bellowing from the train's engine should have masked the sound of the dagger sliding from its sheath, but Lady Kaitlyn Montrose heard the crisp scrape of steel against leather with an intimate brush of familiarity.

Thrusting the document she'd just retrieved into her bodice, Kat twisted to the side as a blade whistled past her and lodged with a thud into the wood paneling of the baggage carriage, barely a foot away from her head.

Spinning around, she found two men blocking the exit through to the other compartments. Both were dressed in rather nondescript brown clothing with scuffed black boots and an inch of dirt caked under their nails. The first was short and stocky, with the meaty fists and squashed nose of a pugilist, and an empty knife sheath hanging from his belt. The dagger thrower, she guessed. The second was tall and lanky, with the bulge near the waist of his jacket suggesting he had a revolver tucked underneath.

The men were a complication.

"Did you miss on purpose?" Kat asked, her eyes flicking to the dagger before returning to the knife thrower. "Or do you have a terrible aim?"

The man blinked and an expression of what could only be disbelief crossed his features. "What the hell did ya just say?"

Kaitlyn sighed. "Are you hard of hearing, too?" She knew saying such a thing would enrage them, but if she was going to have to fight her way out of the small space, then she may as well agitate them.

"Hard of hearing?" the man exclaimed, his whole body jerking like a bull spotting a red flag. He twisted his head over toward his companion. "Ernie, did ya hear what I heard? Did she criticize my aim and then me hearing?"

The second man rubbed his chin, confusion flaring in his long, thin face. "I reckon she did, Tommo."

"The man who 'ired us said ya was odd, but he didn't mention ya were stupid," the one called Tommo said, his eyes narrowing upon Kat as his face turned a mottled shade of red.

"Someone hired you?" Kat leaned forward on the balls of her feet, ready to launch at them if necessary. "I hope for their sake you give refunds for a job poorly executed."

Tommo's jaw clenched tightly in unison with his

fists. "I don't think you're properly understanding this situation, love." The man cracked his knuckles. "'Cause ya should be scared instead of mouthing off. Now, give me the bloody letter."

So that's what they were after. "That will not be happening," Kat replied, her lips twisting into a grim smile.

The one called Ernie stepped forward, his hand hovering close to the revolver tucked into his trousers. "Hand over the missive, and we won't hurt ya. Promise."

Kat could hear the lie in his words. "As I have already said, I shall have to decline." She hadn't spent the better part of a week chasing down this little gem of information to hand it over to these two. "You're very welcome to *try* to retrieve it from me, though I'd warn against it, for both your sakes."

"What's wrong with her?" Ernie directed his question to Tommo. "Is her brain addled or somefink, 'cause she's a redhead?"

"Maybe she needs some sense knocked into that pretty little head of hers." Tommo looked her up and down, a calculating expression in his eyes as they came to rest on her neckline. "No one will hear ya scream from back here, me lady."

They'd just disparaged her hair color and now they were threatening to abuse her? Well, enough was enough. Kat reached across and wrenched the dagger from the wall, and before the men could even blink, she flicked it with precision, aiming it directly at Ernie's shooting hand. It hit its mark, slicing through his palm and lodging deeply in his flesh, blood spilling from the wound. The man glanced down at the dagger before screaming and fainting to the floor.

Tommo peered down at his fallen companion, a glimmer of uncertainty flickering in his eyes as they lingered over the second man's wound. But then he leaned down and twisted the dagger out of his friend's palm. Confidence now replaced the uncertainty in his gaze. "Whatcha gonna do now, love? I got the dagger, and ya ain't got another one to throw."

He was right, she didn't. She could have used her derringer on him, but that would be a waste of a perfectly good bullet, so she rushed at him, closing the gap and catching him by surprise. He waved the knife wildly, but Kat raised her left arm, blocking his swing and catching his wrist in midair. Propelling her forehead sharply forward, she head-butted him in the nose. His head snapped back and the dagger in his hand clattered to the ground.

Blood gushed from his nose and his beady black eyes held hers. "Ya gonna pay for that, ya little bitch!"

"You, sir, are rude." Kat raised her elbow, and with a quick slicing motion struck him across the windpipe. He clutched at his throat and gasped for breath.

She shoved him backward into the wall of the carriage, then swiftly picked up the fallen dagger. As he tried to right himself, still laboring to take a proper breath, Kat stepped forward and slammed the hilt of the dagger into his temple. He crumpled into a heap on the floor and was still.

"There. That will teach you some manners." Taking a deep breath, she swiveled to the other one. He appeared to still be unconscious.

The train began to slow as it neared New Cross Station, the last stop before London. Kat unlatched the side door on the right, facing away from the platform, and dragged the first man and then the other over to the door. When the train came to a halt at the platform, she pushed them out of the carriage and into the hedges lining the tracks. Both moaned slightly as they landed in the bushes, though they didn't awaken. Kat rolled the side door closed, just as the opposite door was unlatched and someone slid it open.

Without glancing back, she strode from the baggage compartment and down the corridor of the train. She focused on calming her breathing and her heart rate. The rush of energy in her body was fading and she knew from experience she'd soon be feeling tired and longing for a good cup of tea.

The conductor's whistle shrilled loudly and a moment later the train chugged toward its final destination, London. Stopping at the door to her uncle's private compartment, she smoothed back some of her wayward strands of hair which had come loose during the encounter. A quick glance at her reflection in the carriage's window satisfied her that she looked presentable enough. She pushed open the door and stepped inside the compartment.

Victor Montrose lowered his newspaper a fraction and peered at her, his eyes tightening slightly at the corners. "Trouble?"

"Two men decided to bother me. Nothing I could not handle, Uncle." Kat closed the door and twisted the lock with a flick of her wrist. Taking a seat opposite him, she relaxed onto the red velveteen cushions and smoothed out the folds of her sapphire skirt. "Why do you ask?"

Victor looked pointedly at her left shoulder. "Your dress has a small slash in it, my dear. It didn't penetrate through to your skin, did it?"

Annoyance flashed through Kat as she looked at the torn fabric. "No. But Madame Arnout is going to kill me." The French seamstress took great pride in her unique creations, so much so that Kat thought the woman fancied each outfit a child of some sort. The seamstress wouldn't like to hear that one of her babies required fixing, again.

"She shall be annoyed only briefly." Victor's

lips twitched as he settled back against his own seat. "Madame Arnout is nothing if not a clever businesswoman who charges me an inordinate amount of money to either fix or replace your special dresses. Perhaps next time, though, you might move quicker? I thought I'd trained you better."

Kat felt a knot of annoyance in her belly. As much as she disliked the reprimand, her uncle was correct—she should have moved quicker. Next time she would. "At least the protective layer below the silk is intact."

Victor nodded, his eyes keenly assessing the incision. "Yes. The special knots and weaves of the cotton create a slash-proof layer, as the good Madame said they would."

"She's also designing me some special detachable skirts, which will allow me to fight more effectively."

"You will, of course, wear trousers underneath, won't you?"

Kat nearly rolled her eyes. Her uncle had spent the past twenty years training her in all manner of weapons, hand-to-hand combat, and a great many other skills never taught to a child, let alone a girl, and he was worried about her wearing trousers underneath? "I shall, Uncle. Though surely you're aware my undergarments do cover my entire legs from my ankles up?"

This time it was her uncle that rolled his eyes.

"Yes, I am aware of that. Though black trousers will blend into the night much better then cream pantaloons. Oh, and do your old uncle a favor, would you, my dear? Please, no more mention of undergarments in my presence. I am progressive, but not enough to discuss such subjects with my niece." His voice held a hint of amusement in its rich depths.

Kat grinned in spite of herself. There was nothing old about her uncle. In his late fifties, he was fitter than most men half his age, and even though his hair was laced with more silver than black he still turned many a lady's head, much to her aunt Daisy's annoyance.

Noticing that the train was slowing, she stood and reached for her valise from the overhead rack, retrieving her black leather knife roll from the bag's depths. Sitting back down, she unrolled it out onto the empty seat beside her, the selection of sharpened daggers glinting in the afternoon sunlight.

"You weren't armed when you faced those men?" Victor asked, his tone stern.

"You are the one who ensured that I am perfectly capable of defending myself without the need of a weapon." The endless hours of training every day since she was four years old were testament to that.

"I also taught you to never be caught without a weapon on your person." His voice cracked like a whip. "Particularly in the confined spaces of a train."

Without warning, Victor lunged forward, drawing his own dagger and pushing her farther back into the chair. He pressed the blade against her throat.

"To not have a weapon in such a constricted area is the height of stupidity." His voice was harsh. "Have I not always taught you to expect the unexpected? Not doing so will get you killed like your mother!"

"Who says I am not armed, Uncle?" Kat cocked the hammer of her derringer and pressed it into his stomach. "You did teach me better than that."

A glint of pride flashed in his eyes as he drew back his blade and re-sheathed it in the custom-made retractable holder hidden up his right sleeve. "Good. I would hate to think all those years of training were a waste. Yet you didn't use it on the men who accosted you."

"They weren't worth wasting a bullet on." She returned her derringer to her pocket, then selected her favorite dagger, a mix of silver embedded with some small rubies, and the first knife her uncle had given to her, for her eighth birthday. She pocketed it too before returning her knife roll to her valise.

Victor retrieved his own bag from the rack above, as the train came to a stop.

Pulling back the curtain to the window, she

glanced through the glass to the platform. "No one is here yet." She'd been expecting to see her aunt and seven-year-old cousin Samuel, along with a retinue of servants, waiting at the platform to meet them.

"I daresay the carriage is caught up in traffic." Her uncle opened the exterior door to their compartment and glanced in both directions before stepping down the few steps onto the bustling platform. "You know how dreadful it is trying to travel through Westminster at this hour of the day. Besides, my wife is never on time for anything."

Kat draped her shawl over her dress before she followed him down. Her uncle was correct; Daisy was always running late.

Victor's brow furrowed as he looked up and down the station while he placed his valise on the ground next to Kat. "I'll go see if I can spot them from the top platform, and if not, I'll rustle up some porters to assist with our luggage once it's unloaded. Then at least we shall be ready to go when our carriage arrives."

She nodded, watching as he strode down the platform, purposeful and dignified as one would expect from the Earl of Harrow. The other gentlemen he passed inclined their hats toward him in acknowledgment and the ladies turned and regarded him with undisguised appreciation, with several purposefully brushing against him as they walked past.

Even though Victor was married and finally well and truly off the marriage mart, women still clamored for his attention. The folly some women engaged in trying to attract a man's attention really was an embarrassment to her entire gender.

Her gaze returned to the carriage as one of the train's porters began unloading their suitcases and bags from the compartment. Kat motioned for him to put them down, then thanked him as he completed his task.

The bustling noises from the station went unnaturally silent for a moment, before several piercing screams ripped through the afternoon breeze, echoing shrilly across the platform.

Kat turned her head toward the sounds, the hairs on her arms standing on end as a chill of dread gripped her. Up ahead, men and women were frozen in shock, looking down at a man lying still on the ground.

Blood rushed to her head as whispers of her uncle's name reached her ears.

Not her uncle. Please, God, no. He couldn't be taken away from her. With a hoarse cry she didn't even realize came from her own mouth, Kat took off running toward him.

She pushed aside the statues of bodies blocking her path until she was crouching down beside him. His shirt was covered in blood; a dark crimson mess, spreading quickly across the once pristine white cloth. His breathing was shallow and he looked deathly pale.

"Someone get a doctor!" she yelled frantically to the onlookers, before yanking off her shawl and balling it up. "It's all right, Uncle." She tried to sound confident, despite the lump in her throat, as she pressed the material tight against what looked to be a stab wound very close to his heart. "You're going to be fine."

"Should have seen it coming. Stupid of me," he whispered. "The Chameleon caught me off guard."

"But that's not possible," Kat whispered. "The traitor's in Europe. The missives all say so."

Victor shook his head, pain mingled with sadness etched on his face. "Said 'The Chameleon sends his regards.' Stupid of me to underestimate—"

"Shh, Uncle, you must save your strength," Kat said, unable to stop the tears from streaming down her face.

He coughed and Kat felt her shawl soak through with his blood. "Have to tell you before it's too late—"

"Don't talk like that!" She pressed down harder against the wound, all but willing her strength into him.

"No, I must," he said, wheezing. "Should have told you long ago but couldn't bear the thought of you thinking ill of me."

"I could never think ill of you. But whatever it is, you can tell me later. You must save your strength."

He smiled softly. "We both know what a mortal wound looks like."

"You cannot leave me." Kat willed all the strength she had into her voice. "Do you hear me? I will not let you die! You must fight."

He coughed again, this time more heavily. "Least I...get to say...goodbye. An inch to the left...and I'd already...be dead." He breathed in a jagged breath, barely able to take in any air. "Still will...do its job."

"No! You will not die, do you hear me!" Kat yelled at him as she pressed down even harder against the wound. *Please, God, please don't take him away.*

"No time to...waste," he rasped, before reaching into his trouser pocket and pulling out a brass key. "Wanted...to tell you...so many...times before."

"Tell me what?" She swiped at the tears clouding her vision.

"Take the key," he urged, pushing it into her hand. "It opens...my safe. Inside... Should have told you sooner."

"Uncle, please, you must fight! You can't leave me."

He smiled softly as he held on to her hand,

his grip feeble. "My brave Kat...always been so proud...of you."

She sobbed as she leaned over and kissed his cheek. "I love you, Uncle Victor. Please don't leave me. I do not know what to do without you..."

"Of course you do. You are a Montrose... I have trained you well." His voice was like steel for a brief moment, before he coughed and the strength drained out of him. "Take care of Sam and Daisy...they're not strong like you."

Kat nodded. "I will, Uncle. I promise."

He smiled again, his eyes unwavering as he looked up at her. He squeezed her hand, though there was little strength left. "Remember...I love you, my darling girl."

His hand went limp in her own as the vacant look of death settled across his eyes.

Kat shook her head. He could not be gone. He was too strong, too stubborn. But as she continued staring at his unblinking gaze, she realized that he was. That an assassin, known only as the Chameleon, had taken him away from her.

Kat felt a bottomless chill settle into the deepest part of her soul. She gripped her uncle's cold hand tighter and leaned down to his ear. "The Chameleon will rue this day, Uncle," she whispered. "There will be nowhere he can run, nowhere he can hide. I promise you, he will bleed as you have, before I send him to meet his maker in Hell."

Chapter Two

Kat swung the grappling hook high into the fog-shrouded air and heard the ting of steel striking stone as the hook's claws latched firmly onto the first-floor balcony railing of the Viscount of Somerville's residence.

Gripping the attached rope with her gloved hands, she began climbing up the stone wall, her leather boots and trouser-clad legs easily finding purchase along the stone grooves, assisting in her ascent.

Garbed in the usual black outfit she wore for her clandestine activities, Kat was glad for the warmth the mask and cape provided against the chill night air, along with the anonymity of both her identity and gender that the trousers and shirt allowed.

She reached the top railing and gripped the ledge. Swinging her body over it, the balls of her feet landed softly on the stone floor of the upstairs terrace. The terrace and house appeared dark and soundless, the thick layer of fog below nicely masking all sounds.

Looking to her left, she counted two doors down to where the French glass doors led into Lord Somerville's bedroom. If all had gone according to plan, her informant should have left them unlatched. But Kaitlyn was never one to trust things to go according to plan, not in her particular vocation. Which was why she never went anywhere without the trusty weight of her lockpick set settled comfortably in her trouser pocket. That and her daggers, of course. One never knew when either would be required.

Without a sound, she strode across the balcony and stopped near the entrance to Somerville's bedroom. The thick drapes were closed across the glass, obscuring her view into the space. Pausing for a moment, she listened for any sounds coming from within, but heard nothing. Carefully, she reached out and turned the door handle. It opened effortlessly.

Silence continued to greet her, so she stepped into the room and left the glass door ajar, ensuring her escape route was easily accessible if needed. Glancing around the barren bedchamber, Kat's eyes drifted across the ancient mahogany bedframe standing like a giant sentinel in the middle of the room. Thick blue drapes hung from the canopy above it, tied haphazardly to each wooden post by a crimson satin sash. A thick layer of dust covered the duvet and what little bedroom furniture was in the musky room.

Clearly, Lord Somerville didn't care to let his servants into his bedchamber often, or else his eyesight had deteriorated to the point of gross inattention. But she suspected it was the former, particularly if what her informant said was true. The man was paranoid to the point of madness, which was probably correct. After all, those who dabbled in blackmail did tend to live rather shortened lives.

Kat spied the painting her informant had mentioned, a bland watercolor hanging almost forgetfully above the mantel, looking about as dilapidated as the rest of the room. She stalked over to it and felt along its edges until her fingers ran over a small button on the underside of the right hand of the frame. When she pressed it, the painting gently swung open from the left side to reveal a wall safe concealed behind, just as her informant said it would.

Assessing the black iron panel of the safe in front of her, she found her interest piqued. Lord Somerville had invested in a safe made by the American company *Day and Newell*. A safe even more secure than its English counterparts, and nearly impossible to open without its custom cut key. Nearly, but not completely. And there wasn't a speck of dust on the thing.

For an old recluse, Somerville obviously had items inside the safe that he was willing to spend a great deal of money to protect and look after, having purchased the best safe money could buy. And if one of those items was a journal mentioning the Chameleon, as she hoped it would be, then she could understand his investment in such a fortified safe.

Fortunately, Kat was a believer in being prepared for any possibility and her investment in private lessons with the world's foremost lockpicking master, the American Mr. Hobbs, would now pay off. The man had, after all, worked for *Day and Newell* and designed the very safe in front of her.

A small smile tilted the corners of her mouth upward as anticipation coursed through her at the thought of cracking open the lock. It was one of her most favorite pastimes. Pulling her small leather lockpicking kit from her pocket, Kat selected the two most appropriate picks and slid them into the barrel; one at the bottom, the other at the top. She began raking the top one carefully backward and forward against the pin tumblers within the casing, adjusting the torque on the pick at the bottom of the lock as she did so.

It took her slightly longer than she had planned, closer to three minutes she would guess, but gradually the tumblers fell into place as she continued to rake the top pick against them, while placing a gentle amount of torque on the bottom one. With a final twist of the bottom pick, the lock made a distinct clicking sound as it twisted open. A sound Kat always found satisfying.

Twisting the handle on the safe, she pulled it open, and there, nestled on the bottom level, was a brown leather-bound journal. Disregarding the other assorted items in the safe, Kat reached in and pulled it out, before flipping through the pages and briefly scanning the contents. Her fingers clenched around the leather when she read the words "my Chameleon" scrawled across several pages.

"I'm afraid that's not yours to take," a deep voice rumbled from behind her.

Kat snapped the journal closed and whirled around. A man stood in front of the now fully opened glass doors, his face concealed by the room's shadows. He was tall and broad-shouldered, and his voice was that of a gentleman, but certainly not that of old Lord Sommerville. He was also strategically blocking her only exit. *How had she not heard him?* A man of his size should have made ample noise to alert her to his presence. *Sloppy work, Kaitlyn. Very sloppy, indeed.*

"A masked bandit. How interesting." He sounded somewhat amused as he took a few steps into the room, his eyes taking in the entire space in a glance.

Kat gasped as the shadows receded from his face. Standing there, his six-foot-four-inch frame engulfing the doorway, was Marcus Black, the Earl of Westwood. Her uncle's most favorite protégé.

He looked harder and fiercer than when she saw him last, when she'd only been a girl of fourteen, and there was an air of grim purpose and danger surrounding him like a second skin. And even now, after all these years, he had the power to unsettle her completely. She was loathed to find herself still attracted to him, her body clenching in recognition and longing as her gaze locked with his.

The young man she'd known was gone. His eyes were different now; they no longer held the laughter and hope they once did. Instead, they were filled with unflinching and impenetrable blue steel.

And no wonder. In the intervening years since she'd last seen him, the man's wife was brutally slain, and his brother, Nathaniel, who Kat had trained with for several years after returning from the ladies' school, had been branded a traitor and then killed in an explosion in Paris.

Each time she thought of Nathaniel, a deep sadness filled her. He'd been like a brother to her in some respects, though she doubted Marcus even knew that she and Nathaniel had trained together. By the time they did so, Marcus was already living in Europe with his new wife, conducting various missions on behalf of the government.

"Now be a good chap and put the journal on the bed," he said. There was no threat in his voice. There didn't have to be. His calm, autocratic demeanor and crisp diction were all that was needed to convey the fact that the man was used to being obeyed.

Kat weighed up her options. He thought her a man, which was good as she certainly didn't want him to know who she was, particularly since after all this time she had no idea if she could trust him or not. And if he was after the journal, too, it meant one of only two things: he was also hunting the Chameleon, or he was the Chameleon.

The latter made her stomach churn, though she doubted it, although nothing would surprise her anymore. Not after Victor's last secret had tilted her world on its axis. One she still hadn't righted herself from.

"It ain't yours, either," she said, disguising her voice with the deepest cockney accent she could muster as she tucked the journal into the pocket of her jacket.

Marcus smiled though the sentiment didn't reach his eyes. "The item may be in Somerville's safe, but in point of fact, it is mine. It belonged to my late wife."

Kat felt a moment's hesitation. "Your wife?" She'd heard about the late and beautiful Countess of Westwood, a woman Marcus had apparently been besotted with.

Taking another step closer to her, Marcus's footfalls were surprisingly silent for a man of his size. At least now, Kat didn't feel so incompetent about not hearing his approach. "Yes, my wife's. As you can see, it does indeed belong to me."

Well, if he was being truthful, then he was correct in that regard. But Kat had hunted the Chameleon for too long to simply relinquish possibly the best lead she'd ever had to find the assassin. She couldn't let the fiend slip through her fingers any longer. And she would fight Marcus to ensure that didn't happen, if she had to.

"I suggest you hand it over now. Otherwise, I will take it from you."

There was a silent promise in the depths of his eyes and an unflinching pledge in his words. This was a man who would intimidate most people, but not Kat. She'd been trained as well as he had, and she knew that under the hardness, there was an honorable man, or at least there had been. "You can try to," she said.

For a moment, it looked like Marcus was amused, but then he sighed. "Must we really do this dance?"

"It seems so." She assessed her exit options, as he was clearly going to try to prevent her from leaving with it. "I warn you though, *dancing* with me will be perilous."

"Consider me warned," he drawled.

Kat saw the intention in his eyes a moment before he lunged for her. She dove toward the floor and tucked into a tight ball, rolling forward and then back onto her feet, just behind where he'd been standing.

He anticipated her move and pivoted, grabbing ahold of her arm. "You're fast, I'll give you that."

Kat twisted her body back toward him and struck him in the chest with her other arm.

He grunted as he was forced back a step, his hand losing its grip on her arm. She twisted to the side and aimed a spinning kick at his chest. He blocked her leg with his left forearm and used his own leg to swing out to strike her.

She managed to avert the full force of his attack using a block of her own, followed by a strike with the back of her arm. Deflecting her, he matched her strikes and blocks as they fought each other, parrying back and forth across the room.

He'd been taught well by her uncle. Kat generally prided herself on her ability to outfight any man, but she was no fool and was loath to admit that Marcus's size and strength were difficult to combat, even for a woman with her height and skills. The very thought she might be bested was surprisingly thrilling, for no man had truly been able to challenge her before. But Marcus could.

Kat cursed when she realized he was maneuvering her close to the wall, where there would be little room left for her to strike. Knowing she would have to resort to another tactic, she paused in her strikes, allowing him to grab hold of her arms and pin her to the wall so she was trapped, his frame pressed hard against her own.

She could feel the strength of him leaning into the soft curves of her body and unexpectedly her breath quickened. His chest was so broad and his muscles so hard, that it made it difficult to ignore the heat and masculinity radiating from him.

His shocked eyes peered down into hers. "You're a woman?"

"Hello, Marcus." Kat smiled up at him through her mask, trying to ignore the ripple of awareness radiating down through to her center, acutely aware of her femininity against his masculinity. "I wish I could say it was nice to see you again after all these years..." She shrugged. "But in the circumstances, I'm not so sure."

It took a moment for him to recognize her voice. "Lady Kaitlyn?"

He relaxed his grip a fraction, though he still did not release her. Instead, he pulled her hands above her head and switched his grip so her wrists were pinned by only one of his hands.

Her breasts were unintentionally pressed farther into his chest, while he removed her mask, and Kaitlyn couldn't help but gasp at the contact.

She heard his swift intake of breath as he scrutinized her face. For a moment, she wondered what he was thinking, but his gaze gave little away.

"You've grown up." His voice was thick, and she could see his jaw clenching. Probably in annoyance, as that had always been an easy emotion to rouse in him when she was a girl. She had enjoyed poking fun at him, after all.

"Twelve years does tend to age a person," she replied. Although, instead of looking aged, Marcus simply appeared more dangerous and harder than he had before. Compelling, in fact, to the point where she found herself slightly breathless, and Kat didn't get breathless for any man.

His eyes narrowed rather treacherously. "What the bloody hell are you doing here?"

"Is it not obvious?" she all but purred, as she tried to return her thoughts to the task at hand. "I've come to retrieve this journal."

"Damn it! I could have hurt you, you foolish woman." His face was mere inches from her own, and she could see small flecks of grey mingling with the blue in his eyes. She'd never been close enough to him before to notice such an intriguing thing.

For a brief moment, Kat found herself slightly mesmerized by the intensity of his stare and the woody scent of his cologne as it engulfed her nostrils. It was a scent of sandalwood and something else she couldn't quite identify. She gave herself a mental shake. *Stay focused, Kaitlyn.* She couldn't allow herself to be distracted, even if this man was making her feel more like a woman than she ever had.

"So," he demanded, "what do you have to say for yourself?"

"That I am truly sorry for what's coming next." And she was, but she could see no other solution to the situation. She had to get away from him, and away from the unfamiliar sensations he stirred up inside her.

Before he could formulate an answer, Kat lifted her right knee up as hard as she could toward the junction between his thighs. Marcus swore when her knee connected fully with his body and then he grunted as pain overtook him and he crumpled to the floor.

Kat stood there for a second, panting from the exertion as she looked down at his face. "I'm sorry, Marcus. Normally, I do try to fight fair, but against a man of your size and experience, a woman must use every weapon at her disposal." Belatedly, she realized she was still calling him by his first name, a habit she'd formed as a girl. She hurried around him to the balcony door. She had definitely overstayed her welcome.

"Damn it! Get back here," he choked out, still

writing on the rug in the middle of the room.

"After I obtain what I need from the journal, I will return it to you." And next time, she'd have these foreign feelings of attraction firmly in check. She looked at him one last time before turning and sprinting out of the door and across the balcony to where she'd left the grappling hook. Swinging herself over the balustrade, Kat gripped the rope and slid to the ground, her feet landing gently in the shrubs.

Seeing Marcus again after all of these years had shaken her greatly, which had to have been the reason she'd been stupid enough to allow him to maneuver her toward the wall in the first place. She'd never permitted such a thing to occur before. It was highly disconcerting. As was the fact that her body seemed to mold against his to perfection, sending a fluttering of awareness through her.

And she never fluttered for any man. In fact, she'd always had little patience for a woman claiming to have succumbed to a man's charms, yet when confronted by the Earl of Westwood, that very thing had nearly occurred with her. It was unacceptable, and she would not let it happen again.

Kat flicked the rope up, and the steel hooks lifted from the balcony railing before dropping to the ground next to her. Gathering up the equipment, she stuffed the items into the bag she'd left by the shrubs. Kat frowned when she noticed her hands were trembling a little. No man had ever made her tremble before. She didn't like it one bit.

She was trained to be better than this. Victor would have expected more. She couldn't let any awareness of Marcus's allure distract her again.

"I will find you, Lady Kaitlyn, make no mistake about that," Marcus said from above. "And I will retrieve that journal from you."

Kat stifled her gasp and looked up to see him staring down at her from the edge of the balcony, his blue eyes filled with determination. He'd recovered sooner than she'd expected. Not surprising, though. Marcus had always been stronger than an ox. "You can try," she stated, picking up her bag. "Though I don't like your chances. At least, not unless I wish to give it to you." She had to portray an air of nonchalance, for if the man sensed any weakness, he would pounce. It's what they'd both been trained to do.

"I'm serious, Kaitlyn," he said. "This is no jest. I will come for you and I will take the journal."

There was a dark promise in his words. And rather than fear, Kat felt exhilarated. But then the reality of the situation intruded and she found herself wondering if the honorable man she once knew was gone. A lot could change a person over the years, and where once there was hope, too easily it could be replaced by the dark shadow of vengeance. That she knew only too well.

"This is no jest for me, either," she replied. "And I'll give you the journal once I'm done with it, providing it does not implicate you as having anything to do with Victor's murder. Because if it does, then I promise you, you will have no need to look for me, for it will be I who will come for you." She pivoted, and without looking back she strode through the grounds of the back of Somerville's townhouse to where her carriage waited. The dark promise in Marcus's words and the intensity of his gaze were fixed firmly in her mind.

The man would not give up, of that she was certain. And the thought thrilled her as nothing else had in a long time.

Chapter Three

Marcus strode through the door into his townhouse and ripped off his gloves. "God damn it," he swore aloud, as the night's events continued to replay in his head, regardless of how he tried to put a stop to them.

How could he have been so thrown off his game that he allowed Kaitlyn Montrose to best him and take the damn item he'd hunted for months? Because he'd been too bloody well distracted by the fierce attraction he'd felt toward her, and that distraction had cost him the journal. "Stupid. Absolutely stupid." Marcus strode over to the entry table.

"My lord, is everything all right?" Crawley, his butler, stepped out from the adjoining hallway, an expression of mild concern on his normally austere face.

And who could blame the man? Though Crawley was used to Marcus's unpredictable and, at times, odd behavior, it wasn't often Marcus would come storming home, blaspheming and chastising himself. No wonder the unflappable Crawley looked somewhat flapped.

"No, unfortunately, Crawley, everything is not all right." A large sigh left Marcus's lips, and he took a moment to rein in his annoyance with himself before flinging his gloves on the table. He had to calm down and approach the situation involving Lady Kaitlyn Montrose with logic, even if he couldn't stop thinking about her curves pressing against him. "Send someone to Lord Cantfield's residence and have him fetched here, immediately."

"The Marquis of Cantfield is already here in your study, my lord."

"Of course he is," Marcus muttered, turning on his heel and heading down the hall to his solitary sanctuary, which had of late become Cantfield's sanctuary, too, it seemed. Handy in this instance, as he had a job for his friend.

"He is happily availing himself of some of Cook's fare," Crawley added as he hurried to follow Marcus down the hall. "Shall I ask Cook to prepare you something, too?"

"No, I'm fine. Thank you, Crawley." Marcus halted at the door to his study, dismissing Crawley with a nod, before swinging the door wide open. Sure enough, his friend Lucas Devereux, the Marquis of Cantfield and future Duke of Carlisle, was comfortably lounged in one of the armchairs by the crackling hearth, *The Times* in his lap, and a plate of cold meats and cheese on the table next to him.

"Glad you're making yourself comfortable," Marcus remarked, striding over to the side table and pouring himself a stiff whisky. He lifted the glass and took a healthy swallow of the smooth amber liquid, though it did nothing to quell the sense of annoyance still coursing through him from the botched evening.

"I take it things did not go as planned?" Cantfield asked from across the room.

Marcus turned to his friend, who'd made a quasi-second home in Marcus's residence, claiming that, apart from their club, this was the only place he was able to get a measure of peace and quiet away from his gaggle of four younger sisters, a younger brother, and his parents.

Marcus approached the fireplace and took a seat in the chair beside his friend. "No. Not a damn thing went to plan tonight." A red-haired vixen saw to that.

"How odd," Cantfield said, looking somewhat baffled. "Our intelligence suggested the journal was in Somerville's safe, but perhaps he moved it earlier in the day?"

"The intelligence was correct. The journal was there." He still couldn't believe he had let it slip through his fingers. He hadn't let a woman distract him in years and yet Lady Kaitlyn had done so, effortlessly. "Somebody got to it before I did."

"It was gone when you got there? That's bloody bad luck."

Leaning forward, Marcus watched the flames dance in the hearth, unable to forget the vivid emerald of Lady Kaitlyn's eyes when he'd pulled off her mask, and how his entire body had tightened in response. She'd grown from a tall and gangly young girl into what could only be described as a stunning woman. A woman he'd wanted to cart over his shoulder and whisk away to his bed. "I arrived just as the journal was being taken out of the safe."

"And you let the fellow simply take it? I suppose you must have had a reas—"

"Dammit, I didn't let her simply take it!" Marcus raked a hand through his hair. "We fought and I lost."

Cantfield nearly choked on the cracker he'd just popped into his mouth. "Her? You fought a female? And she *bested* you?"

Marcus scowled into the flames. "It wasn't just any female. It was Victor's niece."

There was complete silence for a moment.

"Oh…" Cantfield took a sip of his drink. "Well, Lady Kaitlyn is not just any woman, is she? I must say that with her background and the training Victor demanded of her, I'm not all that surprised the Ice Maiden bested you."

"The Ice Maiden?" He'd not heard any lady

called that, though he had been out of the country for the better part of three years trying to hunt the Chameleon in what had so far proved to be a fruitless endeavor.

"God, yes." Cantfield seemed eager to fill him in. "Her reputation precedes her amongst the gentlemen. It's why I haven't sought a proper introduction to her yet."

"A beautiful woman you are yet to be introduced to?" Marcus replied. "What on earth is the world coming to?"

"I do have a reputation to protect." Lucas grinned. It was well-known that Cantfield prided himself on his success with the ladies, and considering his good looks and status as the heir to a dukedom, it was only to be expected.

"Lady Kaitlyn is stunning," Lucas continued. "Yet, why would I wish to jeopardize my reputation with a woman who herself is reputed to freeze a man's ardor with a mere glare, while flaying him alive with her tongue? A shame, really. A woman's tongue should be used for far better purposes."

Marcus's scowl deepened. Her gaze certainly hadn't frozen his ardor. Quite the opposite. "I thought you braver than that."

"Not when it comes to the fairer sex. I live with too many of them to forget how fearsome they can be under their veneer of elegance and beauty." Cantfield stretched his long legs out in front of him. "I must say, I'm surprised you fought her in the first place. You don't normally fight women... Even someone as well-trained as you and I both know she is."

"I didn't know it was her at first, or that it was even a woman for that matter," Marcus replied. He'd been so focused on getting Elizabeth's journal, he hadn't paid attention to the details—to his detriment. "All I saw was a figure dressed in black trousers and a cape, scaling a rope up the side of Somerville's residence. And in my own defense, what woman does that? Let alone a lady?"

"Victor's niece, obviously." Cantfield appeared to be rather enjoying the whole tale. "Though you're normally very observant. I would have thought you'd have deduced the person was a woman. Granted, Lady Kaitlyn is tall for a female, but she has an undeniably delightful figure. *That* I have definitely appreciated from afar."

"The cape covered most of her. And, damn it, don't talk about appreciating her figure. She's Victor's niece, and despite being an obvious hellion, you will show her respect." Marcus needed to remember that himself because, try as he might, he couldn't forget the moment he'd flattened himself against her slender frame and felt the soft swell of her breasts pressing into his chest, while the scent of roses and peppermint had enveloped him. "I still can't believe I let her rattle me to the point of inattention."

"Rattle you? The impenetrable Earl of Westwood?" Cantfield's deep laugh ricocheted through the room. "I should bloody well have enjoyed seeing that."

"It wasn't amusing." Even if he'd found himself more attracted to her in that short space of time than he'd been to any other woman, including his late wife, Elizabeth.

Thinking of Elizabeth always brought back the final image he had of her, of walking into her bedchamber and seeing her lifeless body, tangled amongst the blood-soaked sheets of her bed. The pale, almost translucent porcelain of her skin, a stark contrast to the deep crimson pooling around her. It was an image he couldn't forget. And no matter how unfaithful she'd been, no one deserved to die like that.

Cantfield's laughter brought him back to the present with a jolt.

"Oh, this is brilliant!" Cantfield said. "Though I'm curious to know how the lady bested you?"

"How do you think a woman can physically best a man?" came Marcus's droll reply. He could still feel the searing pain and incapacitation her knee had caused.

Cantfield's laughter stopped for a moment while his eyes narrowed in thought, then he hunched over as his body was once again racked by mirth. "Oh, my Lord, she kneed you in the bollocks, didn't she?"

Marcus nodded. "Yes. And I'm glad you find it funny, for I do not."

"Funny? It's not funny. It's bloody hilarious." Cantfield guffawed. "Probably the most hilarious thing I've heard in a long time. You've never lost a fight before, let alone to a woman."

"Like I said, she's not just any woman." Marcus stood and paced in front of the fire. Victor had trained her to be a weapon since she was a babe, determined to ensure she knew how to protect herself as her mother had been unable to.

Cantfield sighed, his laughter slowly subsiding. "I think I'm half in love with Lady Kaitlyn already. I shall certainly have to make it a point to be introduced to her officially now. I'll even brave her glacial stare for the privilege, and perhaps I shall elicit a smile or two from her."

Marcus's blood boiled at the words. The thought of his friend eliciting anything from Lady Kaitlyn made him furious. "I hope she freezes your bloody nether regions off with one of her glacial stares."

"That's not charitable of you, though I'd prefer a stare to a knee."

"I need to find Lady Kaitlyn and get the damn journal back." Marcus took another sip of his drink, and once again the fluid did nothing to calm him. He placed the glass back onto the side table with slightly more force than was necessary.

"Finding her should be no problem," Lucas remarked. "But why did she want Elizabeth's journal in the first place? Do you suppose she's after the Chameleon, too?"

Marcus paused in his pacing and turned to face the man who had trained and fought beside him for the past eighteen years. A man who was more like a brother to him than simply a friend. "Yes, I think that's exactly what she's after. She's trying to avenge Victor's death, which will only complicate matters."

"Or make them easier." Cantfield leaned forward and tossed the paper onto the table beside his empty plate. "If you're both trying to find the Chameleon then why not team up and work together? I imagine Lady Kaitlyn still has Victor's network of informants."

"Team up with her and put her in harm's way of an assassin? Never." The very idea caused a hard knot of unease in his stomach. "Besides, I think she means to do more to the Chameleon than simply bring the fiend to justice. Not to mention Victor would have had my head for doing such a thing."

"I doubt that." Cantfield shrugged. "Victor was the one who trained her in the first place, and I don't think he taught her to use a dagger to merely cut the Sunday roast. Besides, if she can make a good account of herself against you, imagine what she'd do to the Chameleon."

"As unorthodox as it is, she can fight. There's no doubt about that," Marcus found himself reluctantly conceding. "But I refuse to have anything to do with putting her in the path of one of Europe's most deadly assassins."

"I daresay she'll be doing that herself, with or without your help." Cantfield reached over and picked up his glass of whisky. "Besides, you've been trying to find the assassin for over three years. And I imagine Lady Kaitlyn has been on his tail since Victor's murder over a year ago. Clearly, you've had no luck individually. Perhaps it's time to combine your resources and skills?"

"You've lost your senses, Cantfield, to suggest such a thing." Lady Kaitlyn had already distracted him enough tonight; he could ill afford any more such distractions. "However, I must find the Chameleon. 'Tis the only way to vindicate my brother and prove he was no traitor. I must retrieve Elizabeth's journal. Which means I have to find Lady Kaitlyn."

"I imagine she'll be at Darrow's ball tomorrow night. Everyone who is anyone will be there," Cantfield answered.

"Find out tomorrow morning, and then let me know." A sudden urge burned deep in his gut to find out all he could about the woman.

He hadn't seen her in over twelve years and had only just recognized the girl inside the woman who stood defiantly before him earlier tonight. He remembered a stubborn girl, fierce in her resolve to live up to her uncle's demanding schedule. A girl who'd never really been allowed to be a child, instead living a life of regimented training. But now she was a woman, hell-bent on revenge and better trained in combat and subterfuge than most of Her Majesty's agents.

A dangerous combination.

"Consider it done." Cantfield stood. "Where are you going now?"

"To find Sir William. If anyone has more information about Lady Kaitlyn, it will be him." And he needed to find out everything he could about the woman who'd not only taken the journal from him, but who had stirred a longing in him that he'd long thought was dead.

"True. He knows everything about anything that's going on." Cantfield grinned again. "I must say, I'm looking forward to my official introduction to Lady Kaitlyn. I wonder if she remembers briefly meeting me when she was a girl. I didn't think anything of it back then, but I dare say I probably made a lasting impression on the chit."

From another man, it would sound con-ceited and vain, but with Lucas Devereux it was altogether too true. Women were drawn to him.

"Stay away from her, Cantfield." His friend usually succeeded at wooing whomever he set his sights on—though he usually avoided unwed virgins like the plague.

"You sound rather possessive, old chap," Lucas said.

Marcus couldn't blame him for the surprise in his tone. Ever since Elizabeth's death, he had shown no interest in dalliances, no matter how determined some Society women were to entice him. When one's heart was first crushed, then incinerated, and finally scattered like ashes to the wind, it was all but impossible to resurrect the thing, a fact that ensured he'd never marry again. That had been Elizabeth's parting and everlasting gift to him before her death.

Which was why he was disconcerted at his own reaction to the thought of Cantfield dancing with Lady Kaitlyn. He felt jealous. Damn it. Such feelings were perilous. He'd not reacted this way to a woman in a long time, and he'd be the biggest fool imaginable to ever let another woman get close enough to hurt him again... Even if the memory from last night, of Lady Kaitlyn's soft curves pressing against him, was starting to drive him to distraction. He'd never reacted so much to a woman before, not even to Elizabeth, who he'd been besotted with in the beginning—before he knew her true and faithless nature.

Marcus cursed softly. The very thought of his late wife and her betrayal reminded him exactly why he would never allow a woman to hold that sort of power over him again. Never again, no matter how enticing her curves or her blasted peppermint and rose scent.

Chapter Four

After a restless few hours of sleep, if that's what one could even call the tossing and turning Kat had done, she'd finally given up on the activity altogether when Marcus's ridiculously blue eyes kept swimming in and out of her dreams. She dragged her slightly stiff and sore body from the warmth of her bed, determined to make a head start on the day.

Having finished reading the journal cover to cover before eventually trying to sleep, she had obtained what promised to be the most tangible link thus far to finding the Chameleon, if she could convince Marcus to assist her. Because although she loathed the thought of asking anyone for anything, in this instance she needed a man to infiltrate the club mentioned in the journal, and Marcus fit the bill to perfection.

Obtaining his agreement, however, could prove difficult, especially if her memories of his stubbornness were anything to go by. Well, she'd have to make him agree. No matter what it took. She'd just have to remember not to let herself get distracted by him again. A fact she was starting to think might be easier said than done, given her body's traitorous reaction to him last night. But she would persevere. She had to.

Marching down the last of the stairs to the ground floor of the Montrose townhouse, her purpose for the day clear, Kat stopped in her tracks as the aroma of coffee and bacon assailed her senses, tempting her as little else could. Perhaps a quick detour to replenish her energy reserves before she headed to the *Gazette*'s office in Bethnal Green was warranted after all.

"You're not training this morning, my lady?" Fenton's deep baritone interrupted from behind her.

Kat swiveled around and faced her ever-efficient butler, who was standing as always with his tall frame erect, and not a strand of his white hair nor a thread of his clothing daring to be out of place.

He was more family to her then nearly anyone else in her life, having been in her uncle's employ since before she came to live with them after her parents died when she was three.

"Not today, Fenton. There is much to do." Normally, for an hour every morning she trained with her friend, Master Zhang, who had been first Victor's mentor and later Kat's, training them both in Eastern fighting techniques. But when it came to the Chameleon, sacrifices had to be made.

"I take it your visit to Lord Sommerville's

residence was productive and you retrieved the journal?" Fenton's piercing blue eyes probed her own.

"Indeed, it was, and I did." Kat smiled. He knew her moods better than she.

"Good. Then we are a step closer to finding the Chameleon." Fenton, who had been Victor's most loyal and trusted servant for over thirty years, was in full support of her quest to find the assassin.

"We are, though I shall need the floor plans for the Corinthian Club. Do we have them?" She always liked to study the layout of any premises she intended to pay a clandestine visit to, for it paid to be prepared.

"For such a questionable establishment? Of course." Fenton rubbed his jaw. "Though we only have a minor informant in the kitchens. It's been near impossible infiltrating that club without a more well-placed informant. I daresay it's going to be difficult to get in undetected, if that's what you were thinking of doing."

He knew her too well, for it's exactly what she intended. "I shall have a way in, I just need to lay the groundwork first and obtain Marcus Black's assistance."

"The Earl of Westwood?"

She briefly recounted the tale of the previous night, to which Fenton seemed neither surprised nor fussed over. The man was unflappable and completely dependable, thank goodness.

"Westwood is hunting the Chameleon, too," Fenton said. "I believe the assassin murdered his late wife. The earl could prove useful."

"Oh, he will," Kat said. "He just doesn't yet realize it."

"Your uncle trained him, too," Fenton remarked. "Which will make him a formidable ally, or an equally formidable foe. Do have care when dealing with him, my lady. Though he is a gentleman, he can be ruthless when he must."

Kat could always depend on Fenton to look out for her. "I will be careful."

Fenton nodded. "Indeed, you will. Now, I shall obtain those plans for the club for you and make contact with our informant there. When you do need to infiltrate the place, you shall be well prepared."

"Thank you, Fenton." She reached over and placed a quick kiss on his weathered cheek. "I can always count on you."

He appeared equally embarrassed and delighted with the praise. "Always, my lady. I made a promise to his Lordship that I would assist you and look out for you, and I intend to keep that promise to my last breath."

"I'm grateful for that, for I consider you family." She picked up his hand and squeezed his fingers before releasing them.

"As I do you, my lady." He smiled, which was rare for Fenton. "And don't you worry, we will find the Chameleon."

"Yes. Perhaps with my endeavors today, the path to avenging Victor will finally be within reach." Exhaling sharply, she prayed that would be the case in her so far unsuccessful pursuit of the Chameleon. It had to be. The Chameleon couldn't keep lurking in the shadows forever.

Fenton bowed and then turned on his heel before disappearing down the corridor.

Kat turned in the opposite direction and strode down the hallway, following her nose to the breakfast room. Once she satisfied her belly, then she could get everything in place to ensure Marcus's agreement.

The first thing she noticed when stepping into the room was her aunt Daisy sitting at the table calmly sipping some tea, with not a wisp of her pale blonde hair escaping her perfect coiffure.

Kat absently brushed some of her own recalcitrant auburn locks from her face, wishing not for the first time that her mane would take some lessons from Daisy's. Not that she'd bothered to spend any more than a few moments upstairs twisting it into a knot at the nape of her neck. There were more important things to do than spend hours on one's hair.

"Is everything all right?" Kat asked Daisy, glancing pointedly at the clock on the far wall. It was a rare occasion that her aunt was up before eleven. Practically unheard of.

Daisy's brow arched slightly. "Everything is fine, Kaitlyn. Why wouldn't it be?"

"It's rather early for you to be up, is it not?"

"Perhaps," her aunt replied, a soft smile tilting her lips upward. "Though it seems we are both acting contrary to our normal patterns, does it not? You're up and about a great deal *later* than normal." Daisy gently placed her teacup back onto the saucer with elegant precision, before picking up a white linen napkin and dabbing at the corners of her mouth. "Were you delayed in your return last night from the Bentley soiree?"

There were subtle hints of worry and disapproval in her aunt's tone, as Daisy was perfectly aware Kat hadn't actually been at a soiree, but with the footmen standing to attention on the far side of the room, Daisy was always careful when discussing Kat's unusual activities, regardless of the fact the servants were all aware of the nature of some of Kat's work. They themselves were trained by Fenton in skills unusual for domestic servants, but definitely required in the Montrose residence, where maintaining vigilance and security was paramount. After all, Victor's work within the government hadn't been without risk, nor without accumulating enemies.

"Yes, I did get in late," Kat said as she wandered over to the buffet table and placed a few strips of bacon and some eggs on a plate.

"You know I dislike you attending those sorts of activities, Kaitlyn." Daisy was trying to project a stern matronly voice, but it never had the desired effect, especially considering Daisy was only ten years older than Kat, and more like a sister to her than an actual authority figure.

"I know you don't," Kat remarked as she returned with her plate to the table and sat across from Daisy. "But you also know why I do so."

Daisy didn't actively encourage or support Kat's activities, believing such things were well outside the realm of what a woman ought to be doing, let alone what an Earl's daughter should be. And, of course, by Society's standards, her aunt was correct.

But spying and dealing in information paid ridiculously well, and the estate needed every penny it could get its hands on, especially after they had discovered soon after Victor's death that it was on the verge of bankruptcy. Which was the only reason Daisy put her displeasure aside surrounding Kat's activities. Her aunt was nothing if not pragmatic when it came to finances, contrary to how delicate and ethereal she appeared on the surface.

"I hope you didn't run into any difficulties?" Daisy asked, as Kat took a seat across from her.

Kat chewed on some of her bacon before finally responding, knowing Daisy wouldn't like hearing about her run-in with the earl. "I suppose it depends on what you class as difficulties."

An expression of shock or perhaps horror flickered across Daisy's face. "What do you mean by *that,* Kaitlyn Montrose?"

She couldn't help the grimace that stretched over her face with the knowledge of how truly displeased Daisy was about to be. "Please leave us," she said to the two footmen.

The men bowed and then swiftly left the room through the open doorway.

"It's that bad, is it?" Daisy asked, bringing her hands up to her temples and rubbing them.

"*I* don't think so," Kat began, "but I suspect *you* will have a different opinion. You see, I ran into the Earl of Westwood last night."

"Westwood?" Daisy seemed baffled. "I thought you went to Somerville's last night to retrieve a journal. What does Westwood have to do with any of that?"

"He showed up while I was removing the journal from Lord Somerville's safe. I had to fight him to ensure I kept it." Kat poured herself a cup of coffee, knowing she'd need the sustenance of the brew against what she predicted would be

Daisy's attack of apoplexy at the announcement.

"Kaitlyn, please tell me I heard you incorrectly. You didn't actually fight the Earl of Westwood… As in, *physically* fight him, did you?"

"I did."

Daisy's hand clutched at her chest, while her other hand gripped the handle of her teacup so tight, her knuckles went bone white and Kat thought she would snap the fine bone china. "You physically fought not only a man, but a peer of the realm? Good Lord, you will be the death of me."

"I had no other choice," Kat replied with a shrug. The bruises along her arms and legs were a testament to the sparring and blocking she'd done fighting Marcus to avoid having to hand over the journal to him. "There's no need to make such a fuss about it. I wasn't presented with many other alternatives."

Silence greeted the pronouncement for about a minute, as Daisy digested her words. "I can't fathom that the Earl of Westwood would fight a woman. I would have thought him too much of a gentleman to do so…"

"He didn't know I was a woman when we initially fought."

"Oh, thank goodness." Daisy breathed out a heavy sigh of relief. "Then there's still a chance your reputation is salvageable, if he's not aware of your identity."

"I hate to disappoint you, Daisy, but I'm afraid he's well aware of my identity." It would have been far easier to allow Daisy to labor under that particular illusion, but Kat always believed the truth was the best policy, no matter how painful it might be. She proceeded to tell her aunt exactly what had occurred, and when she finished, Daisy was staring at her as if she had lost her mind, an expression Kat had become familiar with over the last few years.

"You actually *kneed* the Earl of Westwood in his nether regions?"

Kat nodded. "He had me pinned against a wall and it was all I could do to escape his grip." She truly hadn't enjoyed resorting to such a move, but one did what one had to.

"My goodness, if this is ever revealed to anyone, we will be ruined…" With shaky hands, Daisy lifted her cup to her lips and took a sip of the liquid.

"That is a tad melodramatic. We shall not be ruined. As you said, Westwood is a gentleman, so he will not gossip about the matter."

Her aunt placed her cup on the saucer, tea splashing over its edges, her usual finesse clearly shaken. "Melodramatic? Kaitlyn Montrose, your actions are melodramatic. What other lady would ever do the things you do? None, that is who! Why you take such risks is beyond me."

"You know why I take such risks." Kat pinned Daisy's eyes with her own. "Victor must be avenged."

"Your uncle would not have wanted this for you!" Daisy implored. "Fighting a man, at night and all alone. I admit I tend to cling to the past and the etiquette of years gone by, but even this is too much! I fear Victor would be turning in his grave with what you've been getting up to."

Annoyance coursed through her with Daisy's words. Why didn't her aunt understand? "*Victor* was the one who trained me for this, a fact you frequently like to forget."

"Yes, and he realized he'd made a mistake and that you needed lessons in decorum. Which is why he sent you off to that finishing school!" Daisy countered, her eyes flashing with fire. "He wanted you to eventually get married and be happy."

"I'm twenty-six and firmly on the shelf, Daisy. I have no intention of marrying." Kat stood and paced over to the window overlooking the gardens. "Besides, Victor only sent me to that finishing school to appease you, after you married him."

"I make no apologies for that. You were in desperate need of learning the etiquette required of your station."

It was a sore spot between them and one Kat didn't want to dredge up. "What is done is done, including what happened with Westwood last night." Her expression softened as she saw the angst on Daisy's countenance. "The Earl of Westwood is too honorable to talk about it, and besides, what man wants it known that a lady bested him by kneeing him in the bollocks?" She walked over to Daisy and took her hands in her own. "You must trust me on this. My reputation and yours in turn, are safe. I promise."

Daisy sighed and squeezed Kat's hands for a second. "You know I trust you. I just don't know if we can trust Westwood."

"Victor trusted him." And Kat knew that if Victor trusted him, she could, too.

"For a man used to deception and treachery," Daisy said. "Your uncle trusted a great many people he shouldn't have."

Kat glanced down at the small brass key suspended on the gold chain hanging around her neck. Reaching down, she took ahold of it and began to absently twirl it between her fingers. Yes, Victor had been immersed in a world of deception and treachery, and most of it entirely of his own making.

Indeed, he'd even kept the truth of her parentage from her, her entire life. A bitter secret Kat had discovered after opening Victor's safe following his death and reading the letter he'd left her. The secret that she wasn't actually Victor's niece, but instead his daughter.

He'd explained in the letter that he'd fallen in love with her mother, Amelia, shortly after she'd married Victor's brother, the first earl. Victor and Amelia had apparently tried to resist each other, but Amelia's husband had always been distant and inattentive to his new bride, instead preferring to visit London and leave his bride in the country. And one stormy weekend, the two succumbed to their love, after which Victor promptly left the country, guilt wracking him after betraying his brother. But the damage had already been done— Amelia was pregnant with Kat.

Though no one, apart from Victor and Amelia, had ever known the truth of Kat's parentage. Except now Kat. Not even Daisy knew the truth. Part of the reason why she'd never marry. A secret like that had to stay buried. And what man in Society would want to marry a bastard in any event?

"Westwood is an honorable man," Daisy continued, returning Kat's thoughts to the present. "Perhaps he might even consider marrying you, after essentially compromising you?"

The idea was amusing, especially after what she'd just been thinking. "You do understand I wasn't compromised, don't you?" Even if her dreams had been filled with the thought of being compromised by Marcus all night.

The patter of footsteps and Samuel hollering from the hallway was a welcome relief from the tension in the atmosphere, and a moment later in barreled a small white puppy, with flecks of brown on its coat, followed closely by Samuel.

The boy pulled up short seeing his mother and Kat sitting at the table. "Oh, good morning. What are you both doing down here?" he asked, panting, his gaze darting about the room for his errant companion. "Oh no, D'Artagnan! Stop it!" His eyes, the same green as Kat's and every Montrose before them, looked stricken toward the French doors leading to the terrace, where the puppy, whom he'd named after his favorite Musketeer, was now quite happily tugging on the curtain hem, seemingly determined to fight the material to the death. The puppy definitely lived up to his namesake.

"Goodness, Samuel!" Daisy exclaimed, jumping to her feet. "How many times must I tell you that that creature is to be kept outside?"

Samuel darted over to the pup and wrestled him away from the paisley material. "I'm sorry, Mother, he snuck in when I went to feed him." He picked up the wiggling puppy and turned back around to face them. "And he headed straight for this room."

"And who could blame him with the smell of bacon wafting through the house." Kat said as she picked up a piece from her plate and went over to feed it to the wagging ball of energy, who eyed her in adoration.

"Kaitlyn Montrose! Must you encourage them?" Daisy groaned as she sank back into her seat with a sigh and took another sip from her teacup in weary acceptance.

"It's only a little bit of bacon," Kat replied, with a quick wink to Sam, who grinned in reply. "The poor little darling was obviously desperate for some, weren't you?" She rubbed D'Artagnan's head and was rewarded with some furious thumping of his tail.

"He loves bacon," Sam said, before leaning closer to Kat and lowering his voice. "Are we still good to train later today?"

They both knew full well Daisy got particularly upset with the thought of him following in his father's footsteps, preferring Sam to have nothing to do with learning the art of defending himself. Which, in some ways, Kat could understand, even if she didn't agree with it.

Daisy had lost her husband at the hands of an assassin, so it was no wonder she was determined not to lose her son, too. But sheltering Samuel from the harsh realities of the world and preventing him from learning life-saving skills, was a naive and foolhardy decision. Which was why Kat was going to start training him, following on from what Victor had started shortly before his death, regardless of Daisy's dislike of her doing so. After all, he was her only blood family left, and she would do everything to protect him.

She wouldn't lose him as she had lost Victor.

Ruffling the lad's dark blond hair, Kat whispered in his ear, "Unfortunately, not today. I'm chasing a lead. But I promise I'll start teaching you soon." She drew back and twisted the brass handle of one of the doors leading out to the back terrace. Raising her voice again, she said, "Now, why don't you take D'Artagnan out the back for a play."

Samuel nodded in understanding, before bounding out the doors with D'Artagnan in tow.

"I can't believe I let you convince me to allow him to get a puppy in the first place." Daisy sighed.

"He's the happiest he's been since Victor's death," Kat replied, grinning slowly as she watched Sam and D'Artagnan chasing after each other through the gardens at the back of the residence. Sam was still so innocent and unaware of the horrors outside of the walls surrounding him, having had a very different childhood from her own. For Victor had never pushed Samuel as he'd pushed her. Had never forced the lad to train from the age of four, as he had Kat.

In a way, she envied Samuel. Never having the shadows of death hovering at the back of his memories as Kat had. Never waking up, frozen in terror after nightmares filled with the horror of blood being everywhere. Never having to hear his mother's last anguished screams echoing in his head like Kat did.

But that very fact meant Samuel was so underprepared to protect himself. By his age, she'd been capable of throwing a knife from twenty feet away, hitting her target dead center. She'd been able to load and fire a pistol as quick as any of the men Victor had been training. And then, when she was twelve, only four years older than Samuel was now, she'd felt the burden of taking lives. A burden that was always with her, no matter how she tried to forget the fact.

Seeing Samuel grow with a carefree type of innocence, Kat realized she'd never really had a childhood to begin with. Not that she blamed Victor. He'd simply been trying to protect her as best as he knew how, even if that meant she'd never had a puppy to play with, or the freedom to run around chasing it with blissful abandon, completely oblivious to the potential dangers looming around every corner.

"What are your plans for the day?" Daisy asked. "Sending an apology note to the Earl of Westwood, perhaps?"

There was a definite hint of sarcasm and perhaps futile hope in her aunt's voice.

Kat turned back to face her, blinking away the memories and returning her thoughts to what she had to do. "I already apologized to him prior to incapacitating him. I was taught manners, after all, at my finishing school."

"At least you were taught something." Daisy sighed heartily. "Whatever am I to do with you, Kaitlyn? I do hope the Earl is not at the Darrow's ball tonight when you attend."

"Oh, he'll be there, searching for me, no doubt." Which is exactly what Kat wanted. She had plans for the man, and the sooner he knew of them, the better.

Chapter Five

Switching from the tram to an omnibus, and then walking several blocks around the outskirts of Bow Common, until she was satisfied that she wasn't being followed, Kat proceeded down the last few streets to the warehouse that housed the printing press that produced *The Bachelor Bounty Gazette*, a publication dedicated to printing the secrets and scandals of the nefarious bachelors in Society.

Taking such a roundabout route was imperative to maintain the secret location of the *Gazette*, as was not using the Montrose carriage, which was far too recognizable, especially in such a neighborhood.

Her black boots made nary a sound on the cobblestone path as she turned onto Walker Street. In her plain and simple navy woolen skirt and jacket, she was easily able to blend in as just another young woman on her way to work in one of the factories. It was liberating in a way. Her station in life didn't often allow those of her rank the freedom that women from other classes were allowed, though things were changing. Perhaps she should even get herself a bicycle, like she'd seen some women riding past on.

Pausing outside of the green side door to the warehouse, Kat glanced around. Satisfied she wasn't being observed, she unlocked the door with her key and stepped into the building, closing and locking the door behind her. Immediately, the smell of ink and freshly cut paper enveloped her in its familiar and welcoming scent, as the voices of her two best friends in the world, Livie and Etta, travelled down the hallway from the office.

Excellent, they were both here, just as she'd expected them to be.

"Thank goodness you're finally here!" Etta exclaimed from where she sat at her desk as Kat strode through the doorway into the office.

Looking over at her friend, who was dressed in a soft yellow and blue day dress that complement-ed her complexion perfectly, Kat could see the cu-riosity and questions all but radiating from Etta's warm chocolate eyes.

"Yes, do tell us what happened last night. Were you successful? It was Livie who asked the question, her blue gaze intense as she pushed up from her own desk chair and stood, her extremely pregnant belly protruding in front of her.

Seeing her best friend pregnant was always unnerving for Kat. And each time she saw Livie of late, her belly looked like it had grown by a mile. Which meant the babe was probably due any day. Kat would choose a fight any day over Livie possibly going into labor any minute. "Shouldn't you be in bed, resting?"

"You sound just as annoying as Sebastian!" Livie declared, settling her hands on her hips. "Can you believe he wants us to travel to our country estate and relax there for the final month of my confinement?"

"What an absolute monster," Kat replied, completely straight faced as she swung her coat off and hung it on the peg behind the door, before turning to face her friends. "When do you go?"

Livie sighed. "Tomorrow. I can't believe I let him convince me."

"Please," Kat scoffed. "The two of you convince each other to do things all the time. I've never seen a couple more in love. It's rather nauseating. But a trip to the country sounds sensible."

Livie's eyes narrowed. "I shall remind you of that when your turn comes."

"Good God, I'm never marrying and getting pregnant!"

"That is what I used to say, too," Livie replied, a soft smile creeping across her face. "Until I fell in love with Sebastian."

Kat noticed the slight flush that rose up Livie's cheeks at the mention of her new husband, Sebastian Colver, or as he was more commonly referred to, the Bastard of Baker Street.

Her friend had been married for less than

a year, after creating the scandal of the decade when she, a duke's daughter, defied the edicts of Society and married not only a commoner but one of the most feared and notorious men in London. Sebastian was the bastard son of a duke, and a man who had grown up in the slums of London, eventually becoming the undisputed king of the Rookeries, not to mention one of the wealthiest men in England.

A man who despised the profligate members of the aristocracy on account of his father's perfidy and had happily bankrolled their publishing venture to start an anonymous gazette dedicated to dishing the dirt on the disreputable bachelors in Society.

To say Kat received the shock of her life when she returned to England to discover her best friend was engaged to such a dangerous man was an understatement.

Probably why she'd overreacted slightly upon hearing the news and had immediately gone to Colver's club to confront the fellow, disarming several of his men in the process, along with threatening Colver at knife point that if he was trifling with Livie or broke her heart in any way, he would answer to her.

"I still have high hopes that you both will meet the love of your lives, too," Livie continued. "In any event, how *did* you go last night?"

Kat had sent them each a note yesterday,

having to postpone her attendance with them to the Bentley soiree in order to retrieve the journal. There were few secrets between the women, and clearly both Etta and Livie wanted a full account of her evening, which would certainly be much more preferable than any more talk of love. "It didn't go quite as expected."

"Yet, there's a gleam of anticipation in your eyes," Etta murmured, her observation skills keen as usual. "Which I assume means you met with some success?"

Kat couldn't help but smile at the two women. Both more like sisters to her than friends, ever since Kat had been forced to attend Mrs. Morrison's finishing school when she was fourteen years old. And though Kat had fought against going, Victor had agreed with Daisy that it was well past time Kat learned the social skills required of her station.

And in the end, though she hadn't wanted to spend three years at the school, it had been the best thing she could have done as she'd met her best friends there, women she would gladly give her life to protect.

"I had some success, yes," Kat replied, glancing out the glass internal window of the office, into the main indoor space of the warehouse where the printing press stood gleaming in the middle of the room.

Mr. Whitbury and his assistants, who were usually busily buzzing about the contraption, preparing to print the publication for either the next edition or their advertising flyers, were absent. "Where are the men?" She needed them, after all.

"They went out to fetch some breakfast," Livie replied with a wave of her hand. "But they'll be back soon enough. So? Tell us what happened. Did you get the journal?"

Kat summed up her adventures of the night, which ended in both Etta and Livie exhibiting much the same expression as Daisy had. Shock. Though rather than the accompanying mortification that Daisy had displayed, Etta's eyes brimmed with excitement, and Livie peered at her altogether too knowingly.

"I seem to remember you having a slight fascination with the man when you were a girl," Livie said. "Something about how he was the handsomest man you had met?"

"I was fourteen. Any girl would be fascinated with a man as tall and muscular and as handsome as he was, and still is, I suppose."

"Did you really fight Westwood and knee him in his nether regions?" Etta asked, her fingers tapping across the tabletop of her desk. "I know you've taught us that that region, along with the neck and eyes, are the best to target if we are attacked, but I just didn't really think one would ever do it…"

"Well, I had to, and it was extremely effective." Kat shrugged.

"I'm impressed," Etta enthused. "And shall definitely keep such a move in mind, if I ever have need of it."

"I'm glad someone was impressed, for Daisy certainly was not."

"No, I imagine she would have been mortified," Livie said as she sat back down.

They all stared at each other for a moment, before they burst out laughing.

"I can't believe you told her! Goodness, I wish I'd seen her face when you did," Etta said. "I bet she was horrified."

"Completely, though that's not unexpected. When is Daisy ever pleased with my actions?" Kat said, her laughter subsiding as she sank down into her own chair at her desk across from Etta and Livie's. Suddenly, she could feel every ache and bruise from last night with acute intensity. She wondered if Marcus was also feeling the effects of their encounter. Had he been thinking of her, as she'd been unable to stop thinking of him? "In any event, retrieving the journal has placed me a step closer to finding the Chameleon."

"That's wonderful! What did it disclose?" Livie asked.

Kat thought back to the words in the journal,

words that painted a woeful tale of Westwood's late wife, Elizabeth. Her vanity, her spite, her shallowness, her perfidy; all clearly evident from the woman's own scrawls. What had also become obvious was that Lady Westwood had taken a lover, someone she had called 'my Chameleon.'

And that could be no coincidence, particularly not when Westwood himself was one of the masters in the game of espionage. No, it was clear from the woman's words that she was being manipulated by her lover for information on the earl's dealings, yet the poor woman herself had no idea she was being bedded and used by one of Europe's greatest assassins to do so.

No doubt the Chameleon was also the one to have stabbed Lady Westwood to death in her bed after one of their trysts, a fact carefully concealed from Society by the War Office. Even Daisy and Etta didn't know the true circumstances surrounding her death, believing what the rest of Society did, that Lady Westwood succumbed to a fever whilst living abroad with Marcus.

But Kat knew the truth. Her informants had ensured that. After all, Victor had taught her that information was the truest source of power one could have, even more important than combat skills. And over the years, Kat came to realize how accurate his teachings were.

And Lady Westwood's journal contained

some interesting and scandalous information. No wonder Westwood wanted it back. But Etta and Livie didn't need to know the specifics. Besides which, they weren't Kat's secrets to share.

"Suffice it to say," Kat continued, "Westwood wants the journal for the same reason I do. He's also hunting the Chameleon."

"He could prove useful, then," Etta mused. "Particularly a man with his skillset. Not to mention he is rather handsome on the eyes. Don't you still think?"

Kat rolled her eyes as her friends grinned. "I have little interest in his effect on my eyes." Even though he had haunted her dreams all night. The very thought of her breasts pressed against his chest was vivid in her mind. "But, yes, his skills could come in handy. He was trained by Victor, after all. And after reading the journal, I know I'm going to need his help."

"You need his help?" Etta appeared even more shocked with this pronouncement of Kat's. "But you hate asking anyone for help."

She did, and it was going to be especially annoying to seek out the man that Victor had always remarked was his star pupil and ask for his assistance. But she had little choice in the matter. "In this case, I must."

"Why?" There was curiosity rife in her friend's expression.

"Because the Corinthian Club was mentioned in Lady Westwood's journal, as a place where her lover attended regular business dealings."

"It doesn't surprise me that an assassin would have links to such a disgusting club." Etta became incensed whenever the Corinthian Club was mentioned. They all took it as an insult that every time the *Gazette* announced which disreputable bachelors were going to be critiqued in the next month's edition, the manager of the Corinthian Club would send each bachelor an invitation to become a member of the Club. It was an exclusive men-only club on Plymouth Street, home to as many vices and debauched entertainments as a man could possibly envisage.

And it was the only club Kat did not have a well-positioned informant in.

"No, it's not a great surprise, but that's why I need Marcus's assistance. I need to get inside that club, find out what links the Chameleon has to it, and obtain their membership list."

"I'm surprised Lord Westwood is a member of such a…um, *unusual* establishment." Etta rubbed her chin. "He doesn't strike me as the sort to enjoy those activities. He seems rather too proper for them."

"He's not a member," Kat said. "Well, at least not yet, anyway. But he will be."

Livie narrowed her eyes at Kat. "What are you

intending to do, Kaitlyn Montrose?"

There was no escaping that Livie knew her better than even Etta. Kat smiled grimly. "We are going to list Westwood as one of the next bachelors the *Gazette* will be critiquing."

Silence greeted her pronouncement, before Etta recovered her voice with alacrity. "We agreed when we started the *Gazette* that it was to be used to unmask nefarious bachelors!"

"We did," Livie said. "In fact, its entire purpose is to stop other ladies from suffering the same fate as poor Alice did. We can't use it to blackmail Westwood, even to assist you."

Alice had been the fourth in their tight knit group from finishing school, until her murder last year, after having been seduced and then discarded by a scoundrel. Her death had been the catalyst for starting the Gazette, to name and shame the bachelors who thought it acceptable to use and abuse women, and hopefully prevent any other young ladies' lives from being destroyed as Alice's was.

"I have no intention of blackmailing him." Kat frowned at the suggestion. "I simply need him listed so he receives an invitation to join the Corinthian Club."

"Oh…" Etta shook her head morosely. "But if we list him, his reputation will suffer. And particularly after what he's already endured with the

whispers regarding the treachery of his brother…
Do you think it wise?"

"Nathaniel was not a traitor!" Fury engulfed
Kat with the suggestion.

"We know," Livie placated. "But that's what
everyone else believes."

"Everyone else is wrong." She rarely spoke of
Nathaniel, whom she had spent over four years
training with after returning from finishing school
when she was eighteen.

"Why did everyone whisper he was a traitor,
then?" Etta asked.

"They say he fell in love with a Russian and
was leaking British intelligence to her. Though I
didn't believe such a thing for a minute. The Nathaniel I knew would never do such a thing, even
if he was in love." The fight she'd had with Victor
about it was probably one of the worst they'd ever
had. Victor had believed the tale, whereas Kat never had. She was certain Nathaniel had been set up
by his Russian love, or else by the true traitor. Victor had disagreed, saying all the evidence pointed
to Nathaniel and that men did terrible things for
love.

When the War Office tasked Victor with track-
ing Nathaniel down and bringing him back to
England to face justice, Kat had refused to have
anything to do with such a mission. A fact she still
regretted, because if she had gone to Paris with

Victor, perhaps she might have been able to save Nathaniel, and stop him from running into a burning building to save his love.

In the end, though, Victor had realized everything was too convenient in tying Nathaniel to the treachery of selling the government's secrets and had come to regret his part in Nathaniel's death.

The government had tried to limit any gossip from being released regarding Nathaniel's apparent treachery, especially considering his father, the earl at the time, was a close friend of Prince Bertie. But that hadn't stopped the whispers from spreading, even though nothing was confirmed or denied. Many said that when Nathaniel's father died a few months later, it was from heartache over his youngest son's death. Perhaps they were right.

That was when Marcus became the new earl. And, yes, Kat supposed listing him would suggest there were secrets in his past, which would put him firmly back in the spotlight. And though she loathed to do such a thing, what other choice did she have?

Without Marcus being listed, it was unlikely he would be sent an invitation to the Corinthian Club. And Kat needed someone in that club, specifically the manager's office, which she knew from the limited information she'd gathered was always kept locked unless the manager himself was inside discussing membership with a potential member.

"I need Westwood listed." She glanced up at both of them; Etta was biting her lip in concern and Livie was staring steadily at her. "I know it will create further gossip for him, but I can't see any way to avoid it. At least not initially. Once he's offered the invitation to the Corinthian Club, and we find what we need there, we can publish a retraction flyer outlining his virtues and making the public realize he is honorable."

"It sounds like you intend to tell him of your involvement in the *Gazette*," Livie said. "Is that wise, given we decided it is safer if no one else knows?"

She'd thought long and hard about the matter, and though she hadn't seen Marcus in years, she believed she could still trust him. And finding the Chameleon was too important to play it safe on anything. "I don't believe I'll have to tell him. He has the skills, unlike others, to find out on his own who is behind it once he's listed."

"It will still have the same effect of him finding out," Livie added.

"Are you certain, Kat?" Etta said. "I don't think Westwood will be forgiving when he finds out you're the one behind having him listed, even if you have no intention of having him critiqued..."

"Leave Westwood to me," Kat said. "He wants the Chameleon as much as I do, though I daresay he plans to bring the man to justice instead of sending him to hell as I intend. In any event, I think Marcus is thick-skinned enough to weather a few glances and veiled comments, particularly if it means catching his quarry. And I do believe he will keep our secret."

"If you feel this is the only way, then I'm with you," Livie said.

"As am I," Etta said. "Though I wouldn't want to be you when Westwood finds out you're behind it. The man might be handsome, but he's intimidating, too."

Kat heard the door open and close before seeing Whitbury and his two assistants trooping into the warehouse. "Perfect timing. How long until we can get a flyer printed and distributed, announcing his name being added to those critiqued next month?"

"After lunch, perhaps?" Etta answered, sounding somewhat dubious about the project.

"Excellent." In a few hours, all of London would know the Earl of Westwood was listed as one of the next targets of the *Bachelor Bounty Gazette*, which should mean he'd receive an invitation to the Corinthian Club by nightfall. "All will be fine. I know it." She turned to Livie. "Will your husband distribute the leaflets within his clubs? It's imperative word spreads as quickly as possible."

"Of course he will," Livie said. "I don't know

if you realize it, but Sebastian has a soft spot for you after you threatened him with a knife." Livie must've seen the look of bewilderment on her face with that fact because she shrugged. "What can I say? Apart from myself, you're the only other person to have ever stood up to him. He admires such a trait."

"Your husband is unlike most men," Kat said. Because only the Bastard of Baker Street could have a soft spot for someone who confronted him at knifepoint.

"I do hope your plan works," Etta said, an expression of reluctant acceptance and hope jostling over her features. "Westwood isn't the sort of man I'd wish to evoke anger in, and one can only imagine what his reaction will be when he finds out he's been named to be critiqued. I, for one, certainly wouldn't wish to be in the Earl's crosshairs."

"But that is exactly where I want to be." Kaitlyn smiled.

Let the game begin.

Chapter Six

Marcus strode up the steps to the entrance of his club two at a time, only just giving the footman time to hastily open the door as he crossed through the marble arched doorway and entered the grand lobby. Glancing around, he couldn't spy his quarry, Sir William, but the man had to be here.

It was the only place in London Marcus hadn't yet checked, and he'd spent the better part of the early hours of the morning and the rest of the day trying to track down the elusive old man.

Walking past several acquaintances, Marcus nodded in acknowledgment, noting with interest some odd stares directed toward him. He paused briefly at the entry to the lounge area on his right and scanned the room. The establishment was marked by an air of refined elegance, with the fire burning diligently in the large hearth at the end of the room and several velveteen settees and sofas placed strategically throughout, with some tucked into corners to offer privacy, and others out in the open for those wishing to partake in some conversation with the other patrons, depending on one's mood.

You had to give it to the club's notorious owner, Sebastian Colver. The man knew how to do luxury and cater to the aristocracy, even though he'd grown up in the slums of the Rookeries. Colver had turned Club Tartus into the most exclusive establishment in London, where membership was vied for with fervor. There was never an empty glass to be seen and the table of refreshments was always kept replenished. The service, the ambiance, and the gaming was bar none, and there sitting unobtrusively in the far corner, reading *The Times* and sipping a glass of whisky was Sir William Buford. Finally.

A more unassuming man, there wasn't. Nor one whose appearance was so deceptive. Sir William was dressed in navy blue trousers and a matching coat, his white hair brushed back, with an easy smile at the ready and the usual mischievous twinkle lurking in his pale blue eyes.

The man looked more like someone's jovial grandfather who kept candy in his pockets to dish out to all, than one of the most powerful and argu-ably influential men in Europe. An elite spymaster for Her Majesty, he was one of the best-informed gentlemen on the continent—a fact Marcus was counting on. After all, if the man in charge of the War Office's entire intelligence department didn't know what Lady Kaitlyn Montrose was up to, then no one would.

Even the mere thought of the woman was enough to stir him. He shook his head in disgust; he was acting like a randy schoolboy.

It was at that moment Sir William spotted Marcus and waved him over.

"Marcus, my boy!" Sir William enthused as Marcus stalked across the oriental rug covering the parquetry flooring to where the man lounged, glad to be focused again on to his task.

Sir William stood and grasped Marcus's hand with his own, pumping it up and down vigorously. "How are you? Do take a seat." He motioned to the chair across from him.

Marcus waited for Sir William to sit back down before taking a seat on the upholstered armchair. "I've been looking for you for a good portion of the day."

"Have you indeed?" Sir William replied with an indulgent smile. "I've been running from one end of town to the other with various meetings today, so it's no wonder you haven't been able to track me down. Not to worry, though, you've finally succeeded." He smiled as he picked up his glass and took a sip. "Did you wish to discuss the little run-in you had last night, dear boy?"

Marcus raised an eyebrow. "You know of it already?"

"I've heard whispers." Sir William winked before motioning over to one of the footmen. "A drink for you?"

Marcus nodded, and Sir William ordered him a whisky.

"How did you find out?" Marcus asked once the footman had scurried off to fetch him a drink.

Sir William chuckled. "Come, my boy, you know I can't disclose my various sources. I wouldn't be much of a Director of Intelligence for the War Office if I did."

Marcus had to agree. One thing you could always depend upon with Sir William was his integrity and ability to keep secrets. "How is it that with both your own informants and mine, we still can't find the Chameleon?" It was a question he'd asked himself often over the past few years, with the Chameleon seemingly a step ahead every time.

Sir William exhaled sharply, clearly sharing in the same frustration at the failure. "In all of the decades I've been doing this work, I've never faced such a difficult foe. I sometimes wonder if the Chameleon is a ghost. He's so easily able to infiltrate a place and then disappear into the ether, almost as if he never was there. Well, apart from the dead corpses he inevitably leaves behind." Sir William's face hardened while his fingers clenched tightly around his glass. "But the fiend cannot remain hidden forever. Eventually, he will make a mistake, and that's when we shall pounce. So, have faith, dear boy, have faith! We shall find him, and he will face justice for all of his atrocities."

"I intend for him to. Which is why," Marcus said, leaning forward, "I need to know what the devil Kaitlyn Montrose is up to. I can only assume she's chasing after the Chameleon, too. Why else would she take the journal?"

Shock replaced the merriment in Sir William's eyes. "It was Lady Kaitlyn you fought last night?"

Marcus arched an eyebrow. "I thought you said you knew about my little run-in, as you called it."

"I assumed you'd fought the person who took the journal, though I didn't know your assailant was Lady Kaitlyn," Sir William confessed.

"The information you were given was not particularly detailed."

Sir William shook his head. "It was only whispers. But it was Lady Kaitlyn you fought? Are you certain?"

The man appeared slightly confounded, though not surprised. "It was definitely her," Marcus confirmed, a picture of the woman herself, and those glorious emerald eyes of hers, vivid in his mind.

"I do so admire a resourceful woman," Sir William said. "And let us face it, Victor trained her to be formidable. You must have annoyed her greatly."

The waiter returned and deftly deposited a neat glass of whisky on the table beside Marcus, before departing as swiftly as he arrived. Marcus leaned forward and picked up the glass. "What do you mean, *annoyed her*? If anyone was annoyed after last night, it was I. She's the one who got Elizabeth's journal." And kneed him in the bollocks for the pleasure of it.

"No offense, dear boy, but you do tend to upset people with your forthright manner, calling a spade a spade as you are wont to do. But if you didn't annoy her, why else would you have been named?" His voice trailed off as he rubbed the whiskers of his beard in thought. "Unless she's using the announcement as leverage with you."

"Announcement?" Marcus didn't like the sound of this. "What announcement?"

Sir William blinked, an expression of incredulity in his gaze. "Don't tell me you haven't heard yet? Surely, you've noticed the odd stares directed toward you today."

He had, though he'd been too intent on finding Sir William to pay the glances much thought. "I'm not going to like this, am I?"

"Probably not, though I think I'm in for a treat." Sir William chuckled, causing many of the other patrons to eye them curiously. "Tell me, my boy, have you heard of *The Bachelor Bounty Gazette*?"

"Hasn't everyone?" Marcus replied, a sinking feeling slowly dropping into his stomach. "It's the publication that socially ruins whomever it critiques, detailing their sins and secrets. Laying a man's life bare, warts and all, for Society to consume like a veritable scarab beetle. *That* gazette?"

"Yes, the very one!" Sir William clapped his hand on his leg. "My wife and daughters can't get enough of the thing. They send a footman out on the first of the month to line up and get three copies of the latest edition, so they can each have one to read."

"It's a trashy gossip rag at best," Marcus stated. "I've never bothered to read it."

"Oh, but you should. You'd be surprised at how accurate the intelligence it details is." Sir William's laughter had subsided, but his voice was still filled with mirth. "It contains a wealth of factual information and tantalizing truths that sends whomever it critiques into hiding. It has fast become the most popular publication in London."

"And what does *it* have to do with *me*?" he all but ground out, guessing he knew exactly what it had to do with him, but wanting Sir William to verify the fact before Marcus decided to go to war against Lady Kaitlyn Montrose. God help them both.

"I rather thought it obvious," Sir William replied. "You see, a special flyer was printed by the *Gazette* this morning, distributed far and wide across London, announcing to one and all that one more bachelor would be critiqued in next month's edition. *You.*"

It took several moments for Sir William's words to fully sink in and confirm his suspicions. He'd been listed to be critiqued in a gossip rag? "Bloody hell! You can't be serious? My mother and sister will be tarnished by such speculation. Not to mention they'll worry their heads off." And whenever his mother was worried, that of course meant a visit from her, which was always an uncomfortable event since Nathaniel's death.

"The countess and Lady Isabelle seem far too sensible to worry their heads off over anything. How are they both?"

Marcus shrugged, his chest feeling suddenly tight. "Fine, I assume. I haven't seen them in a few weeks."

Sir William was quiet for a moment, his smile replaced with a frown. "They don't blame you for his death, you know." He sighed. "None of us do."

"I do," Marcus growled in a low voice. "If it wasn't for me, Nathaniel never would've gotten involved in our world of intrigue and he'd still be alive. Which is why I must find the true traitor and exonerate my brother's name. Being named as a scoundrel is not going to help that cause, only hinder it."

"I'm sure there's a good reason for it," Sir William said, his mood lightening as he smiled.

"Which no doubt you'll find out."

"You seem to be enjoying this entirely too much." Marcus raked a hand through his chestnut hair. "Lady Kaitlyn is behind the *Gazette*, is she?" It was to be war with the lady, then. He didn't know why he was anticipating it. "And considering I haven't seduced any virgins or broken any poor damsel's hearts, there'd be no reason to list me, unless for another purpose, which clearly Lady Kaitlyn has."

"You were always quick on the money, dear boy." Sir William sighed. "And, yes, she's one of several partners in the endeavor. Her particular contribution is using her network of informants to dig up all of the dirt on the men they expose," Sir William said. "Normally, I'd not disclose that considering her involvement in the thing is so fraught with issues if it was ever exposed. Though I trust you will tell no one else of what you've learned, at least not until you speak with her first and ascertain what it is she seeks by having you listed."

"Speak to her?" Marcus scoffed. "I'll be doing more than simply speaking to her. And what the bloody hell is she doing listing me, in any event? She knows better than anyone I can't have my work for the government exposed."

"No. Such a thing would not be good for the War Office," Sir William agreed. "We can't have the department exposed if any of your escapades are detailed for one and all to read."

"Your concern for my reputation is touching," Marcus noted drily.

Sir William smiled. "Queen and country first, my boy. You know that." He took another sip of his drink. "But I doubt we have anything to worry about, though perhaps you had best speak with her and see what it is she is after. And I would try to tone down your slightly abrupt demeanor... You could even try some charm on the lady and see how that goes." Sir William did not look at all confident with his suggestion. "Actually, maybe ask Cantfield for some tips first before trying that..."

Marcus merely grunted. He never bothered to subscribe to charm when it came to women. He'd done that with Elizabeth and look where it had gotten him. "I'd wager Lady Kaitlyn is not a woman charm will work on."

"I don't know about that." Sir William shrugged. "Most women respond to charm, in some way or another."

"This woman scales balconies with a rope, wears trousers, and quite happily fights someone my size," Marcus said, feeling the need to remind Sir William. "She's not a normal woman. She likes to play with fire."

"Yes, indeed she does. Having all but waved a red flag in your face naming you," the old man conceded. "But, in the end, like I've said, I'd be surprised if she intends to compromise you."

"You're giving her far too much leeway." Marcus smiled, though it didn't reach his eyes. "And regardless of what she intends, she's gone too far, a fact I will be making abundantly clear to the lady tonight at Darrow's ball when I hunt her down."

"I imagine she'll be hunting you down, too, my boy." Sir William sighed. "Just don't start sparring with her in the ballroom. Then there would be some tantalizing tidbits for the masses."

Spar with her? He didn't dare touch her again, not after his body's reaction. No. Marcus wouldn't spar with the lady, but he'd certainly point out to her the error of her ways. He was a gentleman, after all.

Chapter Seven

Kat stood silent and still, patiently observing Lord Darrow's ballroom from the empty alcove above. With her body mostly hidden behind the red velvet drapes that were pulled partially closed across the balcony railing, Kat had a perfect view of the multitude of guests milling about below, all of them none the wiser they were under close observation from above as they danced and gossiped.

It often surprised her how people could be so blissfully ignorant to their surroundings and the possible dangers around them, oblivious to anything but their socializing. Perhaps ignorance was bliss, though Kat could rarely tolerate ignorance, which made coming to these social events so tedious. Probably why she rarely did.

However, there was often a viable source of information amongst all the gossip, and Kat's position in Society got her into places many of her informants couldn't go. It was the only reason she accepted Darrow's invitation, alongside the fact Etta had implored her to attend, too, as her father was forcing her to go as part of his campaign to find her a husband with a title. An effort proving fruitless so far, thanks in part to Etta's resistance.

The smell of lavender wafted along her senses just as the muted sound of wood thumping softly against the carpet reached her ears. Kat didn't bother turning around. "Good evening, Duchess."

"Hmph," the lady harrumphed as she came to stand beside Kat at the balcony, her cane tapping impatiently against the floor. "One can never catch you unaware, Lady Kaitlyn." The woman didn't sound happy with the observation. "I see you're spying on everyone below as you often do at these events."

Kat glanced over to the woman known as the Dragon Duchess, who was also Livie's godmother, and a woman Kat had an odd sort of acquaintance with.

After all, Kat seemed to be the only lady in Society unafraid of the duchess, and likewise the duchess seemed to be the only lady who wasn't afraid of Kat. A mutual respect had been born from that fact—and a mutual rivalry over who could verbally best the other.

It was a pastime at these events that Kat suspected both of them looked forward to.

"Did I get to your spying spot first?" Kat replied with an arch of her eyebrow. The duchess loved nothing more than knowing everything about everyone in Society, even though she'd deny such a thing to her last breath.

"Impertinent gal!" She frowned at Kat. "But, yes, you did. Anything of interest I missed?" Her eyes left Kat's to glance down at the crowd.

"Nothing as of yet," Kat replied as her gaze also swept down again over the crowd. She spied Etta below talking with Lady Marlborough, who was a regular fountain of gossip and unwittingly gave them many leads to chase up for the *Gazette*, but there was still no sign of Westwood. Darn the man. He was meant to be here, and she was getting impatient waiting for him.

"Who is it you're hoping to spot?" The duchess swiveled her altogether too perceptive eyes back to Kat. "A man, I'm guessing, which is most unlike you."

Kat, thankfully, had been well-schooled in keeping her expression carefully blank, even though she inwardly resented that the woman had guessed the truth all too easily. "Why would you say that?"

The duchess raised an imperious dark brow, her wrinkles crinkling up with the action. "There's anticipation in your eyes that isn't usually present. And you've clearly spent time choosing a dress to complement you. The only time a woman does that is when she wishes to impress a man."

Kat's already foul mood darkened with the observation, for she had in fact spent a ridiculous amount of time trying to decide what to wear, something she never worried over. Her maid had impeccable taste after all, but the emerald gown Bess selected for her hadn't seemed right.

In the end, Kat settled on her new sapphire satin gown with sparkling crystals woven along the bodice that was one of Madam Arnout's most stunning creations yet, employing the special metal studs on Kat's specialty garments, sent over by her German dressmaker friend.

The gown consisted of two separate pieces: a skirt and bodice top. The skirt had the studs sewn along the inside seam and waist, which allowed it to be detached from the top bodice and opened in seconds if Kat required her legs to be free. The bustle wires that shaped the garment had also been sewn directly into the material of the skirt itself, so for all outside appearances she was wearing a bustle, though smaller than was the current fashion, but still shaped as expected, with the hidden benefit of detaching simultaneously with her skirt.

"It's a Madame Arnout creation, isn't it?" the duchess said, sweeping her gaze down the dress and back up again. "She does wonderful work, though I have wondered on occasion if instead of a gown you may one day turn up to one of these things wearing trousers and a tailored jacket, as has become the deplorable fashion choice some women are choosing."

"You flatter me, Your Grace." Kat smiled at

her. What the duchess said was true, some women were indeed daring to wear such clothes. They were in the minority, of course, but still daring. If it weren't for Daisy or Samuel, Kat would have rather liked to join them for the convenience of the trousers rather than the actual look. "I've heard some women are even wearing bowlers, top hats, and cravats." Much to Daisy's horror.

"Good gracious, what is this world coming to?" The duchess tittered.

At that moment, in strode Marcus. He stopped inside the doorway of the ballroom as his name was called aloud, heralding his entrance.

Kat's entire body clenched, and her breath caught, her eyes unable to do anything apart from drink in the sight of him. He was resplendent in a black evening suit with tails, and a crisp, snowy white shirt with a matching bow tie. She rarely ever bestowed the term "dashing" to any gentleman, but Marcus was the epitome of the word, a prime specimen of a man, all but demanding a woman's attention. And Kat was powerless to do anything but stare down at him.

It seemed several other women felt the same as they clamored around him, vying for his attention. Jealousy wasn't an emotion she was used to, but unaccountably the feeling began to crawl up her throat, grating against it like sandpaper. Shaking her head, Kat had to control her wayward emotions. She had no right to be jealous because she had no claim to him, nor would she ever.

An involuntary gasp left her lips as Marcus's gaze swiveled upward and caught hers. Even with the distance between them she felt the intensity in his stare, but she couldn't look away. There was both heat and fury in his gaze, and she knew then and there that he was aware that she was behind his naming in the *Gazette*, and he was coldly furious about it.

Hopefully, once she explained her reasoning for listing him, he'd understand why it was necessary. Not that she should worry about Marcus and what he thought of her, especially when she rarely worried about other people's opinions. If she did, she'd be too fearful to do anything in the rigidly structured social world she was meant to belong to.

Raising her chin a notch higher, she refused to look away. For a full minute, they remained still, locked in a silent battle of wills spanning the length of the ballroom, until the Marquis of Cantfield walked in behind Marcus and said something to him. When Marcus's gaze swung to Cantfield, Kat spun around.

"He is rather dashing, isn't he?"

She'd forgotten the duchess was there. Lovely.

"Though slightly tainted now he has been named in the *Gazette*," the lady continued, her eyes assessing Kat thoroughly.

"Oh, there you are," Etta stated, coming up the back stairs into the alcove and stopping short upon seeing the duchess standing next to Kat. "Oh, excuse me, Your Grace, I didn't realize you were up here, too…"

Etta was rather terrified of the lady. All of the women were. The Duchess of Calder could literally make or break a lady's reputation with the snap of her fingers, such was her power and authority in the upper echelons of Society.

"What a marvelous observation, Miss Merriweather," the duchess intoned. "Now, if you will both excuse me, there'll be much discussion below that I have no intention of missing out on. Oh, and that reminds me, I believe I am to play chaperone to you both next week for the theater."

"Yes, Livie mentioned it." Kat had nearly forgotten Livie's irrational worry that her godmother would be lonely in town once Livie and Sebastian left for the country. Perhaps pregnancy was wreaking havoc on Livie's normally sensible nature, because the thought of the Dragon Duchess lonely was rather laughable. The lady took far too much enjoyment in ensuring everyone in Society lived in fear of occasioning her wrath. It was fun to watch, actually.

"Hhmph, the things I do for my goddaughter…" the duchess said. "Having to put up with the two of you."

"The feeling is mutual, Your Grace," Kat said with a smile.

Beside her, Etta gasped softly and the duchess arched an eyebrow, as she was so fond of doing.

"You're entirely outspoken, Lady Kaitlyn." The duchess assessed her for a moment. "I like it. Perhaps the theater shan't be entirely boring." She inclined her head at them before marching briskly from the space and down the stairs, her cane tapping along next to her much like a brigadier general with a sword.

"That woman terrifies me," Etta blurted out once the duchess was out of earshot. "In any event, you'll never guess who has arrived."

"Westwood."

Etta's face pinched with consternation. "Does nothing ever surprise you?"

She smiled at her friend. "My own reactions of late have been a great surprise, actually."

"I hope you're prepared to deal with him, as I've never seen the man look so determined," Etta said. "Do you think he knows?"

"He definitely knows," Kat replied. The look he'd given her was crystal clear. He was furious with her, there was no skirting around that fact. "And I think it will be best to face him sooner rather than later. So, come along. Time to confront the bear." She wound her arm through the crook of her friend's elbow and they headed down the

stairs. "Though I suspect it will be best to be surrounded by an audience when Westwood seeks
me out, for I fear he's rather upset with me at the
moment."

"How correct you are, my lady," the man
himself voiced from the foot of the stairs. "But
you're too late to seek the safety of the ballroom
audience for our conversation."

• • •

Marcus watched as a myriad of emotions crossed
Lady Kaitlyn's face as she caught sight of him
standing at the base of the stairway with Cantfield
beside him, tagging along for his introduction.
Surprise, shock, and anticipation flashed briefly in
those fierce-green eyes of hers, before she deftly
masked them and took the final step down from
the stairs with her friend, coming to stand defiantly
before him.

If he hadn't been paying such close attention,
he would've missed the play of emotions dart
across her gaze altogether. She was excellent at
concealing her thoughts.

"Lord Westwood." She gave him a fleeting
curtsy. "How good to see you again. I do hope
you're well recovered from last night."

Beside him, Cantfield smothered a laugh while
Marcus raised a brow. It didn't seem the ballroom

setting deterred the lady from speaking her mind. "I'm quite recovered, my lady, and your concern for my welfare is touching."

"I did warn you that *dancing* with me could prove perilous." She shrugged lightly, the glow from the wall lights shining upon the crystal beads of her bodice and drawing Marcus's eyes to the soft swell of her cleavage pressing against the neckline of the gown. Dressed as she was, he certainly wouldn't mistake her for a man.

"So you did," Marcus replied, unable to help the corner of his mouth from twitching up at her impudence. He'd never met a woman so bold, and try as he might, he couldn't maintain his fury at her audacity for listing him in her *Gazette*. Her forthright manner, bordering on sassiness, was a surprising breath of fresh air amongst all of the falsities clinging to the other women in the room like second skins. "And you were correct, it was perilous. You need dancing lessons."

Lady Kaitlyn's eyes narrowed with indignation. He couldn't resist giving her a wink, and nearly laughed aloud when an expression of pure outrage crossed her face.

The sound of a throat clearing beside him abruptly reminded Marcus that he and Lady Kaitlyn were not alone, even though for a moment it had felt that way. How could he have forgotten Lucas, who was determined to be properly introduced to the lady before the night was through? The thought of introducing them caused an uncomfortable knot to lodge in his chest. There wasn't a woman he knew who didn't succumb to Cantfield's charm. "Lady Kaitlyn, let me introduce you to Lucas Devereux, the Marquis of Cantfield. Cantfield, this is Lady Kaitlyn."

Cantfield picked up Kaitlyn's gloved hand and bent down over her knuckles, brushing his lips against the material of her glove. Marcus clenched his jaw.

"It's an absolute pleasure to meet you, Lady Kaitlyn." Cantfield's smiled oozed charm as he straightened up, an inch shy of Marcus's frame. It was a smile Cantfield often deployed on the ladies, which always evoked either a soft sigh or a smile from the recipient. "I don't know if you remember me from when your uncle trained me years ago?"

"Actually, I do." She plucked her hand from Cantfield's and regarded the man steadily.

A big grin danced over Cantfield's face at her words and Marcus felt unaccountably annoyed that she remembered him.

"You were the one always looking at yourself in the mirror in Victor's training room," she continued, "always discussing your latest conquests with whomever you were sparring with."

The young woman beside her laughed, quickly covering it up with a hand over her mouth.

"Yes, I suppose that was me… I was somewhat vain in my younger years." Mortification flooded his face. "I didn't know you were in the training room to hear all of that. I never would've spoken of such topics if I had known…"

"I wouldn't have been good at spying on the training when I was a young girl if you knew I was there, now would I?"

Cantfield didn't seem to know what to say. "Um… No, I don't suppose so…"

Marcus couldn't help but grin at Cantfield's bewilderment. It wasn't often that a lady not only rebuffed Cantfield, the future Duke of Carlisle, but also befuddled him. Well, until the Ice Maiden, it seemed—a woman with high standards and quick wit. He liked her all the more for it.

"Hopefully, you don't get as distracted by your own reflection nowadays." Kaitlyn's eyes flicked back to Marcus, essentially dismissing the Marquis within a few seconds of being introduced to him. "As we're doing introductions, let me present to you both my friend, Miss Henrietta Merriweather, whose father is Mr. Henry Merriweather. Etta, this is Lord Westwood and Lord Cantfield."

Miss Merriweather curtsied, her chocolate brown eyes darting between Marcus and Cantfield, seemingly not knowing who to settle upon. "Very nice to meet you, my lords."

Both Marcus and Cantfield bowed to the girl

before taking it in turns to chastely kiss her gloved hand, Marcus first, followed by Cantfield, whose usual charm seemed to be working, at least with Miss Merriweather, who started to blush heartily when Cantfield raised his head.

The ladies were complete opposites. Kat was tall and athletic in shape, whereas Miss Merriweather was of average height, and slightly voluptuous of figure, with chestnut brown hair compared to Kat's deep auburn. And Marcus could never imagine Kat blushing from a man kissing her knuckles as Miss Merriweather had. Though for a mad moment he wondered if she'd blush if it was somewhere else she was being kissed by Marcus...

Instantly, his body tightened as the image of her naked in his bed flooded his imagination. Thoughts of kissing her everywhere filled him and he had to blink hard to bring his surroundings back into focus and pay attention to whatever it was Miss Merriweather was talking about. Something to do with the weather.

"Cantfield was just telling me he wishes to dance," Marcus announced. "Would you do him the honor, Miss Merriweather?"

Canfield rounded his eyes upon him, but clearly understood Marcus's need to speak with Kat in private.

"Of course," Miss Merriweather said, taking

Cantfield's outstretched hand, who then led her back to the ballroom.

Alone at last, though the hallway was still too public for the verbal battle Marcus suspected he was about to have with Lady Kaitlyn. He swiveled his eyes to hers, and they clashed. The most overwhelming urge to drag her into the nearest room and kiss her senseless to see if she was as passionate at kissing as she was fighting came over him. But he resisted the impulse. Just.

"I'm glad you found me." Kat's voice was a welcome distraction, except that it drew his attention to her lips, damn it.

What the devil was wrong with him? He never reacted to a woman like this, not to the point of nearly losing control. Ignoring his wayward thoughts, he returned to the matter at hand. The whole point for his attending. "Surely, you knew I'd hunt you down."

"Hunting me down would suggest I'm prey," Kat replied. "And I can assure you, I am anything but."

"Apex predators hunt other predators, my lady." He took a small step closer to her, but she didn't budge an inch. "Particularly when you've all but invited or perhaps challenged me to do so."

"And how have I done that?" Her green eyes radiated innocence.

"Come, my lady. I thought you more forthright

than that." Marcus reached into his pocket and pulled out the offending flyer that had made its way into the hands of most Londoners by late this evening. "Apart from stealing the journal—"

"Borrowing—"

"It seems you had a hand in my sudden rise to fame, or infamy as most would suggest…" He pressed the flyer into her hands. "I know you're behind this."

Kat glanced down at the paper before returning his stare. "I was confident you'd put two and two together, though I imagine Sir William assisted."

She knew of his relationship with Sir William, did she? The woman was well informed. "He confirmed my suspicions."

"Clearly, we need to talk."

The woman was the queen of understatement. "We need to do a lot more than talk. You need to start explaining yourself before I cart you out of here over my shoulder in front of everyone. At least then I will have earned a reputation worthy of being torn apart by your little gazette."

"You could try, though I don't like your chances."

"Darling, I can do a lot more than try." He squared his shoulders.

Kaitlyn merely shrugged, obviously certain he wouldn't do such a thing.

Tempted though he was, he wouldn't, as doing

so would mean a quick trip down the aisle to redeem both their reputations. And marriage was not an institution he ever intended to partake in again. "Are you not concerned that now I've learned of your little secret, about being one of the owners of the *Gazette*, that I might use it against you?"

"Not at all," her velvet voice drawled. "I expected you to discover it was me behind the move. And if you hadn't been able to do that, you would have been of little use to me."

"I live to be of use to you, my lady." He mockingly bowed before her.

"You will be of great use soon, I can guarantee it," came her pert reply. "And, no, I'm not concerned you will reveal my secret. We have too much at stake to be playing games of tit for tat."

She was right. Marcus sighed. "Then do you mind telling me why the devil you had a special flyer printed listing me as one of the bachelors to be critiqued? I can see no useful purpose in doing so, apart from incurring my wrath."

"I always do things on purpose, my lord, and you can be assured that is certainly the case in this instance." Kat squared her shoulders. "I need your help."

Marcus couldn't stop the laugh of incredulity from leaving his lips. "You need my help?" Was the woman serious? "Let me see if I understand you correctly. First, you knee me in the bollocks.

Second, you steal Elizabeth's journal from me. Third, you have me listed as one of the next bachelors to be critiqued in your gazette, which leads to my reputation being damaged in the short space of only a few hours. And after all of that, you're asking for *my* help? You have an odd notion of how to go about asking for someone's help."

"Perhaps." She lifted her chin, her eyes never leaving his. "Though I disagree somewhat about your reputation. It's only slightly sullied and will be redeemed when I publish a retraction about you being critiqued, after you help me."

"After I help you? Are you blackmailing me?"

"Not at all." She shook her head vehemently. "I'm recruiting you."

Chapter Eight

Her announcement to recruit him went down exactly as a lead balloon would in the Thames— it disappeared into the murky depths and sank to the bottom all but instantly as Marcus eyed her like she had completely lost her wits.

"Recruit me? You seem to enjoy playing dangerous games, Lady Kaitlyn." His voice was deadly and low as he leaned in closer to her, his breath but a whisper away. "For your sake, I hope you know the rules."

There was an unspoken promise in his words and a shiver of anticipation ran down her spine. "I've played dangerous games my entire life, Lord Westwood. So, yes, you can be assured I know the rules." Though she had a feeling when it came to Marcus that the rules would fly out the window. The thought was as frightening as it was thrilling.

"It's back to Lord Westwood, is it?" He quirked an eyebrow. "I thought now we are alone you wouldn't be so formal."

"I slipped into childhood habits when calling you by your given name last night," she replied, eyeing the slight smirk on his face, and knowing that he was enjoying teasing her. "I will try not to do so again. I do know *some* of the proprieties."

"Who would have guessed?" He shrugged. "But there's no need for formalities. You have already kneed me in the bollocks, so call me what you will. Blackmail is an intimate business, after all."

"I'm not blackmailing you." Kat had to resist the urge to stomp her foot on the spot. "I told you, I'm recruiting you. I have no intention of having you critiqued in the *Gazette*, regardless of whether you agree to help me or not." She tilted her head as she stared steadily at him. "However, after you hear what I have to tell you, you will be begging me to assist."

"I don't beg for anything." His voice was smoothly confident as he leaned in closer. "Though you might after we're done."

Kaitlyn gulped. The very words were like a soft caress along her skin, leaving her breathless.

The sound of a woman's laughter echoed down the hallway coming toward the stairway from the ballroom. It was enough to remind them of their surroundings and break the odd spell between them.

"Come," Marcus said. "We need to talk without fear of being overheard." He placed a light hand on her elbow and guided her down the hall. "And you can explain to me your rationalizations for why you did what you did. I'm sure it will prove entertaining if nothing else."

Normally, Kat would take exception to a man touching her, but this was Marcus and his touch did the strangest things to her. Even now as he led her into Darrow's library, she had to work hard to keep her reaction to his touch from showing. The heat radiating from his fingers, even through the material of his gloves, felt like it burned a hole on the bare skin of her upper arm, sending a wave of electricity through her entire body.

She wondered what it would feel like to have him touch her elsewhere... For him to caress her waist, her thighs, her innermost core. The thought was as shocking as it was scorching.

Kat tried to regain her wayward emotions by taking a deep breath, but all she ended up doing was inhaling the woodsy scent of his cologne, which clouded her already clouded senses a great deal more. What was wrong with her? She'd been trained to never allow herself to be so distracted. Not that she'd ever been as attracted to anyone before as she was to Marcus, but still, she knew better.

As soon as they entered the library and it was clear they were alone, Kat wrenched her arm free from Marcus's and stalked over to the fireplace burning cozily on the right wall, opposite a large, gleaming rosewood desk. She was more upset with herself for simply being led along and doing nothing to stop him. But she'd been powerless to stop him, caught up in her thoughts of him touching her.

Marcus followed her into the room, kicking the door closed behind him with the back of his boot, and then marched over to stand in front of the desk, arms crossed over his chest as he faced her.

To anyone else, he'd look menacing, downright fierce even, as he stared at her. But to Kat, he looked enticing. So much so that she was wrestling with herself to resist storming over and demanding he kiss her.

"All right then, talk," he said, thankfully oblivious to her internal struggle. "Tell me this master plan of yours and why you had to list my name, making everyone think I'm some nefarious bachelor who eats virgins for breakfast."

Kat nearly laughed, grateful that the idea of Marcus being some sort of debauched rake, broke the passionate trance she'd half been in. "I needed everyone to think you were going to be critiqued so you'd receive an invitation to become a member of the Corinthian Club. An invitation I believe you should have received this evening."

"How the bloody hell do you know that?" Now it was his turn to regard her with suspicion. "Do you have an informant in my household?"

She bestowed upon him a supremely frosty glare. "No, of course not." Though it would've becn a handy thing, as she preferred to try to have at least one informant in most houses of rank. It's how she obtained a great portion of her information. Servants were a veritable fount of the stuff. "I anticipated you'd receive an invitation, because every other bachelor we have named thus far for critique in the *Gazette* has immediately been sent an invitation to join the Club. In having you named, I was hoping you would be invited."

"Why would you wish for me to be a member of that sort of establishment? It's known for some rather tasteless activities…" Marcus seemed uncomfortable even discussing the matter, which was rather endearing.

"I'm well aware of the Corinthian Club's profligate and debauched activities." Though she didn't have any personal experience with such things, she knew of them. "I believe a man can generally indulge in whatever he wants to there, for a price."

"And again, why do you want me to join such a club?"

This was the difficult part. How much did he know about his late wife? Kat didn't want to crush any memories he had of her, though surely someone with Marcus's skills had to have known about the woman cheating on him. "The Club was mentioned in your late wife's journal."

Marcus gritted his teeth. "You've read Elizabeth's journal?"

She nodded. "I have. Why else would I have taken it but to discover the information inside?"

"Why else." Marcus stalked over to the window overlooking the back gardens.

"It mentions the Chameleon."

"Which is obviously why we both want it." Marcus's hand stilled on the window frame, his shoulders tense. "What did it say?"

"How much did you know of your wife's activities?"

He scoffed as he raised the window frame a few inches, then turned to look at her. "If you're trying to ask if I knew my late wife was unfaithful, then the answer is yes. She started having affairs a few months after we were married, when I was sent over to Spain, though I didn't know it at the time. Elizabeth complained of being bored and lonely when I travelled, so she pleaded with me to allow her to accompany me on my future trips. Considering what I was doing was low-level spying for the government by attending various balls in Europe and discreetly obtaining information, I thought it wouldn't hurt, and would assist in my cover story of traveling through Europe. But Elizabeth soon got bored with that, too, and seemed to think it would add far more enjoyment to take a lover in each city we visited."

"You don't strike me as a man who would condone such a thing." The man standing before her was the epitome of a proud and confident man, one who wouldn't cower to anything or anyone. Traits that Kat was starting to realize she found supremely attractive.

"By that stage, the spell she'd originally ensnared me with had well and truly worn off, and I could see Elizabeth for the vain and shallow creature she truly was." He shrugged as he perched on the edge of the windowsill. "To be honest, her affairs meant she was occupied and left me alone to do my work, so they mattered little after the initial sense of betrayal. That is until they began to impact my work."

Marcus stared into the flames of the hearth, lost in the past, Kat supposed. "They used her to get to you?" It's what was evident in the journal, even if it hadn't been obvious to the lady herself.

He swiveled his gaze back to her. "Yes. I had failed to consider that aspect of her affairs. Elizabeth's vanity and her compulsion to be worshipped were traits easily manipulated and could be exploited by those who knew of the special assistance I provided for the government."

"Which the Chameleon did."

"Yes. I assume the man seduced Elizabeth to gain easy access to the apartments we were lodging in at the time, and break into my safe to steal the notes and dossiers I'd collated on the Russians, regarding the issues we were having with them and the Afghan border. Clearly, the assassin was content with the information he was able to steal and had no need for Elizabeth anymore. I found her dead in our bed, and every piece of information I'd collected was gone."

"Her journal confirmed as much," Kat said.

"Did it mention his name?"

She shook her head. "No. She only ever referred to her lover as her mysterious chameleon who had links to the Corinthian Club. Which is why I need your help."

A rich laugh filled with what could only be described as incredulity left Marcus's lips. "You're serious? You expect me to help you after all you've done?"

"I haven't done that much, really." She lifted her chin a fraction higher in the air and stood her ground. "And I do."

"Victor should have damn well spanked you when you were a child." Marcus shook his head ruefully. "Perhaps that might have jolted some sense into you. Instead, he was far too indulgent with you, especially as you seem to think I'll agree to whatever it is you want my help with."

Kat screwed up her nose slightly. "I know you're not happy with me at the moment."

"How insightful." He walked over to where she stood, almost like a panther stalking its prey in the jungle, before he stopped a foot in front of her.

"What is it you need my help doing?"

Kat paused. Being so close to him had the oddest effect on her senses, almost as if he was befuddling her. She had to stop herself from reaching up around his head and pulling him down to her lips. Catching her breath and her previous train of thought, she said, "I would have thought it obvious. I need your help to catch the Chameleon. The Corinthian Club is the only club in London I don't have a well-placed informant, and this is the best lead I've had so far regarding the Chameleon. We need to investigate it immediately. And considering I know you've been hunting the man for years, as have I, we need to work together. At least until we find him."

"We do, do we?"

The man was being deliberately difficult. "Yes. If we can get into the manager's office in the Club, then we should be able to obtain a list of their patrons. And if the Chameleon does frequent the Club as suggested in Elizabeth's journal, then he would have to be a financially contributing member, so we should be able to narrow down a list of suspects if we obtain their membership list."

Marcus swore and stalked over to the hearth, raking a hand through his hair. "The Chameleon is one of Europe's most formidable assassins. Victor would wring my neck from his grave if I helped you get anywhere near the fiend."

"No, he wouldn't. He trained me since I was a child to do exactly that," Kat replied, glad for the space now between them. She needed to regain her equilibrium if she was to have any chance of convincing him.

"He trained you to protect yourself, as your mother and father were unable to. Nothing more and nothing less."

"You're wrong," Kat said. "And do not use Victor as an excuse either. I will find the Chameleon and have my vengeance, with or without your help. But he will be caught sooner if we work together. And after reading Elizabeth's journal, I know that the Corinthian Club is a key to finding him."

His eyes darkened. "You had no business reading Elizabeth's journal."

"I know, and normally I wouldn't. But I had to see if it contained information about the Chameleon, which my informants suggested it might." She'd been conflicted enough last night, though in the end her desire for vengeance won. "If it's any consolation, I haven't divulged the contents to anyone, nor will I. But I don't regret reading it, as it has provided me with the first tangible clue about where the Chameleon may be found."

Marcus's hands were clenched by his sides, and Kat had the odd impulse of wanting to grab his hand in her own and soothe away the anger. She'd never felt the need to comfort a man before, but suddenly she wanted to comfort Marcus.

"You have no idea of the league you're playing in, Kat." He was using her first name as he said he would, and it sounded so familiar rolling off his tongue that she couldn't imagine him calling her anything but that. "The Chameleon is deadly. No one knows the exact number of his kills, but it's in the hundreds."

"I'm fully aware of the man's deadly abilities." She'd studied her quarry's assassinations and movements intimately, to the point of knowing them almost better than her own recent movements. "If we combine our resources and our skills, we'll find the traitor."

"Skills?" Marcus scoffed. "You got lucky last night with that knee. If I hadn't been distracted with finding out you were a woman, I'd never have let my guard down and you wouldn't have gotten the best of me."

"Knowing I was fighting you was a distraction to me from the start, and the only reason I allowed you to maneuver me into that untenable position against the wall." She raised an eyebrow at him. "And trust me, you haven't seen the extent of my skills just yet."

"You will get yourself killed chasing the Chameleon," Marcus growled.

"I'm capable of protecting myself."

"You can't knee every man in the bollocks."

Kat smiled at him. Clearly, he underestimated her abilities. Perhaps it was time to teach him a lesson in assumptions. "Did you notice the painting on the wall near the entry when we came in?"

Marcus stopped short at the change in conversation. "What about it?"

"How far would you say it is from where I am now standing?"

"Around fifty feet." He shrugged. "Give or take."

"And did you notice the small apple being held by the lady in the picture?"

"What the devil does this all—"

"Did you notice it?"

"Yes."

"Could you aim a dagger and strike the apple from this distance?"

Marcus's face screwed up in exasperation. "No, of course not. No one could."

"Consider this your first lesson in the folly of making assumptions, Marcus Black, especially when it comes to me." Kat reached into her skirt pocket, and before Marcus could even guess what she was about to do, she slid her dagger from the sheath sewn inside and launched it across the room. It landed directly in the apple's center and Marcus swore.

"Do it again," he said, bracing his legs apart,

an expression of defiance in his eyes.

She shrugged, having spent hours upon hours every day for literally years perfecting her dagger skills. "Very well." She reached down and pulled out her smaller dagger from the sheath strapped to her lower calf. "I'll aim for the woman's head this time."

Marcus's eyes snapped down to her lower leg, desire flaring in his expression.

Exposing any part of her body was scandalous, of course, but Kat did have trousers on underneath her dress, and she'd only pulled up the pant leg for a moment to expose her stocking-clad calf.

Lowering the skirt of her dress seemed to snap Marcus out of his daze and he blinked, his eyes finding hers again, a smoldering heat still blaring in them.

She broke eye contact for a moment as her gaze flicked to the target before her eyes returned to his. She threw her knife at the picture. Once again, it landed dead center, lodging in the picture of the woman's head. "Satisfied?" Kat sashayed past him to the painting. "I wonder if Lord Darrow will notice the cuts in the canvas."

She pulled both knives free from the painting and re-sheathed them before turning back to face Marcus. "I hope that illustrates to you I'm capable of handling myself. Though I can demonstrate further, if needed. I'm as good with a pistol as I am with a dagger."

Marcus shook his head. "No, that won't be necessary. Clearly, you are capable with weapons."

She smoothed down the material of her skirt before walking over to perch on the desk to the side of where he was standing. "Trust me, Westwood, this is no game for me. I know exactly what the Chameleon is capable of from firsthand experience. And I have the skills to protect myself."

Dragging a hand through his hair once again, sure to cause his valet distress if he ever caught sight of his employer's tussled locks, Marcus then sighed, a very long, very weary sigh. "And how do you propose we work together to find the Chameleon?" He walked over to the brandy bottle sitting on the side table and poured himself a glass.

A blossom of hope sprang up inside her. The stubborn man might finally be coming around. "I suggest we pool our resources and work together to find him. The first step being to get into the Corinthian Club." She stood and approached him. Reaching past him, Kat picked up the brandy bottle, pouring herself a nip of the liquid in one of the other empty glasses. "He won't escape England this time with both of us hunting him."

He gazed down at her. There was the heat from earlier, but also a question in his eyes. "What do you intend to do when we find him?"

She smiled grimly. "Seek justice, of course." Her form of justice—an eye for an eye. "Isn't that what you also intend, my lord?"

"It is, my lady." His eyes narrowed upon her. "Though I think our notions of what justice is may differ somewhat."

Kat shrugged and lifted the glass to her lips. "Perhaps," was all she would allow, before swallowing the contents. She coughed slightly as the rich fluid burned down her throat. "Oh, that is just horrible."

The corner of his mouth tilted up in a semblance of a smile. "Darrow isn't known for his taste in spirits."

There was still a wariness about him, but he seemed much more receptive to her suggestion. "What do you say, my lord?" she asked. "Shall we partner up on this hunt?"

Reaching over, he plucked the glass from her hand. "If we are to be partners, you should start calling me Marcus again." He put the glass down on the table before turning back to her.

There was such fierce determination in his eyes that she couldn't help but feel as if he was a predator looking upon his next meal—her. Her pulse quickened in response. "So you agree, then?"

He stepped forward, until he was less than a foot from her. "'Tis probably the only way I can ensure your safety. I owe Victor that much."

She scowled. "A moment ago, you conceded that I am capable with weapons."

"I did. But being capable with weapons doesn't necessarily mean you are safe in every situation." His voice was a soft caress as he whispered against her ear. "For example, are you safe now, Kat?"

Her breath hitched in her throat at how intimate the use of her first name sounded on his lips when he was this close to her. How the man seemed to know exactly what to do to get under her skin was maddening.

Well, that wouldn't do. It was time to take the situation into her own hands. Literally. She slid her hands up the front of his shirt and gently grabbed ahold of his lapels, before pulling him up against her. "Fairly safe, I believe."

His lips hovered only an inch away from her own. "We have different ideas of what we consider safe."

"Possibly," Kat conceded. "But as my knee is now safely positioned between your legs once again, and ready to strike, I would say yes, I am indeed safe. Though you might not be."

He blinked for a moment and then threw back his head and laughed.

When he put his hands up in a gesture of surrender, Kat let go of the material of his shirt and lowered her knee, but Marcus made no move to step backward and away from her. "I seem to have a terrible habit of forgetting to protect my most vulnerable parts from your wrath, my dear." He looked at her cryptically for a moment. "Something I shall have to ensure I guard against in the future."

"Perhaps then, *Marcus*, you shouldn't try to intimidate me. If that is what you were attempting to do."

"Intimidate is not the word I would use… I was actually thinking perhaps I need to live up to my newfound infamy."

"And how would you do that?" Her voice was but a breathless whisper as he lowered his head once again closer to her own, his lush lips fully in her focus.

"If we're entering into an agreement together, we should seal the deal with a kiss," he murmured. "It's the polite thing to do."

"Sealing the deal with a kiss is how my friend Olivia ended up marrying the Bastard of Baker Street," she said, annoyed her voice sounded slightly breathless. "I've no intention of following the same path."

"Oh, don't worry, my lady. Neither do I," Marcus all but purred. "I will never marry again. You're safe from me in that regard. Unless, of course, you're scared of a kiss?"

"I'm scared of no man's kiss."

"Then show me."

The deep timber of his voice sent a shiver

through her body and all she could do was nod. What harm was there in a kiss? It might satisfy her curiosity and put the unaccountable sensations she was experiencing in his presence to rest once and for all. "Very well."

She raised her head and pressed her lips softly against his. Almost immediately, a heat began to curl in her belly from the touch, his lips scorching in their intensity. She moaned as he nudged open her mouth with his, and his tongue flicked against hers. Mirroring the movement, she did the same to him and was rewarded with his deep groan as they began to kiss each other with an unrestrained passion she didn't think was possible for her.

Instinctively, she pressed herself closer to him, reveling at the sensations of pleasure coursing through her from his very touch. He was strong and so masculine it made her feel delicate and feminine, which she rarely ever did.

His hands circled around her waist, before sliding lower and cupping her buttocks, pulling her in, tighter against him. Kat nearly gasped when the hardness of his manhood pressed into her lower belly. It was wicked. It was wanton. It was addictive, and she wanted more.

She wound her hands up and around his neck and kissed him back with unrepentant fervor, pressing her breasts more snugly against the broadness of his thick chest. Never had she tasted such sublime wonder as was Marcus.

A throat being cleared from behind them had Kat wrenching away from Marcus and spinning around to face the threat. It was Cantfield and Etta. How mortifying. And Kat never felt mortified by anything, though she'd never been kissed so thoroughly before either, or caught in the act.

"We do hate to interrupt," Cantfield said, unable to fully suppress the small grin twisting his lips. "But Lady Birmingham is mentioning to all and sundry that she saw the two of you sneaking off in here together."

"It's all anyone is talking about…" Etta cringed while she pointed out the fact. "And, well, combined with the flyer today… Kat, they're all whispering that you're in here being compromised by Lord Westwood…"

"Not far from the truth, it would seem." Cantfield's grin grew. He was clearly enjoying the situation.

"Don't push me, Lucas," Marcus growled from behind her. "Damn it. This is less than ideal and entirely because of that flyer, you do realize that, don't you?"

Kat turned to face him and saw the lines of exasperation on his face as he glared at her. Passion replaced by frustration.

"At least it will put you in good stead for membership with the Corinthian Club," she said.

One had to look at the positives and focus on what was truly important in the scheme of things. "Speaking of which, we will need to arrange for you to have a meeting with the manager, Mr. Dartmoore, tomorrow. The sooner we can get in there, the better."

"We?" Marcus's expression turned to incredulity. "How do you intend to get into a men's establishment?"

"Not through the front door, obviously." She placed her hands on her hips and returned his glare. "Once you're taken into Dartmoore's office, I'll arrange for a large-scale distraction which will force Dartmoore to leave the room, while you remain inside. Then I'll slip into the building through the kitchens, undetected, and meet you in the office."

"Even with a distraction, someone is bound to notice a lady skulking through the hallways of the place," Marcus replied.

"Not if I'm dressed as one of the female entertainers that work there."

Marcus closed his eyes tightly. "Absolutely not," he ground out with a clenched jaw, his voice brooking no arguments. "You're not dressing as a trollop and that is final, end of story."

"You have no say in how I dress."

"If you want my help in this endeavor, then yes, I do." His eyes narrowed upon her. "No trollop outfits, are we clear? And you can arrange the distraction, but I will search his office on my own. I'm not risking your pretty little neck for something I can do perfectly well on my own. Understood?"

"Perfectly." If he thought she was going to blindly follow his orders, he really didn't know her at all.

"I mean it, Kat. No dressing as a lady entertainer, or our partnership, if that's what we can even call it, will be over before it has even begun. I'm not having you place yourself in danger."

"No trollop outfits, I promise." And she would honor her promise. She'd just dress in some other costume to blend in, because if the man thought she was going to sit out from searching Dartmoore's office, he was in for a surprise. "What time will you attend the club tomorrow?" She wouldn't have thought it possible that the man could appear even more suspicious, but he did. "I need to know when to set up the diversion."

"I'll go late in the evening, probably around eleven," he gruffly replied, his eyes watching her like a hawk.

"Good. I'll organize the diversion for a quarter past. Make sure you're in his office by then, discussing your membership." Kat pulled out the journal from one of the concealed pockets in her skirt and handed it to him. She'd intended on giving it back to him tonight, and hopefully doing so now would distract him from thinking overly about her easy acquiescence surrounding the club.

Marcus took the small leather-bound book and regarded it for a moment. His lip curled into a slight snarl. "This damn journal has eluded me for years." He shook his head. "Perhaps Elizabeth's folly in documenting her affairs will lead to her killer being apprehended, and my brother's name being restored." He placed it inside the pocket of his jacket. "And then the last laugh will be on the Chameleon, won't it?"

"Once I obtain my vengeance against him for all of the lives he's taken, it will," Kat declared.

"This is no game, Kat. We're dealing with a ruthless assassin who, as far as I know, has a one hundred percent success rate. He's not a person to be playing with."

"This is no game for me, I assure you. I'll have my vengeance and not you or anyone else will stop me. And just as you have, I'm expecting the Chameleon to underestimate exactly what I am capable of. In fact, I'm counting on it. Now, if you'll excuse us." She walked over to Etta, who had been standing with the marquis, appearing somewhat uncomfortable watching Kat and Marcus bicker. "Etta and I will start circulating in the ballroom to try to minimize any gossip this little sojourn in the library has cost us. I suggest you and Cantfield find Darrow's billiards room and play a game or two, and if anyone asks, that is what we shall say you and he have been doing for the past half hour. I'll see you tomorrow, my lord."

"No surprises, Kat."

Kat was never one to do well with heeding warnings. "If you're expecting me to do something unexpected, then it won't really be a surprise at all when I do it, will it?" Unable to help herself, she winked at him, to which he appeared to be at an unaccountable loss for words.

Good. The man was far too confident. It was time he realized who he was dealing with. She linked her arm through Etta's and strolled out of the room, Cantfield's laughter booming behind them.

"If you wanted to bait Lord Westwood," Etta murmured as they walked down the hallway, the sounds of the orchestra getting louder with each step, "then mission successful."

"Bait him? I wasn't trying to bait him. I was giving him advanced notice of what to expect with me." It was the least she could do, given the man's previously well-ordered existence. For a brief moment, she felt sorry for him. But only for a brief moment.

"He has no idea who he's really dealing with, does he?" Etta bit her bottom lip.

"None at all." How she was looking forward to the moment when he discovered she'd paid no attention to his edict whatsoever. The man was going to have his finely ordered world shaken and Kat was going to be there to witness it.

Chapter Nine

The next evening, Marcus was shown into the office of the Corinthian Club's manager, Mr. Lionel Dartmoore, and directed to take a seat opposite the massive mahogany desk taking up the far side of the room.

"Mr. Dartmoore will be with you shortly, my Lord," the man's secretary intoned, before swiftly departing and closing the heavy oak paneled door behind him.

Marcus surveyed the room, noting that the ostentatious decorations and fittings in the entrance of the club had been carried into this office, too. Everywhere he looked there was either gold, crystal, mahogany, or marble somewhere. From the crystal chandeliers hanging above, the gold-trimmed brocade drapes covering the windows, which matched the settees in the middle of the room, to the heavy mahogany desk and the marble fireplace adorning the far end of the room, everything screamed wealth and excess.

He walked over to the glass display cabinet standing prominently in the center of the room. Proudly lining its shelves was an odd collection of snuff boxes. Marcus had never seen such an assembly of so many ornate boxes before; there had to be over a hundred of them. Some were gold and others silver, but all had intricate filigree patterns in swirls on their surfaces and a majority were adorned with glistening gems and jewels.

"A sight to behold, is it not?" a voice asked from the door behind. "The finest collection of snuff boxes in all of England."

Marcus turned as a slender gentleman with slicked back sandy hair and a slightly crooked nose approached. The man was in his late thirties and had a smile oozing from his face as he extended his hand toward Marcus. He was also a good foot shorter than Marcus, and his clothes, though tailored, were rather gaudy in their style. Perhaps the man was trying to emulate the gaudiness of the establishment he was running?

"I'm Lionel Dartmoore, director of the Corinthian Club." He came to a stop beside Marcus at the glass cabinet case. "It's an absolute honor to meet you, Lord Westwood."

Marcus grasped his hand and shook it, surprised at the firmness of the thin man's grip. "Mr. Dartmoore."

"On behalf of the other members and patrons of the club," Dartmoore enthused, "might I say we're honored, my lord, that you're considering our offer of membership."

"I've heard…interesting things about the club," Marcus said.

"I am sure you have. And trust me, you will now need a safe space to come and relax in, without censure or gossip, which is what I'm sure you've been met with since that nasty leaflet was printed yesterday. Oh, but where are my manners?" He all but squealed. "Please do take a seat." The man motioned over to one of the settees across from the display case.

Marcus sat on one and Dartmoore took a seat on the settee across from him. They were oddly delicate little chairs for a gentlemen's club, with white and gold painted wood, and were smaller and more uncomfortable seats than usual, too. He briefly wondered if it would hold his weight for long.

Dartmoore seemed used to them as he relaxed back in apparent comfort, though he was half the size of Marcus, which probably accounted for them being chosen in the first place.

"I was surprised to see you listed as one of the bachelors to be critiqued," Dartmoore said.

"As was I," Marcus muttered.

"Yes, well, it is a publication aimed at ruining the pleasurable activities and pastimes men like us wish to partake in." Dartmoore leaned forward and rested his elbows on his knees. "A travesty, really. But the one positive to be gained from it, is that it has made my job a great deal easier."

"How has it done that, Mr. Dartmoore?" Marcus asked.

"Well, it highlights the sort of men we like to have as members here." The man was beaming at that fact. "Men who can stop worrying about whatever their desires are, and have their needs filled right here in their very own club. It's a fact we pride ourselves on and is why we are fast becoming *the* club to join at the moment."

"I thought Club Tartus was *the* club at the moment."

Dartmoore actually turned his nose up at the suggestion. "Colver's club is only *the* club if your tastes are limited to gaming and conversation. You'll soon see why we are getting so popular. We have so much more specialized entertainment available to our members. Though, of course, we don't simply accept every gentleman who applies to us. No, indeed. We only accept the crème de la crème of society, whose tastes run toward the more adventurous."

"How reassuring." The club sounded more deplorable by the minute. "It has a select membership, then?"

"It certainly does, my lord!"

"Is there a list of your members I may peruse?"

Dartmoore squirmed slightly in his chair, uncertainty crossing his face. "I actually haven't been asked that before." He laughed uncomfortably.

"If I am to join your club—"

"Oh, it's not my club," Dartmoore interrupted him. "The owner is private and likes to keep that same ethos throughout the club, which is why our membership list is held in the strictest of confidences. Of course, though, you are bound to recognize some of our members when I take you on a tour of the premises, but I'm afraid I can't let you see a list of our membership. I am sure you understand the need for privacy, especially with what takes place here."

"Of course." If it had been that easy, the Chameleon would probably have been found long ago. Though finding out who the owner was, was another line of enquiry to be pursued, too. He glanced at his fob watch, noting it was a quarter past on the dot. Where was the distraction Kat had promised?

"Your understanding is much appreciated," Dartmoore enthused, before suddenly springing to his feet. "Why don't you allow me to show you our facilities and amenities, then? That will allow you to look over some of our guests before I show you the array of entertainment on offer. Then you can make an informed decision as to whether you will accept my invitation to join."

Damn, where was that distraction? To say no would only invite suspicion. "Very well."

"Excellent!" The man placed his hand up to the pocket of his waistcoat and removed a timepiece from its confines. "Wonderful, we shall be in time for a special show scheduled in the entertainment room."

Marcus raised an eyebrow. "You have an entertainment room in the club?" Perhaps he could keep him talking for a bit.

The man nodded his head and smiled proudly. "Oh, indeed we do, and let me tell you it is for that reason we are so unique. Without ruining the surprise, let me just say that you will have never seen so many delectable ladies all in one place."

Now the rumors of the club and its unusual entertainment were becoming clear. "I rather thought the purpose of a gentleman's club was to be a safe haven of sorts for a man, away from the ladies?"

"Oh, goodness no, we do not allow ladies in the club. No, no, no. These ladies are for entertainment purposes only. There are no female members here."

The man began to walk toward the door and Marcus slowly stood to follow him, making note of the fact that the location of the office and the actual size of the room didn't match his observations from the outside of the building when he'd first entered the establishment.

The wooden paneling on the far wall behind the desk looked suspiciously like it may contain a hidden door, to what Marcus suspected was Mr. Dartmoore's true office. Now all he had to do was figure out how to get back to it, without

Dartmoore, which could prove difficult if the man always locked the door behind him, as Kat mentioned he did.

But then the door opened, and a footman hurried in. He rushed over to Dartmoore, carefully avoiding looking at Marcus. Dartmoore stopped mid-stride, his face scrunched up. "What is going on?"

The footman whispered something hurried in the man's ear. Whatever was said had all color leaching from Dartmoore's face. Perhaps this was the distraction Kat had promised.

Dartmoore quickly glanced up at Marcus, unable to disguise the panic in his eyes. "I am terribly sorry, my lord, but a slight emergency has come up that I must see to immediately. Would you please wait here? I shouldn't be too long."

Marcus nodded easily. "Of course. Attend to whatever you must."

The man nodded and then turned his eyes on the footman. "Fetch his Lordship a drink and then come and assist in the lobby." He then strode out the door, closing it swiftly behind him.

Marcus looked up at the young man. "I've no need of a drink, thank you. You may leave."

The footman bowed and smiled. "Yes, my lord."

Marcus narrowed his eyes. That smile seemed familiar.

He watched as the footman turned toward the main door but instead of stepping through it, he simply opened it a fraction before peeking out. Clearly satisfied by what he saw, he closed the door and stepped back into the room, then turned back to face Marcus.

"Do not just stand there." The footman's voice had suddenly turned into that of a lady's. "We have to get into his office before he returns."

Chapter Ten

Marcus swore vehemently. "I'm going to spank you until you're black and blue, woman! Damn it, I told you, you were not to be involved with anything to do with the Corinthian Club! You broke your promise to me."

"No, I did not. I promised you I wouldn't dress as a trollop. And as you can see"—she waved her hand down at her footman's costume—"I'm not dressed as one. You couldn't even tell it was me." Kaitlyn smiled from beneath the beard and wig, enjoying his annoyance more than she should.

She ripped the facial pieces off one after the other, stuffing them into her trouser pockets, before pulling out the wads of cotton from inside her mouth that she'd used to create a squarer jawline. "You can be upset with me later."

"How the devil did you even get in here?" Marcus growled, watching her like a hawk. "And dressed in the clothes of a footman, no less! Could you have gotten any more scandalously tight pants to wear?" His eyes trailed down the length of her legs, lingering on them.

"My butler was competent enough to obtain

the uniform for me, and I already have a large array of wigs and facial disguises." She felt a slight blush creep up her cheeks at his continued perusal of her legs, which suddenly felt unaccountably bare, when only moments before she'd felt liberated wearing the pants in public.

Deciding to ignore his close scrutiny, she continued, "I have an informant here who is a scullery maid, so though she can't assist greatly with providing any sort of information, she left the servants entrance unlocked for me. I came in through there, letting loose a little diversion in the process."

She watched him shake his head as he dragged his eyes away from her pants, muttering something to himself before he sighed loudly.

"How long do we have until he comes back?"

"That will depend on how long it takes them to wrangle a dozen piglets, ten geese, and seven rabbits from the main lobby and rooms flowing off from it." She shrugged. "Now on to more pressing matters, if my calculations are correct," she began, glancing over to where the desk was positioned over on the far side of the room. "The room is shorter from the inside than the outside—"

"Meaning there's most likely a concealed room containing Dartmoore's true office," Marcus interrupted. "Yes, I had managed to already figure that out, without your help." He began to walk over to the desk.

Kat followed close behind him, her eyes drifting down to appreciate the musculature of his backside before she could help herself. He was a fine specimen of a man. There was nothing wrong with her appreciating that. At least that was what she was trying to convince herself of. "You're quite welcome for the distraction, too, by the way."

He simply grunted as he trailed his hands along the wooden wall paneling, obviously searching for a panel that would open the concealed room.

Her gaze followed his fingers, almost hypnotically, and she found herself wondering what his fingers would feel like trailing over her own body with such deftness. Heat flooded her face just thinking the scandalous thought.

"Success!" He glanced back at her and smiled. Then he frowned. "You look all flushed. Are you all right?"

Thankfully, he couldn't read her mind, but his words did bring her back to the present with a thud and she shook her head free of the images. There was work to be done. There was no time to daydream about taking him as a lover. "I'm just hot. It's this outfit, I think." She tugged at the collar of the footman's jacket and shrugged.

Marcus nodded and then pressed the panel his hand was resting on. A loud click sounded and a door to his right swung inward. He grinned at her, then stepped into the small chamber. Kat followed him through. The room was about a quarter of the size of the main room housing it, and it contained several filing cabinets and a large desk scattered with papers.

Marcus began searching the desk while Kat started to look through the cabinets. The filing system was fairly organized and held folders that contained some dossiers on some important people.

"There's got to be hundreds of files in these drawers!" she exclaimed, quickly going from one to the next, in search of hopefully a master list of the club's membership. She pulled out one file and opened it, revealing several sheets of parchment with neat writing scrawled across the pages.

"I've found something," Marcus said. He was holding a small, red leather journal and was quickly leafing through the pages. "It looks to be possibly some sort of transaction ledger, but what's intriguing is it's written in code." He glanced back to her. "Any luck with the files?"

She shook her head and closed the file she had open, returning it to the drawer. "There's certainly all of the members' files within, I would say. But we have no time to go through them all."

"Oi! What's going on in here?" a rough voice from the concealed doorway barked.

Kat glanced over at the brawny man blocking the door only a few feet from her. He had close-shaved dark hair and appeared as if he'd come straight from the slums, even though he was dressed in a suit, ill-fitting as it was. Clearly, he was one of the men that Dartmoore paid to perform security duties at the club.

"Stay there, Kat," Marcus said as he slowly stepped out from the desk toward the doorway. "I'll deal with this."

Kat smiled at Marcus. "What, and let you have all of the fun tonight? I think not."

Before he had a chance to cross the space to where the guard was standing, Kat launched a flying front kick toward the guard, which landed squarely in his chest, knocking him back several paces into the outer room.

Kat frowned; the man was still on his feet. Well, he was built like a brick, so it would probably take a few more hits to knock him out. She ran through the door and launched herself directly at him.

The guard wore an incredulous look as Kat smiled at him, before landing another spinning kick to his side.

He expelled a breath at the impact and cursed. "You're a bloody woman?"

"Good of you to notice." She blocked one of his strikes and used the heel of her palm to strike his chin from underneath.

The man cursed again as his head jolted backward.

"Damn it, Kat, move away," Marcus yelled from behind her.

But Kat paid Marcus no heed as she continued to kick the brick. The man fought back and when his fist managed to glance the side of her torso, Kat exhaled as a jarring pain lanced up the side of her body. She narrowed her eyes and threw a volley of strikes at his head. The man clearly had skills in the boxing ring and was protecting his head well with his forearms. But this wasn't boxing.

Kat swung her leg in a side kick with all her might and landed a blow to his midsection, hoping to strike his liver. She guessed her aim had been true when he collapsed into a heap on the Persian rug, out cold.

She turned to Marcus who was standing there staring at her with an expression vacillating between extreme vexation and admiration.

"Do you ever listen?" he asked, tucking the red leather journal into his jacket pocket.

She took a second to catch her breath before answering. "Not unless I like what I hear."

"That is obvious."

"And did you observe how I disabled him without the need to knee him in the bollocks?"

"Lucky fellow," Marcus remarked. "Come, we need to get out of here."

He strode past her and grabbed her hand in his own and gently tugged her toward the door.

She didn't argue, somewhat winded from the recent exertion.

Opening the door a fraction, Marcus peeked out, before nodding back at her, then heading out into the hallway. The club was in chaos. Little piglets darted everywhere across the foyer and several geese flapped about wildly trying to evade the servants dashing around, madly attempting to catch them. Kat even caught sight of a few bunnies scurrying under some feet in the pandemonium.

"You like to make a statement, don't you?" he whispered into her ear as they strode around the circular corridor, skirting around the lobby.

She grinned up at him. "You're beginning to understand me."

He simply shook his head, a semi-smile on those lips of his, as together they dodged past the mayhem and slipped out the front door. Following him down the street and around the corner, there was a carriage waiting for them, though the crests of it were hidden under black material.

The driver scampered down and opened the door to the compartment. Kat nearly groaned when she saw it was Lord Cantfield dressed as a carriage driver. It seemed she wasn't the only one in costume today. She quickly averted her head and thankfully he didn't seem to recognize her, though he did peer at Marcus oddly as Kat proceeded ahead of him into the carriage.

Marcus barked out orders to take them to the rear of the Montrose residence before slamming the door closed in the man's face.

Kat heard the stairs outside being flipped up, before Cantfield climbed back onto the driver's perch and set the carriage in motion. She sank wearily onto the soft seat across from Marcus, grateful for the plush padding of the chairs as she was only now feeling the aches and pains occasioned from her run-in with the brick.

"You disobeyed me." Marcus's voice was soft and measured.

Kat sat across from him and smiled grimly. "When? By attending the club or failing to listen to you about fighting the brick?"

"The brick?" Marcus looked confused for a second.

"The guard I fought, who was built like a brick," she said.

"Oh…" Marcus nodded. "Yes, both I suppose. You disobeyed me twice."

"Actually, you're incorrect. I didn't, in fact, disobey you even once." It seemed all she was doing was enlightening or correcting him of late. "You see, I'm not yours to order about, so I can't disobey you, as you can't give me any commands in the first place. The quicker you understand that important aspect of our partnership, the easier it will be to deal with each other."

"Damn it, Kaitlyn!" he growled, his notorious control slipping. "I told you not to come near the club today."

"Yes, you did. But as I have already explained, I'm not yours to command. I've been running my own show for far too long now to start taking orders from anyone."

"You need a lesson in applying some common sense." Marcus ran a hand through his hair. "The way you're carrying on, anyone would think I was being an ogre when I'm only trying to keep you out of harm's way."

"I choose my own path, Lord Westwood," she hissed at him. "I'll let no man try to decide *anything* for me!" Even a man she was ridiculously attracted to, beyond all reason.

"Well, somebody should, because clearly your own decisions make you a candidate for Bedlam!"

Kat narrowed her eyes at him. "Is it your pride that's upset because I fooled you with my disguise? Or because I, a woman, could defend myself without need of a man to protect me?"

"Did you not see the danger that you were in?" he roared.

"And did you not see how I could protect myself from that very danger?" she yelled back at him.

"Damn it, I did!" He dragged a hand through his hair. "And bloody effectively, too."

"Then what's the problem?" She stared at him, exasperation mounting in her entire body.

"I'm not used to seeing a woman fighting a man to protect herself, at least not when I'm there and should be the one protecting her…"

He appeared so lost and confused, all her anger with him vanished. Marcus had been raised a gentleman through and through, and she imagined that accepting a woman could take care of herself to the point of defending herself against a man would probably take some time to get used to. "And I'm used to protecting myself, without the need for anyone else to defend me."

"I'm beginning to realize that."

She reached over and took his hand in hers, giving it a gentle squeeze. And as she glanced up at him and smiled in reassurance, their eyes locked, and a deep awareness charged the air. Kat felt powerless to do anything but stare at him as her heart started thrumming wildly, while his fingers began to softly trace along her palm.

How could such a simple touch send a wave of desire to her very core?

And right in that very instant, Kat wanted nothing more than to feel his kiss again. Without thinking, she leaned across and pressed her lips to his.

Chapter Eleven

The sensation of his lips against hers was hot, hard, and so deliciously wanton that Kat automatically wrapped her hands around his neck and urged herself closer against him.

Since last night, she'd been able to think of little else but the feel of his mouth against her own. Images of him, and the sensations his touch had evoked, were always in the back of her mind. It had taken a great deal of effort to push them to the side this evening for the mission, but she'd managed to do so, or at least she had until he kissed her again.

Now, it was as if her body craved him and couldn't get close enough as his mouth created a delicious sensation of heat and energy that curled within her. She moaned softly, surprised at the gentleness yet thoroughness of his onslaught.

The only other time she'd allowed a man to kiss her was when she was eighteen and she'd all but dared his brother Nathaniel to. That had been after Nathaniel told her news of Marcus's engagement, which for some reason had bothered her greatly. Nathaniel's kiss had been nothing memorable, and it completely paled in comparison to the kisses Marcus had given her last night and was pleasuring her with now.

These kisses were leaving her completely breathless and wanting more, so much more. They were sweet yet so sensual and she was certain no man would ever live up to the kisses Marcus was enthralling her with.

For a second, Kat thought about trying to resist and putting some space between them, so she could calm down and compose herself, but she was so tired of fighting everyone and everything, that for this one moment she was going to allow herself to let go and simply feel.

"So delicious," he murmured in a breathless whisper before he coaxingly teased her mouth open and his tongue flicked inside her depths, caressing and stroking her. Then his hands went from encircling her wrists to curling around her waist, pulling her firmly to him.

The action emboldened her, and she pressed her chest to his while her tongue began to explore his own.

When one of his hands slid from her waist up to her chest and began flicking open the buttons at the front of her footman's coat, Kat thought she would combust then and there. Marcus scattered kisses down her neck while his hand was busy peeling back her jacket to reveal the white cotton shirt she wore underneath, then with nimble fingers he unbuttoned her shirt, too.

He pulled back from her slightly, staring down at the binding covering her chest. "That looks uncomfortable."

For a moment she felt self-conscious, but then with sudden clarity she realized this might be as close as she ever got to truly bending the rules and experiencing some passion. She'd never really believed in the emotion before, but now, after Marcus and his touch, she wanted more of it. And she wasn't getting any younger at six-and-twenty. What was one more risk, in a life of so many? "It is." And then she reached behind her and began to unwrap the binding.

Marcus drew in a harsh breath and his eyes flared with desire. "Kat, we shouldn't be doing this…" There wasn't a great deal of conviction in his voice as he continued to stare hungrily at her, as bit by bit the material unraveled.

"I want to do this." Her voice was much more confident than the nerves running rampant in her belly. She'd never exposed herself to any man before, and then her chest was bared to his view.

She almost covered herself up again, but when she saw the unadulterated desire pulsing in his eyes, a heady sense of womanly confidence swept through her.

"So perfect," he mumbled, reverently reaching

up to caress first one breast and then the other.

The pads of his fingers were slightly rough, which only increased the waves of pleasure careening down to her center. Her nipples peaked into hard buds, and she arched her back, pushing more of her breasts into his eager hands.

"So soft," he murmured, his mouth beginning to trail kisses down the side of her neck once again and going lower down her chest.

She saw the heat in his eyes as he gazed at her a moment before he lowered his head and covered her nipple with his mouth. Kat nearly bolted from his lap at the feeling of his mouth feasting upon her breast, sucking and licking the nipple until she didn't think she'd be able to stand it.

With his other hand, he stroked down the side of her hips and then her thighs, until it skimmed across her trousers and settled between the junction of her legs. Kat couldn't help but moan as he began to softly rub his hand against her. It was thrilling and completely wanton, and she didn't understand the increasing sense of urgency building within her. Urging herself even closer against his hand, Kat instinctively began rocking her hips back and forth.

Marcus brought his lips back up to hers and kissed her hungrily, the stubble along his jaw making Kat feel deliciously feminine. Suddenly, Marcus swore and tore his mouth from hers as the carriage door swung open. He quickly pulled her jacket across her breasts and pulled her off his lap, onto the seat next to him.

Kat hastily began to button the jacket, belatedly realizing the carriage was stationary and must have been for a minute or so. Oh, good lord, what had come over her! She'd lost control of herself. Swiftly, she pushed herself further away from Marcus, across onto the corner of the opposite seat. She finished doing up the buttons on her top, thankful the darkness of the night hid what had to be the absolute mortification currently adorning her face.

"Really, Cantfield, could it not have waited?" Marcus's voice was abrupt.

"I did not wish to interrupt…" Cantfield's normally amused voice sounded shocked as he looked from the darkened corner of the carriage where Kat now sat, back to Westwood. "But you were taking a rather long time in here, so I was wondering if something was amiss. I didn't realize you were…um…occupied?"

Marcus threw back his head and laughed. "The dissolute bounder is shocked for once. I can't believe it. How amusing."

Cantfield screwed up his face. "You could have at least warned me you would need some privacy. Not like you've ever carried on like this before… And with a footman, too. Rather unexpected behavior for you, actually."

Marcus laughed harder.

"Oh, for goodness sakes!" Kat declared as she leaned forward into the light shining into the carriage from the gas lamps lining the street. "I'm no footman, Lord Cantfield."

A look of recognition swamped the man's face. "Lady Kaitlyn. Well, that makes more sense. Uh, it is…um…so good to see you again. Why are you dressed as a footman?"

Kat was profoundly grateful that that was the topic he chose to ask about. She peeked her head out past Lord Cantfield and recognized they were indeed stopped in the laneway at the rear of her residence. "I have been assisting Lord Westwood, to ensure he did the job correctly."

Behind her, Marcus scoffed, then he leaned over her. "Give us a minute, would you, old chap?" He reached across her and closed the carriage door in Cantfield's face.

Kat sat back against the seat and regarded him steadily. The man appeared to be calm, except for the knowing expression lurking in those far too handsome eyes of his. The cad! Whereas she surely had the bright stain of mortification plastered across her cheeks over the fact that Cantfield had essentially caught them in a compromising position. Again. She was hoping the man would keep that fact to himself.

"He won't tell anyone," Marcus stated, almost as if he was reading her mind.

"I hope he does not, otherwise you can let him know he will regret doing so." Etta was itching to have Cantfield listed in the *Gazette*, having taken an extreme disliking to the fellow after their dance the other evening. "What are we to do now?"

"I shall take the ledger to the War Office tomorrow and see if it can be decoded." Marcus shrugged. "Hopefully, we will learn something relating to the Chameleon and not just the club itself."

"Jerome Fullbrink should be the one to decipher it." He was, after all, the only man fit for the task, as he could decipher it swiftly and accurately. It also helped that he was smitten with her, so he did tend to ensure work for her was done with extra speed and accuracy.

Marcus narrowed his eyes. "You know Fullbrink?"

Kat smiled. "Of course. He's the best cryptologist in England and has helped me and Victor on many past occasions. An accommodating man. You could take lessons from him."

"Accommodating?" Marcus raised a brow. "Falls all over himself trying to please you by saying yes all the time, does he?"

"Indeed, he does." Kat shrugged. "Like I said, *you* could learn from him."

"Please," he scoffed. "The man is a ninny when it comes to women. But he is the best when it comes to cryptology, so yes, I shall get him to look at it."

"Excellent! I will accompany you on the morrow, then," Kat declared. "My presence will ensure the task is done with haste and eagerness."

"No, you will not be accompanying me," Marcus countered, crossing his arms across his chest.

"The same way you declared I couldn't go to the club with you?" She arched an eyebrow. "That edict didn't work too well, now did it?"

"Unauthorized personnel are not permitted in the War Office," Marcus ground out, the patience sapping from his face like quicksand. Not that he'd had much to begin with, Kat imagined. She was doubtful that the Earl of Westwood was at all used to being disobeyed by anyone.

Kat grinned, relishing what his expression was about to change to. "Isn't it fortunate then, that I already have the proper security clearances with full authorization to enter the building."

"The devil you do…" Marcus all but roared. "Who would give you access?"

"Who do you think?" What was he trying to suggest? That she'd stolen access, or had tricked someone into giving it to her? "Sir William gave me authorization, of course."

"But he can't have given you that." Marcus appeared baffled. "Only those working for the

War Office can ent—" He stopped short, his eyes staring at her in accusation. "Bloody hell... You're an agent for him, too?"

Kat raised her chin a few notches. "On occasion. Sir William at least appreciates my skills and does not care what my gender is. So, yes, I do take assignments from him."

"What the devil was he thinking recruiting you?" He raked a hand through his hair. "You are an earl's daughter, for goodness sakes. A lady. Not some bloody spy, as much as you may wish to be."

A rage unlike any she'd known started to rise up through her. She'd had enough of everyone thinking she wasn't capable of carrying on in Victor's footsteps because she was a woman. "How dare you!" she growled at him, leaning forward in her seat and poking him in the chest with her finger. "After all you've seen me do, you still think I'm not capable? Are you narrow-minded? Or simply unable to see beyond the dictates of Society and your own limited concepts of what a woman can and can't do?"

They sat there glowering at each other, their breathing heavy, neither prepared to give an inch.

"Your uncle was murdered, Kaitlyn," Marcus said, his voice suddenly soft. "And he was one of the best trained men I've ever known, but the Chameleon still got to him. *Anyone* can be killed, no matter how skilled."

"I know that, intimately," she replied, matching his whisper with her own. "I was there when Victor was stabbed. I was the one trying to stem the blood gushing from his chest. I was the one who saw death take him from me."

"Victor would not want the same fate for you." Marcus's face softened. "You meant everything to him."

"You know nothing about what I meant to Victor." Kat felt her heart constrict with the pain of knowing that if she had truly meant anything to him, he never would have lied to her for her entire life and he would have told her the truth, that she was his daughter. But Marcus had no idea of what Victor had done. She alone bore that burden and always would. "Victor has nothing to do with your unwillingness to accept that I am far more capable of hunting the Chameleon than anyone else."

"Victor has everything to do with it!" Marcus grabbed ahold of her upper arms. "He was like a second father to me and I can't in all good conscience allow the person he loved above everyone to place herself in danger, all in some quest for vengeance. I am duty bound to protect you."

"What a load of nonsense. You men and your honor. You happily brandish it about when it suits you, and when it doesn't, you pretend not to notice it." Kat shook off his hands. "I've managed to survive well enough up until now without you to protect me. And you have no say in what I do or do not do in my life. No say whatsoever."

His eyes shuttered. "Tell me this, what is it you intend to do when we find the Chameleon?"

Kat glanced beyond him to stare out the window. "I think you know perfectly well what I intend to do." She'd known ever since Victor had died in front of her what she had to do. What she must do to avenge him and lay his ghost to rest. "I intend to kill the Chameleon. It will be an eye for an eye."

Marcus was silent for a while. "You don't know what it's like to take a life. To have their blood on your hands."

"Actually, I do." Kat laughed without humor. "You see, the Chameleon will not be the first life I take, Marcus. My hands are already dirty with the blood of others. They have been for years." She swiveled back to face him, her eyes holding his own. "I know exactly what it feels like."

His body stiffened with the nearly imperceptible tightening of his jaw and the rigid brace of his shoulders. "Then you know that taking a life stays with you, always."

"I do." Memories of the small cabin on the ship she and Victor had commissioned in the South China sea brimmed to life in her mind's eye, so vivid in texture and color, no matter how she'd tried to bury the memory over the years. "And

I'm fully prepared to kill again when I find the Chameleon. What is it you intend to do when you find him? Have a tea party?"

"I intend to bring him to justice, and for him to be tried for his crimes."

"Is justice truly all you intend to seek?" Kat asked. "The Chameleon murdered your wife and was partly responsible for framing your brother as a traitor. I would think if anyone intended to exact an eye for an eye, it would be you."

"I know what he did." Marcus was unflinching. "But I will not stoop to his level to have my revenge, and Victor would not want you to either."

"Please, that's exactly what Victor would have done himself if I had been the one killed instead of him." Kat paused for a moment and then sighed. "This is a pointless conversation, Marcus. You can't change who and what I am. And you can't change what I intend to do. I can go to the War Office, with or without you, at any time. I had hoped we could work together. But if we can't, then we had best part ways now."

Marcus peered down at her for what seemed an eternity, before he appeared to come to some internal decision. "You are right, I cannot stop you."

"So, we are to part ways then." Kat couldn't account for the sense of disappointment that surged through her.

"No. We shall work together and find the Chameleon." He shook his head decisively. "In doing so, I shall accept all of your rather *unusual* talents for a female."

"My, how generous of you."

He merely raised a brow and continued, "We do need to trust each other, though, to work effectively together to catch him."

She could appreciate the logic in that. "Very well."

"I would have you promise me two things, though."

"*Two* things? Asking rather a lot aren't you?" she countered. "Well, what are they?"

"Firstly, I must have your word you will not lie to me. *Ever*. Elizabeth constantly lied to me, to the point I started questioning everyone's truth. If I am to truly trust you, I need to have your word."

"I am no liar. Marcus," she said. "You have my word. And what is the second promise you seek from me?"

"Promise me that when we catch the Chameleon, you won't kill him."

"My whole purpose in finding the assassin is to avenge Victor." How could she let the man behind Victor's death live? She would never have closure knowing the assassin was still alive and could potentially escape at any time. "You ask something of me that I can't give."

"You must. I need to find out who the true traitor was that framed my brother and sold the government intelligence to the Russians. Information that only the Chameleon knows, as he was the one to broker the deal. Do you see why I need him alive?"

Unfortunately, she could, as much as she didn't like the fact. "I want justice for Nathaniel, too. He was a good friend to me."

"So, you agree then?"

"No." She shook her head. "But I will promise not to kill the man until you obtain the information you need. Unless, of course, I have no other option. Will that suffice?"

Marcus nodded. "Very well. Perhaps, in the meantime, I can convince you that justice can be served without blood on your hands."

"Blood is already on my hands." She shrugged one shoulder. "Your efforts would be futile."

A grim smile spread over his mouth. "I'm a stubborn man, Kaitlyn, and I intend to save you."

"I don't need saving from the Chameleon."

"It's not the Chameleon I intend to save you from." His expression was fierce. "It's yourself."

Chapter Twelve

"My Lord? Her ladyship is here to see you."

Glancing up from his breakfast, Marcus watched as his mother swept past his butler and into the dining room. She stopped on the opposite side of the table and surveyed him, her blue eyes, identical in color to his own, creased in worry.

As usual, his mother was dressed impeccably, as befitting a countess. Her blue day dress was cut to perfection and her rich brown hair was styled in an elegant upsweep, with her bonnet set at such an angle to offset her classic profile to precision. For a woman in her fifties, his mother was the epitome of a lady of class and style.

But, as usual, there was the ever-present sadness in her expression that had been there since Nathaniel's death, and only made worse after his father's death. A sadness she couldn't disguise from Marcus, no matter how she tried.

"It's nice to see you, Mother," Marcus said, uncomfortable at the formality he detected in his own voice as he stood to greet her. "Please, do take a seat. Coffee?"

"Yes, thank you," she replied, sitting on the

chair across from him, while one of his footmen filled a cup of coffee and handed it to her. "I am sorry to barge in on you like this."

"I know why you're here." Marcus forestalled her. "The *Gazette*."

She nodded her head, her hands gripping the coffee cup like a vise. "Yes, I received the news last night and I had to come and see how I can assist in refuting such lies."

"I don't think the pamphlet mentioned any details, did it?" he murmured, taking a sip of his own drink.

"It didn't have to." His mother's smile was tight as she returned the cup to its saucer. "A man needs only to be mentioned as one of the future bachelors to be critiqued and everyone assumes the worst of him."

"Then let me put your mind at ease," he replied. "I'm not going to be critiqued in the *Gazette*."

"You're not?"

"No," Marcus confirmed. "They will be printing a retraction shortly, and then, hopefully, my reputation will be restored."

"Oh, that is marvelous." She sighed heartily, her hands pressing up to her chest. "I was worried. Not, of course, about any suggestion that you are a scoundrel! But something like that could drastically hamper your future efforts to marry."

And there it was. The other reason he avoided

seeing his mother. "You know I have no intention of marrying ever again, yet you always mention it."

She bit her bottom lip and for a moment Marcus felt himself weaken.

"I know Elizabeth's lies and infidelities struck at your core," she began. "But not all women are like that, Marcus. You could find a lovely, demure, polite, and docile lady who would make a perfect countess. You have such a big heart, with so much love to give—"

"If that is all, Mother, I must leave for a meeting." He put down his cutlery and wiped his mouth with his serviette.

"No, please don't go. I'm sorry to have mentioned it. I just want to see you happy..."

"Happy?" Marcus all but scoffed. "My last marriage was filled with misery and ensured my heart was well and truly annihilated. Trust me, I have no love left to give."

"Then you've let Elizabeth win, my son." His mother stood and smiled sadly at him. "And that is truly a tragedy because you would have made the most wonderful husband and father."

Her words struck a hollow place in his heart and he had to control himself from slamming his fist down on the table. "Similar to how I made such a wonderful brother and son?"

"You must stop blaming yourself for Nathaniel's death." She raised her chin high. "And for your father's. You know he had a heart episode. It had nothing to do with you."

"He died because of heartache over Nathaniel's death," Marcus growled. "We all know Nathaniel was his favorite and part of father died the day he learned of Nathaniel's passing."

"Maybe," his mother conceded. "But your sister and I are still here. You rarely visit us, and your sister misses you, as do I…" Her voice trailed off as she looked uncomfortably away from him. "And the house does belong to you, after all."

After Nathaniel's and his father's deaths, he'd bought another residence, unable to stand the memories in the walls of the place he'd spent a good portion of his life in. Unable to bear seeing the pain in his mother and sister's eyes every time they looked upon him.

"Can you honestly tell me you're not reminded of Nathaniel and his death every time you see me?" Marcus asked her.

She was silent for a moment as she pressed her lips together. "Of course, you remind me of Nathaniel, he looked so like you… How could I not be reminded of him? And, of course, I sometimes wonder if he'd still be alive if he never followed in your footsteps, always wanting to be like his big brother. But that doesn't mean I blame you, Marcus. I've never blamed you."

"Well, I blame myself."

"I know." Her eyes had gotten moist and she was quick to look away from him. "I'm hopeful that one day you'll be able to forgive yourself for something that was not your fault. In any event, I'm sorry to have troubled you this morning, though I did also wish to tell you Isabelle and I will be travelling to the country estate tomorrow. We both need some respite from the antics of the season and the London air. We would love for you to visit, if you get a chance in the next few weeks. I know the tenants around the estate would love to see you, too. Stay safe, Marcus."

And then she swept from the room, the familiar scent of lilacs following in her wake.

Marcus closed his eyes and sighed. He loved his mother, but there would forever be the pain of Nathaniel's death between them, as much as she hoped otherwise.

"My lord?" his butler intoned from the doorway. "Your carriage is ready."

He glanced at the clock on the far wall and realized that it was time to leave. He had to meet Kat at the War Office, and knowing her, if he was even a minute late, she'd go ahead without him. Patience, it seemed, was not her strong suit.

He stood and strode to the front of his house and awaiting carriage.

For the entire trip, Marcus couldn't stop thinking of the conversation he'd had with his mother.

Always mentioning him remarrying was arduous, though he doubted his mother would push for matrimony if Kat was the intended bride. Certainly, she was an earl's daughter, so his mother couldn't complain about her suitability in that regard, but that's basically where it ended. Kaitlyn would make the most unsuitable countess according to his mother's standards of demureness, politeness, and docility. Kat was anything but those things.

Not that he was considering marrying her. No, he would never marry again, he'd made that clear. The idea had simply popped into his head because of his mother's comments about the subject.

Perhaps he should pretend to be engaged to Kat, then when she supposedly cried off his mother would be so relieved, she'd never bother him about marriage again. The idea had some merit. Though he imagined that if he even suggested such a thing to Kat, she'd knock him onto his backside before he could even blink. The thought brought with it a grin.

Thirty minutes later, Marcus was standing beside the lady herself at the entrance to Cumberland House, which housed the War Office. The building was as magnificent as it was imposing, fashioned in the Palladian style as was so popular in the eighteenth century, when it was built. The grand, white columns stood proudly in the center of the edifice under the watchful eye of Her

Majesty's guards, who stood to attention along its perimeter.

"Ladies first." Marcus motioned for Kat to go ahead through the entrance, his hand brushing against her arm, the very touch sending a sharp pang of desire through him.

Trying to ignore the visceral reaction, they both pulled out their identification paperwork, which the guard checked before opening the door and allowing them inside the building.

As they strode through the grand foyer, he found himself aware of the woman beside him, almost to the exclusion of everything else. He had to get a hold of himself. Such a distraction was dangerous.

He focused on his surroundings, the freshly polished marble floors and the familiar scent of lemon that permeated the entrance. The building itself was a treasure, with the classic circular design of the lobby and the two ornate stairways on either side curving up to both the east and west wing, lending an air of elegance one wouldn't expect from a building housing the War Office. Though considering the building itself had originally belonged to the Duke of York and then the Duke of Cumberland, ornate was to be expected.

He peered up at the round glass pane built into the top of the roof over the lobby, not sure which of the dukes had had it installed, but as usual he marveled at the sight of it.

Though the edifice only distracted him for a moment before he found himself once again glancing out of the corner of his eye to Kat beside him. She was dressed in an emerald green skirt and matching jacket that set off the auburn in her hair and molded her body to perfection. With her regal bearing and height, she was a sight to behold, and he'd barely been able to look at anything else apart from her since seeing her waiting for him.

He was having to work damn hard to keep his hands to himself, especially after what they'd been doing together only last night after the Corinthian Club escapade. The very memories of which had invaded his sleep and lingered far too potently in his mind this morning.

Knowing he couldn't compromise her further, and had already gone too far, was all that was keeping his hands from reaching for her. If he went any further with her, he'd be duty-bound to marry her, and he couldn't do that, not after Elizabeth had soured him to the institution for life.

Which was why he still couldn't understand how he'd let himself and the situation with Kat get so out of hand. It was out of character for him. He didn't lose himself to passion, ever. At least he hadn't before Kaitlyn Montrose, who seemed to ignite the emotion in him as if he was tinder. Damn it.

They walked over to the right staircase leading to the west wing.

"After you, my lady." He held out his hand and motioned toward the stairs, which stretched up two levels above. He only just managed to resist brushing his hand against hers once again.

Kat inclined her head and led the way up. Apart from the "good morning" she had said in greeting to him when he'd arrived, she'd barely said a word to him all morning. Odd, but he actually found himself missing her bossy but sultry voice.

Something had to be wrong with him to enjoy verbally sparring with the lady. Shaking his head at his own ridiculousness, he followed her up to the second floor, where Fullbrink's office was.

A frown crossed Marcus's face when he realized Kat clearly knew the way, as she navigated the hallways and headed straight for the man's office door without hesitation.

"Let me deal with him," he said. "Fullbrink can be overly slow when it comes to decoding missives, unless he's directed to do so by someone with authority."

Kaitlyn raised a brow at his comment, while she rapped briskly on Fullbrink's door before a cheerful voice bid them to enter. "I've never had to direct him to do anything to get a job done quickly. Watch and learn, Marcus Black. Watch and learn."

As she pushed open the door and preceded him into the room, Marcus couldn't stop his eyes from glancing down at the enticing sway of her hips as she sashayed inside. Right at that moment all he wanted to do was pull her back against him and cart her over his shoulder, back to his carriage. He shook his head over the notion. He was becoming a bloody Neanderthal when he was around her.

Following her into the room, his scowl deepened at the adoration currently dripping from Fullbrink's face as the man caught sight of Kat. No wonder she didn't have to do anything, Fullbrink was besotted with her.

"Lady Kaitlyn!" Fullbrink enthused, rushing around his desk and reverently grasping her hand. Fullbrink bowed low, his blond hair falling forward over his glasses as he placed a chaste kiss across Kat's knuckles. "It is an honor to see you again!"

Kaitlyn smiled. "You too, Mr. Fullbrink." She had to gently extract her hand from his grip, while Marcus had to restrain himself from ripping the man's hand from his body.

The young man continued to smile goofily at her. "An absolute honor to have you here."

"You've already said that, Fullbrink." Marcus couldn't believe what a fool Fullbrink was making of himself, fawning all over Kat. Marcus would never be caught making such a fool of himself over any woman, not even one he wanted to pleasure until she was screaming in delight. He cleared his throat. "We're in a hurry."

"Ah, Lord Westwood!" Fullbrink exclaimed, finally realizing that Marcus was there, too, as he regretfully tore his eyes from Kaitlyn and gave his attention to Marcus. "Good to see you again, too. How may I help you both today?"

Pulling out the red journal from the pocket of his jacket, Marcus pressed it into the man's chest, causing Fullbrink to stumble back a step. "We need you to decipher this." Watch and learn, would he? He'd show her how he got things done.

Fullbrink's eyes lit up at the request as he grabbed ahold of the book. There was nothing the man loved more than deciphering a coded message, and this was a whole ledger. Flipping open the cover, he began leafing through the pages as he returned to the chair behind his desk. "Hmm… interesting. Very interesting," he muttered, sitting down on the well-worn seat. "Some sort of cipher, but not a usual one I'd readily recognize. It might take me a bit of time to decipher it."

"How long?" Marcus asked.

The young man shrugged. "Maybe a few days? I have to work out the cipher key first, and then decode it all."

"We need it sooner," Marcus told him.

"It's a difficult cipher, my lord." Fullbrink continued to rifle through the pages. "I shall do my best to have it to you sooner, but I can't promise anything."

Kat wandered over and perched on the edge of Fullbrink's desk. "Mr. Fullbrink, it's dreadfully important." She stared steadily at the man. "Lives are at stake, you see."

Marcus's frown deepened as Fullbrink started nodding like his head was about to fall off.

"The information in that journal," she continued, "must be decrypted in the shortest possible time. And you are the best cryptologist in the country, so if *anyone* can have it done sooner, I am confident it's you."

Marcus felt a low anger start to burn in the pit of his stomach, as the young man stared at her like a goddamn puppy, his eyes straying to her décolletage on far too many occasions. Marcus was going to smash the young pup's face into the damn desk if he didn't stop looking at her bosom.

"I would consider it such a favor if you could," she said with a gentle smile tilting up the corner of her lips.

Fullbrink all but started drooling, Marcus was sure.

"Of course, I will make it my main priority!" Fullbrink declared. "You can count on me, Lady Kaitlyn. I should have something for you in a few hours. I'll get to work on it straight away."

"I knew we could rely on you, Mr. Fullbrink."

She straightened and stood, shooting Marcus a satisfied "I told you" smile in the process, just as the door to Fullbrink's office opened and a tall, thin man rushed in.

"Lord Westwood! Thank goodness I caught you before you left."

Marcus glanced over as Neville Glouster, the Secretary of State for War's clerk, came to a stop in front of him.

"We only just arrived, Glouster," Marcus said. "What's wrong?"

The man heaved a sigh of relief. "Lord Danbury and Sir Albert wish to speak with you immediately, in the Secretary's office, my lord. It's urgent."

It was always urgent with Lord Danbury. The man thought himself the most important person in England, aside from the queen, being that he was in charge of the entire War Office of the British Empire. Marcus sighed. The true power, though, belonged to his two deputies, Sir Albert Tanning who was the Under Secretary of State for War, and Sir William, who was in charge of the Intelligence section of the Department.

Lord Danbury was more a mouthpiece for the position, which was appropriate as the man loved to hear his own voice.

Marcus had hoped to get in and out without a fuss, but that was not to be. He turned and shot

Fullbrink a hard glare. "You work on the ledger, and you"—he turned and eyed Lady Kaitlyn—"come with me."

Glouster held up his hands. "Oh no, my Lord. They requested to see you. There was no mention of Lady Kaitlyn."

"If they wish to speak with me, then she's coming, too." He wasn't going to leave her with Fullbrink. The poor man would think himself smitten if he did. "She has the required clearance, does she not?"

"Well, yes, she does…" Glouster looked highly uncomfortable but nodded in resignation.

"Is Sir William going to be there?" Marcus asked him.

"No, he received an urgent missive earlier and had to rush off. If you will follow me." Glouster ushered them out the door and indicated for them to follow.

Marcus placed a hand on Kat's elbow and they followed Glouster down the hallway. "Have you met Lord Danbury and Sir Albert Tanning before?"

"Not personally, no," she replied, her steps staying in stride with his. "All of my dealings with the Department have been through Sir William."

"Do try and behave yourself, will you? They will not be as easily swayed by you as young Fullbrink was."

He was completely wrong.

The woman had barely been introduced to them both before she had charmed the two old codgers as if it was child's play. After meeting them, and subtly reminding them she was Victor Montrose's niece, whose resources regularly helped the Department, she then proceeded to flatter the men with a deftness bordering on genius. She had them completely wrapped around her finger and their previous concerns about her presence allayed in under two minutes flat. Marcus had counted.

Who would have thought Kat was so charming? Obviously, she only employed such a skill when she wanted to. She'd never tried to charm him. Though, in all truth, he rather preferred her bluntness.

It was disheartening to see two such experienced men fawn all over themselves in an attempt to impress Lady Kaitlyn. Darn right embarrassing, actually. But he had to give it to the lady, her skills were impeccable.

Marcus shook his head in reluctant acceptance. The woman had a gift. She seemed able to send a man scuttling away with a glance, or have him hanging off her every word, depending on what she wanted from him. A useful skill for a semi-spy. That fact made her dangerous, and not simply because of her deadly aim, with both her knee and dagger. No, she could use her wiles to manipulate men. Just like Elizabeth. At least he wouldn't be stupid enough to allow himself to be manipulated a second time.

Marcus smiled briefly, wondering what the two men would do if she demonstrated her knife skills. It was one thing for them to be charmed by her smile and words, quite another to experience the extent of her other abilities firsthand. The two men, who prided themselves on their impeccable manners, would be shocked if not scandalized, Marcus was certain.

"You both wished to speak to me about the Chameleon?" Marcus decided to put a stop to the nonsense before it went on any longer.

Lord Danbury raised a quizzing glass up to his right eye and glanced at Marcus. "Quite right, Westwood, we did. But there is a lady present." His voice sounded slightly put out to have had his flirtation with Lady Kaitlyn cut short.

"She's working with me on the matter, Danbury," Marcus curtly informed him. "And her resources will only assist us in finding the man quicker."

There was an expression of perhaps distaste in the man's eyes at the thought of a lady assisting, as the man was well-known as a conformist for the proprieties, but Danbury didn't have the nerve to say anything further on the matter in front of them. "Very well, then. Sir Albert, fill them in."

Sir Albert nodded his balding head and leaned forward from where he sat, glancing first at Marcus, then Kat. He lowered his voice somewhat. "We've received some reliable whispers that the Chameleon has returned to London and has been provided with a list of seven targets to assassinate."

Marcus raised an eyebrow. "Seven? That's a lot."

"Yes, whoever hired him must be extremely wealthy, which is something we're looking into," Sir Albert said. "Unfortunately, the man I had tasked to attempt to retrieve a copy of the list of names was unsuccessful. His body was found floating in the Thames this morning."

The room was silent for a moment.

Sir Albert caught his eye. "We must stop the Chameleon. He has killed too many Englishmen and sold too many secrets to the Russians. We can't allow him to succeed and kill more Englishmen, not on our watch."

"Goodness, no," Lord Danbury added. "We cannot let an assassin have free rein in England. It is not to be tolerated. We would look like a bunch of fools."

Marcus refrained from advising Danbury that the man already appeared quite the fool without the Chameleon's help. "Tell me what you know," he said to Sir Albert, who actually would know.

Sir Albert sighed, his rotund figure slumping a little in the chair. "Not much, I'm afraid. Two days ago, I received word the Chameleon had met with someone here in London and was given a list of names to assassinate. Subsequently, I sent an agent to make some inquiries, but, regretfully, he was met with a bullet between his eyes for his efforts."

Marcus shook his head. Another life to be added to the Chameleon's ever-growing list of kills. The assassin had to be stopped, but how did one catch a ghost?

Sir Albert stood and began pacing across the oriental rug covering the floor. "We must thwart his plans before he can assassinate another person."

"We need to know who the targets are," Kaitlyn said from where she was seated beside Lord Danbury. "Do we know any of the names on the list?"

Sir Albert paused before hurrying on. "Not yet. We've only heard of the list."

Marcus and Kat shared a look. The man wasn't telling the truth.

"Dreadful business, this!" Lord Danbury waved his hand in the air as if to emphasize his displeasure. He pinned Marcus with his beady gaze. "You must put this situation to rest and find this darn fellow! We can't have men assassinated on my watch. The queen would not be impressed, and I could lose my position."

"How dreadful that would be," Marcus remarked drolly.

"Yes indeed!" Danbury agreed, clearly not

recognizing the sarcasm in Marcus's comment. "Now I must be off. I have an appointment at Westminster." He stood and bowed over Lady Kaitlyn's hand. "It was a pleasure to meet you, my lady. Please, though, do not get too caught up in this game. Best leave it to the men to handle." He patted her hand.

Marcus very nearly laughed at the look of haughty rage Kaitlyn directed at Lord Danbury's obtuse face as she deftly pulled her hand free from his grasp.

Lord Danbury turned to Marcus, oblivious of the mental daggers Kat was shooting him. "Westwood, do keep Sir Albert informed of your progress. I expect you to control this situation."

"You do, do you?" Marcus stared down the man.

The War Secretary paled under the intensity of Marcus's gaze, before he turned and hurried from the room.

Marcus turned to Sir Albert, who regarded him with concern. "What are you not telling us?" he asked without reservation.

"I can't get anything past you, can I?" Sir Albert appeared happy with that fact. "And, yes, I wasn't telling you both the full truth." Sir Albert sighed. "Though it's true my informant didn't find out all the names on the list before he was murdered, there was a note found in his waistcoat pocket suggesting he may have discovered one of the names. The ink had run but the word was still legible enough on the parchment, though I did not wish to mention it in front of Lord Danbury."

"Why?"

"Because it would have only panicked him." He looked between Marcus and Kat with an expression of reluctant acceptance on his face. "It was his name on the paper. So, I rather suspect that that makes the Secretary himself a target of the assassin."

Chapter Thirteen

Twenty minutes later, Kaitlyn had excused herself from the undersecretary's office, as Marcus and Sir Albert were finalizing the details on the clandestine security to be assigned to Lord Danbury.

Besides being unable to stand the cloying scent of stale cigar smoke that had seeped into the tapestry of the room itself, she was eager to stretch her legs. She was never one to sit still for long, and being contained in the same room with Marcus, while all she wanted to do was kiss him again, had been torture.

Why the man was affecting her so much was as frustrating as it was concerning. Distraction of any sort when trying to hunt the Chameleon was a dangerous recipe, and one she couldn't afford to indulge in.

Striding out of the room and past the antechamber which housed his assistant's desk, she went into the outer area overlooking the grand foyer. Walking over to the balustrade, she peered down at the hum of activity below. The majority of the foyer had been cordoned off from the entry and turned into an efficient hub of desks for the various clerks that worked for the War Office. It was as orderly and precise as ever, as the men all went about their duties of deciphering, filtering, and disseminating various intelligence to keep Britain safe.

Sighing, Kat turned back to look through the antechamber to the closed door of the undersecretary's office. Hopefully, Marcus wouldn't be too much longer. There was much to be organized when she returned home. Indeed, she was eager to set her own informants to the task of finding out as much information as they could regarding the possible assassination targets.

The sound of hurried footsteps clipping across the marble floor had her turning to her left. She saw Mr. Fullbrink hurrying along the passage, carrying the little red book in his hands and waving it about in excitement.

"Good news, my lady," he enthused as he came to a stop in front of her. "I have partially deciphered the key that will allow me to decode the contents!"

Kat smiled. The man was a genius with codes. "Mr. Fullbrink, that's wonderful news! And so quickly, too."

A stain of red began to creep up the man's cheeks. "Yes, well, I mean, I still have to decipher it fully and then properly decode the journal, but I thought you still might be here and would want to know of my progress. You did say it was important to you."

"It certainly is, and I do thank you for making it a priority. Were you able to make any sense of it, though?"

"I took a look at the last few entries, as I thought they may be more recent and hence of more assistance to you."

"And what did you discover?" Marcus's deep voice asked from her right.

Kat jumped slightly and felt the hairs on the nape of her neck prickle at his nearness. She inwardly cursed herself for not being aware he had exited the office. She was getting sloppy when he was near, and she couldn't allow herself to make those sorts of careless mistakes. Or continue to feel this sense of attraction to the man. So much so that when he was near, she had to restrain herself from grabbing him and demanding he kiss her again.

Fullbrink glanced up at a coldly furious Marcus. "Well, it is a bit odd," he replied, tugging at his collar as if it was constricting his neck. "On a cursory glance, bearing in mind I have only partially decoded the cipher, I would guess that the entries in the journal may be transaction details. Lists of some sort, with possible names, sums of money and dates for each entry. Though, what was of particular interest is the list on the last page. I am still to decipher it fully, but I think the Secretary, Lord Danbury himself, may indeed be named on the list."

Kat and Marcus looked sharply at each other.

"What makes you say that?" Kat asked him. It couldn't be a coincidence that the man's name was in a ledger and also listed as one of the Chameleon's next targets.

"I partly decoded some of the words, and though I won't know for certain until I do finish decoding the cipher in full, one of the words I'm fairly certain will be Danbury... So that's why I thought it might be in reference to our Secretary of State of War, Lord Danbury, as it's not that common a name."

"Are there other names on that page?" Marcus asked.

"I think so, but I won't know until I'm done," he replied. "I'll work on the last page first, where I think Danbury's name appears, along with other entries."

"There are other names listed, along with Danbury's?" Kat couldn't contain the anticipation in her eyes as she glanced to Marcus. This could be the breakthrough they were after.

"Possibly, though I won't know for certain until I'm done decoding. What I did find odd is that these last entries appear incomplete in comparison to other similar pages. There are letters in what I assume is the name column, but the other column has no numbers, like the other pages do."

"Almost like incomplete transactions?" Kat asked.

"Potentially." Fullbrink nodded.

"You're to make deciphering the last page of that journal a priority, Fullbrink," Marcus's voice was stern. "Drop all other projects you're working on. We must know the rest of its contents immediately. Sir Albert will approve my direction."

"Very well," the young man said. "What should I do once I complete the task?"

"Tell Sir William and Sir Albert what you discover, and then find us immediately," Marcus told him.

"Where will you be later tonight, then?" Fullbrink tentatively asked.

"At the Lyceum Theatre," Kat said. "I'm attending with Etta and the Duchess of Calder."

"The Dragon Duchess is playing chaperone to you both?" Marcus seemed surprised. "I thought you and she didn't get along?"

"We might bait each other with our words, but we respect each other, and we do enjoy trying to verbally best one other." Kat shrugged. "Besides, I think Livie has asked her to keep an eye on Etta and me while she's in the country." She returned her attention to Fullbrink. "Can you locate me there? It does get crowded."

"It will a pleasure to find you again, my lady."

Fullbrink bowed to her and then Marcus before

turning on his heels and hurrying back down the hall to his office. She turned to face Marcus and observed the thoughtful expression on his face. "Potentially, Danbury's name, along with others, incomplete on the last page of a transaction ledger. Somewhat of a coincidence, do you not think?"

He rubbed his jaw. "Too much of a coincidence. But we shall have to wait for Fullbrink to decode it fully before we leap to any conclusions."

Kat scoffed. "There are incomplete entries on a ledger we find in a secret room in a club with links to the Chameleon, who we now find is tasked with assassinating seven men. Do you know what this means?"

Marcus nodded. "We may have found a transaction record of the Chameleon's assassinations."

"I can't see what else it would be," Kat admitted. "But as you said, Mr. Fullbrink will unravel it and then we shall know for sure."

Marcus scowled at her.

"What has got you in a flutter?" She picked up the skirts of her gown and began walking down the staircase.

He kept pace next to her and growled low in her ear, "Must you flirt with poor Fullbrink every time you see him?"

"I was not flirting with him. I was being less ornery than my usual self. And I may have smiled at him once or twice, which I don't often do. At least not unless I like the person."

"That might be so," Marcus grumbled in concession. "But still, it's downright cruel to the poor fellow."

"But effective." She grinned up at him. "And look, now I'm smiling at you, too."

His scowl turned even darker and she laughed aloud.

"Oh, do relax, Marcus. We have learned a great deal this morning."

"We have. Clearly, the Corinthian Club is more involved with the Chameleon's activities than we knew."

"Yes. I do believe we'll have to pay Mr. Dartmoore another visit."

Marcus nodded as they made their way through the foyer and out into the sunshine. "No doubt. But we shall do so after Fullbrink decodes the thing. More ammunition that way."

"Let's hope he decodes it soon." Kat didn't like the new information that the Chameleon was potentially targeting seven men, because it meant that with each passing hour a man's life was slowly running out.

Chapter Fourteen

Marcus watched Kaitlyn from across the carriage seat as they made their way back to the Montrose townhouse from the War Office. She could sense his regard upon her, even as she looked pointedly out the window and ignored his scrutiny.

Kat felt her pulse speed up as images of what they'd been doing together last night, in this very carriage, leaped unbidden into her mind. She could still taste his lips on hers. Could still feel the gentle roughness of his stubble rubbing against her throat as he skimmed kisses along the sensitive hollow of her neck. Could still feel the tightness in her core as his hand began caressing between her thighs and his mouth swept over her nipple.

"I've barely been able to think of little else except how soft your lips were under mine, and how I want nothing more than to taste them again."

Kat gasped at Marcus's words, which all but mirrored her own thoughts. She swiveled her head until her gaze pinned his. "You can't say such things!"

"Why not?" He shrugged. "'Tis the truth. Even if I know nothing further can happen."

"And why can't anything further happen?" She couldn't resist asking, even though she suspected it was because he would feel honor-bound to marry her if something did. And marriage was something she'd never agree to. A husband, especially an earl, would never allow her to continue her clandestine activities, which was something she would never tolerate. But perhaps they could come to another sort of arrangement. Livie had told her of the rubber sheaths that were available.

"You know perfectly well only a scoundrel would ever compromise a lady and then not marry her. Hell, you run a scandal sheet dedicated to ruining the men who do that very thing."

"I do," Kat said. "But only those who seduce a woman with false promises of love and marriage are exposed in the pages of the *Gazette*. I see nothing wrong if a woman decides knowingly to have an affair with a man, without any expectation of love or marriage."

"That's not how I was raised." Marcus pressed his lips together and took a deep breath. "Starting anything with you would lead to marriage, and that's an institution I'll never take part in again."

"You are entirely arrogant, assuming I'd ever accept a marriage proposal from you." She lifted her chin, glad they were laying their cards on the table. "You would be far too controlling a husband for me. In fact, any man would be. Which is why I will never enter such an antiquated institution."

"Good, we're in agreement, then."

"About marriage, yes. But perhaps not about improper behavior."

"Lady, you are improper behavior personified."

"That may be true." Kat knew she pushed the boundaries of what was and wasn't acceptable on a daily basis. Some would consider her riding in a carriage alone with Marcus inappropriate.

Though her status as a spinster, especially at six-and-twenty, allowed her a certain level of freedom that the younger ladies of Society were not afforded, at least in the world of rank and privilege. Ladies from the lower classes could happily walk the streets alone or ride their bicycles about. Such freedom without worry would be bliss.

"*May* be true?"

"Society has to witness improprieties for them to be aware of them, and luckily for me, none of them are awake at this hour of the morning to even see me in a carriage with you. They live in ignorance of what I get up to. In any event, we have more important things to discuss than my behavior or what happened last night." She crossed her hands over her chest. "At least for the moment."

He leaned forward, his knees brushing her own above her skirts. "You're right, of course, and I've been telling myself that repeatedly, but for some reason I can't stop thinking of how silky your skin felt underneath my hands…"

She closed her eyes for a second and then opened them, locking gazes with him. "Why are you telling me this if you have no intention of following through?"

His eyes seemed tormented, lust and honor clashing in their blue depths. "I don't know. I realize we can't repeat what happened." His eyes broke contact with hers and he sat back with a sigh. "To do so would have consequences that neither of us are prepared to accept."

"I think you're overestimating the consequences." The loss of the contact from his knee and thigh sent a sharp pang of disappointment through her. The man's presumption over what would or wouldn't occur was starting to annoy her. "Because, once again, you assume if we did anything further, we would have to marry, which is not the case."

"Marriage is a consequence a man must face if he compromises a virgin."

"Why do you assume I am a virgin?"

"What the devil did you just say?" Marcus roared.

Kat screwed up her nose at the look of fury on his face. "Oh, do calm down."

"Who took your virginity and didn't do the honorable thing?"

She felt like rolling her eyes, though in the

circumstances she thought it best not to provoke him further. "For goodness sakes, I'm still a virgin, you baboon!"

"Then why did you say you were not!"

"I didn't say I wasn't, well, not exactly. I was simply questioning your assumption. There is a difference." She shrugged. "You should know better than to assume anything."

"I'm going to spank you over my knees!" he said, before pulling her onto his lap.

She grabbed hold of his shoulders to stabilize herself and found herself trapped in the heat radiating from his eyes. Oh, blast it! Why did his body have such a pull over hers? To the point where all good reason and thought fled her mind when she was physically touching him.

Without considering her actions, she pressed her lips to his and pushed her chest against him, something she'd been wanting to do all day.

If she wanted to experience passion, then she would! She would not let his prudish notion of what should happen after, stop her from doing so. In fact, the more she thought about it, an affair sounded just the thing, particularly as the man clearly knew what he was about in that department.

He tore his lips away from hers and swore. "What are you doing? I told you we can't do this again."

"I'm kissing you. You can't talk about last night and then simply say that's the end of it. Why bring it up in the first place if you didn't want to repeat it?"

He half swore, half groaned. "Damn it, stop wriggling your buttocks against me."

"You're the one who pulled me onto your lap." Kat didn't know what came over her, but an insatiable curiosity and a certainty that she must experience what he could offer, all but consumed her. Slowly, she began unbuttoning his vest, then his shirt.

"Damn it, stop that…" There was little conviction in his voice, as his eyes followed her fingers, as button by button was popped open.

"I'm exploring your chest as you did mine last night."

"God help me," he muttered, his hands dropping to the side in surrender.

As she undid the last button, she pulled aside the white shirt and marveled at the sight that greeted her. His chest was all muscular planes and angles, athletic and lithe, with a smattering of chest hair that she couldn't help but reach up and stroke her fingers across.

A groan from deep in his chest was her reward.

Emboldened by his response, she leaned down and flicked her tongue across his nipple, which tightened in response, while her hand danced across to caress his other nipple. His breathing become ragged and his nipples hardened.

The carriage pulled to a stop, which, thankfully, this time she felt. Hastily, she scrambled off Marcus and onto the opposite seat, while he swore black and blue, and quickly buttoned up his shirt. He glanced at her and there was accusation in the depths of his eyes. "What game are you playing, Kaitlyn? I've told you we can't keep doing this."

"And why is it that you alone get a say in that?" She took in a somewhat shaky breath, trying to return her wildly beating heart back to its normal rhythm. "Surely, my wants and views should be taken into account."

"Oh God, don't talk to me about your wants," he groaned, dragging his fingers through his hair, frustration all but vibrating from him. "We can't do such things again because if we continue, I won't be able to stop, and the consequences of that are too large to ignore… Not after Elizabeth."

"You must have loved her…"

"In the end, I despised her. Which is why I will never marry again."

"Then everything is fine," Kat declared. "Because as I have repeatedly assured you, I have no intention of marrying. But I have decided I'll take you as my lover."

For half a second, he blinked, seemingly not

quite understanding her for a moment, until her words fully sank in. "The devil you will!" he roared as the carriage door was opened by one of his footmen.

"Oh, I will," Kat said as she straightened up her skirt before stepping out through the door. "It will be either yourself or another man." She threw the words over her shoulder as the footman closed the carriage door.

"It's not going to be another man," Marcus said from the window.

Kat smiled to herself before she turned back to assess him. "Excellent. Then we're in agreement. I assume I'll see you tonight at the theater. We can then discuss the logistics of what is to be our new arrangement."

Chapter Fifteen

"Lady Montrose did not feel like some Shakespeare tonight?" The Duchess of Calder snapped open her fan with precision, before deftly beginning to fan herself in an effort to cool down in the overcrowded grand salon of the Lyceum Theatre.

"No, she's not a fan of the theater," Kat confirmed. "Or of crowds."

"Nor of having to monitor you in such a throng, I'd wager," the duchess pronounced, before turning her sharp gaze to Etta. "Don't just stand there, Miss Merriweather! Fetch me a glass of water, and do hurry up, gal. It's stifling in here and I am parched."

"Yes, of course, Your Grace!" Etta rushed out, before swinging around and pushing through the crowd toward the refreshment table as if she was being chased by farmers with pitchforks. Which probably was rather close to describing the duchess, Kat thought with a smile.

"And what are you smiling about?" The duchess turned back to assess Kat, thumping her cane on the ground. "Hoping the Earl of Westwood will be in attendance?"

Kat narrowed her eyes on the woman. How had the dragon known that? "You've always had very good sources when it comes to information."

The duchess merely raised her brow as she glanced across at the crowd. "And this surprises you? Good gracious, girl, I didn't come to be feared by everyone in this room without knowing all of their little secrets. So, go on then, go off and find him."

"Aren't you meant to be my chaperone?" The woman was encouraging her to find Marcus? Had she lost her senses?

"You're six-and-twenty, Lady Kaitlyn, hence firmly on the shelf," came the lady's biting reply. "If you don't have a bit of fun now, you never will."

As trained as Kat was, she couldn't help her jaw from dropping open. The staid, completely proper arbitrator of what was suitable behavior in Society was telling her to go and have fun with Marcus? "Are you serious?"

"Oh, good gracious, child," she chided. "I was young once, too. Now go. This conversation is boring me greatly, and I shall shortly have to put up with Miss Merriweather's timidity when she returns. Unless Cantfield attends too, then I can have him entertain her, and be left in peace to do what I do best."

"Terrorize everyone?" Kat couldn't help herself from saying.

But rather than take offence, the duchess

smiled. Or at least Kat thought the upturning of her lips was what could be classed as a smile from the woman. "You're finally starting to understand me, I think. Good. Now off you go." She shooed her into the crowd with her fan, which Kat allowed, somewhat stunned by such a development.

Who would have thought the Dragon Duchess would prove to be the most wonderful chaperone someone like Kat could have asked for?

Now all she had to do was find Marcus. Kat paused for a moment as she scanned the gathered crowd. The theater was one of London's largest, spanning over three levels and seating over two thousand people. And, unfortunately, it appeared to be a full house, which made spotting Marcus a great deal harder, though he usually towered over everyone, so she should be able to see his head above others. He obviously hadn't arrived yet. So much for arranging to accidentally bump into each other before the play started.

Not that she really needed to do so now, as the duchess had happily sent her off to do what she wished.

The salon area on the second level was only open to patrons who held permanent boxes within the theater, but even so, the room was an absolute crush and though normally Kat disliked crowds, tonight she was glad to be surrounded in seeming anonymity.

She sensed Etta approaching before she saw her.

"Oh my goodness, that woman is a nightmare. Livie's godmother or not!" Etta declared in a whisper as she came to a halt beside Kat, a glass of water in her hand. "I don't know how Livie can say she's sweet underneath all of her verbal brutality."

"Actually, I don't mind her." Kat shrugged.

"Not you, too?" Etta all but whined. "By the way, you look stunning tonight."

Kat looked down at the deep emerald gown she was wearing. Madame Arnout had indeed done a marvelous job on the creation, seamlessly combining a fitted bodice covered with thousands of crystal beads, to fit perfectly over a matching custom designed detachable skirt with a sewn in bustle, as the woman had fashioned all of Kat's new outfits. "Madame Arnout is a genius."

"She is. Have you tried them out yet?" Etta glanced curiously at the skirt of Kat's dress, which she knew was one of the special detachable ones.

"Not in the real world, at least not yet, anyhow," Kat replied. "But I've experimented in my bedchamber and the speed that the skirt detaches and allows my legs the freedom to move about unobstructed is nothing short of marvelous. It takes but a few seconds to unsnap the fasteners with one hand."

"That is marvelous. You're wearing trousers

underneath though, aren't you? Just in case you need to kick anyone?" Etta appeared slightly troubled at the thought.

The comment reminded Kat of her conversation with Victor when she mentioned them to him on that fateful day of his death. It was a bittersweet memory. "Of course."

"I do hope you don't have much need to remove your skirt," Etta said, the normally frivolous expression in the brown depths of her eyes replaced by a solemn seriousness. "Now tell me, have you heard anything further from Mr. Fullbrink yet? And what of the earl?"

Kat had given her a brief overview of the investigation in the carriage before they'd been cut short by picking up the duchess on their way to the theater. Though in her retelling of events, she'd been careful to leave out the kissing she'd been doing with Marcus in the carriage. Even just thinking about it, Kat felt an unfamiliar warmth creep up her face.

"Are you blushing, Kaitlyn Montrose?" Etta exclaimed. "You *are* blushing! What on earth happened between you and the Earl of Westwood today?"

Kat cleared her throat. "Nothing."

Etta laughed. "You little liar!"

"I don't know what you're talking about." With a snap of her wrist, Kat flicked open her fan and began to wave it in front of her face. The theater was suddenly hot. "Don't you have a drink to deliver?"

"Did he kiss you again?" Etta asked, ignoring her. "Though I must say, he doesn't strike me as a libertine... He's fairly stiff and correct in his manners I would have said, but he is very handsome. Mind you, he is friends with Cantfield, who is a terrible flirt, so perhaps he's more of a ladies man than I'm attributing to him. Oh, you simply must tell me what happened, I cannot stand the suspense!"

Kaitlyn rubbed her temples. Goodness, how was she going to divert Etta's nattering over the subject? "Why is it you don't like Cantfield? I thought you were partial to dark haired men who look like fallen angels."

Etta instantly tensed up. "He was rude while we danced the other night."

"What exactly did he do to make you so outraged?"

Etta's normally expressive eyes shuttered over as she looked out across the crowd. "What didn't he say. Firstly, he said I had a fine figure. Secondly, he maligned the *Gazette*, and thirdly, he criticized my political writings!"

"He knows you write as Mr. Henry T. Barton?" No one apart from Livie and her knew Etta was one of her father's celebrated political commentators that regularly featured in his newspaper. Not even Etta's father knew Mr. Barton was in fact his own daughter.

"No, of course not." Etta shook her head rather too vehemently as some of the curls slipped from her chignon. "He was talking about the feud that plays out on the pages between Mr. Barton and that pompous idiot, Mr. Ignatius Reginald. Cantfield was extolling the virtues of Mr. Reginald's political ideals, calling Mr. Barton a naive dreamer for his, or rather my, opinions, though he didn't know he was criticizing me. Even though he was! So, you see, he's an absolute bounder. I think he should be critiqued in the Gazette."

Kat raised a brow. "You wish to vilify him in the *Gazette* for saying you have a fine figure and disagreeing with your political writings, even though he didn't know he was criticizing you?"

"He also maligned the *Gazette*," Etta added, her eyes narrowing upon Kat. "Besides, you named Lord Westwood and he hasn't even done anything to warrant it!"

"You know he was named for a purpose," Kat said. "Do you really wish to destroy Cantfield because he gave you a compliment and disagreed with your political leanings?"

"He had no right to comment on my figure," Etta said. "He is a complete scoundrel to have done so, which makes me think he might have skeletons in his closet that need to be unearthed. Besides, I know my curves are somewhat larger than Society's standards, which is why I'm certain he was being sarcastic with his comments."

"I doubt that. The man adores women and has no qualms about making it known," Kat replied. "Etta, you can't think he was being sarcastic. Too many times you have degraded your figure when I have seen the majority of men admiring it greatly." Really, Etta was so sensitive of her figure and in particularly her overly large bosom, but most men Kat had seen look at her held a definite glint of admiration in their eyes when doing so.

"Please," Etta scoffed. "Next to you, I look like a short, stuffed cream puff."

"And next to you, my chest looks like a flattened pancake."

They looked at each other and burst into laughter, but then Etta glanced up and stiffened beside her.

Kat followed her gaze and saw Cantfield sauntering over to them, a grin covering his attractive face. One couldn't deny the man had charisma. It just wasn't a charisma that attracted her. In fact, no man had really attracted her notice, except for Marcus. Even as a fourteen-year-old, she'd been intrigued by him, and still was.

"Why is he coming over here?" Etta pointedly turned away from the approaching man in question.

"He obviously wishes to talk to us," Kaitlyn said.

Etta narrowed her eyes. "You watch, the first thing he will do is compliment you with some sort of sickly sweet clichéd phrase."

"Good evening, ladies," he said as he stopped a few feet from them and bowed. "How magnificent you both look. Why, just like diamonds sparkling amongst pebbles."

"See!" Etta told Kat, before she turned to Cantfield and shot him a look of utter distaste. "I would have thought a man of your reputation would come up with less of a completely hackneyed phrase than that. Or is that the extent of your compliments?"

Kat had to stifle a laugh at the sudden look of consternation creasing the corners of Cantfield's eyes.

He stiffened up perceptibly. "Excuse me, Miss Merriweather, are you really suggesting my compliment was hackneyed?"

"No, not at all," Etta said. "I wasn't suggesting anything. I was telling you it was *completely* hackneyed. There is a great deal of difference."

The man's jaw clenched and his eyes narrowed, but Etta didn't appear worried at all. Instead, she seemed to be in her element and in control of the situation. A good thing, too, as Kat imagined it was a rare occasion that anyone, let alone someone without rank, would dare say such a thing to the future duke.

As Etta and Lucas continued to exchange veiled insults, Kat excused herself and went in search of Marcus. The blasted man better be here.

She began walking through the milieu of the crème de la crème of society, her eyes wandering over the crowd. The ladies were all garbed in gowns dripping with jewels and fripperies, while the men were dressed in their evening regalia, sporting elaborate black suits and bow ties, with most having even more absurd hairstyles than the ladies.

"Lady Kaitlyn!" a voice exclaimed from behind.

Kat turned to see Mr. Fullbrink hurrying over to her, an expression of both pleasure and anxiety warring on his face all at once.

"Mr. Fullbrink? You found me in this crush. Does this mean you have news?"

"Indeed, it does. Is the earl with you?" There was a question in his eyes as he hurriedly smoothed down his day suit.

"No. He has not graced us with an appearance yet, I am afraid."

Fullbrink's face fell somewhat. "I'd hoped to share the information with him, too, as he will need to know."

"Come," Kat said, gently grabbing his forearm and guiding him toward the back of the room, to one of the empty alcoves. "You can tell me and then I'll pass it on to Westwood."

The man allowed himself to be steered into the alcove and unobtrusively, Kat pulled one of the sashes holding the velvet drapes, and the ruby red cloth cascaded down, covering half of the entry.

"Tell me what you have learned," she said.

The man's eyes twinkled with excitement in the glow of the wall lamp beside him. "I've decoded the ledger, my lady! And you will never guess it, but I believe it to be a list and transaction record of all of the Chameleon's past *and* future assassinations."

Her heart started to pound faster. It was exactly the news she'd been hoping for. "Go on."

"Well, the book is filled with the names of dead men, with the dates of their deaths in one column and a monetary amount in the other. And a majority of them are all men whose deaths have been attributed to the assassin. All except the last seven entries, which have names and amounts of money next to them, but no dates. The names I do recognize are all still alive. At the moment, anyhow." He shrugged his shoulders. "So perhaps they are the future targets of the Chameleon…"

"And who are the seven names listed, Mr. Fullbrink?"

The man smoothed back his hair before taking a hearty breath. "I hate to say it…but the first is the Secretary of State of War himself, Lord Danbury, as I had suspected."

"And the others?"

He scrunched his face up and twisted his hands together. "Sir William and Sir Albert are also listed."

"Are you certain, Mr. Fullbrink?"

"Yes, my lady." There was a hesitance in his voice, almost as if he didn't want to believe such a thing. "Then there is a Mr. Silas Morriset, Lord Newtown, Lord Burton, and a Ms. Bellis Perennis."

Kat had met both Newtown and Burton, but she'd never heard of Mr. Morriset or Ms. Perennis before.

"And what did Sir Albert and Sir William say when you told them this?"

"I um…well, I didn't get to tell them. They'd already left by the time I finished decoding it all." He pulled out a notebook from his pocket. "Here's the copy of the decoded ledger."

Kat placed the notebook in one of her pockets, noting the fear blanketing Fullbrink's eye, which she could understand. The three men essentially in charge of running England's War Office were listed as the Chameleon's assassination targets. Not to mention two lords and two other unknown persons. It wasn't a good situation.

Suddenly, she sensed a presence on the other side of the curtain. Pushing Mr. Fullbrink backward, she swiveled to face the entry, simultaneously grabbing her dagger from her skirt and holding it at the ready by her side.

The curtain was pushed aside and Marcus stepped into the alcove, his features calm and composed except for the grumpy glare in his eyes. She was getting rather good at reading his emotions. Though he did seem to be grumpy a lot in her presence, which was perhaps why she recognized the look so readily.

"My Lord." She curtsied, swiftly returning the dagger to her pocket. "Good of you to finally attend."

"Lady Kaitlyn," he said, a slight raise of his eyebrow as he glanced at the pocket of her skirt, where she'd returned the dagger. "What are you doing sequestered in here with Fullbrink?" He looked between them and his frown became fierce even in the dim light as his gaze rested on Fullbrink before returning to Kat.

"What do you think I'm doing in here with him?" Kat asked, bristling somewhat at his unspoken suggestion. "Fullbrink, fill him in please."

The poor man stepped nervously forward and repeated what he had just told Kat.

Kat returned Marcus's stare in full, not budging an inch.

As Fullbrink finished his report, Marcus finally glanced across at him. "Tell this to no one else at the Department."

"But, sir? No one at all?" Fullbrink shifted from foot to foot. "But what of the Secretary? Not to mention the undersecretary and Sir William? Surely, they should know their lives are in danger?"

"Be assured I will see to their safety. Can I rely on you, Fullbrink?" Marcus asked him.

Fullbrink nodded so sharply, Kat feared his glasses would rattle off. "Indeed, you can."

"Good." Marcus jerked his head toward the curtain. "Now leave," he commanded.

The man gave a quick bow to them and then hurried out of the alcove.

"We need to find them and warn them," Kat said, taking a step to leave the alcove, but Marcus placed his hand across her body, gently halting her.

"We do," he agreed, stepping in front of her and slowly maneuvering her up against the wall, well away from any prying eyes. "But, first, I must do this," he whispered against her ear.

Kat inhaled sharply at the contact, the heat from his body penetrating through the bodice of her gown, sending a wave of longing to her core. She noticed he was breathing deeply now, too, a hot fire burning in his gaze as his lips descended upon her own.

Her whole body melted against his as she opened her mouth up to him, savoring the feel of his lips against hers. She wrapped her arms around his neck and leaned in closer as she returned his embrace in equal measure.

One of his hands skimmed up her body to gently tilt up her chin as he deepened his kiss, while his other hand cupped her bottom and pulled her in tightly to him. She could feel the hard length of him pressing against her lower belly, enticing her. She urged herself closer still and moaned softly.

He reluctantly pulled his lips from her and rested his chin to her forehead, inhaling a shaky breath.

"You do the damnedest of things to me, woman," he whispered into her hair. "I seem to forget everything else when I see you."

Kat took in several deep breaths herself, her whole body feeling electrified, her every sense alert and magnified by his touch. She took in another breath, only to breathe in his intoxicating scent. "I'm glad you have finally seen reason and are agreeing to my earlier proposal to become my lover."

The hazy mist of passion in his eyes was instantly shuttered, only to be replaced by an unfathomable stare. "I haven't said that."

"You don't have to say anything," Kat replied. "Your actions speak louder than words."

"I don't want to compromise you."

"It's not compromising me when I fully agree to it." She raised an eyebrow.

He ran a hand through his hair and swore under his breath. "You're an impossible woman."

"You're not the first to say so. But we have more important things to discuss at the moment, like finding those on the Chameleon's list."

Marcus shook his head. "You're right, damn it. We can start with Burton. He has a box on the third level here and is somewhat of an aficionado when it comes to the theater, so he's always in attendance."

"We had best go and check his box, then," Kat said. "His very life could be at stake."

Chapter Sixteen

Marcus followed Kaitlyn up the stairs toward the third landing of the theater. He couldn't help a frown from marring his face, even with the particularly pleasant view of Kat's hips swaying from side to side as she climbed the dimly lit staircase.

The play itself had just commenced and thankfully the crowd had taken to their seats or boxes for the performance. Lord Burton would most likely be annoyed at the interruption, as he was known for his passionate appreciation of the theater, but Marcus had no doubt that once he heard of the possible danger he was in, he wouldn't be too upset.

There were still a few waiters scurrying about, glasses of champagne balanced delicately on trays as they ducked in and out of the various boxes, in a concerted effort to ensure the patrons comfortably sequestered within had all their wishes satisfied.

Marcus saw one waiter back carefully out of one of the alcoves ahead, his hands empty except for a large white napkin draped over one hand. The man turned and paused upon seeing them climbing the stairs. He bowed to them from the landing above, then straightened but kept his head low and deferential as he clambered down the stairs and rushed past them.

"Where is Burton's box?" Kat asked, looking back at Marcus.

"Up ahead I believe, box sixteen," he replied, coming abreast of her. There was something odd about the waiter that Marcus couldn't quite put his finger on, but when he turned back to look, the man was already gone.

They passed several more boxes, the sound of the show careening through the thin material covering the opening of each, offering a somewhat limited measure of privacy. Then, as they came to a stop outside Burton's box, Marcus realized it was the same one the waiter had exited.

His whole body braced in alert as he pushed open the curtain and peered inside. Lord Burton was the sole occupant of the space and was sitting on one of the plush red velvet chairs, which was inclined at a slight angle toward the front of the stage. His eyes were closed, and he looked asleep, slumped over to the side.

Striding forward, Marcus took in the deathly stillness of Burton's chest. He rushed to feel for a pulse on the man's neck. There was none.

He turned back to Kat. "He's dead." His voice was flat, a sense of rage and helplessness washing over him for a moment. They had been too late!

"The Chameleon got here first?"

Their eyes locked and they simultaneously said, "The waiter!"

Kat ran through the curtain and back into the hallway, Marcus following closely on her heels. They careened down the staircase to the ground floor, passing several other waiters down the stairway, but not the one they were looking for.

They came to the ground-level entry where there were still a few staff members left to maintain order while the performance was on. Marcus scanned those assembled but cursed when he realized their quarry was not amongst them.

"Have you seen a waiter of slim stature and brown hair pass through here?" Kat asked them.

Most shook their heads, but one of the older waiters stepped forward. "If he was a staff member, my lady, he may have gone through the back stairway, located off the first floor just up the stairs to the left. You would have passed it as you came down."

Marcus had already started back up the steps as Kat thanked the man and followed behind him.

He turned at the top of the stairs and saw another staircase farther down, which was roped off with a sign on it saying FOR USE BY STAFF ONLY.

Ignoring the sign, he unlatched the rope from the hook before racing down the much less elaborate stairwell than that of the main staircase, Kat following closely behind. They came out down the bottom, into what was a bustling hive of activity as servants and waiters alike dashed about with trays of food. A man who was clearly in charge rushed over to them.

"I am so sorry, but this is for staff only!" The man tried to smile politely but clearly was not used to having any guests race down into the bowels of the place. "I shall have to ask you to go back to your seats."

"Lord Burton has been murdered," Marcus said.

The man gasped and brought his hands up over his chest. "Murdered? Surely not. Not in the Lyceum Theatre."

"Did a waiter come rushing down here a minute or two before us?" Kat asked the man.

He nodded earnestly. "Yes, the darn fellow wouldn't listen to me when I asked him to take a tray to box twenty-four." He pointed over to a hallway down the corridor. "He ran down there toward the back alley."

"Get the police here immediately," Marcus said. He looked at Kat, unaccountably pleased to see she had already armed herself and was holding her dagger discreetly by her side. There was something to be said for a woman confident in being able to protect herself.

He pulled out his own pistol from the holster hidden under his jacket and then, without a word passing between them, they headed toward the hallway the man had pointed to.

The carpet was threadbare down the darkened corridor, with only a few gas lamps lit on the walls. They came to the end of the hallway where a back door led into the alleyway behind the theater. The door was made of wood and painted a sickly green color.

Carefully, Marcus turned the handle and cracked the wood open but an inch. He glanced through the small gap but couldn't see or hear anything. His eyes sought out Kat's and she nodded in silent acknowledgment. With a returning nod, Marcus kicked the door wide open.

The alleyway was deserted and dark, but there was a gleam of silver and glass from an object lying on the ground to his right. Retrieving a handkerchief from his pocket, Marcus bent down and picked the item up. It was a glass syringe, with a small amount of liquid residue in the bottom.

"Poison, perhaps?" Kat was peering at the vial.

"Yes, we may have found Burton's murder weapon. But, unfortunately, our quarry got away from us. God damn it!"

Chapter Seventeen

Two hours later, after dealing with the aftermath of the events from the evening and ensuring Kat had been safely returned to her residence, despite her protests to the contrary, Marcus sat down on the edge of his bed in his mostly darkened bedchamber, the wall clock's soft ticking the only noise to be heard in the silence permeating the near-empty house.

Silence was what he'd thought he needed to get his jumbled thoughts and emotions sorted. But for some reason he couldn't relax as the frustration of always being a step behind the assassin rose to the surface, threatening to consume him.

He stood abruptly and began to pace across the rug as a sense of restless energy filled him, both from being unable to save Burton, and from the physical frustration of spending so much time in Kat's vicinity but unable to do anything to satisfy his desire to have her in his bed.

Because even though she said she'd decided to take him as her lover, the girl had no idea what she was talking about. She was a virgin, and Marcus had no intention of compromising a virgin, let alone Victor's niece. But then her words suggesting she'd find another man to fill such a role echoed in his head and he found his fists automatically clenching by his side.

Take another lover, would she? The lady was bluffing. She had to be. Though Kat wasn't really the type to bluff. The woman was nothing if not completely stubborn when she had her mind set on something. And if she had the idea in her head that she wanted to experience pleasure, there was no one to stop her from doing exactly that.

Except him.

If she was so determined to do something as outrageous as that, then who was he to stop her? It was her life and her choice what she did with it. And as she'd quite rightly reminded him several times, he had no say in what she did. The thought was infuriating.

A soft rustling from outside the window drew his attention. He strode over and pulled back the curtain a fraction to look down into the dark night below. The moon was nearly full and cast enough light for Marcus to make out the shape of a person.

He swore when he recognized the red hair and slim figure climbing up the drainpipe attached to the stone brickwork of the residence. The woman was utterly outrageous, and he could see her special detachable skirt pooled into a pile on the ground beneath, as her trouser-clad legs carried her up to the second level.

From his vantage point, he did have to admit that the curve of her backside was mesmerizing. He shook his head and swore again. He really was going to spank her this time.

He opened the window and she paused in her climbing and looked up at him.

"Good, you're still awake." She grinned and continued her ascension. "I assumed you would be."

"Why the devil are you climbing up my drainpipe?" he all but yelled before lowering his voice. "You should be at home and in bed."

"We can't really start an illicit liaison if I'm there and not here." She resumed climbing until she reached the window. Marcus pulled her over the sill and into the room.

"What? No black mask and matching outfit?" he asked as he helped her stand, but did not let go of her upper arms.

"There was no need to disguise my identity this time." She shrugged. "Besides, why bother changing when you're going to remove my clothes shortly, anyway?"

Marcus groaned. "I've never met another lady like you. You're completely outrageous, you know that?"

"I know," she happily agreed. "But I'm only outrageous about passionate matters with you."

He stared down into the green depths of her eyes as she looked up at him, and God help him, he was lost. There was an inquisitive openness in her gaze he couldn't resist, and instead of chiding her as he should, all he could think about was kissing her.

She opened her mouth to say something further, but he couldn't help himself and his mouth landed hungrily down upon her soft lips.

A low moan came from her as he plundered her mouth with his tongue, teasing and tasting in turn. He'd never savored anything sweeter or more addictive, and he realized that he'd never wanted anything more than to taste and feel her against him. To make her his.

He brought one of his hands across to cup the small curve of her breast, while his other hand traced down the side of her body to nestle under the edge of her buttocks. He pulled her in tightly against him for a brief moment, before reluctantly wrenching his lips from hers and releasing her.

Taking a step back, he breathed in deeply, immensely satisfied by the look of dazed passion replacing the normally sharp alertness in her eyes. "If we're going to do this," he began, taking in another breath, "we need to set up some ground rules."

"At least you're finally agreeing to my proposal," she said, bemusement replacing the passion in her gaze. "But you know I'm not very good at following rules. Unless they suit me."

"I like rules," he drawled.

"Yes, I know."

He narrowed his eyes. "I'm serious, Kat. I'm already compromising my principles by agreeing to this, so there have to be some parameters around what we're about to embark on."

"Do there?" she murmured, while her hands reached up to the tiny buttons of her bodice and slowly started undoing them, one by one.

Marcus was unwittingly mesmerized by each deft flick of her fingers, as slowly the material of her dress parted, revealing the cotton of her chemise underneath, along with the enticing swell of her cleavage. He cleared his throat and dragged his eyes up to hers. "Pardon?"

"The rules of yours," she said, innocence radiating from her expression as she flicked open the last button and her bodice dropped to the ground. "What are they?"

"You're not wearing a corset..." He could barely restrain his hands from touching her.

"Madame Arnout sews the boning into the bodices of my gowns," she said. "I didn't realize how convenient not wearing a proper corset would be, until right now."

His eyes strayed back to her hands which were pulling up her chemise, inch by agonizing inch, slowly revealing the silky cream of her bare skin underneath. Marcus was hard-pressed to even think of what he'd been talking about, let alone articulate it. The woman was driving him mad with desire.

She pulled off her undergarment with a flourish and the moon's light bathed her skin with its soft caress. He'd never seen a more perfect set of breasts.

Standing proudly before him, he saw a hint of uncertainty in her gaze, an expression he'd never seen on the bold and fearless lady. It was his undoing and he knew there was no way on earth he could resist this woman. He was tired of trying to live by the rules. Tired of always trying to do the right thing. Tired of fighting his attraction to her.

She wanted to be pleasured? Then pleasured he would make certain she was.

• • •

Standing there, with her breasts bared to his gaze, Kat felt completely exposed, with the ramifications of her actions finally starting to sink in. There'd be no going back after tonight. She was going to become Marcus's lover, and she was going to experience what it felt to truly be a woman.

"You're stunning," Marcus said, his voice gruff as he dragged his gaze back to her eyes.

His words brought a smile to her mouth. "Then come and kiss me, as it's all I've been able to think of."

He groaned but took a step closer to her and bent his head to hers. His mouth was hot and delicious. Kat opened her own to him fully, entwining her hands in his hair and pulling him closer. The hard expanse of his arousal pressed against her belly while his mouth continued to explore and devour hers.

Sensations of pleasure snaked through her entire body and she pushed her breasts flush against his chest. The groan that rumbled through him filled her with euphoria. She was doing this to him. She was creating this desire within him. It filled her with such a sense of satisfaction. But then he yanked his mouth away from hers and she frowned.

"Are you sure about this, Kat?" he panted, his breathing slightly uneven. "We can stop now, if you want."

She wrapped her hands around his neck. "Yes, I'm certain, Marcus Black. I want you to be my lover."

"Then so be it," he murmured as his lips captured hers once again, and then he scooped her up in his arms and carried her over to his bed. He lay down beside her, and Kat eagerly pushed aside his dressing gown.

"You're naked," she exclaimed, and even though it was dark in the room, with only the moon's light shining in from the window, she could see he had no clothes under his silk dressing gown.

He grinned. "Have I shocked your sensibilities, my lady?"

She gulped but couldn't resist peeking down the length of his body. And what a glorious body it was. Though she wished in a way there was more light so she could see him fully, but then that would mean he'd see her naked, too, and no man had ever seen her fully naked before. "Perhaps a little."

Her hesitancy was short-lived when he started kissing her again and she ran her hands over the hair of his muscular chest and up over his shoulders. He was so broad and deliciously masculine. She wanted to touch all of him. On impulse, her hands began to drift lower down his body and he groaned in response.

"Can you feel what you do to me?" he whispered into her ear as his hand took her own and placed it onto his cock.

His shaft was hard, hot, and so unbelievably silky smooth. She couldn't help but caress him with her fingertips. In reply, his hand moved to the top button of her trousers and he flicked it open with ease, before he pushed the material down over her thighs.

She wiggled her hips, helping him to remove her trousers. He flung them from the bed and turned back to gaze down at her. The shadows in the room wouldn't have been helping him to see her in full, but he obviously could see enough because his cock leaped and was jutting out proudly. Kat felt the very core of her tingle, almost as if it were about to boil over. She wanted this man with an urgency bordering on frenzy.

When his hand gently reached toward her center and pressed against her curls down there, she nearly jumped from the bed. Then when his fingers began to caress her little nub, she moaned aloud and grabbed the bedsheets with both hands.

"Does that feel good?" he murmured as his hand continued to caress her.

Good? Good was too tame a word to describe what she was feeling. "I feel like I'm about to explode…"

"It's meant to feel that way," he whispered, as his other hand reached over and began kneading her breast.

Kat found her hips rocking of their own volition against his hand. Sensation after sensation rippled through her, and then just as she felt like she was about to burst, Marcus withdrew his hand and replaced it with his cock, gently rubbing it against her instead of his hand.

She'd never felt such wantonness, such desire for anyone.

"I want you so badly," he said as he reached over and pulled something out of his bedside drawer.

"I want you, too, Marcus," she replied, watching as he began to roll whatever it was he'd retrieved over his penis.

"Is that a rubber sheath?"

He nodded, and then pressed his cock against her opening. "Are you sure about this, Kat?" he asked, little beads of sweat on his brow as he positioned himself above her. "I can stop if you want me to."

"Why would I ever want you to stop?" She grabbed his neck and drew his head down to hers, kissing him with all the passion she was feeling. Then she wrapped her long legs around his buttocks and pulled him inside her.

She gasped as a stinging pain hit her.

"I'm sorry," he whispered. "The hurt should go soon."

"It's fine," she said, and slowly the pain started to fade. It disappeared completely when he reached between their bodies and rubbed her nub again while he slowly started to grind his hips against hers, pumping in and out of her. "Oh goodness," she couldn't help uttering as she began to crest that peak again.

"That's it, my darling."

She met him thrust for thrust, the pleasure building until Kat didn't think she could stand it. And then everything around her seemed to combust as wave after wave of pleasure careened through every pore of her body and she screamed in ecstasy.

Marcus groaned as he pumped himself inside of her, and then collapsed on top of her. He pushed himself to the side so he wasn't crushing her, but he made no move to withdraw from her.

Kat wrapped her arms around him and marvelled at how she felt. She'd never experienced such intense satisfaction before. Not even throwing her daggers felt as good as this. "We're going to need to do this again and again."

He half laughed, half groaned. "I'll need some time to recharge."

"You will? That's a bit disappointing."

This time he did laugh. "I'm glad you enjoyed it so much."

"I did." A very satisfied grin spread over her face, but then she frowned. "Did you?"

"So much so that I can't believe I'm starting to stir again."

"Stir again? What does that mean?"

"Let me show you, my dear…"

And he proceeded to do exactly that.

Chapter Eighteen

The next morning, after the chaos of the night before at the theater and then the ridiculously wonderful experience of becoming Marcus's lover, Kat finally crawled into her bed sometime after four in the morning.

She'd slept for a few hours, relatively well, though that was only to be expected after Marcus had kept her busy and thoroughly exhausted with his bedroom skills. And now that she'd awoken, she had to focus and get her mind back on her task, which reminded her of the decoded ledger she still had to read.

She changed into a simple day dress and strode over to her skirt from last night that was still hanging haphazardly from the chair. She pulled out the notebook from the pocket and flicked through the pages, noting several men's names whose deaths were indeed attributed to the Chameleon, but then there were also other men listed whose deaths had been ruled accidental. Perhaps not so accidental after all?

Alongside all the names was a date of death and a sum, which Kat assumed was what the

Chameleon had been paid to kill them. A nagging voice in the back of her mind had her flipping the pages until she reached the date of Victor's murder. There, glaring back at her in stark black ink was Victor's name, with a sum of five thousand pounds alongside it.

Utter numbness filled her as she began to comprehend what his name in the ledger meant. Someone had paid to have Victor killed?

She'd always assumed Victor was targeted by the assassin because he was getting too close to discovering the Chameleon's identity. But now, in the face of what was before her, it seemed that assumption was incorrect. Gradually, the numbness was replaced with a hollow rage.

Five thousand pounds was all it cost somebody to have Victor killed? The thought kept repeating in her mind, coiling inside her like poison. She barely heard the knock at her door before it opened and in walked Daisy.

"I hate to intrude." Daisy stopped at the entrance, a slight frown of worry creasing her forehead. "But Fenton told me what happened at the theater last night and I wanted to check you were all right."

Kat turned to face her. "Five thousand pounds, Daisy." Her voice sounded hollow, echoing exactly how she felt.

"What are you talking about?"

Marching over to the window overlooking the gardens, Kat rested her head against the glass as her fist pounded briefly against the wooden frame. "It only took a measly five thousand pounds to end Victor's life." Taking in a deep breath she pulled away from the glass and swiveled to face Daisy.

Daisy stumbled over to the chair Kat had just vacated and sank into it, her face blanching of all color. "But I don't understand. I thought the Chameleon killed Victor because he was getting too close to uncovering the assassin's true identity."

"As did I." Kat turned and began pacing across the floor, her bare soles oblivious to the cold seeping through the wood, while she briefly explained the discovery of the ledger. "Victor's name was on the list."

"Someone paid to have him killed?" Daisy exclaimed, her head dropping down into her hands. "Who would do such a thing? Did the ledger say who it was?"

"No. But I *will* find out when I find the Chameleon," Kat said as a sudden urge to hit something, hit anything, came over her.

"Who had reason to kill him, though?" Daisy asked.

Kat shook her head. "I don't know. He made many enemies over the years in his choice of vocation."

Daisy's eyes swam, bright with unshed tears.

"I used to plead with him to retire from the spying game…he promised me he would, he just needed a little bit more time, he used to say… But then it was too late, and he was gone."

Kat stopped pacing and walked over to Daisy, placing a hand on her shoulder. "I promise you I will find the Chameleon *and* the person responsible for Victor's death."

"No! Do you not see?" Daisy turned toward her and grabbed both of Kat's hands in her own, her grip like a vise. "That's why Victor was killed. He was too immersed in this ludicrous game of cat and mouse, just as you have become!"

"This is no game." Kat's voice turned cold as she shook free Daisy's hands and took a step back. "I would think you of all people would want to find the person responsible for your husband's death."

"Of course, I do. But it will not bring him back. What it could do is take you away from us." Daisy stood up, regarding her as her silent tears continued to flow down her pale cheeks. "Victor wouldn't have asked this of you. He loved you more than anything."

Kat clenched her teeth together, willing the tightness that was lodged in the middle of her throat to subside. Since his death, she'd questioned whether Victor had loved her or not. How could he have kept the secret that he was her father for all those years if he had? Taking in a shaky breath, she walked back over to the window. "Victor would be avenging me if our places were reversed."

"Perhaps," Daisy intoned, her voice flat. "And though Victor would have given his life for you, he would never have wanted you to give your life for him."

"How dare you presume to know what he would have wanted!" Kat spun around to face her aunt. "You were married to him for what, ten years before he died? I was with him since I was four, Daisy. Over twenty years he trained me for this. I travelled with him, I fought with him, I was with him when he died. And though he wouldn't have asked me to seek vengeance, he would have *expected* it. If you had spent as much time with him as I did, instead of shopping and socializing, you would know that."

Instantly, she regretted the words. Daisy looked defeated, her delicate frame wilting under the harsh words. Kat exhaled roughly. "I am sorry. I didn't mean that."

"Yes, you did." Daisy straightened and squared her shoulders. "It is true. I know I didn't share the bond you and Victor had, nor did I go on your missions and trips to the Continent. But I do know this: he loved you more than anyone and anything." She smiled sadly.

Kat breathed in deeply. "He loved you, too."

"No, he didn't. At least not in the way that counted, for he was never in love with me. His heart had been given to another, long ago. And then broken by her death. I sometimes think he only married me to obtain an heir and because of my linguistic skills."

"That's not true…" Kat's voice lacked a ring of conviction, and they both knew it. The truth was that Victor only paid his wife any real attention when he had need of her skill of speaking three languages, to assist him in translating foreign correspondence.

Daisy's eyes were bright with further tears. "It is true, but in his own way he did care for me at least. But he loved you, and I know he would not want you to give your life for his ghost."

Kat felt a stray tear slide down her own cheek. She pivoted around to look anywhere but Daisy. She hadn't shed a tear since the day of Victor's death, not even at his funeral, and she wouldn't do so now. If she did, she feared she might never stop. "I must find his killer, Daisy. I'll not rest until I do."

The sound of Daisy's soft-heeled boots clipping across the parquet flooring as she walked over to where Kat stood echoed surprisingly loud in the silent room. She picked up Kat's hand and gripped it in her own. "Please do not do this, Kaitlyn, I beg you. Stop looking for the Chameleon. No good can come of it, no matter what happens."

"I can't do that." Kat shook free of Daisy's fingers and stepped away from her.

"The Chameleon is an assassin, Kaitlyn. Perhaps killing even before you were born." Daisy drew herself up to her full height, a good three inches shorter than Kat's. "It's madness to go after such a creature, and it will not end well. Please do not jeopardize us all. Samuel and I have already lost Victor, we cannot lose you, too."

"I have no intention of dying."

"Don't be foolish, Kaitlyn!" Daisy raised her voice, the gentle persuasive tone turning harsh. "Victor certainly did not intend to die, but he died just the same."

"He let his guard down." Kat didn't blink as Daisy stared at her with anger and accusation in her eyes. "I will not make that mistake."

"You are so like him." She raised her hands in the air and stomped her foot. The action was so completely at odds with Daisy's normally genteel manner that Kat knew she was beyond upset. "So stubborn that you also refuse to listen to reason, just as Victor did! You will end up dead if you continue down this path, just like he did."

A lump formed in her throat at the vehement statement. "I do not wish to quarrel with you, Daisy."

"Then don't," Daisy pleaded, the anger leaving her eyes only to be replaced with desperation.

"Stop this madness before it gets out of hand and you die!" Daisy swiveled on her heel and strode over to the door. She stopped at the entry and turned, looking back at Kat. "I know I'm not your blood relation, but Samuel is. Think about him and the danger you're putting not only yourself into by chasing an assassin, but the danger you put him in as well. That you put all of us in. You risk breaking this family apart, Kaitlyn Montrose, because of your desire for vengeance at all costs."

They stood staring tensely at each other before Daisy whirled around and disappeared down the hallway in a swirl of blue skirts, leaving lavender perfume in her wake.

An overwhelming helplessness washed through Kat as her eyes lingered on the empty doorway. Though Daisy had always been the voice of opposition in Kat's rather peculiar activities, eventually she supported her. But Kat had the uncomfortable sensation in her stomach that they had just come across a chasm and were on separate sides.

Glancing at the window, Kat took in a deep breath. She knew what she had to do because contrary to what Daisy thought, they would never be safe until the Chameleon and whoever paid him to murder Victor were no longer a threat.

For a brief moment, Kat found herself wishing Marcus was there with her. That he would wrap his arms around her and take all of her worries and fears away. The longing for his embrace so deep, it pulled at her. She'd never needed anyone before. Had never really wanted anyone before. But she found herself quite desperately aching for him. The thought scared her as nothing else had in a long time.

"Excuse me, my lady?" Fenton said as he stood outside the room, holding a small silver tray with an envelope on it.

"What is it, Fenton?" She forced a small smile, trying to allay the concern she could clearly see gleaming in his eyes. "Have our informants discovered anything?"

Before retiring to bed, she'd filled him in on the events of the evening, except of course what happened with Marcus after. Fenton had no need to know that. Then she'd tasked him with finding out all he could regarding Lord Burton and the other targets.

"I put out the feelers as you requested, and Mr. Gingham has sent a note, my lady." He handed her a small envelope.

"I can always rely on you, Fenton." She deftly opened the gummed backing and pulled out the paper from the envelope. "It says he has information regarding a certain party's funding and who is behind it." Excitement filled her, lifting the tightness that had been pressing against her chest only moments earlier.

Fenton narrowed his eyes and hesitated for a moment. "Gingham has had useful information in the past, but to know who is behind everything? I think it is doubtful."

"True." Kat shrugged lightly. "However, I shall find out soon enough when I meet him at his bookstore at eleven thirty this morning."

"Will you request the company of the Earl of Westwood?"

She felt her heart speed up at the mere mention of Marcus's name, but it was an odd question from Fenton, who knew she mostly did everything on her own. "Why would I?"

He smiled slightly. "I know only too well how you can take care of yourself. However, after last night's events, having him about gives me an even greater sense of comfort regarding your safety. The Chameleon is getting bolder, killing a lord in his own theater box in front of hundreds. Such recklessness concerns me. And I do worry over you."

Her heart was touched by the statement. They might not share a drop of blood, but Fenton was family, and she worried over him, too. "Very well." She owed Fenton so much that the least she could do was lessen his concerns, especially as he wasn't asking her to give up her quest.

"Send Westwood a note and tell him of my movements. Oh, and would you also send Etta a note requesting her presence at the bookstore? Gingham has a soft spot for her and will most likely be much more forthcoming with her there than without, saving me some pounds he will be sure to try to negotiate."

"I shall, my lady," he said, his lips lifted at the corners. "And my thanks. I know you normally prefer to do things on your own, especially since his lordship…left us."

Talking of Victor's death had always been hard for them both.

"You mean a great deal to me, and I respect your suggestions." The man was almost like a second father to her, aside from Victor. And considering Fenton was as stalwart as a rock, if he was worried, it wasn't something to be ignored. "On another topic, though, we need to find out what Lord Burton knew or was involved in, that warranted someone paying for his death. And what connection he has with the others on the list. We also need to find out who this Silas Morriset and Bellis Perennis are."

"I must say, the names sound familiar to me." He rubbed at his jaw. "I'll start making enquiries immediately after sending off the notes to his lordship and Miss Etta. If you will excuse me, my lady." He bowed and turned on his heel, before departing down the hallway.

She watched his retreating form and frowned

when she saw he was favoring his left side. The arthritis in his right knee was obviously flaring up again and as he liked to say, he certainly wasn't getting any younger. She bit her bottom lip. She did not like that he was getting older. Not one little bit.

Kat really wouldn't know what she'd do if she lost Fenton, too.

Chapter Nineteen

"You have done exactly what I asked you *not* to!"

Lord Danbury flicked his beady black eyes over the piece of paper and then up and over toward Marcus and Lucas, both of whom he'd summoned to the War Office in light of last night's events. "You have let the whole situation get out of hand! Imagine my surprise last night, upon hearing that a peer of the Realm was murdered at the theater. Absolutely terrible. Which lord was it again that was killed?" He waved his arms about, asking his question to Sir William and Sir Albert, who were also present.

Marcus refrained from a scathing response at the man's inability to even remember Lord Burton's name. Danbury was an incompetent fool, a fact Marcus should be used to by now, but was still hard to swallow.

A glimpse of weary acceptance passed between Sir Albert and Sir William, who were both sitting on the settee to the side of Danbury's desk, which Marcus and Lucas stood in front of, while Lord Danbury reclined in his chair behind the desk.

Sir Albert cleared his throat. "It was Lord

Burton, my lord. He did some work for us a few years back."

"Ah yes, so it was," Lord Danbury exclaimed. "And to top it all off, the two of you were there and unable to stop such an occurrence." His ire was directed solely at Marcus and Lucas. "What on earth happened? Why did the two of you let this blasted Chameleon kill him? Very bad business indeed. Reflects poorly on the entire department, even if neither of you are official employees as such."

"Well, Westwood?" As predicted, Lord Danbury directed his attention onto Marcus, his asinine face peering at him in suspicion. "What can you tell me of this debacle?"

"Apart from what's in the report, Danbury, there's not a great deal more to tell." Honestly, the man was pushing his already pushed patience to the limit. He didn't assist the government on occasion only to be subjected to such ignorance by Danbury. "Perhaps you should be more concerned over your own safety and the others on the Chameleon's list."

"My own safety?" Lord Danbury furrowed his brows and scowled.

Marcus was somewhat taken aback at the man's confusion. "I thought I made it plain in my report."

"There's your first mistake!" Danbury exclaimed. "You didn't expect me to read the thing, did you? Good Lord, that's why I asked you in here, to give me a verbal report instead."

"You summoned me in here to have me read my report aloud to you?" Marcus clenched his fists by his sides.

The man stiffened. "Steady on now, Westwood. A peer of the realm was just assassinated. Clearly, I must have a report in person. I need to know who is responsible for this debacle. The queen expects a full accounting from me regarding the situation."

"Then perhaps a good starting place for you would have been to actually read the report I wrote in the first instance, instead of lazily asking me for a verbal one," Marcus thundered.

"I never!" Danbury gasped.

"And if you had read the report, you would know you, too, are on the Chameleon's assassination list." Marcus looked over at both Sir William and Sir Albert, who were extremely used to Danbury's drivel. "I have no time to waste on this nonsense. There's an assassin on the loose who is targeting all of you. Do you really want me in here wasting my time with this fool, or out there trying to find him?"

Lord Danbury spluttered, "How dare yo—"

"How dare I?" Westwood turned his eyes back to Danbury and roared, "If you dare to ever summon me here again to give you a verbal reading of my report, you will damn well be sorry."

"Westwood," Sir Albert interrupted as he

jumped up and stepped forward with his hands held up in surrender. "Lord Danbury is just trying to—"

"Waste my time? Well, he's doing a good job of it."

Beside Sir Albert, Sir William began to laugh but quickly covered it up with a cough.

Lord Danbury pushed back his chair and stood to his full five feet nine inches. "Westwood, I will not tolerate this insolence. We may be of the same rank, but in this office, I am the Secretary of State for War. You will respect that. And stop trying to pretend I'm on some assassin's list. I do not find such a jest in good taste at all."

Marcus stalked over to the other side of Danbury's desk and grabbed the man's jacket lapels, hauling him off his feet. Danbury's mouth flopped open, apparently at a loss for words. Finally. "It is no damn jest, *Secretary*. You're one of the Chameleon's targets. As are Sir William and Sir Albert."

Danbury could only utter a squeak and shake his head. Returning him to his feet, Marcus let go of the man's jacket and stepped backward.

Lord Danbury cowered where he stood, no courage to do anything but mumble, "I didn't realize I was a target…"

"You are, and you have wasted enough of my time here." Marcus straightened and turned on his heel. He marched over to the door and indicated with a nod of his head for Lucas to follow. He stopped and turned back to face them. "Security has been arranged for all of you. Don't be stupid and do keep your eyes open. I'll send word if there's news and I'll speak with you two later." He directed the last part at Sir Albert and Sir William.

Stepping out into the corridor, he strode away. What a bloody waste of time that had been. He shook his head, wondering not for the first time, what the queen had been thinking when she appointed that sniveling fool to the position. The world wouldn't be a worse place without the man in it, that was certain.

Lucas hurried to catch up. "That meeting was a smashing success! I particularly liked the part where you had him dangling in the air for a moment. Don't think that's ever happened to him before."

A few seconds later, a voice called out from behind them, "Westwood! Cantfield!"

They both paused in mid-stride and turned back to see Sir Albert's rotund frame rushing down the corridor toward them. "Do wait a moment, please!"

Marcus folded his arms across his chest as the man hurried over, stopping a few feet from them. Sir Albert, though practical and usually level-headed, was still Danbury's right-hand man.

"I'm sorry for Lord Danbury's lack of…" His

voice, which was slightly puffed, trailed off. "Well, um his...everything. He's currently mulling over the new information."

"Cowering in a corner of his office, is he?" Marcus asked.

"Goodness no!" Sir Albert reprimanded. "Under his desk." He smiled at them. "He'll be easy enough to sort out and will gladly accept the security detail arranged for him. However, Sir William is not being equally as compliant."

Marcus raised an eyebrow. "Refusing to accept his life is in danger?"

"No, he believes that," Sir Albert replied. "He just doesn't believe he needs any security."

"The man is stubborn," Lucas chirped in.

"Yes." Sir Albert paused. "Are you certain the three of us were listed? Fullbrink didn't make some sort of mistake?"

"When does Fullbrink ever make a mistake?"

"Yes, true." Sir Albert seemed troubled, which was to be expected of anyone who'd only recently found out they were on an assassin's list of targets. And not just any assassin either, but the Chameleon. "All of the resources of the Department will be at your disposal. Anything you need to find this villain you will have. Just come to me, not Danbury. I daresay his mind won't be on the job until the situation is resolved."

"Good," Marcus affirmed. That meant he'd be

dealing with someone who could get things done. "If anything did happen to the three of you, who would be in charge of the War Office?"

"I'm not sure," Sir Albert said, his eyes wide with the possibility. "Surely, you can't suspect someone from the Department itself has paid for these assassinations?"

"It's a possibility," Marcus replied. "The three of you hold the most power, so who would benefit from your deaths?"

Sir Albert tapped his foot on the floor for a moment as he considered Marcus's question. "No one, really. You see, if something were to happen to Danbury, then I would be in charge, and then if something were to befall me, Sir William would take the reins. And if something were to also happen to Sir William, then I imagine one of the other department heads would be appointed for a short period until a new secretary was decided upon. But you see, no one would permanently get the position, after Sir William. Even then, my appointment or Sir William's would only be final if confirmed by the queen."

"Hmm…" Marcus rubbed his jaw as he thought over Sir William's words. Nothing quite made sense. "Burton's death is an outlier. He had nothing to do with the chain of command, so why was he murdered? What work did he do for the War Office?"

"Nothing of significance, well, except for a few

ycars back, when he brought Sir William some information." Sir Albert paused, his eyes probing Marcus. "We didn't tell you at the time as we didn't wish you to seek any sort of revenge, but considering Burton is now dead, I don't think it will hurt to tell you."

"Tell me what?" Already, Marcus was annoyed at the thought of being purposefully kept in the dark.

"Burton was the one to witness your brother selling secrets to the Russians."

It felt like a dagger had been shoved into his stomach, but outwardly Marcus's only reaction to the news was to inhale a slightly sharper breath. "You believed him?"

"I didn't interview him," Sir Albert confessed. "Sir William did, and apparently the evidence he presented was convincing enough to warrant action, particularly considering Nathaniel had already fled the country to Paris. Which is why Sir William sent some men to retrieve him to answer questions regarding treason, and the Earl of Montrose was the one chosen to lead the team."

"You should have sent me." Marcus had been in Germany at the time hunting for the Chameleon after Elizabeth's murder.

"Would you have been impartial?"

"No, because my brother was no traitor. He was framed." The cold, hard anger always simmering below the surface regarding Nathaniel was threatening to spill over. And the fact that the man who had accused him was now dead at the hands of the Chameleon could be no coincidence.

Sir Albert sighed. "Which is why we couldn't send you. And I know you want to believe the best of your brother, but the evidence was overwhelming regarding his treachery. It was all we could do to suppress the matter after his death to stop your family suffering any further shame. Let the past rest, Westwood. No good comes of dredging it up. In any event, we need to get back to the matter at hand, which does require an urgent response. The War Office seems to be under attack, albeit covertly. We must catch the Chameleon."

"It's my priority." Catching the Chameleon would most certainly let the past rest, as Marcus would be damn certain to get answers from the man. Then the true traitor would be revealed, and his brother could rest in peace.

A look of grim acceptance filled Sir Albert's face. "Good. Now, what do you need? Just say the word. Though, before we do anything else, can you both come and speak to Sir William with me? We must convince him to allow us to place a security detail upon him, for his own protection. You know how stubborn he can be about such things."

Pulling out his fob watch from his pocket, Marcus noted the time. He'd received a note from

Kat's butler earlier, explaining that she was visiting a bookstore in Paddington following a lead, and had asked him to attend. But Sir William's life was in jeopardy and the man would take some convincing to accept a security retinue, of that, Marcus was certain.

Marcus nodded curtly. "Very well, we'll accompany you to speak with him." And after, he would go and see what sort of mess Kat had gotten herself into, for when did she not get into some sort of trouble? The woman was a veritable magnet for the stuff, and though he was coming to accept she could protect herself, he still didn't like the thought of her out and about, traipsing through London while an assassin was on the loose. It was troubling, just like the woman herself.

Particularly after what had occurred between them last night, which had completely changed the dynamic between them, and even though he'd felt protective of her before, it was nothing compared to how he felt now. But, hopefully, she wouldn't get into too much trouble in a bookstore.

Chapter Twenty

Kat and Etta stood outside of the front of the cobblestoned bookstore, staring into the dark interior through the cobwebs and thick film of dust embedded across the glass window panes.

"It doesn't even look open," Etta said, pushing her nose closer to the window as she peered inside. "Are you sure this is where we're meant to meet Mr. Gingham?"

"Yes. Mr. Gingham rarely frequents any other place," Kat replied as she strode to the old wooden door, the paint of which had partially peeled long ago. "The bookshop is his pride and joy after all."

"His pride and joy?" Etta questioned, a note of disbelief in her voice. "The place doesn't look like it's been cleaned in years. I wish we'd been able to meet him in the park, like we did last time, at least then I wouldn't have worried about any rodents scurrying around."

"Mr. Gingham isn't the best when it comes to housekeeping," Kat said before reaching for the handle, noticing a few small flecks of dried blue varnish valiantly clinging to the wood. She turned the knob and pushed the door inward, the bells on it chiming and heralding their arrival.

The bookstore was housed in a small space that embraced the notion of appearing as old and dusty as the second-hand books it held. Kat stepped into the dimly lit shop, followed by Etta. She stopped and listened for a moment. Not a sound. Odd. Gingham was usually quite fond of muttering to himself.

Kat walked across the creaking floorboards toward the counter at the rear of the space. "Mr. Gingham?" she called. "Mr. Gingham, are you here?" Nothing but silence echoed in the space.

"We're slightly early," Etta said, picking up one of the books from a pile near the door and blowing several inches of dust from its jacket. "Didn't he say eleven-thirty?"

"Yes, we're ten minutes ahead of schedule, but he still should be here," Kat replied, while her eyes scanned the space. A prickling sensation began to twitch at the base of her neck when she saw drag marks etched into the layer of dust on the floor, suggesting a body had been dragged through to the back room. "Etta, wait outside."

"Is something wrong?" Etta placed the book back onto the pile, her eyes darting around the shop with concern. "I do suppose it would be unlike Mr. Gingham to leave his shop open and unattended."

"Very unlike him. I'll check out the back for

him while you wait in the carriage," Kat said, also noting some large boot prints etched in the dust, too. Several pairs of them.

"I'm not waiting in the carriage," Etta declared, crossing her arms over her chest, a mutinous expression on her face. "You might need my help, in whatever limited capacity I can assist with…" Her bravado faded as she, too, caught sight of the drag marks through the dust. "Oh dear."

"Indeed. Now if you're still insisting on staying, stay behind me."

Etta nodded and walked around behind her.

Slowly, Kat followed the trail toward the back room of the shop. There was a possibility she was jumping to conclusions and Mr. Gingham had dragged a rug or something through to the backroom and hadn't heard them enter, but she doubted it.

Walking through the open doorway of the back room, Kat stopped just inside the space. The room was small and cramped, with an L-shaped bench running along the back wall, and a doorway that led out to the back alley to the right of where the bench ended. There was also a large workbench in the center of the room. Both surfaces were covered with odds and ends, along with paper and books scattered about on nearly every inch of available bench space.

"He's been burgled!" Etta exclaimed, coming

to a stop just behind Kat.

"Actually, it usually looks like this," Kat said as she searched the room for any signs of Mr. Gingham. The floor in the backroom was covered with a rug, so the dust marks had stopped. But there was no body lying on the floor, which was a good sign, though something was definitely not right. Gingham was always in his shop or in this back room.

"Well, you were right about his housekeeping skills." Etta sniffed the air with a grimace. "They're practically non-existent."

Kat walked over to the far bench, spotting a cup of tea sitting on the wooden surface beside the back door, steam still curling up from its depths. "He was obviously here not too long ago."

A dull thud from the back alley echoed beyond the door and Kat glanced sharply toward it. She held up a hand to signal to Etta to stay put while she hurried over to the door and positioned herself to the side of it. Her fingers reached out and inched back the lacy curtain covering the small window in the center of the door, just a fraction so she could glance out. There were three men in the alley surrounding something on the ground. One of the men pulled back his leg, then swung it, kicking whatever was on the ground in front of him.

A moan of pain reverberated. Good lord, it was Mr. Gingham being assaulted while lying on the cobblestones out the back.

"Find a weapon but stay inside!" Kat said to Etta in a harsh whisper as she unsheathed her dagger, then ripped off her detachable skirt to reveal her trousers underneath before she wrenched open the back door. Without hesitation, she stepped into the alley as the three men swiveled around to face her.

They were holding no weapons, instead preferring to use their fists and boots on poor old Mr. Gingham who was curled in a ball on the ground, groaning, with splatters of his blood littering the cobblestones around him.

"Well, well, well. Look what we have here, boys," the biggest of the three men sang out as he cracked his knuckles together, a tight smile plastered across his leathered face. He was obviously the leader of the group, with the two other men looking slightly uncertain. "A lady interrupting us, and by Jove, wearing trousers no less and holding onto a gleaming dagger, too." His dark eyes darted down to her right hand. "I reckon you'd best drop the knife, love, before you get hurt."

"I'm not your love." Kat smiled grimly at him. "And I suggest you and your friends leave now before *you* get hurt."

The man stared at her a moment before bursting into laughter, his two companions joining him a moment later. Gradually, the men's laughter receded, and the leader took in a deep breath before glancing back at her. "*You* must be Lady Kaitlyn. I was told you were unusual, but I don't think that description comes close to describing you."

"It seems as though I'm at a disadvantage." Kat arched her brow at the leader. "You know who I am, but I have no idea who the three of you are."

"Just call me Jimmy, love." The leader grinned. "To my right is Mark and to my left Scotty. I'd intended to make your acquaintance inside the shop, but you're a bit early and you've interrupted the fun we was having here with this chap." He drew back his boot and kicked Gingham again in the ribs.

The old man moaned, curling even more tightly into a ball.

"Touch him again and you will regret it." Kat flicked the dagger up in the air and caught it by its handle, her eyes never leaving the leader's as she did so. It was a skill she'd perfected when she was ten, and never failed to impress or intimidate.

And in this case, it intimidated. All three of the men blinked and straightened up, adopting defensive postures, clearly realizing she was serious and knew how to handle a knife.

"Now, I suggest you all leave, unless you wish to test how sharp my dagger is," Kat said, letting the sunlight catch the edge of the blade and gleam brightly at them. "I'll not be giving you another chance."

"Afraid we can't do that, love. You see, you're the person we've been paid to collect, and if we don't collect you, we don't get paid. Mr. Gingham obliged us in helping get you here, though he took some convincing to do so." Jimmy winked at her. "Now, be a good little lady, and put the knife away. I wouldn't want you to get hurt."

Kat slowly smiled. "A good little lady? Oh, my dear Jimmy, I'm about to show you just what sort of good little lady I can be. I hope you're ready."

The man called Jimmy smiled at her without humor. "You'll be a good little lady when I'm done with you." He narrowed his eyes at her before glancing over to his right shoulder at his sandy headed companion. "Get her, Mark."

"But she's got a knife," the man whined.

"Then use your ruddy pistol!" Jimmy barked.

Kat saw the man reach into his jacket pocket, starting to pull out his pistol. Reluctant as she was to disarm herself so soon, she launched her dagger at him, the blade piercing through the flesh and bones of his palm.

"What the bloody hell!" Jimmy yelled, seeing the dagger protruding from his companion's hand. The man himself screamed and dropped his pistol to the ground as he fell, moaning in pain on the ground.

Kat faced the other two and saw the intent in their eyes a second before they both charged at her. She pivoted and threw a spinning side kick into the man named Scotty's chest, throwing him backward into the path of Jimmy. The impact sent both men skittering toward the wall of the shop.

Kat raced over to Mark and struck him across his neck with the side of her palm. He crumpled back to the ground, unconscious. The other two got back to their feet and charged at her again. Kat swiveled around to face them, disappointed they hadn't learned their lesson. Jimmy was the first to reach her. She spun out of the way just as he was about to slam into her, then she did a jumping kick to his rear, propelling him headfirst into the wooden fence on the other side of the laneway.

She heard the one called Scotty clamber toward her and she wheeled back around to face him. He threw a punch straight at her. She ducked, then slammed her fist into his groin. He howled in pain a moment before sagging to the ground.

Kat glanced up sharply as Etta came flying out of the door into the alley, brandishing a fry pan above her head.

"Get back inside!" Kat yelled at her. Her neck prickled in warning and she turned, just missing the thrust of Jimmy's arm as he tried to punch her in the head, the blow instead glancing off her shoulder as she stumbled backward.

He came at her, throwing another punch, which she blocked, though the reverberation ran through her blocking arm, sending a shaft of pain up to her shoulder. She regained her footing and volleyed several strikes at his throat.

Jimmy swore as one of her thrusts struck him and he fumbled backward and gasped.

She glanced back at Etta to see her hitting Scotty with the fry pan, until he, too, sank onto the ground and passed out.

Satisfied Etta was safe, she turned back to Jimmy and advanced on him. He lobbed several punches toward her, but she blocked them with her forearms, though each hit from his fist sent a further jolt of pain slicing through her arms and down into her shoulders. Fighting always hurt, but it was a mental game to push through. Victor had taught her that. She pivoted back and swung her leg up to kick him to his chest, but the brute grabbed her knee and twisted.

She yelled in pain but pulled herself in close to him and used her elbow to slam it hard into the side of his head. He swore at the impact but didn't let go, instead he tried to twist her knee harder. Kat struck him again with her elbow and used her other hand to claw at his eyes. The man yelled as her nails tore through his flesh. He let go of her leg and pushed her away from him.

Kat stumbled back a few steps before righting herself. She was breathing heavily but kept her attention on the man in front of her.

He leaned down and pulled out his own dagger from a strap at his ankle and spat on the side of the road. He dashed away some blood dripping from the deep gouges her nails had inflicted on his face. "You little bitch!" he yelled as he came rushing toward her.

Kat rushed at him, too. Surprise washed over his face at her bold move and he lost his momentum for a second. He clearly had no idea that the only way to win a knife fight was to get in as close to your opponent as possible.

She used his confusion to drop down onto all fours and then sweep her right leg out in an arching kick toward his ankles, the movement knocking his legs out from under him.

He fell backward onto the stones beneath with a hard thud. Kat jumped up and kicked at his hand, sending the dagger skittering across the ground and out of his reach. Her next kick landed in his ribs before she grabbed his wrist and bent it back. He screamed and tried to twist free. She applied more torque and he passed out from the pain.

Taking in a shaky breath, she stood over him for a moment before carefully stepping away. She looked over at the other two assailants. One had come to slightly and was groaning in agony, while the other was still happily passed out. Before she could truly catch her breath, Etta rushed over to her and grabbed her in a hard hug.

"I was so scared for you!" Etta cried before she let her go and stepped back. "But that was simply amazing what you did! You saved us!"

"What happened here?" Marcus exclaimed from the rear doorway.

"It looks like a warzone," Cantfield's incredulous voice added.

Kat glanced up as Marcus strode out into the lane, his eyes taking stock of every detail, while Cantfield followed behind, his eyes similarly scanning the scene.

"I knew you'd be getting into trouble." Marcus's voice was resigned. "At least tell me you're not hurt."

"I'm fine." Kat shot him a rather annoyed look as she tried to push back some of her wayward red curls that had made use of her exertion to escape their confines. "I was here to see Mr—Oh no! Mr. Gingham!" she exclaimed, remembering the poor, fallen man.

She rushed over to where he was laying on the ground, curled into a tight ball still. Kat crouched down beside him and used her sleeve to gently wipe away some of the blood on his face. He was whimpering. "It's all right. You're safe now. No one is going to hurt you anymore."

Kat glanced up as Marcus knelt beside her and regarded the man.

"He'll live," Marcus said. "But we will need to

get him to a hospital. My carriage is out front."

"As is mine," she said, standing. "But what are we going to do with these three?" She peered down at the men scattered on the alley floor. "Apparently, they were here waiting for me."

Marcus's jaw tightened as he also stood. "It was a setup?"

Kat shrugged. "They said someone paid them to take me, but to where or to do exactly what with, I'm not certain."

"You took on these three men by yourself?"

"I couldn't let them continue to hurt Mr. Gingham."

He swore, then pulled her roughly into his arms, and kissed her then and there. It was quick but firm, and right in front of Etta and Cantfield, too. The man didn't appreciate that an illicit affair was meant to stay a secret from others.

Kat dazedly held onto the lapels of his jacket as he pulled back from her.

"You're going to send me to beyond Bedlam," he muttered, shaking his head.

Her pulse raced from his touch and she felt her cheeks warm at the notion that he just kissed her in the cold light of day. What on earth had the man been thinking? He really had to be far more circumspect about the fact they'd embarked on an affair. Luckily, only Etta and Cantfield were witnesses and wouldn't tell anyone.

"Lucas," Marcus yelled over to Cantfield, who was deftly trying to avoid looking at them, though had a somewhat awestruck expression on his face when he glanced over at Kat. "Fetch my footmen and tell them to bring rope. Also, tell the coachman to hail a hackney and get it to wait outside."

"*You* did all this damage?" Cantfield asked Kat, sounding astonished. "To three men? By yourself?"

"I had a little help," Kat responded, nodding toward Etta. "Etta valiantly finished up that one with a fry pan to the head."

"I had to do something to help," Etta mumbled, appearing rather flustered.

Cantfield continued to gaze at Kat in complete awe. "I assumed you were skilled in combat, given your training with Victor and besting Marcus, but I didn't fully appreciate the extent of your—"

"Damn it, man, stop standing there gawking at her and blabbering," Marcus commanded. "Go and do as I asked, please!"

Marcus's bark penetrated through the man's astonishment, at which he shook himself out of his daze before turning and walking through the door to do as requested.

A minute later, he emerged from the shop's gloomy interior, bringing with him two of Marcus's burly footmen, one of whom was carrying a length of thick rope.

"Search the three men and take any weapons

off them," Marcus directed his men. "Then tie up their hands and feet with the rope and load them up into the hackney. You two and Cantfield will take them to the War Office to be held for questioning until I get there. Once they are secure in cells and guarded, return home."

The footmen nodded as they set about their task, clearly used to some odd requests made by their employer, judging by their nonchalance.

"I intend to take Mr. Gingham to the hospital and then go back to the War Office to question the men," Marcus said to Kat. "Would you like to accompany me?"

Kat had to stop her mouth from dropping open. Westwood asking her instead of telling her? That was a new development, as was wanting to include her, too. She rather liked it. She should have commenced an affair with him days ago if this was his new attitude after. "Yes, I would. Thank you."

They stared at each other and for a brief moment, Kat felt her world stand still as a deep longing welled up inside her. For one moment, she imagined what it would be like staring into his eyes, always.

She shook her head and looked away. She could not start daydreaming about things that could never be. Her independence was far too important to ever give up, not to mention she would make a terrible countess. The thought was laughable. She may be an earl's daughter, but she'd never been bought up as one. Having an affair with Marcus was all she could have.

A glint of silver caught the corner of her eye. Her dagger! She wrenched it from the man's palm as a footman carried him past, then wiped the blood off on her pants and sheathed it. It was one of her favorite weapons, after all.

"Do you need me to do anything?" Etta asked beside her.

Kat felt guilty for a moment, having completely forgotten about her friend. "No. I'll accompany Mr. Gingham and Marcus to the hospital. Will you be all right using my carriage to take you home?"

"Absolutely." Etta nodded. "Just one moment, though." She twisted on her heel and dashed into the back room of the bookstore. A second later she returned, triumphantly holding Kat's detachable skirt. "You might want to put this back on before you go anywhere. Wearing trousers about will attract unwanted attention."

"Ah, yes." Kat took the skirt from Etta's outstretched hand and draped it around her body, before clipping up the special metal fasteners. Her legs already felt trapped with the material once again surrounding them.

Both Marcus and Cantfield looked at her skirt for several seconds, their brows furrowed in consideration.

"How did you do that?" Cantfield asked, a note of wonder still in his voice.

"It's one of Madame Arnout's custom creations for me." Kat shrugged. "She's an absolute genius when it comes to *special* attire and uses some special fasteners that one of her German inventor friends designed and sent across."

"Madame Arnout? She's a highly sought-after designer." Cantfield rubbed his chin. "Do you think you could recommend me?"

"What? Are you wanting some skirts made for yourself?" Etta asked pertly. "I suppose you'd look pretty in them."

Cantfield swung around to face her and narrowed his eyes. "How very droll, Miss Merriweather. Actually, I was thinking if she could do that to a skirt, perhaps she could rig some jackets or pants for me."

"Do you really need help to get your pants off quicker than you already do?" Etta asked. "One would have thought that with all your experience as a lothario, you'd have it down to a fine art by now."

Cantfield's eyes almost bulged out of his head and Kat couldn't help but laugh. She'd never heard Etta speak so boldly to anyone before, let alone a man who was to be a future duke. Usually, the aristocracy intimidated her friend, especially with her father continually making overt attempts to marry her into it.

"Come on," Marcus said as he carefully bent down and picked up the old man. "We need to get Gingham to the hospital. Lucas, after you've secured the men in cells, place a guard to watch them and then I want you to go the Corinthian Club and bring in Mr. Dartmoore for questioning, regardless of if he wishes to or not."

Lucas nodded as he lifted one of the firmly trussed-up men onto his shoulder.

"Miss Merriweather." Marcus spoke to Etta. "Would you do me a favor before you head home? Would you stop by the Montrose residence first and inform Fenton and Lady Montrose of this development? Tell Fenton he must increase the security at the residence, considering it looks as though Lady Kaitlyn is being targeted."

"That will only worry them." Kat crossed her arms over her chest and scowled.

"It will prepare them," Marcus countered. "And will ensure Fenton is on the alert for any potential surprises."

"Fenton is always prepared for surprises. The whole household is."

"Wouldn't you want to know if either of them were being targeted?" Marcus watched her and Kat got the sense he wasn't really asking a question.

"You know perfectly well I would," Kat replied. "But it's not the same."

"It is, Kaitlyn, so stop being contrary." He

turned to Etta. "Will you tell them?"

"Of course," Etta confirmed, an expression of "I'm sorry" emanating from her eyes to Kat, before she turned and strode through the back door into the shop, followed by the footmen and then Cantfield, carrying the third assailant over his shoulders.

"I don't like you dictating orders to my friend that impact my family," she said over her shoulder to Marcus, as she too walked into the shop, her knee paining her somewhat, while Marcus followed her, carrying Mr. Gingham.

"I know you don't," he said. "But you know it's the safest course. Besides, as we've embarked on this affair, I have a vested interest in your safety."

She sighed. "You do. Somewhat. Which is the only reason I'm allowing such high-handedness from you. Now come on, we need to get Gingham to the hospital."

The pause of his footsteps and the undecipherable cursing from under his breath from her pronouncement was enough to bring a big smile to her face. If Marcus Black thought to dictate what was happening in her life, then he could certainly get used to her dictating his. And as much as he might protest, they both had a vested interest in protecting each other.

Now all they had to do was find the time to continue their affair, which was proving difficult to fit in amongst chasing down an assassin. But Kat had always believed where there was a will, there was a way. And she definitely had a will, so they'd simply have to find a way.

Chapter Twenty-One

While Lucas and the footmen lumbered into the hackney with the assailants, and Etta departed in Kat's carriage, Marcus carefully placed Mr. Gingham onto one of the seats of his carriage before he and Kat settled on the opposite seat.

He told his coachman to take them to the closest hospital, which turned out to be Saint Mary-le-bone, only a short carriage ride away, and they stayed with Mr. Gingham until he was assessed by a doctor and deemed out of the woods. Gingham was concussed, though badly battered and bruised, but the doctor confirmed it was nothing life-threatening and that a night in the hospital would do the world of good for him.

Marcus was a bit frustrated that Gingham couldn't seem to even remember being assaulted let alone remember contacting Kat regarding any information over the Chameleon.

"Hopefully, his memory comes back soon," Kat said, as he helped her into his waiting carriage.

"I wouldn't count on it." Marcus sat down next to her, and almost immediately had to restrain his hands from pulling her onto his lap. She'd just been through a traumatic incident and the last thing she'd be thinking about was being ravished, even though somehow, amidst all this chaos, that was at the forefront of his mind.

"In a way, it was indeed fortuitous those men were there for me," Kat said as the carriage steered its way through the early afternoon traffic of the cramped London streets, heading to the War Office.

"How so?" Marcus asked.

"Well, they stayed until I arrived." Kat shrugged. "And we now have them in our custody, so we can question them and find out *who* sent them."

"The very fact you were targeted is unacceptable." Marcus grunted. "This entire situation is getting out of hand."

"How so?" She mimicked his words back to him.

He narrowed his eyes. "Lord Burton was murdered last night, and then you were attacked today and had to fight off three men on your own. It's got to be related."

Kat sighed heartily. "Trust you to only see the dangers instead of the progress we have made."

"Progress? Kat, I don't want to see you getting hurt." The very thought was like a vise around his chest.

"You can't wrap me up in cotton." She placed her hand over his as it rested on his lap.

The touch instantly calmed him, and he

intertwined his fingers with hers. "I have to keep you safe, especially now."

"Now that we're lovers?"

"Yes." He turned to face her, expecting to see perhaps sarcasm in her eyes, but instead there was an earnest truth radiating from her gaze. "The idea of you hurt is… I don't know… It's troubling. Intolerable."

She smiled softly up at him and cupped his cheek with her other hand. "I'm fine, Marcus. I can protect myself. If those men were paid to either attack me or kidnap me, then it means someone is worried. That's a good thing."

"Your definition of the term, and my own, differ greatly."

"Yes, I'm beginning to see that." She sighed again and dropped her hand from his face, though she didn't move her other hand from his. "Why did you ask Lucas to have Mr. Dartmoore brought in? I know we need to speak to him, but won't he refuse to talk if we make things too official, bringing him to the War Office?"

The loss of her touch from his cheek was strangely disappointing. "Did you notice the rings the men were all wearing?" Marcus asked, trying to get his mind back onto the priorities.

"No."

"They were the same rings as the one Dartmoore was wearing, a ring with the Corinthian

Club symbol on it."

"That must have been the extra jolt of pain I felt when that one called Jimmy hit me."

His jaw clenched. "You were hit?"

"Yes, it was a fight, after all," she said, her hand squeezing his. "Truly, his fist only glanced my side."

"Perhaps you should wait outside while I question him." His voice was clipped as a fury unlike any he'd experienced washed over him. Someone had dared to hit his Kat?

His Kat. The thought stopped him cold. She wasn't his. He couldn't think of her like that. He wouldn't. Simply because they'd embarked on an affair together didn't mean he had any claim to her. Nor did he want any claim to her. A claim meant something permanent, and that was the last thing he needed. He was angry at himself for even thinking it.

He cleared his throat and returned to the matter at hand. "Who was the one that hurt your knee?" He'd noticed her slight limp as they'd left the bookshop. "Was it this Jimmy, too?"

"Why? Are you planning to teach him a lesson for daring to strike me?" she asked. "If you are, I'd like to watch."

The comment seemed to wash away his anger and he couldn't help but smile. "You truly are incorrigible."

She grinned back at him. "Completely. Now,

how long do you think it is before we arrive at the War Office?"

Marcus glanced out the window of the carriage to the thick traffic of a London afternoon. "At least forty minutes or more, I'd say. We haven't even got through Piccadilly yet."

"Perfect," came her silky reply, as she closed the curtain next to her and then reached across him and did the same with his.

"What are you doing, Kat?" He gulped, having a rather good idea of what she was up to, but wanting to check all the same.

"I was just thinking to myself earlier that starting an affair in the middle of hunting an assassin was going to prove difficult," she began, her hand letting go of his and starting to trail across his thigh, toward his waist. "Especially in terms of finding the time to actually continue our affair. As we have at least forty minutes alone together in your carriage, I think we should make productive use of the time. Don't you?"

"Here, in my carriage?"

She grinned. "Why not? Can't it be done here?"

"Of course," Marcus grumbled. "But I don't have any rubber sheaths on me."

"Luckily, I do." She pulled out a tin from her reticule.

Marcus felt a throbbing pain at his temples.

"Why?"

Shrugging, she opened the tin, and sure enough there was a brand-new rubber sheath inside. "After you used one, I was curious, so I went and bought one from the apothecary before I met Etta at the bookstore. I must admit, I thought it could come in handy at some point between us, and it seems I was right."

"You went into a shop and purchased one of these?"

"Don't worry, the man behind the counter didn't know who I was," she rushed to assure him. "Though he did nearly faint when I asked for one."

Marcus drew in a long breath and then let out an equally long sigh. "I can honestly say I've never met another female like you."

"Thank you." Her whole face lit up.

"It wasn't necessarily a compliment."

"You know it was." She gave him a gentle tap on the cheek with her hand, then reached down and picked up the rubber sheath. "Now, do you want to put this thing on, or do you want me to?"

The thought of her rolling the thing on his cock instantly had him as hard as a rock, his shaft straining against the material of his trousers, begging to be released. "You're maddening and so goddamn desirable that I can't say no to you."

He grabbed her by the waist and swung her onto his lap.

The soft sound of her laughter brushed along his ear, and it was then he knew he was lost. This woman could get him to do anything, of that he was certain. The thought scared him like nothing else, but then she wiggled her delightful derrière against him and his fear was replaced with desire.

· · ·

Kat was thrilled when he pulled her onto his lap, and she gripped his jacket as his lips met hers and gently coaxed them apart. His tongue stroked hers, all but demanding a response, which she was happy to give him.

Ripples of pleasure coursed through her, much like they had the other night when he'd bought her to the peak of her climax again and again. She wiggled her bottom against the hard length of him.

He groaned and then with a flick of his wrist, ripped off her skirt. "Remind me to thank Madame Arnout when I next see her. Your special skirts are brilliant for this sort of thing."

"I don't think it's what she had in mind when designing them," Kat replied with a grin, as she helped him unbutton her trousers and then his. "But they certainly are extremely practical for an affair, aren't they?"

"Very much so," Marcus murmured as the pads of his fingers began to rub against her undergarments at the junction of her legs. He kissed her again, and slipped a finger into her wetness.

"I want you so much," she whispered.

"You can feel how much I want you, my lady," he said, panting as he slipped the rubber over his thick, pulsating shaft. "Straddle me, darling."

"Like a horse?"

He chuckled lightly. "Yes, just like that. Guide my cock into you when you sit on me and then ride me."

"Oh. So that's how it's to be done in a carriage?" How fascinating. She straddled him as he'd instructed, until she felt the tip of his shaft pressing against her. She couldn't stop the moan from her mouth as he slid inside her and filled her completely.

"You can set the pace, my darling."

Kat had never felt so bold as when she slowly moved herself up and down on his cock, the bliss from doing so starting to build sharply inside her. "Oh, Marcus, you feel so good inside me."

"I know," he grunted. "You're tight and wet for me."

The feeling of pleasure was too intense. It felt like she was about to fall from some great height. She began squirming against him.

"Yes, that's it, my darling," he whispered against her lips, his hips thrusting up to meet hers. "Allow the sensation to consume you."

Deeper and deeper he moved himself inside her, and she returned his thrusts with equal fervor. Reaching the peak together, Kat closed her eyes in surrender as her whole body clenched and surges of pleasure erupted within her.

She managed to peek up at Marcus, who had his eyes closed but was wearing an extremely satisfied smile on his face.

"I think we've found another excellent location to conduct our illicit affair." She knew she needed to get off him and get her clothes back on, but she didn't want to feel the loss of him from inside her just yet.

"I can honestly say you've brought out the caveman in me," Marcus replied as he opened his eyes. "I've never done that in a carriage before."

"Really?" Kat asked as she reluctantly pushed up and off him, grabbing her trousers and fumbling them on.

"Yes, really." He pushed aside a small portion of the curtain and peeked outside. "Damn, we need to make haste. The carriage is nearly at Cumberland House."

"Excellent," Kat purred, swinging on her skirt and beginning to clip up the fasteners. That meant it was nearly interrogation time. And considering the wonderful mood she was in, which usually seemed to follow an encounter with Marcus, she might just go easy on them.

Chapter Twenty-Two

Marcus lifted the already lit kerosene lamp from the wall and held it aloft in front of him as he began the descent down the steep stone steps into the dungeons below. He still couldn't believe he'd made love to Kat in the back of his carriage, but it seemed when it came to this woman, he was doing all sorts of things he normally wouldn't.

Whether that was a good thing or not, he still wasn't certain. But it had made the trip one he'd never forget and did open a great many possibilities for how they could conduct their affair in the future.

"Rather antiquated and a touch melodramatic, is it not?" Kat's smooth voice broke into his thoughts, as she walked beside him while they journeyed down to the basement. "Keeping our guests in the dungeons and using kerosene lamps to light the way? One would think the War Office's budget could have extended to installing gas lighting in this section of the building as they have throughout the rest of it."

"When does the department ever spend more than the bare minimum? Besides, what better way to welcome our guests than having them brought down to the dungeons, kerosene lamps and all." Marcus grinned fleetingly, his mind firmly back on the task at hand.

"True, I suppose." She laughed and the melody of the sound sent a jolt of pleasure through him.

His reaction to the woman was getting decidedly harder to disguise with each moment he spent in her presence. Not that he had to disguise such reactions from her anymore, but he got the feeling that the more Kat knew of how she physically affected him, the more she might use such knowledge to her advantage. His cock definitely had a mind of its own when it came to her, and didn't seem to care or acknowledge Marcus's thoughts on the matter.

He had to get a grip on his unruly emotions and physical reactions, otherwise he'd be heading for some dangerous territory, territory his heart wasn't ready to face. Shaking his head, he continued his decent down the stairs, with Kaitlyn following silently beside him.

The curved stairway leading below held a damp musty smell and as they got further down, the light from the few windows high above in the tower barely pierced the blackness creeping up from beneath.

"I appreciate the chilling atmosphere the darkness would create for any *guest*, but is it always so dark?" Kat asked. "It seems somewhat perilous to have no lighting down such a steep stairway."

Marcus frowned. Antiquated it may have been, but there still should have been wall lamps lit every so often to shed light down the stairway. Yet, currently it was pitch black, apart from the light from the lamp he was carrying. "There are normally lamps, they have been extinguished for some reason. Come on." He motioned with his head and continued downward.

They wound their way to the bottom, but before they entered the passageway, they stopped on the last step and listened for a moment. The sound of dripping water against brick echoed around the corridor, but no other noises were audible.

"Something is definitely not right," he whispered to her. "Take the lamp and go back upstairs to raise the alarm."

Kat arched her eyebrow at him and the fierce expression in her gaze told him she was going nowhere. "I thought you knew me better by now."

He considered trying to reason with her, but there was no time and the stubborn set of her jaw all but proclaimed it would be an impossible endeavor, in any event. Marcus sighed in reluctant acceptance and placed the lamp in an empty holder on the wall. "At least stay behind me, all right?"

"I had intended to," she whispered back.

He was pleasantly surprised for once.

"You've been here before and know where you're going," she added. "Whereas I do not. Otherwise, I probably would have taken the lead."

"Of course you would," he muttered. The woman was slowly driving him mad. There was no other way to describe the sense of vexation she caused him. How he could want to pull her into his arms and kiss her senseless one moment, and then the next feel like putting her over his knee and spanking some sense into her, quite baffled him.

Shaking his head free from the distracting thoughts, he motioned to her, indicating the left passage, before silently stalking down the dark corridor. He couldn't hear Kat following behind, but he could sense her.

It took a moment for his eyes to adjust to the inky darkness, but he'd been down here so often over the years he knew exactly where he was going.

They came to the end of the passage and turned the corner to the right, continuing down the dark stone corridor that led to the rooms where the three men were being temporarily imprisoned. The wall lamps along this passageway were also absent of any flames, though there was a flicker of light shining from the darkness ahead, at the very end of the corridor where the cells were located.

They followed the winding corridor, until they got closer to the end of the passage. There, up ahead, one lamp was still burning, casting its light over the guard who had been posted to watch the men yet was now lying flat on the floor, unmoving.

Three cell doors along the right side at the end of the passage were all ajar. Marcus pulled out his pistol and quietly cocked the hammer. Turning to face Kat, he saw she was pulling her dagger from its sheath. Their eyes held in silent understanding before Marcus turned back and they stealthily made their way toward the dead end. As they approached the first of the three doors, Marcus held up his free hand, signaling his intention to stop.

He halted just before the door and bent down to the guard, who was staring blankly up at the ceiling with glassy eyes, a copious amount of blood oozing from his chest onto the stone floor beneath. Marcus reached down with his left hand and felt the man's pulse, while his right hand held his pistol steady and aiming forward. The man was dead, as Marcus had known he was, but he'd still wanted to be certain.

A slow anger began to burn inside of him at the guard's senseless death. How could the War Office have been compromised like this? It was simply unheard of. But there would be time enough later to work out how someone had infiltrated the almost impregnable building and killed one of their own.

Standing, Marcus positioned himself with his back against the wall alongside the first cell door. Kat moved herself next to him. Ducking his head around the frame, he peered into the dark cell, pulling back equally as quick. He could barely see anything in the deep gloom, the lamp at the end of the corridor not shedding enough light into the room itself to effectively see much of anything.

"I need the light," he whispered to her. "Stay here and if anything moves, use your brilliant aim."

She nodded tersely. "I have you covered."

He didn't hesitate to dash over to the lamp, knowing with a deep certainty that Kaitlyn Montrose did indeed have him covered. It was then he realized quite astoundingly that he trusted her, when he'd thought he'd never be able to trust another woman after what Elizabeth had done.

Grabbing the light from its wall bracket, Marcus swiveled to face the last door he now stood in front of. With his pistol in one hand and the light in the other, he pushed open the door fully and rushed into the room, hunched down low. The room was empty, except for one of the men he'd hoped to question, who was lying on the floor, deathly still, a large pool of blood beneath him.

Marcus checked the other two cells while Kat stood vigilantly ensuring he wasn't attacked from behind. The same image greeted him in the two cells as it had the first. All three men and the guard had been killed. And obviously not long ago, as the bodies were still warm. "God damn it! We're too late. They're all dead."

Kat's gaze flicked from the guard's lifeless body up to Marcus. "You do realize what their deaths mean."

Marcus nodded grimly. Unfortunately, he did. "Not only are our best leads to finding the Chameleon now dead, but the very fact that they are means someone has either managed to get into the building and past security undetected, or there's a traitor within the War Office."

"It must be a traitor," Kat replied. "Someone with an intimate knowledge of this area of the dungeons."

Her words sent a chill through his heart, because he knew she was right. He'd already had to deal with the fact that his wife had been a traitor and because of his ignorance to that fact, men had died. But if there was a traitor in the War Office then that meant the entire Empire could be compromised, with not only hundreds of lives in jeopardy, but thousands.

He couldn't let that happen again. Not ever. "If the murderer isn't someone from within the department, we need to lock down the building in case the assailant is still here."

With a last look at the scene, death clinging to

the atmosphere with a ghastly grip, Marcus and Kat made their way back to the upper levels to raise the alarm.

Two hours later, after the War Office had been fully searched for the unknown assailant, with no one found, the building was reopened to allow personnel back inside and out. The fact that the search had yielded nothing was lending credence to their theory that it'd been an inside job, but with over eighty staff alone currently in the building, it might as well be anyone.

Marcus felt like kicking something, anything really. He hadn't experienced this sense of hopelessness since the day of his brother's death. It seemed as if he'd been robbed. Robbed of not only interrogating the men and trying to discover more details of the Chameleon, but robbed of being able to punish the three of them for daring to touch Kat. When he thought of the danger she'd faced confronting them earlier, essentially on her own against three men, he felt both in awe and sick to his stomach.

How could one woman get into so much personal danger? He never thought he'd be grateful to Victor for training a lady how to fight, but after today he was starting to think that perhaps women should be taught how to defend themselves. Nothing as much as Kat, but skills to at least help themselves if ever faced with a dangerous situation.

If Victor was still alive, Marcus would've kissed the chap for the unusual upbringing he gave his niece. Because if it had been any other woman, the men would have gotten her, and God knows what they would be doing to her now.

The thought terrified him. He glanced over at Kat, who was sitting next to Sir William on the chaise lounge in the man's office, recounting what had occurred at Gingham's store leading up to the men's deaths. Sir William was very still and the usual mirth dancing in his eyes was absent as Kat recounted the morning's events in precise detail.

As she spoke of the one called Jimmy drawing his dagger and lunging for her, Marcus felt his fists clench unwittingly by his side. It was bloody lucky the man was already dead, as it saved Marcus from having to explain himself out of a murder charge.

"Who knew you were going to meet with Gingham this morning?" Sir William asked.

Kat nibbled on her bottom lip as she thought over the question. "No one else apart from Etta, Daisy, Fenton, and Marcus. And poor Mr. Gingham, of course."

"How well do you trust Gingham?" Sir William asked as he poured a cup of tea from the pot sitting on the mahogany coffee table in front of him and then handed it to Kat.

She took it from him and sipped it heartily, to which Marcus found himself smiling. There was nothing missish about his Kat. Damn. There was that *his* again. He had to stop thinking of her like that, even though they were lovers. She'd never be his, she couldn't be by his own admission, no matter how tantalizing the idea of such a thing was. He'd enjoy whatever this temporary affair was and then move on.

He stood and walked over to the tall window overlooking the front of the street, then turned and perched upon the sill as he watched Kat and Sir William.

"His information has always been reliable," Kat answered as she placed the cup and saucer down onto the table. "But in terms of trusting him? There are few people I trust."

"Trust is one of the scarcest commodities in our occupation, I'm afraid." Sir William smiled sadly. "As the head of intelligence, I've learnt that only too well."

"Are you certain it was actually Gingham that sent you the note?" Marcus said, straightening from the window and walking back across to where they were sitting. There was something about the whole situation that didn't sit well with him.

She shrugged. "No. Not entirely. It was on his usual stationery and signed with his name, but I would have to go back and compare his previous notes to confirm if the handwriting was his or not."

The door to Sir William's office burst open and

in marched Lord Danbury, trailed by Sir Albert. Danbury held himself like a stiff poker, outrage all but radiating from his every pore, while Sir Albert appeared harried from most likely trying to calm the man.

"What on earth is going on?" Lord Danbury screeched, coming to a standstill a few feet from where Kat and Sir William were sitting. "Four men, one of them a guard of the War Office, murdered in our own building? How could such a thing occur? Especially when three of us in this room are targets of an assassin!" His eyes darted between all of them. "Well? I'm waiting for someone to shed light on such an unacceptable situation!"

Beside him, Sir Albert wore a rather apologetic yet resigned expression. Sir William, on the other hand, leaned back against the cushions and sighed heartily.

"What do you think happened, Fox?" Sir William used the Secretary's first name. "They were stabbed, and in our dungeons, no less. It was either an inside job or someone got past all our security. Neither is acceptable, which is why you can't attend the opera tonight with your new paramour."

Lord Danbury appeared taken aback, whether it was from the use of his first name in front of others, because of the situation, or the mention of his paramour, it was hard to tell.

"I certainly will be attending with her tonight.

I haven't worked so hard wooing her to cancel at the last minute! You will all simply have to accompany me and see that I am safe."

"You're not the only one on the list, Fox," Sir William reminded him. "And as we either have a traitor in our midst or someone slipped past our security, both place us all at risk. Most especially you."

"Why most especially m-me?" The color leeched out of Lord Danbury's face.

"As you're the Secretary of the State for War, one would assume whoever is trying to kill the three of us would want you out of the way first."

"Oh… I hadn't considered that aspect of it, actually." Lord Danbury's voice trailed off, terror flashing in his eyes before he abruptly slid to the floor in a dead faint.

Marcus shook his head. Wonderful.

"Goodness, William." Sir Albert sighed, looking first down at Danbury on the floor and then across to Sir William. "Did you really have to say that? The man is as nervous as a flea already."

"He should be." Sir William shrugged. "I have no idea what the man is thinking, planning to attend the opera tonight with his new paramour. He's an idiot."

"What did I miss?" Lucas's voice rang out loudly from the doorway as he strolled into the room. "And why was the whole place put in lockdown?

And what's Danbury doing on the floor?"

Marcus walked over to the fallen man and motioned for Lucas to assist him "Grab his legs, would you?"

The two of them moved Danbury over to the settee across from where Kat and Sir William were sitting, while Marcus quickly filled Lucas in on the earlier events. After he'd finished, Lucas wore an extremely somber expression, one Marcus hadn't seen in a long time on his friend's normally sardonic features, though the somberness was soon replaced by raw fury.

"Damn it! I should have questioned them when I had the chance," Lucas exclaimed, a muscle twitching in his jaw. "I should have stayed with them, then they would still be alive for us to question."

"You weren't to know, my friend," Marcus assured him. "How did you go at the Corinthian Club in any event?" Marcus asked him. "I do not see Mr. Dartmoore with you."

Lucas frowned and ran a hand through his thick hair. "Mr. Dartmoore was pulled from the Thames this morning, a stab wound in his chest."

A collective sigh filled the room from the news.

"Does anyone feel as if we are chasing our tails?" Kat asked as she stood and wandered over to perch on the edge of Sir William's desk.

Marcus laughed without humor. "It feels

like I've been doing that for the past three years hunting down this bloody assassin."

"We all feel the same." Sir William walked over to the side table and began pouring glasses of brandy for them all.

"Indeed, we do." Sir Albert sighed as he happily took one of the full glasses from Sir William. "No escaping the fact that this Chameleon has thus far been one step ahead of us every time." He looked over at Marcus. "What's the likelihood that the Chameleon slipped into the War Office and murdered those men?"

Marcus shrugged. "It is possible, though he'd have to have known the layout in advance." He looked around at each of them. "I think it more likely the killer came from inside the department on this occasion."

Chapter Twenty-Three

Kat strode up the steps to the Montrose residence and smiled gratefully when she caught sight of Fenton standing at the entrance waiting for her. Reliable, steady, and supremely efficient Fenton. He really had become her rock since Victor died.

He stood stiffly in the early afternoon sunlight, a frown marring his features. Fenton never frowned. In fact, his face rarely revealed any emotions, which was what made him so effective in all of his varied roles.

"Miss Merriweather told me what happened," he said without preamble. "Are you all right?" There was worry in his glance as it swept over her. It was also rare to see such an emotion in the light blue depths of his eyes.

"I am fine." Kat stopped in front of him, touched that he was so concerned for her.

Sagely, he nodded his head, seeming satisfied with her answer. "Good." He walked over to the front door and opened it for her. "I'd suspected as much, though one can never be entirely certain when Miss Merriweather is trying to recall the details."

Stepping through the threshold and into the entrance hall, Fenton closed the door behind them and twisted the lock. He always believed that the townhouse should be secure, day or night.

"Fenton, do you still have any contacts within the War Office?" she asked, as she walked over to the mirror and regarded her very disheveled appearance. Oh goodness, what Marcus must have thought at the sight.

"I do." He walked over to her and stopped a few feet from the table. "Did the men provide information, then?"

She swiveled around and faced him. "No. Unfortunately for us, someone decided they shouldn't be questioned and eliminated them before the earl and I arrived."

To an onlooker, Fenton's bland expression changed little, but Kat could see the tightening at the corner of his eyes and a definite expression of worry passed over his countenance. "Murdered?"

Kat nodded. "Stabbed in the heart, all three, as was the guard watching them. But of particular interest was that there was no sign of any struggles."

"Which would suggest they either knew their killer or else felt comfortable enough with whomever it was to relax their guard," Fenton said.

One could always count on Fenton to assess a situation quickly. "Yes. I think it was an inside job."

"Someone certainly didn't want you and

the earl speaking with them." He looked at her sharply. "Is what Miss Merriweather said true, that the men were waiting for you at the back of Gingham's shop?"

"That is what one of them said."

For the first time Kat could ever remember, the unflappable Fenton looked scared. "I will make some inquiries immediately with some of my old contacts in the department." He bowed to her and began walking down the corridor. He stopped suddenly and turned around to face her. "Please do take care, little miss, dangerous times are afoot. I fear you may be right and there is a traitor in our midst."

Kat watched him glide off down the hall. He hadn't called her "little miss" since she was ten. It was somewhat disconcerting to see him so worried. A cold chill fleetingly ran through her, but she shook it off and turned toward the sitting room.

Daisy was standing at the door looking at her, worry knitting her brows together. "I've been fretting dreadfully about you." She rushed over and gave Kat a hug, clearly no longer holding on to their argument from the other day.

"Not you, too!" Kat briefly returned the embrace and then stepped back.

"Fenton is right to be worried," Daisy said, turning and walking back into the room, with Kat following. "What does he mean by a traitor in our midst?"

"What is this about a traitor?" Etta spoke up from where she was sitting on the lounge.

"You didn't go home?" Kat walked over to the lounge and gratefully sank down onto the soft cushions next to Etta and sighed. It had been a trying day and she was only now starting to feel every single ache and pain slicing through her body from her earlier clash. A nice hot bath would be just the thing. Her knee was really starting to pain her.

"I couldn't, not until I knew you were home safe." Etta tapped her toe somewhat impatiently, as Daisy took a seat across from them both. "How did it all go?"

Kat recounted the afternoon's events to the two of them. Both women stayed completely silent during the telling and indeed said nothing for a full minute after she was done.

Daisy was the first to speak. "That's unfortunate, particularly for the innocent guard, though I can't say I'm sorry about the three other men. They clearly deserved to die."

"Daisy!" Etta exclaimed. "I've never heard you speak a bad word about anyone."

Daisy looked uncomfortable at her bold words as she smoothed out the skirts of her dress. "Goodness knows what they'd have done to our Kaitlyn if they'd succeeded in capturing her."

"That may be the case," Etta agreed. "But being killed is perhaps a tad harsh."

"I'm starting to come around to the idea of an eye for an eye," Daisy primly replied, her eyes catching Kat's. "Some people do deserve to die, I am beginning to realize. And besides, they would have gone to the gallows for daring to touch an earl's daughter. Whoever killed them simply sped up the process."

Kat leaned over and took a biscuit from the plate on the table in front of her. "They could have at least waited until I'd questioned them," she muttered, taking a bite of the crumbly deliciousness.

Etta shook her head at both of them and helped herself to a biscuit, too, sighing in contentment after the first bite.

Daisy picked up her teacup and took a dainty sip. "Kaitlyn," she began, "I wish to be taught how to shoot a pistol and maybe even how to throw a knife."

Kat paused, her mouth gaping with her biscuit still midair, while Etta began choking on her mouthful. Kat had to thump Etta's back several times to stop her friend from choking on the thing.

"You want to do what?" Etta got out after her coughing had subsided.

Daisy raised her chin high in the air. "You heard me!" She turned to look at Kat. "Well? What do you say, will you teach me?"

"But you have never had any inclination to learn before," Kat said, still digesting the request. "In fact, you have always been against any form of defense being taught... We only just recently argued about it."

"Well," Daisy began, "today has shown me that knowing how to protect oneself may indeed be necessary. If you're a target, then Samuel and I might also be. I can't keep burying my head in the sand as I wish I could."

Kat inclined her head and regarded Daisy intently. "Are you certain you want to learn?"

There was a slight pause before she answered. "I am."

"Very well, then. I shall teach you," Kat said. "I'll get Fenton to teach you how to shoot a pistol first. He's an expert at it, and I'm going to be busy hunting the Chameleon. Is that acceptable?"

"It is."

Wonders would never cease. Daisy wanting to learn to shoot and throw a dagger. Maybe there was hope for Samuel to be properly trained up, yet. "Do you wish to learn fighting techniques, too, then?"

"Oh, goodness no!" Daisy said with disdain. "That would be going too far. No. I only wish to learn shooting and throwing a dagger."

"You don't care anymore about it being unladylike?"

Daisy scrunched up her face. "Well, it's not as if I shall be advertising learning such a thing. Can you imagine the looks I'd get if anyone knew I was doing so, or they saw me doing it, for that matter?"

"Actually, I think they'd look upon you in wonder, as Cantfield did today with Kat," Etta said, rather softly.

"He did?" Kat asked, perplexed.

"They all did." Etta folded her hands over her chest and an annoyed expression washed across her face. "Cantfield especially. It was as if he couldn't believe a woman could do such a thing. That bounder needs to be shown that women are not to be treated as play things that can't think. That we're more than capable of protecting ourselves and don't need a man to do so."

"You get passionate when you talk about Cantfield."

Etta grimaced. "The man makes me so angry."

"I've noticed." It was odd, too, as Etta really only ever got angry about social injustices and her father's attempts to marry her off to a title. "In any event, we all need to get ready to go to the opera."

"The opera?" Daisy blinked. "Surely, you're going to rest this evening after what happened today."

"Lord Danbury is going to be in attendance, against the advice of nearly everyone," Kat said. "And I imagine it'd be a wonderful venue for the

Chameleon to strike. Though you'll both be quite safe in Westwood's box, as he and Cantfield will also be there. Which is why I do particularly need a chaperone tonight."

Daisy arched one of her blonde brows. "A chaperone? You happily lark around London through the day on your own, or with Westwood, it seems. Why on earth would you need a chaperone for anything?"

"Sarcasm does not become you," Kat said. "Besides, you know I can get away with it through the day, but at night, especially at the opera and in front of the eyes of high Society, I'm not quite so fortunate. So, what do you both say? Ready for a night of entertainment? You'll enjoy The Mikado. I've heard it's thoroughly entertaining."

"Goodness, Kaitlyn, yes, I shall accompany you," Daisy said. "Though I swear you're going to be the death of me."

"Yes, you've said that before." The only person Kat wanted to be the death of was the Chameleon, which could even be tonight, if her quarry showed his hand. With the amount of security Marcus was arranging to protect Danbury, it was unlikely, though one could always hope.

Chapter Twenty-Four

The lights of the opera house were dim as the performance of The Mikado was enacted in grand splendor on the stage below. A spectacle of sights and sounds, keeping the majority of the audience enraptured.

Except for Kat, who could barely focus on the production. Not while Marcus was sitting next to her, causing her body all sorts of troubles, while she had to keep her attention on scanning over the crowd, trying to spot anything unusual.

Her skin tingled when Marcus leaned over and whispered into her ear, "She's been watching us like a hawk all night." He motioned over his shoulder to Daisy, who, along with Lucas and Etta, sat behind them in the second row of his theater box. Thankfully, though, their seats were far enough back that they couldn't overhear the specifics of Kat and Marcus's hushed conversation.

"What do you expect, you goose?" she whispered back. "You insisted I sit next to you and all but dragged me in here. What else is she to think but that you're courting me, though in a very Neanderthal way?"

She smiled at the chagrin that came across his gaze.

"I wasn't thinking of how that might appear when I did it," he gruffly replied.

She shifted in her seat, her eyes looking back down onto the stage below. "Obviously. You're going to have to be far more circumspect as we continue our affair, which I hope will be later tonight," she whispered.

Marcus coughed loudly. "What?"

Kat had to hide her grin at the look of irritation warring with alarm on his face. "Hopefully, I'll be able to sneak back to your residence later."

He grunted beside her and she couldn't help the small smile from tugging at the corners of her mouth. She knew such talk shocked him, but she was having too much fun to stop.

"You're incorrigible," he murmured.

"Yes, you've told me that already. Many times. But on to more pressing matters. Surely, the Chameleon would've struck by now, if he was going to. The extra security you have everywhere has obviously scared him away." Her eyes perused the theater as the crowd erupted in laughter around them at the antics going on on the stage below. "We should be asking questions at the Corinthian Club, especially after Dartmoore's death."

"We will go there after," he replied. "But Lord Danbury could not be reasoned with and insisted on attending tonight. Sir William thought it prudent we attend and keep an eye on him."

"I rather thought Danbury of all people would be keen to keep himself out of harm's way?"

Marcus chuckled lightly. "So did I. Though, you'd be surprised what lengths a man will go to when there's a woman involved." He gave her a rather cryptic look.

"And what woman is involved with Danbury?" Kat asked. "Sir Albert mentioned earlier he had a paramour, but to be honest I was doubtful of that. Who would want to be romantically linked with a man like him?" Her nose squished up at the thought.

"Lady Brighthope, apparently."

"Really?" Kat's jaw dropped slightly. "The Siren is his new paramour?"

Marcus shrugged. "I would think so, considering she's sitting in his box with him."

Kat lifted her theater glasses up and focused in on Danbury's box across the other side of the theater. Though the lighting was dimmed for the performance, the wall sconces in the boxes were still lit, shedding enough light into each box to ensure the occupants could comfortably be seen and see others, which to most patrons was the most important reason for attending any event such as this.

Sure enough, there sitting next to Danbury, and smiling coquettishly up at the little man, was

Lady Brighthope, or the Siren, as all of Society called the great beauty. Kat had never met her in person, as an unmarried lady didn't associate with a courtesan, as much as Kat did in fact want to meet her. "So that's what she looks like."

The lady was indeed beautiful, her rich ebony hair piled high atop her head in an artful arrangement that showed off the delicate length of her neck. She was blessed with full rosy lips, cheekbones that looked sculpted by Michelangelo himself, and smooth alabaster skin. No wonder the woman was reportedly the most sought-after courtesan in London.

Kat was certain Lady Brighthope would be a wealth of information, having been a paramour to some of the highest ranking men of the nobility, men in positions of great power and influence in the House of Lords. She would've made an excellent informant in Kat's network, but how did one get introduced when the social conventions normally forbade it? Not that Kat was one to let social conventions get in the way of any of her plans. Perhaps tonight could prove useful.

She watched as Lady Brighthope raised her theater glasses, too, and then looked directly at her. Or perhaps she was looking at Westwood? It was hard to tell. Kat narrowed her eyes when the woman lowered the contraption and then very definitely smiled toward the earl's box, tipping her head in acknowledgment.

Lowering her theater glasses, Kat peered over at Marcus. "How are you acquainted with Lady Brighthope?"

Marcus glanced at her sharply. "What are you talking about?"

"The lady just smiled and nodded toward us," Kat said. "As she and I have never met, I'm assuming she was acknowledging you and not myself."

"Assumptions can be perilous."

"Do you know her or not?" Her eyes narrowed upon him.

He grinned and leaned closer to her ear. "Jealous, my dear?"

She crossed her hands in front of her chest and pointedly looked down to the stage below. "Do not be stupid." Even though she was. Completely so.

Marcus chuckled. The sound ensured that several hushing noises were aimed in their direction, along with many looks of annoyance from the patrons of the surrounding boxes.

"You are jealous," he whispered once again in her ear.

"And you still have not answered my question," Kat said in a harsh whisper.

He laughed again, garnering even more hushing sounds and vexed looks. "I'm not acquainted with her. Well, at least not really." He shrugged one shoulder.

"For goodness sakes, what does 'at least not really' mean?" she asked. Kat was beginning to suspect that perhaps he did indeed know the lovely Lady Brighthope. The thought was disheartening. How did one compete with perfection?

He sighed. "I've met her on occasion, while in Europe with Elizabeth. Lady Brighthope was hanging off the arm of one diplomat or another at the various balls and galas we all attended. That's the only reason I know her, I promise."

"She is very beautiful," Kat added, looking back at him superciliously.

"She is."

That was not the exact answer she had wanted to hear from him. Though, if he'd denied what was obvious to all, she would not have believed a word he ever said, so at least he was telling the truth, even if a part of her would have preferred he lied.

"Your wife was beautiful, too." She felt him go still beside her. Though she'd never met the late Countess of Westwood, she had seen her from a distance once. The woman had looked like a graceful, petite angel, and been considered a diamond of the first water. It was no wonder Marcus had married her.

Kat didn't know what prompted her to mention his late wife, but an underlying curiosity about the woman who had betrayed him was gnawing at her. From all accounts, he'd fallen head over heels in love with the woman, who broke his heart and betrayed him. She felt her heart sink, wondering if part of him was still in love with her. Why she should care, Kat didn't know. It wasn't as if she and Marcus had a long-term future together. They were simply embarking on a passionate affair.

"She was beautiful," was all he said.

"Did you love her?"

Silence greeted her question. Kat thought he wasn't actually going to answer her, when finally, he did.

"I was young, and I thought what I felt was love." His voice was low and somewhat chagrined. "In retrospect, it wasn't. It may have been at the start, but it certainly wasn't at the end. It was the opposite."

"Have you read her journal yet?"

"I have," came Marcus's curt reply.

"Did it shed any light?"

He looked sharply at her before his eyes hooded over. "On what?"

"On the Chameleon."

He shook his head. "No, apart from the reference to the Corinthian Club and the fact that Elizabeth obviously began her torrid liaison several months before her death, I found no other useful information."

"I know it's of little comfort." Her voice was

soft but passionate as she looked at him. "But some people forever seek thrills, constantly trying to attain what they perceive they do not have, remaining oblivious to what is right in front of them." She paused and searched his gaze. "She didn't deserve you."

The blue depths of his eyes were impenetrable, and Kat thought he wasn't going to say anything more on the subject. But he did.

"Initially, I was captivated by her beauty and apparent kindness. She carried herself with such poise and accomplishment. She could captivate everyone in a room with her presence. I thought she would make the perfect countess. It wasn't until after we were married that it became apparent it was all on the surface and that underneath she was nothing but a spoilt and vain woman unaccustomed to playing second fiddle to anyone. She quickly became resentful of the assistance I provided to our country and equally as quickly found solace in the arms of several other men.

"I did the honorable thing, at least I thought so at the time, and fought several of her lovers. But she seemed to delight in the spectacle of it all, only encouraging her further. That was when I decided not to bother paying attention to her liaisons. Perhaps if I had, her affair with the Chameleon would not have led to her death and all of those innocent others."

"It wasn't your fault."

"It was," he countered. "My inattention most certainly led to the events occurring as they did." He looked at her cryptically for a moment. "I realize with Elizabeth that I was only looking at what she wanted me and Society to see—a beautiful, captivating, picture-perfect lady, with impeccable manners and decorum. She was everything I thought a wife should be. But I soon discovered it was an illusion. Unfortunately, by then, it was too late. We were married. She still continued to charm everyone with her beauty and poise." He paused for a moment. "You are as different from her as night is from day."

Kat felt her heart sink upon hearing his words and she turned away from him. She didn't need to be reminded that she was not as beautiful or as captivating as his late wife had been. Not to mention she was completely unconventional for an apparent earl's daughter and would make a terrible countess.

The theater lights brightened, heralding the intermission. She stood and, without looking at him, mumbled about having to powder her nose and fled from the box. She needed some fresh air and couldn't think straight when he was around.

She made her way down the stairs to the lobby and then pushed past the glass doors leading out onto the street. She strode over to the small garden area to the right of the entrance and breathed in the chill night air while she closed her eyes for a moment, steadying the sinking feeling in her stomach. Why it should matter that he'd been captivated by the beautiful Elizabeth, Kat didn't know. But for some reason it did, and the thought caused a knot to twist in her stomach.

Kat swiveled around as she heard the door to the theater hall open, and out stepped another woman Kat was certain also captivated all men in her radius—the Siren, Lady Brighthope.

Chapter Twenty-Five

"Lady Kaitlyn Montrose, is it not?" Lady Brighthope inquired as she wandered closer to Kat, her voice equally as beautiful as her face, with a slight European lilt gracing her accent. If it was put on to add allure to her overall impression, she was doing a very good job of it. The woman smiled at Kat and her brown eyes sparkled with an inner merriment that was almost infectious.

No wonder the woman was so sought after; men would be unable to resist such a combination of feminine wiles and playfulness, Kat was certain. "It is," she answered, wondering how the woman knew who she was. "Lady Brighthope, I take it?"

The woman grinned widely. "You know who I am, too. Good. That will simplify matters."

Lady Brighthope had matters to discuss with her? How odd. "What matters would those be?"

The woman's soft laughter floated through the space. It was equally innocent and seductive all at once. *How did one do that?* Kat shook her head. Clearly, there was a lot to be learned about being a courtesan.

"I'm glad you're as forthright as your

reputation would suggest," Lady Brighthope said. "I saw you in Westwood's box and I knew I had to speak with you."

Kat raised her eyebrow. "You followed me out here? I'm intrigued." A courtesan wishing to speak with an earl's daughter was unusual, even for Kat.

Lady Brighthope grinned. "I have information for you about the Chameleon."

Kat was able to keep her expression free from any surprise, even though inside she was reeling. How did a courtesan, whom she had never met, know about the Chameleon? And even more importantly, how did the woman know Kat was after him? "The Chameleon? What an odd name for someone."

"Now do not be coy, Lady Kaitlyn, for it does not suit you," Lady Brighthope tittered. "You're hunting the Chameleon and I fully intend to help you find him."

"Let's pretend for a moment I knew what you are talking about," Kat said. "Why would you want to help me?"

A dark light seemed to burn in the woman's eyes. "Because it is time for the Chameleon to die. The assassin is responsible for the death of the only person I have ever truly loved."

"Lord Brighthope?"

The woman shook her head and then laughed lightly. "Oh, you are delightful. No, not Lord

Brighthope. My late husband was not someone I loved. He was a means to an end, and unfortunately unbeknownst to me, had gambled away our fortune before falling down the stairs at our residence while drunk. The fool broke his neck, and though I was happy about that part, I was not happy to learn the estate was penniless."

A situation she and Daisy had very nearly faced, too.

The woman shook her head and continued, "That was why I was forced into my current occupation. I had to maintain the lifestyle I was used to, you understand." She smiled at Kat. "It's amazing what men will pay for the privilege of my company."

Kat was not sure how to respond. She'd never spoken to a courtesan before, let alone had such an in-depth conversation with one, about such a topic either. "Actually, I hadn't considered such a thing before."

"No woman does, until it becomes a necessity." Lady Brighthope shrugged. "In any event, when Lord Danbury let slip earlier tonight that you and Westwood were chasing the Chameleon, I knew I could help, and in some small way obtain justice for my love's death. I must say I was impressed to hear that a lady was doing such dangerous and potentially ruinous endeavors. It's heartening for all us women to hear."

Kat frowned. Marcus would be livid to discover Danbury had revealed such information. After all, the Secretary of War should know better than to discuss such matters with his paramour. "How did you think to help?"

The woman pursed her lips. "I have information regarding the list of targets I believe you are after."

"Danbury told you of the list?" Was there nothing the man hadn't told Brighthope about?

"Yes, he mentioned it last night in bed. Men will talk about practically anything once they're satisfied. A rather useful thing, I've found." She grinned.

An interesting thought. Perhaps she should try it on Marcus?

"And in light of Burton being murdered the other night," Brighthope continued, "I knew I had to talk to you. You see, one of my more recent clients is a man with a great deal of influence and resources. When I get such a client, I always find it prudent to know as much about him as possible. To do so, I often take the liberty of looking through his discarded clothing while he slumbers."

"Risky but clever." If Kat had been in the same profession she would have done so too.

"Inside this gentleman's jacket pocket was an envelope." She paused and leaned even closer to Kat. "And within that, there was a list of names along with several thousand pounds in bank notes. I recognized all but two of the six names. It wasn't until last night when Danbury disclosed that Lord Burton's murder was being attributed to the Chameleon, and that Danbury himself was one of several on a list to be assassinated, that I realized the significance of the list I'd seen."

"How so?"

"I specifically remember that Lord Burton's name was at the top of the list, then Sir William, then Lord Newtown. But my gentleman started to stir, so I didn't read the rest, but I did retrieve the list and hid it while I occupied the man again until he was satisfied." The lady shrugged with a look of smugness on her beautiful features. "What can I say, except I'm extremely good at what I do. In any event, when he was dozing again, I summoned my maid and told her to copy the thing and then return the paper to the envelope inside his pocket, while I made certain he wouldn't need to dress for some time."

"Who is this client of yours?"

Affront screamed across the woman's face. "I can't reveal my client's name. If word got out my services were not completely confidential, I'd be ruined. Besides the fact that my life would be at risk if he found out. He's powerful and does not forgive."

"How do you know your client is not the

Chameleon himself?"

"He's not," Lady Brighthope replied. "But I think he may be employed by him."

"Then this client of yours knows who the Chameleon is. You must tell me his name."

"I've told you I can't." Lady Brighthope crossed her hands over her chest. "But I can get a copy of the list my maid copied and give it to you at Newtown's house party this weekend. I assume you and Lord Westwood will be there, considering Newtown is on the list."

"Danbury should've kept his mouth shut." Kat was furious with the man. She hadn't known Newtown was hosting a house party, but she certainly would be going if he was.

"Darling, it's my job to ensure their mouths open, amongst other things." The lady appeared amused by her own words. "So, will you be in attendance?"

"Probably." She'd have to get Marcus to secure them an invitation, and she'd need to get a chaperone to go with her. Daisy, perhaps, although she rarely liked to travel and leave Samuel. Maybe the Dragon Duchess felt like a trip to the country? She'd proven herself as an excellent chaperone of late.

"You do realize I'm putting myself at great risk talking to you about this. And for me, that's not something I would normally even contemplate. But vengeance is a funny thing."

Yes. It certainly was. "I do appreciate your gesture, and I hope you will stay mute on the subject when talking to others."

Lady Brighthope arched one of her perfectly sculpted black brows. "Discretion is my middle name. Well, not really." She laughed. "But rest assured, I have no intention of jeopardizing your hunt for the Chameleon."

"Good, now are you certain there were only *six* names on the list?"

Lady Brighthope nodded, the diamonds that were dripping from the earrings she was wearing dancing in the moonlight with the movement. "Yes. Danbury mentioned seven, but I still thought it too much of a coincidence that the three names I read on my list are also names on the list Danbury spoke of."

Kat couldn't help but roll her eyes. "Good Lord, is there anything Danbury didn't tell you?"

"I doubt it." Lady Brighthope grinned. "The man will tell me anything to get me into his bed." Her sigh was long and drawn out. "But I did over-hear something I found interesting. My other cli-ent, only the other night, was discussing the matter with one of his servants. Something about Morri-set being the key and he had to be found…" She shrugged. "I don't know what he meant, but he mentioned something about how the list must be followed in the order given."

"In the order given?" That was interesting. As was the discrepancy in the numbers. Particularly, as there were seven in the ledger Fullbrink had decoded.

"Yes. Burton was first, Sir William next, followed by Lord Newtown." The lady shrugged. "I hadn't even thought of the list since finding it the other week. But now I'm curious as to who the three after them are."

"Are you positive you will not tell me who this client of yours is?"

"Absolutely certain." The woman was firm and there was steel in her tone. "There are many other things I could tell you, about a great number of other influential gentlemen, but if this particular one found out I told you anything, I would wind up in the Thames. Truly, what I've already told you is enough to ensure a ride there."

"The Thames seems to be a frequently mentioned method of disposal lately."

"Goodness knows what's down in that murky abyss." She turned up her nose with the thought. "It would be a perfect place to dispose of a body, wouldn't it? Though it's not a place I would wish to end up." The woman grinned wickedly at her. "It may well be my resting place, considering all of the secrets I've amassed over the years in my occupation."

The woman's words were intriguing. After all,

once the Chameleon situation was sorted, Kat could resume her quest to ensure dishonorable bachelors were exposed, and Lady Brighthope in her unique career involving influential gentleman could prove useful. "Yes, I would imagine you find out all sorts of intriguing information in your position…"

"Most intriguing. You'd be amazed at what I have learned over the years. I could tell you some fascinating things…"

"I believe you could." Perhaps the lady could prove to be a good source of interesting facts for the *Gazette*.

"Kaitlyn." Marcus's deep voice carried across the night breeze, interrupting her before she could even broach the subject. "I've been looking for you." He stood in the doorway, a definite frown marring his brows as he glanced between the two of them.

"Lord Westwood," Lady Brighthope purred. "How good to see you again and looking as deliciously robust as the last time I saw you in Vienna."

There was an underlying familiarity in the woman's words, much more than Kat would've expected, given what Marcus had said earlier about his acquaintance with the woman.

"Lady Brighthope." Marcus inclined his head toward her. "Danbury is leaving and fretting over your whereabouts. You should get back to him."

Brighthope pursed her lips as her eyes wandered over Marcus from top to toe. "'Tis a shame *you* were never in a position to fret over me. I should have enjoyed that greatly."

Kat's whole body tensed with her words as Brighthope languorously strolled over to Marcus, the side of her body brushing against his ever so slightly. Then, she trailed her fingers along Marcus's jacket sleeve.

"Perhaps we still can enjoy each other?" Lady Brighthope smiled coquettishly, batting her ridiculously long dark lashes up at Marcus.

Gritting her teeth, Kat had to make an active effort to stop herself from launching at the woman and wrenching her as far from Marcus as she could.

"Stick with Danbury, Lady Brighthope," Marcus said bluntly, the woman's words and touch clearly having no effect. "You'll have success with him, whereas you never will with me."

A red flush infused Brighthope's cheeks as she narrowed her glare at Marcus. "That will be your missed opportunity." She glanced back over to Kat. "You seem far too progressive, my dear Lady Kaitlyn, to tie yourself to a man with such little adventure or passion in his soul. Nevertheless, we'll talk again for I sense you and I are kindred spirits." Then, without sparing them a further glance, Brighthope swept past Marcus and disappeared through the doorway back into the Opera House.

"What were you doing out here with her?" Marcus demanded, his gaze steadily upon her, his words more an accusation than a question.

"I was talking to her. What of it?"

"What of it?" There was a definite hint of mocking in his tone now as he took several steps and stopped in front of her. "Did it escape your notice that she is a courtesan?"

"I'm perfectly aware of her occupation." Kat fisted her hands on her hips as she glanced up at his eyes. "It's one of the things she was about to start elaborating on when you interrupted."

"My timing was impeccable, then, wasn't it?"

"That is a matter of opinion," Kat countered. "Regardless, at least she told me some interesting information before you did interrupt."

Succinctly, she filled him in on the details, including the house party on the weekend. His jaw grew tighter with every word.

"Danbury told her all of that?"

"Apparently."

"The man is a bloody fool! He needs to be horsewhipped for disclosing such confidential information."

"Is it true then that men are more inclined to talk after they experience pleasure?" Such a thought was fascinating. Was that how some of her most proficient lady informants obtained their

own intelligence? "You've never been overly talk-
ative after we've been together."

Marcus grunted. "Most men bloody well fall
asleep after coitus, not chat about state secrets."

"She must be good at her job to get him to do
so." Perhaps Kat could recruit her as an informant
for the *Gazette*.

"If the man had been doing *his* job right in
the first place—" Marcus took a step toward her,
bending his head down until his mouth was but
inches from her own. "Then they both would have
fallen into a satisfied slumber. Didn't you have
good sleeps each time after I satisfied you?"

"I might have," Kat said, her breath starting to
get wispy as she breathed in the fresh masculine
scent of his skin.

"I would expect so. You did, after all, experience pleasure multiple times…" Marcus's voice
trailed off, and there was an intense charge of energy crackling between them. "There are still so
many things I want to show you. So many things
I want to do to you until you scream in pleasure
over and over again."

His words cascaded through her and Kat could
feel the heat radiating from his skin against hers in
the chill night air. More than anything, right then,
she wanted to pull his head down until their lips
pressed together, and she could taste him with
sweet abandon.

And just as she was about to reach out and do that very thing, Marcus shook his head and cursed. "Damn, you distract me, woman."

"Distract you from what?" Perhaps she could start her seduction of him here. After all, they were alone on the terrace, and it was dark.

"From why I came to find you. We need to leave now."

"What's happened?" She could sense the change in him. Tension, but also a sense of anticipation.

"Sir William has been attacked."

"Is he —?"

"He's fine." Marcus was quick to assure her. "But he might very well have survived an attempt by the Chameleon."

"He was the target tonight, not Danbury?"

"He was attacked at his house, a half hour ago. I've sent Cantfield ahead to ensure he's safe until we get there." He paused for a moment and stared at her. "You know what this means, don't you?"

Kat nodded as the same anticipation she was sure was coursing through Marcus began to run through her. "It means Sir William might be the only person alive who can finally identify the Chameleon."

Chapter Twenty-Six

Thirty minutes later, Kat followed Marcus over the threshold into Sir William's study. Her eyes automatically surveyed the subdued surroundings. The room was a mess, with some chairs overturned, papers scattered on the floor, and broken furniture upended on the rug. The only light came from a desk lamp and the blazing hearth on the far side of the room.

But, thankfully, sitting near the hearth was Sir William, seemingly all in one piece albeit looking a bit disheveled with his hair messed and his jacket ripped, while he nursed a glass of whisky in his hands. Cantfield was sitting next to him and both stood as she and Marcus approached.

Sir William glanced between them, his eyes narrowed with concern. "Are Danbury and Sir Albert safe?"

"They're fine. I've sent a retinue of men back with them to their houses," Marcus replied. "You should have listened when I tried to have men stationed here."

"I know." Sir William sank back down in his chair with a weary sigh. "It was arrogant of me to think the fiend wouldn't be so bold as to attack me in my own residence."

"Did you see who he was?" Kat asked, her every sense anticipating the possibility.

Sir William shook his head. "Unfortunately, no. Not only was he wearing a mask, but, as you can see, the lighting in here was minimal. I can tell you he's tall and muscular, though I doubt I'd be able to pick him out. His physique was rather like the both of yours." His eyes flicked over to Cantfield and Marcus.

Confusion swamped her. The physique Sir William was describing was not that of the waiter they'd chased at the opera the other evening after Burton was murdered.

"Are you certain that was his physique?" Marcus asked, clearly thinking the same thing as Kat.

"Positive," Sir William confirmed before taking a somewhat shaky sip of his drink.

"Tell us what happened," Kat asked.

He glanced across to his desk. "I was working on some files when I got a niggling sensation at the back of my neck that something wasn't right."

It was a feeling Kat had learned never to ignore.

"I pushed my chair to the right just as the blade of a dagger whistled past me," Sir William continued. He raised his arm and pointed to the far wall behind his desk where a dagger was lodged firmly in the wood paneling, right behind where his desk chair would have been, and at chest height. "I looked over to the door and saw a masked man standing there, reaching for another dagger. That's when I dove to the ground, grabbed my own hidden pistol from where it was strapped under my desk, and got off two shots."

Striding over to the door, Kat saw the two bullet holes marring the wood of the door frame. "You didn't hit him."

"No. I was rattled, and my aim was off, though the shots did as I intended and deterred him as he fled down the hallway."

"We need to question your staff and find out how he got in, and if anyone saw him leaving," Marcus added, while Kat crossed the room to examine the only piece of evidence left, the dagger.

Her steps faltered as she got closer and she swallowed away the large lump that had gathered in her throat.

"What's wrong?" Marcus murmured as he came up beside her.

She took a step toward the weapon and stared, almost mesmerized by the thing. "It can't be…"

"Kat, what is it?"

There was concern in Marcus's voice, as he placed a gentle hand on her arm.

"I recognize the dagger," she managed to utter, noticing that Sir William and Cantfield were now also standing around her and Marcus, looking at the knife, too.

"Who does it belong to?" Sir William asked.

"Victor."

Silence greeted her pronouncement for a good ten seconds.

"Victor's dagger?" Sir William exclaimed, after the shock had passed. "How is that possible?"

"Where is it normally kept?" Marcus asked.

"He gave it away a long time ago." She remembered the moment as she'd been slightly envious that Victor had given it to someone else rather than her. "He gave it to Nathaniel."

Sir William pressed his lips together. "Then that means we do indeed have a traitor within the War Office."

"It does?" Cantfield said. "I'm not following."

"After he was accused of being a traitor," Marcus answered, "all of Nathaniel's belongings were confiscated and taken to the War Office, with only his personal effects ever returned to my mother."

"Yes," Sir William confirmed. "His dagger should be safely sealed with the rest of his belongings, in the secure vault of the War Office. Clearly, that's not the case. I must admit I didn't truly believe I was a target."

"Why would you say that?" Kat swung around to look at him. "When you're listed in the journal as one."

"I found it a bit far-fetched that all three heads of the War Office were targets of an assassin." Sir William made his way back over to the armchair by the hearth and slowly sat down. "But after tonight, it's obviously not so far-fetched at all. And though it's certainly not the first time I've been a target, it is the first time I've been one of many targets within a conspiracy, which is what I find fascinating."

"Fascinating?" Kat wrenched the dagger from the wall and peered down at the ivory handle.

"Completely," Sir William replied. "The top three in charge of the War Office, targets of an assassin. Makes you wonder who would benefit from our deaths."

"And who would?" Kat asked him.

"That's the most fascinating thing. You see, there's no true successor if all three of us died." Sir William smiled at her. "Though, when you add in Burton and Newtown's names, along with Nathaniel and Victor's dagger, then perhaps a clearer picture emerges."

Marcus sat on the other seat next to Sir William, and Kat couldn't help but think he appeared fatigued. All she felt like doing was wandering over to him, plunking herself down in his lap, and holding him. The thought had her shaking her head. What was wrong with her? These sorts of sentimental feelings were becoming a nuisance.

"What clearer picture?" Marcus asked as Cantfield handed him a small whisky.

"As you're no doubt aware now, Burton was the one who observed your brother selling secrets to the Russians."

"Yes, Sir Albert mentioned it." Marcus's fingers clenched around the glass and for a moment Kat was sure he was about to snap the thing, but he took a breath and released his harsh grip, placing the glass down on the table next to him and standing. "What of Newtown, though? What does he have to do with it all?"

Sir William took a sip of his whisky. "He was sent with Victor to bring Nathaniel back to England."

That was news to Kat. She knew Victor had assembled a team and had grumbled about being forced to take certain people he'd rather not, but the War Secretary had insisted. Perhaps Newtown was one of those Victor hadn't wanted on the trip?

"Though the last two on the list throw a spanner in the works." Sir William sighed. "We haven't found who they are or where they're located."

"Are they aliases?" Kat asked.

"Most likely," Sir William said. "If they were real names, we should have found them by now, or the Chameleon would have. So, it could be a good thing, for if we can't find them, perhaps the Chameleon can't either. Now, though I'm loath to admit it, I'd probably serve a better purpose if I left England for a short period until the situation is resolved. You won't have to worry about keeping an old man like me alive then and can focus on saving others."

"Where will you go?" Marcus asked.

Sir William shook his head morosely. "I'm not certain. A holiday in Europe with my wife would be just the thing, I think." He walked over to Kat and took her hand in his. "Do be careful, my dear. I know you can defend yourself, otherwise I never would have brought you into the Department. But when emotions are concerned, they tend to skew our more rational thought processes."

He bent down and placed a kiss on her gloved knuckles, then turned and walked over to Marcus, who was leaning against the far wall.

"There's a traitor in our midst, my boy." Sir William lowered his voice as he spoke. "Have a care and do not trust anyone who isn't in this room, and I do mean anyone."

A short time later, they'd arranged to move Sir William and his wife to a more secure location, and one not even the Chameleon would dare breach, Club Tartus.

After all, no one risked incurring the wrath of Livie's husband, the Bastard of Baker Street. And even though the man himself wasn't at his club, or even in London for that matter, his men were, and they would ensure Sir William was safe until he could make sail on the morrow and leave the country.

Marcus had also spoken to Lord Newtown using Sir William's new desk telephone and had organized invitations for all of them to attend his house party tomorrow. Which was why he was now on route to the Lavingham ball to find the Duchess of Calder and convince her to accompany them all to the house party. And that shouldn't be too difficult to accomplish as Kat had told him to mention anyone who was anyone would be there. The old dragon wouldn't be able to resist such a challenge.

Kat would have gone with him but seeing the dagger had rattled her a lot more than she'd let on. It brought back memories of training with Nathaniel, and the feeling that she'd never been quite good enough for Victor. Especially when he'd given Nathaniel the dagger of his that had belonged to his own father, knowing how much Kat had wanted it.

It was silly, she knew, but at the time as a young impressionable seventeen-year-old, it had hurt her, and she couldn't express such feelings to Victor as he would have seen it as weakness. So, she'd kept the pain hidden and got on with training.

When Marcus had suggested Cantfield escort her home while he saw to securing the Duchess' agreement and ensuring Sir William and his wife got to Club Tartus safely, Kat agreed without a word to the contrary. She suspected her easy capitulation had surprised him, but she couldn't help the feeling that she was missing something. And, really, if she wanted to clear her head and think properly, she needed to steer clear of Marcus for a bit. The man unbalanced her normally sharp senses, especially when he was physically near her.

The carriage she was in with Cantfield came to a halt at the back of her residence, and before the footman could open the door, she did, bidding farewell to a bemused Cantfield in the process. The carriage clattered away down the street as she pushed open the back gate and began the trek to the back door.

When she was a few feet away, a tingling sensation danced along her spine, and she knew she wasn't alone. In one swift move, she spun around toward the bushes and pulled out her dagger as a man stepped from the shadows.

"Hello, Kat," his deep voice rumbled. "It's been a long time."

Shock tore through her. She was seeing a ghost. "This isn't possible... You're meant to be dead."

Chapter Twenty-Seven

"Death is slightly overrated, even if it is useful."

Nathaniel Black stepped farther out from the shadows until he was a few feet from Kat, an expression of grim weariness on his stubble-covered face as he stared at her. "However, as you can see, I'm very much alive. Slightly scarred and certainly not the trusting fool I once was, but alive nonetheless."

Her eyes darted to the mottled patch of his skin stretching along the left side of his neck up to the lower portion of his mouth. Burn marks, and bad ones at that. Scars that hadn't been there when she'd last seen him alive three years ago.

"It's good to see you, Kat. I've missed you and our sparring rounds." He glanced down at the knife she was holding. "And I see you still prefer your dagger."

Surprises didn't usually trip her up as she'd been trained to adapt to the unexpected. But this was something else entirely. This was Nathaniel, back from the dead. "Everyone thinks you died in a bomb blast in Paris…"

"I know."

It was as if she was looking at a ghost. A ghost bearing remnants of the young man she'd trained with. A young man she'd laughed with. A young man she'd shared her first kiss with. But gone was the lighthearted adventurer and in his place was a man with eyes haunted by vengeance and sorrow. An expression she recognized, having regularly seen it herself in her own mirror.

"You'd better start telling me what's going on," Kat said, her fingers clenching the hilt of her dagger tighter.

"I can explain." He held up his hand, almost in a placating manner.

"Then do so, for my patience is wearing thin."

A brief smile flicked up at the corner of his lips. "You were never patient when it came to anything, except of course for your training."

"You remember correctly." She smiled before swiftly moving in toward him and pressing the knife to his neck, while simultaneously grabbing her second dagger with her free hand and pressing it against the junction of his legs. Light enough not to cut him, but close enough that she could do so with barely a movement. "But you've clearly forgotten what I do to those who try my patience." She emphasized her words by pressing both daggers a bit closer to him. "Was it you that tried to kill Sir William?"

There was a hint of confusion as he peered at

her. "I don't know what you're talking about."

"The old dagger Victor gave you just so happened to be used in an attempt on Sir William's life, and here you are only an hour or so later, back from the dead. Too much of a coincidence I'd say."

He pressed his lips together. "I didn't try to kill Sir William."

"Then tell me what you're doing here, and stick to the truth, Nathaniel." She stared intently into his eyes, willing him to see how serious she was. "You know I could always tell when you were lying. And you know what I do to those who lie to me."

He didn't flinch. "I will tell you the truth, Kat. At least as much as I can. But, first, you must promise not to tell anyone I'm alive. And I do mean anyone. Not even Marcus."

His words answered a silent question she'd been wondering herself. "He really doesn't know you're alive?"

"Not a clue."

"What about your mother and sister? Sir William?"

"No one knows, except you."

"Why me?"

"Because I've information for you, but I must have your word first."

She paused for a second, then shook her head. "I can't promise you anything, at least not until I know what's going on. And do start talking soon, for my hands are tiring and I'd hate for them to accidentally slip." She emphasized her words by pressing her blades closer to him.

But rather than balk, he laughed. "You always did have pluck. I'll give you that. But lower your weapons a little, would you?" he murmured, glancing down at the knife near to his nether regions. "A man can't really think when his jewels are threatened."

It was something the old Nathaniel would have said, and for a second a bittersweet nostalgia rose in her throat. She did miss those days. Lowering both daggers a little, she nodded. "You do realize everyone believes you're a traitor who sold secrets to the Russians."

"Yes. I know." He smiled, though it was in self-deprecation rather than happiness. "But I don't care what anyone thinks anymore. I stopped caring after Paris. I probably never would have returned to England except for you."

"Me?"

"Yes." Nathaniel went to say something but stopped for a moment. "You're in danger, Kat."

She arched an eyebrow at him. "That's not particularly news. I'm regularly in danger."

"You don't understand." There was an urgency in his voice. "The Chameleon has taken an interest in you. Perhaps even become obsessed with you…

And when the Chameleon is obsessed by something or someone, it never ends well."

In an instant, she flicked her knife back up against his throat and glared at him. "How would you know that about the Chameleon, unless you know who he is. Or you are the Chameleon?"

"Do you really think I'm Europe's deadliest assassin? Me?"

"Are you?"

"No."

Kat didn't know why, but she believed him. "Then do you know who he is?"

"That doesn't matter."

"Actually, it does." She pressed her dagger closer against his neck, until a thin line of blood appeared just on the skin's surface. "The Chameleon killed Victor, and if you're in league with the assassin that makes you my enemy."

"I'm not your enemy, Kat, nor am I in league with anyone," he snarled. "Especially not the Chameleon, who helped to set me up as a traitor. The Chameleon was partly responsible for the death of the woman I loved."

There was truth radiating from his eyes and words. But could she really trust him? Once, she would have done so blindly and with her life. But now? Now she didn't know. "I've been hunting the assassin since Victor's death, so if you know anything about him, you will tell me."

"Or what? You're going to slit my throat if I don't?"

Kat took in a harsh breath and lowered her knife, slipping both daggers back into their sheaths and stepping away from him. "No. But you know what Victor meant to me, what I thought he meant to you, too. If you know anything about the assassin who took his life, you must tell me."

Nathaniel took a deep breath in. "I can't."

A sinking sensation pooled in her stomach with his words. *He did know something.* "Can't or won't?"

"I made a promise a long time ago that I'd neither hunt the Chameleon nor assist anyone else to."

"Victor meant so little to you?" Her heart dropped but then anger replaced the sadness.

"He was like a second father to me."

"What nonsense!" Kat exclaimed. "You'd be out for vengeance if that was the case, just like I am."

"Things are not so black and white, Kaitlyn!"

He dragged a hand through his dark hair, in much the same manner as Marcus did when he was frustrated, and Kat was struck by the similarities between the brothers, much more pronounced now that Nathaniel was older. Though Marcus was an inch or two taller, and his chest was broader than his younger brother's.

"You can't assume anything about the Chameleon," Nathaniel continued, "nor underestimate the assassin's abilities."

"You better start explaining yourself." Kat's voice was raspy with emotion. "Why have you stayed hidden and pretended to be dead for the last three years? Why did you not send word you were alive?" The question was suddenly eating at her, demanding to be answered. "I could have helped you."

"Initially, I couldn't. I was literally in a hospital bed for four months recovering from my injuries after the bomb. The bomb that killed the love of my life." He laughed without humor. "Everyone thought I'd died along with Irena, and that's how it had to stay."

"Four months…" Kat felt sick with the thought of him all alone in a foreign hospital, knowing his love was dead and that if anyone knew he was alive, he could be killed, too. "If you had sent word, I would've helped you."

"I know." He took in a deep breath and exhaled. "You've always been a rescuer. But it was safer for all of you if you thought I was dead. Besides, after that I was busy in Russia for a period."

"Russia?" Were the rumors he was a traitor true?

Nathaniel was perfectly still for a moment as he peered off into the distance. "Yes. Some Russian operatives did not take well to discovering me in the Kremlin trying to discover who the English traitor was. They were hospitable and allowed me to spend the better part of the last two years in their dungeons. So, you see, I was rather tied up. Quite literally, too." He laughed for a second, but Kat could see the pain in his eyes as his fists clenched by his sides.

"They beat you." It wasn't a question. The stories she'd heard of the conditions the Kremlin kept their prisoners in were almost unimaginable.

"Every day." A wry grin split across his face. "They also had rather dismal accommodation, food and activities, actually. I don't think I'll choose to stay there again. Very poor service, indeed."

Her throat clenched at how casual he sounded, when in fact he'd been in hell. "Did they torture you greatly?"

His smile grew fierce. "Clearly not enough, as I eventually escaped in one piece." The smile vanished. "I found sanctuary with Irena's family on their farm in Russia for a bit, at least until I received word about what was taking place back here. I knew then I needed to come back to warn you and uncover the true traitor before all the witnesses had been killed. And until I discover who that is, I need you to keep my secret. You can't tell anyone I'm alive, especially Marcus." Nathaniel sighed heavily. "His life depends on it. My mother and sister, too. Please, Kat, you must promise me."

There was a rigidity to his posture as he awaited her answer.

Was the man serious? "You can't turn up back from dead and ask me to promise not to tell anyone else you're alive. Marcus needs to know. In fact, he has a right to know. He's trying to exonerate you and is putting himself in harm's way doing so."

Nathaniel crossed his arms over his chest. "Like I said, his life would be at risk if he knew. Great risk."

"At risk from whom?"

"Whoever it is that's getting rid of everyone involved in setting me up in the first place. It's someone close to him, I feel it. And whoever it is has already gone to great lengths to hide their involvement, and has the money and resources to get rid of anything or anyone who gets in their way. The money to hire the Chameleon."

"Why is it you revealed yourself to me, then?" Kat narrowed her eyes upon him. "Why have you suddenly reappeared, and don't tell me it's because I'm in danger, because you know I can protect myself."

"You can only protect yourself if you know there's a threat. And if the Chameleon has taken an interest in you like my sources tell me, then you're in danger, and not just from the Chameleon."

"Who am I in danger from then?"

"I don't know, not exactly, though I have my suspicions. As soon as I can confirm them, I'll let you know, but I had to warn you nevertheless."

"That's not good enough, Nathaniel. You can't expect me to keep such news from Marcus without anything more substantial than 'I have my suspicions.' Losing you eats away at him constantly. He blames himself for your death."

"You seem to know my brother a great deal."

An odd sense of discomfort ran through her at the look of speculation in his gaze. "Marcus and I are working together to find the Chameleon. We're partners of sorts." She couldn't very well say she was his lover.

"You've teamed up with my brother?" For a moment he seemed shocked, but then he started laughing. "Oh, that's grand. My staid and predictable brother dealing with whirlwind Kaitlyn. How is he coping with that? Not very well, I'd say."

She'd forgotten the nickname he used to give her. "He's coming around."

"Of course he is. When you put your mind to it, you can convince anyone to do anything. You're an extraordinary woman. Do you want to hear something funny? I once thought myself a bit in love with you."

The news was like a cannonball exploding. "What?" They'd shared a kiss when she was eighteen, but only because she'd been annoyed to hear Marcus was getting married. She hadn't ever really had any feelings for Nathaniel, apart from that of a very close friend, almost like a brother. Mostly because he'd never been able to take anything too seriously, but that was not the case now. The man standing before her was changed to the point she didn't really know him anymore.

"I did," he confirmed with a wry smile. "But don't worry, my heart was broken with Irena's death, and I know I'll never love again. Now, I've already been here too long, but before I go, you must promise not to tell Marcus I'm alive." Nathaniel stepped closer to her. "If he finds out, it will place him in danger, especially as he'd try and find me. You know he would."

What Nathaniel said was true. If Marcus knew, there was nothing he wouldn't do to find his brother.

"And besides," he continued, "this is my mess to fix. I don't need my big brother charging in and saving the day like he always used to. Promise me you won't tell him. Let me redeem my honor for myself."

As much as a little voice inside her was telling her not to, she slowly nodded. "I won't tell him. At least not yet. You have a fortnight, Nathaniel, to tell him yourself or I will." It felt so wrong to promise not to tell Marcus something, but the memories between her and Nathaniel deserved one promise.

"Very well. Oh, and one thing, Kat. In this quest for vengeance of yours, be careful not to let it consume you as it's done me. You can never fully return to the living if you constantly surround yourself with memories of the dead."

She saw the darkness close over his eyes, and a deep foreboding came over her as she saw the truth of his statement mirrored in his expression. The man had seen and done things that clearly tormented his soul.

Standing there, out in the dark with him, she realized Nathaniel's scars ran a great deal deeper than his skin. The Nathaniel she used to tease and torment was long gone. In his place was a man she didn't truly know or recognize.

He took a step in front of her and gently placed his hand under her chin, tilting up her face to his. And she let him. Nostalgia for their shared past was almost palpable in the air around them.

"Stay safe, Kat." He pressed a brief kiss on her cheek, then released her, before he turned and fled through the garden.

As she stood watching where his shadow had disappeared, guilt clawed at her over the fact that she'd given him her word not to tell Marcus he was alive. What had she just agreed to? And how was she going to keep such a secret from a man she was growing to care for a great deal? A man who did not countenance lies and had extracted a promise from her to always tell him the truth.

A sinking feeling pitted in her stomach, because she knew if he ever found out she was keeping such a thing from him, he'd never trust her again.

Chapter Twenty-Eight

The next day, Kat found herself ensconced in the Duchess of Caldwell's luxurious train carriage with the lady herself, along with Etta, Cantfield, and Marcus, as the train steamed ahead, on route to Bramsfield Village, the closest town to Lord Newtown's country estate.

Thankfully, she was seated at one end of the carriage along with the duchess and Etta, while both of the men were seated at the bar on the opposite end, discussing something amongst themselves. The space between Marcus and herself was much needed at the moment, as she didn't think she was ready to have a normal conversation with him in light of what she'd learned last night.

Luckily, Etta had kept up a constant stream of dialogue, and with the duchess's somewhat acerbic tongue adding snippets here and there, Kat barely needed to speak, giving her time to think about what happened last night and her promise to Nathaniel.

Even just thinking about her promise and the resulting betrayal it could cause if Marcus ever found out made Kat sick to her stomach. The guilt was horrid. She didn't know how to face him, not without him realizing something was wrong.

"You seem distracted today," the duchess said from her seat across from Kat. "Most unlike you, Lady Kaitlyn."

"My head is paining me, Duchess," she replied with a little more bite in her tone than she'd intended.

Rather than take offense, the lady peered at Kat with even more scrutiny. "Hmm, do you have a fever, too?"

"What's this?" Etta asked, overhearing the question. "Are you unwell, Kat?"

"We shall have to watch her carefully," the duchess said. "It could be scarlet fever or possibly the measles. You don't have any spots on you, do you?"

"I'm fine," Kat ground out. The pain in her head started to pound further with all the chatter.

"Hmm, we shall have to keep an eye on you." The duchess plainly didn't believe her. "Do let me know if your symptoms worsen. I have some medicine in my travel bag that you may require."

"I said I'm fine." Kat tried to smile, but all she could manage was a tight grimace.

"You know a great deal about illnesses, Your Grace," Etta enthused.

"I should. The dear girl I'm sponsoring, Miss Charlotte Hastings, has the most unusual notion of following in her father's footsteps and becoming a doctor. All she ever talks of is diseases and remedies. I've gotten rather good at knowing the symptoms for a variety of ailments." The duchess sounded vexed, but Kat could see the gleam of pride in her eyes. "I really don't know how I shall find her a husband with such conversation regularly coming from her lips."

"Perhaps she doesn't want a husband," Kat said. "Not every woman does."

"My dear girl, you don't strike me as naive," the duchess replied. "A woman might not want a husband, but in this world, if she wants a decent life and a measure of freedom, at least as much as her husband will allow, marriage is the only option. Which begs the question, how am I to find you two husbands, as well?"

Kat merely blinked while Etta nearly stumbled off her chair.

"I have no wish to marry," Kat bit out.

"Neither do I," Etta declared, regaining her balance.

"Ha! Please," the lady scoffed. "The way the two of you have been making eyes at the two of them?" Her hand waved over to Marcus and Cantfield. "You might be succeeding in fooling yourselves you don't wish to marry, but you can't fool me. Looks don't lie. And I've been alive long enough to know just what sort of *looks* have been going on."

"There have been no looks going on," Kat countered, knowing full well she'd barely been able to look at Marcus all morning.

"Certainly, there haven't been," Etta added, a rather cranky expression creeping over her countenance. It was rare for Etta to ever get cranky. "Besides, I wouldn't marry such a profligate rake if he was the last man in the world!"

The duchess merely raised her eyebrow. "I'd rather marry a young and handsome rake than an old degenerate lecher like the Earl of Edmington, whom I hear your father is very close to settling upon as a husband for you."

"The Earl of Edmington..." Etta's voice trailed off, her already porcelain skin becoming even whiter. "But he's eighty if he's a day."

"Eighty-four, actually," the duchess corrected as she picked up a small appetizer from the side table and placed it into her mouth. "And as for you." Her eyes homed in on Kat. "You've been doing all you can to avoid looking at Westwood today. It speaks volumes."

Kat shook her head in exasperation. "How so?"

"From my observations, you're not one to normally avoid anything. You'd rather face things head on. The fact you can't do that with him"—she inclined her head in Marcus's direction—"like I said, speaks volumes."

"And from my observations of you, you're entirely too observant." Darn the wily old woman.

The duchess laughed, though it certainly sounded husky, as if she rarely used her voice for such a thing. "Oh, you remind me of myself. Except for carrying weapons about. That I never did." She glanced pointedly down at Kat's skirt and the outline from the pockets of her sheaths inside. "But if you're still in denial about your feelings for Westwood, who am I to correct you? You'll eventually come to the realization. I only hope it's not too late when you do. I made such a mistake when I was younger and have forever regretted it."

The duchess stood, her cane by her side. "Now if you will excuse me, I shall freshen up, as I do believe we'll be arriving shortly." With a regal nod, the lady turned and wandered through the carriage door into the adjoining compartment.

"Can you believe the nerve of that woman!" Etta exclaimed. "How dare she suggest I have feelings for Cantfield. Though she was right about the way you and Marcus look at each other. But she wasn't right about me. Goodness, I hope she wasn't right about what my father is up to. I shall have to make some inquiries as soon as we return to London."

Kat sighed. "She knows practically everything

that goes on in Society. Though her eyes must be aging if she thinks either of us wish to marry either of them." Her eyes darted over to the two men, and it was at that moment Marcus's eyes caught hers.

Quickly, she looked away, but whatever it was he'd seen in that brief glance had him pushing back from his chair and walking over to them.

"Ladies," he acknowledged with a nod. "Is the duchess well?" He motioned to the woman's empty seat.

"Her tongue is as acidic as ever," Kat replied, finding it difficult to even meet his eyes. Eyes that seemed to see deeply inside her. "So, yes, she's well, she's simply freshening up before our arrival. Which I might do, too." She stood and started toward the same doorway to the other carriage.

"Kat, wait." Marcus followed her, gently placing his hand on her arm.

She stopped and pressed her lips together before taking a deep breath and turning to face him. "Yes?"

"Is everything all right?" There was concern and confusion on his face. "You don't seem yourself. Almost like you've been avoiding me."

He was far too perceptive for a man. But most spies were observant. "Last night unsettled me." Which was the truth. And suddenly she realized she didn't have to lie to him at all. She could tell him the truth, but just not tell him about

Nathaniel. That wasn't lying to him, was it? "See-ing the dagger brought back a lot of memories of the past." Again, another truth.

"For me, too," he replied, releasing her arm, only to drag his hand through his hair. It was a gesture of his she was quite fond of watching. "It feels as if the Chameleon is trying to bait us, using Nathaniel's dagger."

"Yes, I suppose so." Nathaniel had denied he'd been the one to throw it, and she'd believed him. If that was the case, then what Marcus said was true. Because what other purpose had there been in trying to kill Sir William with Nathaniel's knife? Unless the Chameleon knew Nathaniel was alive, and was trying to frame him?

Excitement surged through her with the thought. That could very well be it. She opened her mouth to share her theory with Marcus, and then realized she couldn't. Not without telling him, which she couldn't do just yet. She'd given Nathan-iel a fortnight to do so, and he should be the one to tell Marcus what had happened.

The excuse sounded weak to her own mind.

"Is something else troubling you?"

For a moment, she considered telling him, but Nathaniel had been right. If she did, he wouldn't stop looking for Nathaniel, and he could become distracted by the news, and potentially careless with his own safety. She wouldn't allow that, so she shook her head in reply. "I'm just feeling slightly nauseous. Perhaps it's from the slight bumping of the carriage against the tracks."

"All right. We'll be there shortly. Newtown has organized for one of his carriages to meet us all at the station and take us to the manor." He took a step closer to her and raised her chin with his finger. "Hopefully, the country air will make you feel better."

Kat closed her eyes and breathed in the woodsy scent of him. There was nothing she felt like doing more at that moment than burying her head in his chest and having him hold her tight. But they weren't alone, so she opened her eyes and found him staring at her.

Her heart quickened as she saw the hunger and heat scorching in his eyes. It felt as if he was stripping her naked and she was intoxicatingly trapped in his gaze, unable to look away. But the duchess harrumphing from behind broke the spell, and Kat swiveled around to face her.

"Yes, there's no particular looks going on between the two of you, whatsoever, is there?" Derision and a touch of smugness all but oozed from the woman's every word as she stepped around them and returned to her seat, a light chuckle following in her wake.

"What's she talking about?"

"I think the Dragon Duchess is trying her

hand at matchmaking," Kat said. "I think she'd have an attack of the vapors if she knew what has already taken place between us."

"The Dragon Duchess, matchmaking?" Marcus whispered, before he laughed, too. "Please, 'tis rumored the woman eats debutants for breakfast. I doubt she's trying to play matchmaker."

"There are a lot more depths to the woman than meet the eye." Kat was beginning to realize that fact herself. The woman was uncannily observant and knew all of the goings on in Society. Why on earth had Livie never suggested using her godmother as an informant for the *Gazette* before? The duchess would be perfect for the role.

"Much like you, my dear," Marcus added with a wink.

The wink was the last straw. If she stayed in his presence any longer, she'd either blabber out the truth of Nathaniel, or pull Marcus into a passionate kiss in front of them all. And though the duchess was a pragmatic sort of lady, even she would draw the line at such a display.

Kat excused herself from Marcus and pushed open the door to the next carriage, fleeing inside. She took in a deep breath and unclenched her hands. She had to get her emotions and her guilt under control. The house party would present a perfect opportunity for the Chameleon to strike and kill Lord Newtown, so she couldn't allow herself to be further distracted. There'd be a raft of unknown servants and new help from the village, as well as numerous guests, making the house itself a veritable hive of activity with a plethora of unknown faces. Such a combination would make sneaking into the residence all the easier for someone with the skills possessed by the Chameleon.

Their mission was simple and completely complicated all at once. They had to find and stop a ghost. And Kat had to get her mind off Marcus and the way she wanted to grab him when he was near, and back onto the important task of exacting her vengeance.

Chapter Twenty-Nine

"Oh my goodness!" Etta rushed into the bedchamber Kat had been allocated, less than thirty minutes after they'd all arrived and were shown to their rooms to change and freshen up. "You'll never guess who is here!"

Kat turned from where she was directing her maid, Bess, to hide her daggers and faced Etta, who seemed as if she had run the entire length of the corridor from her assigned room. "Who?"

"Bertie!" Etta gasped.

"The Prince?"

She nodded her head confidently. "And you'll never guess who his special companion is!"

"What? It's not the princess?" Kat's voice held an edge of sarcasm as she resumed pulling out some of her more interesting items of subterfuge. She put her special lockpicks, which were disguised to be used as hair pins, into her chignon.

"You know he wouldn't bring his wife!" Etta looked around superciliously. "His companion is the Siren. Can you believe the Prince brought a courtesan to Lord Newtown's house party... Clearly, she's moved on from Danbury."

Kat shrugged. Brighthope hadn't mentioned she was attending with the prince, not that it made any difference to her. Though there'd be more security around. Perhaps the Chameleon wouldn't risk assassinating Newtown now? "He is the prince and does as he pleases. You know that."

"I do," Etta agreed. "But I've never been to a house party while he's in attendance." Etta narrowed her eyes as she looked at Kat. "You're not going to try to speak to that woman again, are you?"

"I have to," Kat responded. She'd told Etta all about her encounter the other evening with the woman, and Etta had been less than impressed. "She has a list to give me."

"Kat, you can't speak to her."

She smiled at her friend. "You know Bertie expects his companion of the moment to be treated with the utmost respect. This is in actual fact the only time I can converse with the woman in front of others, without censure. It's perfect really."

Etta frowned. "Trust me, even though they won't be able to chastise you openly, the other ladies will certainly be doing so behind your back if you do speak with her."

"You know I care little for other people's opinions." Kat shrugged again.

A long sigh left Etta's mouth. "Unfortunately, I do."

Kat walked over to Etta and grabbed her hands in her own. "Everything will be all right, you must trust me. Now, come on, we have a luncheon garden party to attend."

They walked along the corridor and down the grand staircase, making their way to where lunch was being served on the terrace. Kat's eyes glanced over the grand statues in the entrance hall and lining the passageway leading to the terrace, and for a moment, even she was taken aback.

Newtown seemed enamored with ancient Grecian statues in the nude style, and also favored somewhat gaudy paintings in a similar style.

As they arrived at the terrace, Kat realized Lord Newtown was continuing the Greek theme for the festivities over the weekend, as several of his footmen and the maids were dressed in Greek togas. Kat looked across at Etta, who was having a hard time keeping her mouth closed at all the bare flesh displayed by the servants.

Even though it was nearly summer, the wind whipping along the outside terrace was somewhat chilly. She couldn't help but feel sorry for those of his poor serving staff forced into wearing the costumes, especially as it seemed a storm was brewing.

The guests themselves, around fifty, were dressed in their best day wear, and having a grand time flirting with each other, as they sipped on champagne and nibbled the food from the trays being taken around.

Kat spied Marcus and Lucas leaning against the balustrade at the far end of the balcony, their long legs occupying a great deal of the space in front of them. Marcus had changed into buff-colored trousers and a matching jacket, with a crisp white shirt and a deep blue waistcoat underneath. She hated to admit it, but every time she looked at him she was struck by just how devastatingly handsome he was. Not that the man seemed at all aware of his looks, and more often than not sent women scurrying away with a glare. It was something Kat enjoyed seeing more than she ought to, considering she had no claim on him.

To an observer, Marcus's casual pose suggested he was supremely relaxed and rather blasé about the whole affair, but Kat could see the sharpness in his gaze as he superciliously surveyed the assembly. He was assessing everyone present. Then, his eyes came to rest upon her own. He inclined his head and his mouth tilted up into a half smile as he watched her and Etta approach, weaving their way through the gathered guests.

"Ladies." Marcus bowed to them both as they stopped in front of him and Lucas. "Refreshed from the journey, I hope?"

"Admirably so," Kat replied as she curtsied back. There, she sounded back to normal with him, she hoped.

"Yes, quite refreshed." Etta smiled as she curtsied, too, before turning to Lord Cantfield, who had a decided glower across his countenance. "Are you ill, my lord?" she asked him.

Lucas's glare only increased. "I'm fine," was his clipped reply. "But I think perhaps you forgot to wear your fichu, my lady."

"I have no need to wear a fichu, Lord Cantfield," Etta ground out, glancing down at her décolletage, which was on prominent display, though tastefully so. And which a fichu would have completely covered up. "It is completely ungentlemanly for you to have mentioned such a thing, though completely expected from a rake of your ilk."

"Any news on the man that attacked Sir William's residence yet?" Kat hastily interrupted, trying to divert them from killing each other, which it appeared they were about to do, going by the expressions of fury in both their eyes.

Marcus shook his head. "Unfortunately, no. I have my informants making some enquiries but it looks like he disappeared into the night. What we need to do is work out what the motive is." Marcus folded his arms across his chest. "If we can do that, it will potentially narrow down who the man is that funded the assassinations."

"True," Lucas said, finally flicking his eyes

over to Marcus instead of glaring at Etta. "It's got to be someone who has a grudge against the War Office. We know Burton had links to the Office and was the man who supposedly witnessed your brother selling secrets to the Russians. Perhaps it's the Russians seeking revenge? Or to silence those involved in selling those secrets to them?"

"The Russians wouldn't hire an assassin, they would send their own men," Marcus replied. "But what does Newtown have to do with selling secrets to them?" He ran a hand through his hair, messing the style up wonderfully. His poor valet would be frustrated at the end of each day.

Kat had to resist the urge to step over to him and run her own hands through his locks and kiss him. They hadn't kissed since last night, and already it felt like too long. But then she felt angry with herself for even thinking about kissing him, when so many lives were at stake. She had to return her thoughts to the situation at hand.

"We could always ask him," Lucas said. "Because it does seem that everyone named, apart from those two last names we don't know, are linked in some way to your brother and the selling of the secrets to the Russians or his apprehension."

Just then the tap of the duchess's cane echoed on the stone floor and a moment later, she had insisted on whisking Etta and Cantfield away to the refreshment table. And no one, not even

Cantfield who was to be a duke himself, was brave enough to say no.

Kat turned back only to find Marcus staring at her. His eyes were intent but unfathomable. She felt herself start to feel somewhat hot beneath his gaze. Why did the man affect her so?

"Lady Kaitlyn," the velvet tone with a hint of an accent purred from behind her.

Swiveling around toward the voice, she found Lady Brighthope standing there, an expression of bored amusement dancing in her eyes. She was dressed in a sapphire blue day dress dripping with small jewels sewn into the bodice, and in the very fabric itself there seemed to be some sort of tiny sparkling objects interspersed throughout, making it appear as if she was shining. Her hair was swept up and piled high atop her head, with some ringlets cascading down her neck. The woman really was stunning; it was no wonder she was known as the Siren.

Kat couldn't help but glance down at her own emerald outfit. Next to Lady Brighthope, she looked rather underdressed and dull. Though looking around, it appeared the woman had that effect on all of the other ladies present. Lady Brighthope knew how to live up to her nickname, as no one shone as bright as the Siren.

"Lady Brighthope," Kat said, "it's good to see you again. I was hoping we might have another chance to speak."

"I did enjoy our little chat last time." Lady Brighthope smiled at her and then she batted her eyelashes up toward Marcus. "Lord Westwood, we meet again. Have you changed your mind about my suggestion?"

She watched as Marcus gazed at Lady Brighthope, an expression of disinterest visible in his eyes. For some reason, his obvious lack of interest in the woman made Kat feel like smiling.

"No," came his curt reply. "Now, tell me, who was the man with the list?"

The woman laughed lightly, the sound both innocent and seductive all at once, yet there was an edge of uncertainty to it. The woman was obviously not used to rejection. "Oh, you're still as blunt and inflexible as always, aren't you, Westwood? Where's your sense of adventure and fun?"

"Long gone, my lady, as I'm sure you're aware." He straightened off the balustrade. "Who had the list?"

"You're like a dog with a bone." Lady Brighthope tossed one of her curls over her shoulder. "I'm sure Lady Kaitlyn has already told you that I shall not disclose such a thing."

"You will if you don't wish to end up in Newgate Prison."

Lady Brighthope narrowed her eyes at him in glittering menace. "You'd be wise not to threaten me, my lord. Have you not seen whom I'm accompanying this weekend? One word from me and you'll find yourself in a great deal of...what is that saying? Hot water, I think?"

A thin smile stretched across Marcus's lips. "Threats do not work on me."

"And what makes you think they'll work on me?" Lady Brighthope demanded, squaring her shoulders.

"My threats have the power of being carried out." Marcus shrugged.

Lady Brighthope's jaw clenched and for the first time she didn't look beautiful at all.

"Is that so? You know, I did bring the list with me this weekend, and had intended to give it to Lady Kaitlyn at some stage," the woman began, "but if this is how I am to be treated, then I see no reason to assist further."

Kat rushed to step between them and placed a gentle hand on the woman's upper arm as she commenced turning away. "Please pay him no heed. You know what men are like, they get fixated on something and can think of little else."

Somewhat mollified, Lady Brighthope lifted her chin and nodded. "What you say is true. Men always underestimate us, don't they? Thinking they can bully and threaten us. But, ultimately, we're the ones who control them." Slowly, her practiced smile replaced the look of fury as she pulled Kat over to the side and away from Marcus.

Brighthope leaned in close to Kat and whispered in her ear. "But I think the name of the man who had the list isn't the only thing Westwood is fixated on." The woman eyed Kat up and down. "He hasn't been able to keep his eyes off you ever since you came downstairs. Which must be the reason he's turned me down. Which is understandable as you're beautiful and intriguing. No wonder he's smitten."

Kat felt her face redden and had to force herself not to glance over at Marcus. Thank goodness he was far enough away not to have heard. "Let's stop playing games, Lady Brighthope. Do you have the list?"

"Yes, but not with me. It's up in my room." The woman glanced around before returning her attention to Kat. "I've heard whispers that tonight may be the night that the Chameleon assassinates Lord Newtown."

"At the ball?"

The woman nodded. "But you may be able to prevent it. There's an inn in the village where a man by the name of Charles Tremont is staying. He might have some further information about all of this."

"How did you find this out?" Kat asked her.

Fear seemed to grip Lady Brighthope's eyes for a moment. "I'm already risking much by being seen speaking with you in public." She took ahold of Kat's hand and squeezed. "Do be careful, Lady Kaitlyn," she said, an expression of intense urgency replacing the coyness normally present on her face. "I should hate to see anything happen to a woman as worthy as you, but the Chameleon is closer to you than you realize. *You* are in danger."

Chapter Thirty

Kaitlyn rode her horse over the field, the sprightly mare she'd been given for their trip into the village happily keeping abreast with the large stallion Marcus was riding beside her.

After she'd told him what Lady Brighthope had said, they'd both agreed that the information warranted following up, though as far as trusting the woman, well, that was another story entirely.

They'd rounded up Etta and Lucas, with Etta agreeing to keep watch on Lady Brighthope's movements, while Lucas would look out for Lord Newtown, which would then allow Kat and Marcus to ride covertly into the village to see if they could find this Charles Tremont fellow.

The ride into Bramsfield village wouldn't take them more than thirty minutes and would hopefully be quick and uneventful. They cantered through the dense forest bordering Newtown's lands, passing an abandoned hunting lodge before coming out onto an open field.

Marcus reined his horse to a halt and Kat did the same.

"The road to the village lies beyond the field

over that crest." Marcus pointed to the end of the stretch of grass. "Shall we race there?"

Kat peered across at him. "You want to race our horses? Like children do?"

He grinned broadly across at her. "Scared you can't win against me? Bearing in mind you're using a regular saddle and can't claim you were hampered by a side saddle."

She mimicked the duchess's deft arch of her brow and stared at the man. "This doesn't sound like the normally sensible Earl of Westwood. Who are you and what have you done with him?"

"Very funny," he drawled. "So, are you up for a race to the village or not?"

"Surely, by now, Marcus Black, you know I'm up for anything." She couldn't help but wink at him before she kicked back her heels on her horse's flanks and urged the horse into a gallop.

"You little cheat!" Marcus grumbled from behind her as she dashed ahead of him, the wind whipping her hair and a sense of freedom unlike anything she'd experienced in some time washing over her, filling her with joy and happiness.

She peered over her shoulder and laughed. He was trying to catch her, but she had a good head start. For the first time in a very long time, all of Kat's worries and fears disappeared, as she and Marcus raced. She stopped thinking about catching the Chameleon and began to simply enjoy racing through the fresh country air, an extremely determined Marcus trying to catch up.

Cooped up in London, as much as she loved the energy and how alive the very city itself was, she had missed the exhilaration of riding hell for leather. And racing Marcus was the icing on the cake. She'd never raced anyone before. Nor had she ever enjoyed anything as much before, either.

She glanced behind her and saw he was nearly upon her. "Come on, darling girl," she yelled to her horse. "Fly for me."

"I will catch you, Kaitlyn Montrose," Marcus yelled from behind. "I will always catch you!"

"You can try, Marcus Black," she yelled over her shoulder with a smile. "But I don't like your chances."

She could see the town's name sign up ahead only a hundred feet away, just as she saw the head of Marcus's horse edging up next to her from the corner of her eye.

"Come on, girl," she hollered. "We can beat them!"

A few seconds later, with the head of her horse passing the name sign a second before Marcus's, Kat won her first ever horse race.

She reined her horse to a halt and grinned at Marcus. "That was simply marvelous! We have to do it again another time."

Marcus pulled his horse next to hers. "You

are marvelous." And then his lips pressed down against her own, and he kissed her with such desire that Kat thought she might fall from her saddle, such was the delicious sensation shooting down her body from his touch. "I want you so badly," he murmured when he finally pulled his lips from hers. "Can you feel how I burn for you?"

He took her hand and placed it on his manhood, which was hot and hard as it strained against his pants.

Kat groaned. "I'm burning for you, too."

But then the reality of their situation hit when a farmer's cart lumbered past them, with the farmer driving the thing looking at them as if they were lunatics escaped from an asylum. Which she supposed wasn't too far from the truth, given what they were doing on a country road. She laughed aloud and Marcus grinned.

"This is the most fun I've had in a long time," she said, realizing just how true that was. "Thank you for giving me this. It's what I needed." She smiled slowly at him, and the most overwhelming feeling of caring for him came over her. Not only was she attracted to the man, she really liked him, too. "And thank you for letting me win. I've never won a horse race before."

"Let you win?" He arched his eyebrow. "You forget you gave yourself a decent head start, my dear, which was the only reason you did win.

Come on, we need to head into town and find this Tremont fellow."

He was right, and as they trotted down the country laneway leading into the village, they began to focus again on their purpose.

As they neared the main street, Kat pulled her cloak over her head, wishing to maintain her anonymity. It would not help if she were to be recognized, especially as she was unmarried and accompanying Marcus with no chaperone.

The inn itself was located in the heart of the village, which was a surprising hive of activity for a relatively small town. The villagers bustled in and out of the stores, cheerful expressions on their faces as they went about their business. In the center square was a cobblestone building, with a wooden sign hanging above the door, declaring it to be the Bramsfield Inn.

The inn was wedged between two other buildings, and even though it looked old, the windows sparkled and there was a new coat of paint along their sills and the wooden door. Some pots of flowers adorned both sides of the entrance, giving it an inviting feel.

Reining their horses to a halt in front of the inn, Marcus whistled to a stable boy from across the road and motioned him over. The young boy dashed across the street and took the stallion's reins as Marcus deftly dismounted, his boots landing lightly on the dirty street.

He walked over and helped Kat dismount. His hands reached up and circled her waist as he effortlessly picked her up from the saddle. His touch seemed to electrify her senses and he held onto her for a moment longer than was necessary, before setting her feet down on the street.

There was a burning heat in his gaze as he stared down hungrily at her. She gulped at the intensity and wicked promises in his stare, her heart starting to thunder in her chest.

Reluctantly, he moved his hands from her waist and cleared his throat. Kat was grateful he seemed physically as affected as she was from the contact, for the pulse in his throat throbbed.

He tossed the mare's reins over to the boy before throwing him a guinea, with instructions to look after the horses and keep them ready to be brought around.

The boy's face lit up as he caught the coin thrown to him. "They'll be the best looked after horses in the village! And don't worry, I'll keep 'em close," the boy said before turning and leading the horses back across the road to the stable house.

Marcus looked down at Kat. "Did that woman say anything about what to expect with this Tremont fellow?"

She shook her head. "Not a thing."

"Bloody Brighthope and her sense of the

theatrical," Marcus said. "The woman is a menace. I don't trust her as far as I can throw her."

Kat shrugged a shoulder. "True, but think of all of the information she's privy to. She'd be a tremendous informant for the *Gazette*."

Marcus scoffed. "You've got to be joking."

Kat pursed her lips. "That was essentially Etta's reaction, too."

"Etta's a lot smarter than anyone gives her credit for."

"I know," Kat said. "But the information Brighthope is privileged to, is unparalleled."

Marcus narrowed his eyes at her. "You have enough informants as it is that you don't need to bother getting immersed in Brighthope's world of intrigue and debauchery."

"I don't know… A little debauchery might be fun." She grinned at him. "Perhaps we can experience more of it ourselves together this weekend…"

"You're incorrigible, Kaitlyn Montrose. But I'm sure we can," he said, his voice nearly a growl. "But back to what I was saying, I'm serious, Brighthope has no morals. You should stay away from her."

"I'm well aware of her nature," Kat said. "But in capturing the Chameleon her purpose has aligned with ours, it would seem."

Marcus merely grunted as he began walking toward the entrance of the inn.

"I do admire her ability to captivate others," Kat continued, as she followed him to the door, "and you have to admit, she is beautiful."

He stopped with a hand on the handle and looked back at her. "Beauty is in the eye of the beholder. And trust me, that woman's beauty is all external, with no substance underneath. You're a thousand times more beautiful than she could ever wish to be."

For a moment, his words stopped her in her tracks. He thought she was more beautiful than the Siren? Her heart melted with the knowledge, and she couldn't help but grin.

Marcus turned the handle and pushed open the door. "Come along, let us see what surprise we may be walking into."

"Ye of little faith," Kat admonished as her grin turned into a cringe when she caught sight of a group of ladies and gentlemen walking toward them. She pulled up the hood of her cloak and all but pushed Marcus through the entrance of the inn. She closed the door shut and peeked out the window, watching as the group passed by, none the wiser.

"What was that about?" he asked.

She continued to watch as the group wandered down the street. "Some of the guests from Newtown's house party look to be partaking in a day trip. Oh goodness, Bertie and Brighthope are amongst them. So is the undersecretary. What is Sir Albert doing here?"

Marcus peered carefully out of the window. "He's trying to convince Bertie to leave. We don't want to have the heir to the throne anywhere near the vicinity of an assassination. Once he does convince him, Sir Albert will return to London with the prince. In the meantime, he's completely safe in amongst all of the prince's guards."

"Doesn't look like he's having much luck convincing Bertie, does it?" Kat remarked as she saw the undersecretary whisper something to the prince, only for the prince to vehemently shake his head.

Marcus shrugged. "Sir Albert can be highly persuasive, trust me."

They turned back to the interior of the inn. It was as well-kept as the exterior, with the floors spotless, and not a hint of dust to be seen on the furniture. There was a lovely little vase of flowers on the inn keeper's desk area to the right of the entry.

Marcus walked over to the alcove where a portly man with spectacles was issuing instructions to a maid. He looked up as they approached and smiled jovially.

"Welcome to the Bramsfield Inn," he said. "I'm Mr. Heffron, the proprietor of this establishment. How may I be of assistance?"

"A friend of mine, Charles Tremont, is a guest

here." The lie slipped off Marcus's tongue with smooth grace.

"I didn't know he was expecting more guests, my lord!" Mr. Heffron exclaimed. Then he looked uncomfortably over at them both. "He mentioned only one guest, I'm afraid, so I only prepared the private dining room with two settings. But not to worry." He hit the desk with enthusiasm. "Something that's easily remedied."

Kat looked across at Marcus and saw her own expression of consternation mirrored in his eyes. Tremont was meeting with somebody?

"If you both wish to follow me, I shall take you to the private dining area on the first floor where Mr. Tremont and his friend are luncheoning," Mr. Heffron continued. "Then I'll fetch an extra place setting for you both." He walked around his desk and motioned them to follow him up the stairs.

Marcus gave her an imperceptible shrug and they followed the innkeeper up the stairs to the first-floor landing and then down a corridor to the private dining room at the end of the hallway.

Mr. Heffron stopped outside of a door and rapped on the wood, but without waiting for a response, he opened the door wide and stepped into the room, with Kat and Marcus following behind.

Kat gasped. A gentleman wearing a blue day suit, with tousled blond hair and baby blue eyes was holding a dagger dripping with blood. He stood behind a man who sat in a chair, slumped face down on the dining table, a pool of crimson pulsing from his neck and staining the tablecloth beneath.

Mr. Heffron shrieked aloud.

The man with the knife smiled at them all before drawing his arm back and launching the dagger directly at them. Kat dove to the side, while Marcus pushed Mr. Heffron to the floor. The assailant's knife whizzed past where they'd been standing, landing with a loud thud in the corridor wall outside the door.

Glancing up, she saw the man launch himself through the open window. She scrambled up and over to the window, catching sight of the man landing in the shrubs beneath. "He's getting away!"

"Move!" Marcus yelled as he vaulted over the window sill and dropped down into the shrubbery below, then straightened and ran after the assailant.

Kat raced back to the man slumped over the table and checked for a pulse. Nothing. He was dead. She wiped the blood coating her fingers on her skirts before striding over to the innkeeper, who was still on the floor where Marcus had pushed him, staring dazedly at the body of the dead man on the table.

Bending down in front of him, she blocked his view from the sight. "Who was that man with the blond hair?"

Mr. Heffron peered up at her, his eyes completely blank for a moment. "Um... That was... Why that was Mr. Tremont's guest... I don't remember his name though..." Mr. Heffron wailed a moment before fainting.

A scream tore through the room. She glanced over to the doorway to see two maids standing there, one in hysterics and the other looking stricken. Kat stalked over to the women. She ignored the one screaming, instead focusing on the other.

The maid looked up at her, fear plastered over her face.

"Run and fetch the constable," Kat said in a loud and clear tone of voice. "Now!"

She watched as the maid scampered down the corridor, passing many nosey faces peeking out the doors of their own private dining rooms to see what all the fuss was about.

"A man has been murdered," Kat's voice rang out clearly down the corridor. "Stay in your rooms."

She hurried down the hallway toward the stairs, only to see Marcus striding up them. "He got away?"

He nodded tersely as he came to the top of the stairs. "He had a horse waiting for him and rode off before I could catch him." He angled his head down the corridor. "Is the man dead?"

"Yes. It was Mr. Tremont apparently."

"Damn it! Another senseless death." Marcus narrowed his eyes. "Well, let us go and see what the late Mr. Tremont and his room can reveal, and perhaps we can obtain justice for him."

Chapter Thirty-One

After the police constables had removed Mr. Tremont's body from the room, Marcus and Kat spent the next half an hour sifting through the late man's lodgings, but found nothing that would assist in either revealing the Chameleon's identity or exactly how he was going to make an attempt on Lord Newtown's life.

All they discovered was a small suitcase containing some men's clothes, shoes, and toiletry items, and a lone violin leaning against Tremont's trunk. Nothing to suggest Tremont was an assassin or at all immersed in a world of cloak and daggers.

Marcus felt the usual frustration at being too late roll around inside him. Damn it, if they'd only been a few minutes earlier, they might have saved the man's life.

Mr. Tremont's pockets hadn't been all that forthcoming either. He'd had little in the way of interest in them, except for a business card in his bill fold to none other than the Corinthian Club. Though what the man had been doing in Bramsfield and what role he was potentially meant to have played in the events unfolding was anyone's guess.

The innkeeper was too traumatized to say much apart from what a nice fellow Mr. Tremont had been and that he'd checked into the inn two days ago under extremely positive circumstances. The man had apparently been ecstatic about a new job offer.

From the corner of his eyes, through the windowpane, he saw Sir Albert climb into his carriage to depart for London to make some more inquiries on Mr. Tremont and how he was linked to this whole mess. Marcus had given Sir Albert a quick briefing only a short time ago, and the man had used that information to finally convince the Prince to return to London posthaste, though his companion Lady Brighthope had insisted on staying for the festivities. The woman did seem to thrive on the dangerous.

The local constabulary had sent patrols through the village and neighboring countryside to look for the assailant, but it appeared he'd long since vanished.

The man's face was vivid in Marcus's head. Had they just seen the Chameleon? Was that the man who killed Elizabeth and played a part in framing his brother as a traitor? Frustration rolled through him like a freight train.

Unable to help himself, he walked over to the door of the room and slammed his fist into the wood, the action helping to release some of the

pent-up anger inside him, though it did send a jolt
of pain down his forearm, damn it.

"Are you all right?" Kat asked as she finished
looking through the man's trunk.

"No, I bloody well am not." He couldn't seem
to control the restless energy surging through him.
"We nearly had him, Kat! But he slipped through
our fingers again." Marcus clicked his fingers. "Just
like that, he was here, then he was gone."

She walked over to where he stood by the
door and placed a calming hand on his arm. "Trust
me, I've thought of nothing else since. He fit the
description Sir William gave to us of the man who
attempted to kill him."

"I know."

"We will catch him," Kat replied. "Though, we
need to get back before we're missed, and a good
ride will help."

Yes. He needed some exercise to get rid of this
sense of listlessness and bitter disappointment that
rolled around his mouth like a sour grape.

A few minutes later, after they'd mounted
their horses, they cantered out of the village just
as dark clouds began to sweep in overhead like a
perfect reflection of Marcus's mood.

"Do you think that was the Chameleon?" she
asked, glancing back over her left shoulder at him
as they made their way through the woods back to
Newtown's estate.

Marcus sighed. "I don't know. A face is easy to disguise but one's stature is not. He certainly fits the size of the man Sir William described, but he's a great deal larger than the waiter at the opera."

Kat pursed her lips. "Yes, I'd made that same observation, which begs the question, is the Chameleon working with others? And if that's the case, then we are well and truly in the dark."

Marcus's face was stormy. "We need to get more answers from that damn woman again, and this time she'll be wise not to refuse to answer them. We need to know the name of her client." Brighthope knew more than just the man's identity, Marcus would place money on it.

A flash of lighting illuminated the trees surrounding them, and was quickly followed by a crack of thunder that rumbled through the forest. A second later, heavy drops of rain began to pelt down from the heavens above.

Marcus pulled up his horse alongside her own. "We can't stay in this."

"There was that old hunting lodge not far away," Kat said. "We could seek shelter there."

He nodded in agreement, waiting for Kat to precede him, before he too urged his horse forward through the downpour.

About five minutes later, they arrived at the abandoned lodge, dripping wet and cold to the bone. There was a rather dilapidated thatched stable leaning to the side of the cottage, which they rode their horses into. It provided a reasonable amount of protection from the storm, though still had several leaks in its roof, which the rain poured through.

Marcus dismounted, his coat plastered to him and dripping wet puddles on the rough earth beneath as he tied up his stallion and then helped Kat dismount. She quickly began to tie her horse up while Marcus strode over to the main hunting lodge to check it was safe. He opened the door and peered inside. Apart from not having been used in years, with covers on everything and an inch or two of dust everywhere, it looked fine.

"All clear," he hollered to Kat and then motioned her inside.

She ran out from the shelter and splashed through the mud-covered ground, before dashing inside the cottage.

Following her inside, Marcus closed the door behind him. As with the stable, the roof of the cottage had seen better days and the sound of water dripping onto the wooden floor echoed around the space. From the shape of the furniture under the dust covers, it looked as if there was a table in the center of the room, with some chairs underneath, and in the far corner was the outline of a bed.

Suddenly, the gravity of the situation hit him. He was alone, in an abandoned cottage with

Kaitlyn Montrose, without any rubber sheaths to offer protection.

He was in trouble. Big trouble.

• • •

"I saw some wood outside in the stable," Marcus abruptly said before he cleared his throat. "I'll get some to start a fire. We need to dry off before we catch a chill."

Kat watched as he stood staring at her for a moment, before abruptly turning toward the door and stalking outside, almost as if a band of cutthroats were on his tail.

He must really be cold, then as she glanced around the room, she became aware of the intimacy of the location. Surrounded by a storm, with not a person around for miles, except for her and Marcus. She glanced down at her clothes, which were plastered to her skin from the rain.

Hmm, perhaps she could take advantage of the situation? After all, she'd been craving to be with him again, but everything had been so hectic she'd been doubtful they'd get another chance, at least not until they'd apprehended the Chameleon.

She walked over and began removing the dust covers from the lounge beside the fireplace. She caught sight of a double bed in the far corner of the room.

The door creaked behind her and she glanced at Marcus as he stepped over the threshold carrying a pile of kindling and wood in his arms. He'd managed to use his coat to shield most of it from the downpour.

He followed her gaze to where she'd been looking and a dark glare fell over his face. She also thought she heard him swear softly under his breath, though wasn't certain. Without looking at her, he walked straight to the fireplace and began loading it with what was in his arms. Once he'd stacked the wood and kindling into a small pile in the hearth, he stood and plucked a box of tinder from off the mantel and set to work lighting the fire.

The man didn't look back at her the entire time.

It was rather strange, as she'd thought he'd also want to take full advantage of such a situation. She'd have to fix that. She unbuttoned the top clasp of her cloak and dragged the dripping garment from her shoulders. The rain had soaked through the fabric of her dress and chemise, all the way through to her skin.

Even her boots squelched with water as she padded over to the small kitchen area, while Marcus lit the fire. She draped her cloak over a chair and then bent down and unlaced her black leather boots before pulling them from her stocking-clad legs.

The soft sound of wood crackling was a

welcome one, and she looked over to see Marcus standing next to the hearth, doing all he could not to look at her, it seemed.

He pulled out his pocket watch and stared down at its face. "Ten past four. Even if the rain continues for a while, we should still have plenty of time to get back in time for dinner, with no one the wiser of our predicament."

"And just what predicament is that?" Kat asked as she slowly began unbuttoning the small buttons at the front of her jacket. "I consider our situation fortuitous."

"What are you doing?" His voice was slightly hoarse.

"What does it look like?" She raised an eyebrow but continued with the process. "I'm taking your advice."

"I never told you to take your clothes off," he practically groaned.

"You told me not to catch a chill, and I'm soaking wet and starting to get cold," Kat said with a hint of exasperation. "Stop being such a prude. You should take your clothes off, too."

"I don't have any rubber sheaths with me," he whispered under his breath. "And unlike last time, I don't see you carrying your reticule with one inside."

"We'll adapt." She eyed his dripping pants and shirt, and the growing puddle of water on the floor where he stood. "Now start undressing. We can't afford for you to catch a chill, either."

"Are you always so bossy?"

She grinned over at him. "You know I am." But then a thought stopped her cold. "Don't you want to continue our affair?"

He frowned fiercely back at her. "Of course I damn well do. But sometimes I can't control myself with you. My body is addicted to yours, and in all truth, that scares me."

"I'm glad to hear it." She grinned at him while she finished unbuttoning the jacket of her riding habit and peeled it off. Then she pulled open the snap studs on her special skirt and tugged it away from her body, revealing a pair of her specially tailored black trousers beneath, which hadn't been spared the brunt of the downpour.

"This isn't amusing, Kaitlyn." He stomped over to the hearth and yanked his jacket off. "What if you fell pregnant from our escapades?"

"Are there ways to prevent a pregnancy without rubber sheaths?" She draped her skirt over one of the chairs in the kitchen area.

"Yes." He reluctantly tugged off his waistcoat before beginning to unbutton his white shirt.

Her eyes were drawn to the thatch of dark hair on his chest as the fabric of the shirt was slowly removed. She turned around quickly, looking away from the sight. As much as she'd teased him, seeing his flesh in the broad light of day was more than she'd expected. And she realized he'd soon be seeing her naked in daylight, too. The thought was disconcerting, but not in an unpleasant way. "Then all will be fine, won't it?"

Marcus grunted, now completely bare chested.

His arm and chest muscles were a sight to behold, especially with the flames from the hearth casting a golden glow across them. She wanted nothing more than to run her hands across the expanse of his chest once again, her fingers trailing over every muscle on his body.

The man was hard muscle all over. Not an ounce of flabbiness on his finely-crafted form. Her hands trembled as her gaze travelled down the mane of his chest hair, which tapered down and disappeared in a line past the belt buckle of his pants.

Never one to be patient, Kat approached Marcus where he stood. He sucked in a deep breath when she stopped a foot from him, his eyes seemingly glued to her chest. Following his gaze, she could see that through her wet chemise, the buds of her nipples were pressing tightly against the material, the rose color of them visible through the wet garment.

"You're still not wearing a corset?"

"I have no need to." She shrugged. "Madame Arnout sews the boning into all of my tops, or in this case my riding jacket. It maintains the shape but doesn't restrict me as much."

"This is not a good idea," he muttered, still unable to look away from her chest.

Kat felt a wonderful sense of her own power as a woman. She pushed her chest out slightly and he groaned. "You said you don't need a sheath to protect us, so I intend to take advantage of you." Kat pulled her chemise over her head, exposing her naked breasts to him. It had been different the first time with him, as that had been in the depth of night. This was in the bright light of day. "Who knows when we'll get another chance?"

He gulped, his eyes feasting on her breasts. "Why am I even bothering to resist?"

"I really don't know."

"Neither do I." With a hoarse moan, Marcus took two steps toward her and pulled her into his arms. His mouth crashed down hungrily onto her own as he began kissing her with barely restrained passion.

Kat reached her hands up and wound them around his neck, pulling him in even closer against her. Opening her mouth, she met his tongue with her own, matching him thrust for thrust. She pressed her naked breasts up against his chest and marveled at the feel of his chest hair rubbing against her nipples.

He cupped her bottom and pulled her snug against him. Kat could feel the hard length of him through his pants. But that was not nearly good enough. She fumbled for the buttons of his trousers, and slowly pulled them away from their button holes, one by one, until she was able to pull his trousers down and over his hips.

His manhood stood proud before her, a thick smooth shaft begging to be touched. She couldn't resist, and her fingers drifted across the hard length of him. "You've missed me."

Marcus groaned, his cock leaping in response. "You invade my dreams every night."

Emboldened by his words, she began stroking her hand across him, marveling at his smooth silkiness. Her very touch elicited a deep growl of pleasure from him.

Before she knew what was happening, he scooped her up into his arms and strode over to the bed. He set her down gently onto her feet, before quickly grabbing ahold of the dust cover and pulling it aside. Some dust flew into the air and Kat laughed.

Marcus grinned back at her, before lifting her into his arms again, and carrying her over, placing her down on the bed with care. He lay next to her and his eyes met hers. "Do you know how hard you make me? How much I want you?"

"I feel the same." She brought her lips to his as she reached for her trousers and began to pull them off, to which he helped.

She moaned when his hand slid down the side of her now naked body, to rest between her legs. His fingers stroked her while he eased his lips from hers and began nuzzling her neck with his mouth.

She arched her body as one of his fingers teased its way into her passage and his thumb rubbed on the little bud at the juncture of her womanhood. The usual sense of overwhelming wonder came over her, like it had the last time. Her hips slowly gyrated against his hand.

His mouth travelled lower and trailed kisses over her chest, before he took one of her nipples into his mouth. Her skin prickled with thousands of bumps and she couldn't help but moan.

Marcus raised his head and gazed down across her body. "So beautiful. I've never wanted another woman more," he muttered, before he lowered his head to her other breast, eagerly paying it the same attention as he had the other.

Before she knew what he was about, Marcus pulled his mouth away from her breast and lowered his head between her thighs, his mouth now replacing where his hand had just been stroking. Kat nearly bolted off the bed as she felt his lips kiss her very center, his tongue flicking lightly across her flesh.

She moaned loudly as the feel of his lips devouring her sent a sensation of pure pleasure surging through her entire body. Her hands gripped his hair, urging him even closer against her. Kat felt a deep pressure building up inside her as the last vestiges of her control began to slip away.

"No, don't stop," she said when he tore his mouth from her, but was quickly silenced as he raised himself over her and his mouth returned to her lips, whilst his hard shaft pushed into her passageway. "I thought you didn't have a sheath."

He stopped kissing her and looked into her eyes. "I don't, but as long as I pull out before I spill my seed, it should be fine. Is that all right?" he asked her, his voice sounding strained. "If you want me to stop, I can. Just tell me."

"Don't you dare stop. I've been looking forward to having you inside me again for days." She wrapped her legs around his waist and arched herself against him, forcing him inside of her.

He began to thrust in and out of her, which she met with equal vigor. Urging her body closer, she knew she was on the edge of that delicious precipice he always took her to.

"That's it, my darling."

"Marcus," she cried as he plunged into her again and a deep pressure in her center built to the point she thought she was going to burst. She could feel him starting to pull out, but she gripped his shoulders with both hands, her nails pressing down hard into his skin. "Stay inside me," she begged as wave after wave of rapture began to cascade through her, and her whole body began to convulse around him as he groaned and continued to pump inside her.

A tingling wave of satisfaction burst within her as Marcus collapsed on top of her, his breath ragged and his body hot.

It felt as if she was a million miles away, floating high above everything, yet his body pressed against hers was a warm and gentle anchor returning her awareness to him. She wrapped her arms around him and felt his pounding heartbeat thrumming through his chest.

Having him inside of her was bliss, and his strength and heat calmed her as nothing else had in a long time. But then he gently pushed her away from him and sat up. She caught a glimpse of his face and realized he was wearing a frown, a very deep and cold frown. "What's wrong?"

"I just came inside you."

"Oh…" She had begged him to. "Yes, that was my fault, I didn't want to lose the feeling of you inside me."

"I'll make the announcement tonight."

"The announcement?" She had a very bad feeling with where he was headed with this.

"That we are engaged." His words brooked no argument. "I'll obtain a special license and we can marry within a few days."

It took her a moment to fully comprehend

him. "No. We most certainly will not!" She jumped out of the bed and stalked over to where her clothes had been tossed to the floor. With sharp motions, she pulled them on, knowing she wouldn't feel comfortable arguing with him while she was naked. And argue they were definitely about to do. "I'm not marrying you because you spilled your seed inside of me."

From where he sat on the edge of the bed, Marcus regarded her steadily. "You could be pregnant because of it."

"Surely not just from one instance." She shook her head vigorously.

"It only takes the one time," he bit out. "We will marry and that's the end of it."

"You said you never wanted to marry again."

"And I don't. But I will marry you after what I just did."

She couldn't marry. If he ever found out the truth of her parentage, he'd never forgive her, or the scandal she could bring upon him. It would be like a cloud hanging over their heads. And she refused to lose her independence for any man, not even Marcus.

A long, heavy sigh came from his direction as she shoved her chemise on and then pulled her drawers and pants over her thighs. She glanced at him as he stood, but unlike her, he seemed comfortable arguing with her while nude.

For a second, she found herself distracted as she drank in the sight of him fully naked. She tamped down on the ridiculously feminine sensations she was beginning to feel simply from gazing at him. Surely, she was more sensible than to be overcome by looking at a male form. Even if his form was fine indeed.

Shaking her head, she narrowed her eyes and made herself stare directly into his eyes, and only his eyes. She wouldn't allow herself to be distracted, which she had a feeling he knew full well his nakedness caused. "I told you I was prepared to have a liaison with you, not marry you. Besides, I'm sure it will be fine," Kat said, praying it would be so. She turned and collected her damp skirt from the chair, then walked over to the fireplace, and stood in front of it, holding her skirt aloft in an effort to dry it and the trousers she was wearing.

"It's not fine," he growled, stooping and picking up his clothes, too. "You will marry me, Kaitlyn Montrose, and that is that."

The man needed a lesson that she was not one of his servants to be bossed around. She arched an eyebrow. "I will not marry you, Marcus Black. And you can't demand that I will and expect me to happily acquiesce to your proclamation."

"When have you bloody ever acquiesced to anything I've told you to do? Never! That is when."

"Well, then," she pertly responded. "It should

come as no surprise that I will not do so now either. Why you are even trying to push the matter, I do not know."

"You're impossible," he grumbled. "What if you are pregnant?"

"Then we shall reassess the situation."

He pulled on his trousers, his movements rough and hasty. "If you are with child, then we will marry, regardless of what we want."

His words unexpectedly tugged at her heart. She knew he didn't want to marry her but hearing him say so was another thing. It was only out of some misplaced sense of honor that he was demanding they marry. Well, she'd never marry anyone because of such a reason. Never.

Wrapping her skirt over her trousers, she clipped up the studs before walking across to where she'd draped her bodice over the chairs. Caring little about the damp material, she stuck her arms through the sleeves and did up the buttons on its front. Then she retrieved her boots and put them on, the wetness of everything only adding to her annoyance.

"What are you doing?" Marcus asked. "It's still raining."

"I'd rather put up with a thunderstorm," she continued, pulling her cloak from the chair and swinging it on over her shoulders, "than endure listening to your preposterous demands and edicts for a moment longer."

"Prep—for goodness sakes, I'm trying to do the right thing here, and you call it preposterous." He shook his head in resignation. "Run away all you like, but this conversation is not finished."

Stopping on her way to the front door, she glanced back at him. "I'm not running away. Instead, I'm leaving before your arrogance and high-handed manner cause me to do something I might regret. I have a temper, you know."

He laughed. "As if I did not already know that!"

She narrowed her eyes at him. "Perhaps then you should continue to remember my temper and the fact that I'm usually armed, and how annoying it would be to live with, day in and day out, if you continue to insist upon marriage!"

And with that, she stormed out the door and slammed it behind her.

There, that showed him.

She marched over to her horse, caring little for the rain washing over her as rage fueled her each and every step. Demand they marry, would he? The man had clearly underestimated who he was dealing with, so she was just going to have to show him how unsuited to marriage she really was.

And while she did that, she was also going to have to continue to remind herself quite sternly of that fact, too, because suddenly the idea of marrying Marcus wasn't so repulsive at all.

Chapter Thirty-Two

A few hours later, after Kat had warmed up with a hot bath and dressed in new clothes, she stood staring into the dressing table mirror and narrowed her eyes. She truly was a woman of the world now after having been with Marcus a third time.

Hmm… She looked exactly the same. Perhaps there was more of a sparkle in her eyes, but that was more likely lingering anger over his earlier edict, than truly appearing any worldlier than when she'd last looked at her reflection this morning.

Rather disappointing actually.

Oh well. She shrugged to herself. There were a great deal more important things to do tonight than to dwell on whether or not one could tell she'd been thoroughly ravished for the third time in as many days.

A gentle flush crept up her cheeks at the thought of seeing Marcus again. How was she to maintain a calm composure and look him in the eyes in the clear light of day after what they'd done that afternoon? Every time she even thought about it, which was nearly every second since his terse goodbye as they'd parted ways upon returning to the stables, she felt the weirdest sensation tingle through her.

The rapture and pleasure she'd experienced from his touch, his kiss, his being inside her again, had been even more marvelous than she could have imagined possible. And then he'd gone and ruined it with his talk of marriage. The blasted man.

Sucking in a deep breath, she turned away from her own reflection. There was time enough to be annoyed with him later, for now she had to return her attention to the matters at hand. Hurrying over to her trunk, she opened up the secret compartment and pulled out her dagger roll, then spread it out onto the bed.

She raised her right leg onto the foot stool, swept up the skirt of her gown, and placed one of the smaller daggers in the sheath already strapped at her ankle, underneath her trousers. She lowered her foot before selecting another knife, and then slid it into a portable sheath tucked into one of her skirt's hidden pockets.

Straightening, she smoothed down her gown and gave a nod of satisfaction. That would do nicely. She rolled up her dagger roll and deftly tied the ribbon to secure it, before returning it to her trunk. But then she stopped. She wasn't alone.

"I hope you don't intend to threaten me with your daggers again," a deep voice rumbled from behind.

Kat stilled and took in a deep breath before turning to see Nathaniel lounging against the back of the bedchamber door. He was dressed in footman livery, wearing a wig, along with some face padding that fleshed out his cheeks. "Your disguise won't be enough to fool Marcus if he sees you."

"I know. I had to be careful coming here." He straightened from the door and walked a few steps toward her.

"What are you doing here?" Kat searched his face.

"I've heard the Chameleon may attempt to get Newtown this weekend."

Kat walked over to him and before he could blink, she simultaneously pushed him back against the wall, while pulling out her dagger and pressing the blade up to his throat. "I know about Irena, and how you think Victor is responsible for her death. Did you pay the Chameleon to kill Victor?" Part of her was terrified of his answer, knowing that if he had done so, she was going to be faced with an impossible decision.

Slowly, a sad half smile crossed his face. "Would you kill me if I did?"

Her whole chest tightened. "*Did* you?"

"No. Though I thought about killing him several times while I was lying in that hospital bed." He took in a deep breath. "For the longest time, I blamed him for setting the bomb that killed Irena."

"Victor would never have done that. He would never have killed an innocent."

"He would have always done what he had to if it served the greater good."

"No, he wouldn't. Victor was ruthless, but he had limits." Kat knew that to the bottom of her soul.

"You've always been blind when it comes to your uncle's virtues," Nathaniel said.

"Perhaps. And perhaps I've been blinded by others around me. You, for example." She pressed her knife closer to his skin, nicking the flesh a little. "Somewhat of a coincidence, isn't it, that the Chameleon has been paid to kill men who all had something to do with your downfall, and then you show up, arisen from the dead?"

Nathaniel pressed his lips together. "I'm back because I heard whispers that the man who set me up had hired the Chameleon to clean up shop. And, yes, some on the list do deserve to die."

With a scoff that couldn't hide her disgust, she lowered her dagger and stepped back from him. "Are you the Chameleon, Nathaniel?" Nothing would surprise her at the moment. After all, the Chameleon was rumored to be a ghost, and here Nathaniel was, back from the dead.

"No. The Chameleon is someone I'm probably going to have to kill." There was such simplicity in his statement and Kat reluctantly believed him.

"You'll have to get in line, because that's what

I'll be doing." She re-sheathed her dagger. "Why do you want him dead?"

"The Chameleon was working as a Russian agent and helped the true traitor frame me. Actually, I think it was probably the Chameleon's idea to do so to get me away from Irena, who the Chameleon loved. Which is why I want both the Chameleon and the traitor to suffer for what they did. I want to destroy them both as they destroyed me. And I have a feeling the traitor is someone at the top of the War Office."

"Surely not. Sir William and Sir Albert are as true to Britain as I've ever seen." She'd seen them both in action now, and they didn't strike her as willing to sell secrets to the Russians. Though, one never fully knew a person, she knew that. "And Danbury is simply too stupid to concoct such a plan."

"You're probably right about Danbury, but I think you're seeing Sir Albert and Sir William too kindly, for both have made ruthless decisions in the past." Nathaniel dragged a hand through his hair, reminding her so much of Marcus for a moment that she had to look away. Even thinking of him, she felt guilty knowing she was talking to his brother and he had no idea. Keeping such information from him did not sit well at all.

"Sir William was the one to believe Burton when he presented the supposed evidence to him of my guilt," Nathaniel continued. "And Sir

William isn't one you can pull the wool over his eyes. Perhaps he is the true traitor?"

Everything inside her rebelled at the thought. "No. I've worked with Sir William. He was one of Victor's closest friends and a true patriot. He wouldn't betray England. He wouldn't have laid the blame at your feet."

"A man will do almost anything to protect himself, Kat." There was sorrow in his eyes. "You know that. Not to mention if Danbury and Sir Albert are killed, he'll be in charge of the whole War Office. Such power in the hands of a man with such a network of intelligence operatives behind him… He'd be unstoppable."

A knock at the door startled them both. "One moment," she called out, as she grabbed Nathaniel and pulled him over to her window. "You must let no one see you, at least not until you tell Marcus you're alive first." She opened the window and motioned to the tree branch. "Shimmy down that and go find Marcus and tell him you're alive. The three of us can work this all out."

He stood stubbornly in front of the window, making no move to leave. "I can't tell him, Kat. I won't, not until I can exonerate myself."

"He doesn't believe you're a traitor," she whispered harshly to him. "And if you don't tell him, I will."

"Just give me a day or two, all right?"

"Why?"

"Because I'm hoping that's all I'll need to catch the traitor. I'm very close."

The knock sounded again.

"My lady? Is something wrong?" It was her maid Bess yelling through the wood.

"Just another moment!" She glanced back at Nathaniel. "Two days and that's all. Now go."

He nodded, then turned and began shimmying down the branch.

She closed the window and snapped her curtains shut before hurrying over to open the door. "Yes, Bess, what is it?" She hoped the smile on her face at least looked somewhat real, when inside she felt as if she were knotted up.

"Miss Merriweather has a headache and has decided not to attend the ball, my lady," Bess said, stepping into the room. "She said to go down without her."

"Okay, thank you, Bess." But instead of leaving, the girl still stood there, peering at her rather oddly. "Was there something else?"

"It's just, my lady, I heard the most ridiculous rumor belowstairs."

"What did you hear?"

"That you're engaged, my lady, to the Earl of Westwood."

A few minutes later, with thoughts of killing Marcus firmly in her mind, Kat marched downstairs to the ballroom and through the gathered guests.

"Clearly, my chaperone skills need work," the Dragon Duchess's precise tones enunciated to Kat's left, "if you've gone and gotten yourself engaged in the space of an afternoon ride in the woods."

The woman tapped her cane on the marble floor in a militant fashion as Kat swiveled around to face her. The duchess appeared decidedly unimpressed, with a haughty brow raised and her lips pursed in a thin line, but there was also a hint of curiosity, with perhaps even amusement, buried in the woman's gaze. "You've heard wrong, Duchess. I'm not engaged."

"Hmph." The duchess shrugged. "That is not what I am hearing, but we shall see, I suppose. Now, where is that girl, Miss Merriweather?" She peered over Kat's shoulder into the throng of the crowd.

"Apparently, she has a headache and has decided to stay abed."

"A headache?" Her voice bristled. "That simply will not do, for I intended for her and Cantfield to entertain me."

"Entertain you? All they do is bicker with each other." Perhaps that was the amusement the duchess was referring to? The woman did, after all, have an unusual sense of humor.

"For someone so observant with nearly everything in your surrounds, you are blind when it comes to emotions, my dear girl." The duchess shook her head and sighed. "They bicker as they are attracted to each other. Like I mentioned earlier."

"Etta can't stand rakes such as Cantfield. She's not attracted to him, she hates him."

"Care to make a wager on that?" the old lady asked, a hint of challenge in her eyes. "You see I'm getting rather good at assisting couples of late."

"I knew you were trying to play matchmaker." The very idea that the Dragon Duchess was trying her hand at assisting couples to find love was as confusing to Kat as it was amusing.

"I've done extremely well at it lately." The duchess smiled smugly. "Just look at my darling niece, Livie. She and Colver have turned out to be a perfect match. In any event, I shall go and check on Miss Merriweather, that is if you can keep out of trouble for a little bit?"

"I think I can manage it." Kat smiled back at the woman, making certain the sarcasm was clear in her voice.

The duchess merely raised an eyebrow. "Well, you supposedly got engaged when I left you alone for a few hours today. Who's to say when I return in ten minutes you won't be married? Or, knowing you, more likely arrested for killing the earl for daring to spread such a tale."

And with that, the duchess inclined her head regally to Kat, before gracefully turning and striding from the ballroom, her cane clipping on the floor as she departed.

The woman was right on that account; when Kat found Marcus she was going to strangle him. Perhaps not actually strangle the man, but give him a piece of her mind.

Returning her attention to the ballroom, Kat scanned the assembly and spotted Lord Newtown fawning over several of his guests near the far balcony doors, to the right of the small chamber orchestra.

The host himself was dressed in the height of fashion, wearing jet black tails, with a bright red silk waistcoat and an ivory, starched shirt underneath. The man's trousers had a trim of military red ribbon on their outer seams, that matched his waistcoat.

"Do you notice how he surrounds himself with men?" Lady Brighthope's smooth voice held a hint of derision. "Do you wonder why that is?"

Kat turned around and saw the woman watching her with rather assessing eyes. "If you haven't managed to charm him, Lady Brighthope, then I suspect he keeps their company as he must prefer men over ladies."

Lady Brighthope laughed aloud. "Shame that a man who dresses so well prefers other men. He would have been a lovely trophy to add to my mantel. But aren't you a clever little cat, deducing that."

"Just an observant one," Kat replied.

The woman grinned. "But what about an

adventurous one, my dear?" Blatantly, she began looking Kat up and down, a gleam in her eye. "You would make a wonderful courtesan." Lady Brighthope winked at her. "Especially with your interesting skillset."

Kat raised an eyebrow. "I must say that is the first time someone has suggested such a thing." She didn't know whether to be flattered or insulted.

The woman laughed as she casually brought up her hand and placed it on Kat's upper arm. "You have no idea of the power you can hold over a man in such a position." She then leaned forward and whispered in her ear, "I could teach you everything you'd need to know about how to seduce and pleasure a man until he worships the very ground you walk on, and would do anything for you. I'm sure it would help secure Westwood's affections. A little nudge with the right techniques and you'd have him eating out of your palm until he was but a lovestruck fool."

The idea of love was terrifying. Whenever Kat had loved someone, they died. "I don't want him to love me."

"Lust, then." The woman waved her hand around. "Whatever you want to call it. But I can teach you how to make him burn for you. Worship you, to the point of obsession."

Reluctantly, she was intrigued with idea. "How would you teach me such things?"

Lady Brighthope's hand stroked down Kat's arm for a moment. "I would pleasure you myself, of course."

Kat sucked in a deep breath and hastily stepped away from her.

Lady Brighthope laughed. "You look so delightfully shocked. Women pleasure each other all the time, my dear. Did you not do so in finishing school?"

Kat shook her head firmly. "Certainly not!"

The woman shrugged one of her dainty shoulders. "What a shame. You missed out on such fun. Are you certain you aren't at all interested in my proposition? A female is so much softer and more sensual than a man. I think you and I could enjoy each other a great deal."

Kat could only stare at the woman. Was she playing with her, or was she serious? Obviously, Kat knew women did such things together, but it was not something she herself had ever contemplated.

"What proposition would that be?" Marcus's deep voice echoed from behind them.

Swiveling, Kat saw him standing there, a scowl on his face as he glanced between her and Lady Brighthope. The thought that perhaps he'd overhead their conversation filled her with mortification and her cheeks reddened with the memories of the woman's scandalous offer. How was she to explain such a thing to him? She simply wouldn't.

Some things a man did not need to know.

"It is nothing, my lord," Kat replied curtly.

The man was resplendent in his evening regalia. Unlike the other men, he was dressed in all black except for his crisp white shirt. Kat felt herself aching to be pulled into his arms and kissed senseless by him. But then she remembered how annoyed she was with him.

"Nothing?" he asked, his whole body stiffening a fraction. "I rather think it is something when a courtesan is speaking to my fiancée about propositions."

"I'm not your fiancée," she furiously whispered up at him. "And if you keep saying so, I will happily knee you in the bollocks again, right here, in front of everyone. Do you understand me?"

"Oh dear," Lady Brighthope tittered. "Perhaps I should let you two lovers sort out your tiff in private."

"You're not going anywhere, Lady Brighthope." Marcus motioned his head behind her to the two men that had made their way to stand behind the two women. "If you do not cooperate and follow me and Lady Kaitlyn down the corridor and into the library, these men will escort you there by force."

Lady Brighthope gasped. "Once Bertie hears of what you have subjected me—"

"Bertie is aware of my intent, my lady,"

Marcus stated, his voice entirely matter-of-fact. "Who do you think authorized these men from the War Office to assist me tonight?"

Lady Brighthope stood with her mouth slightly agape. "Assist you with what?"

"To do whatever I must to keep Lord Newtown alive, madam. And if that includes assisting me to get you to talk, then so be it."

"You would not dare force anything from me!"

"Trust me, I would," Marcus stated blandly, motioning with his arm for her to precede him out of the ballroom entrance.

The look in his eyes must have convinced the lady, as she gave a somewhat stilted nod and began walking out of the room, her head held at a high angle as though she was carrying a stack of books on her head.

"You." Marcus pointed to the closest of the two. "Follow her and make sure she goes straight to the library." He turned to the other man. "You, go and keep a watch over Newtown, I shall return after questioning Lady Brighthope."

The men nodded and went to do as Marcus directed, while Marcus himself looked at Kat with weary yet possessive eyes.

"After you, my lady," he said, motioning toward the door. "For I assume you intend to come while I question Brighthope."

"Of course I do. But don't think for a moment

you will not pay for spreading false engagement rumors." She narrowed her eyes and gave him her fiercest glare, before sweeping from the room, too. As if she wouldn't wish to be present, and he knew that fact perfectly well, too. The cad.

She walked down the corridor and into the library. The room wasn't really what Kat would have called a library so much as a space designed to show off Lord Newtown's somewhat ostentatious and scandalous volumes of erotic literature, if the titles she passed stacked in the bookshelves lining the room were any indication.

And now perched on one of the dainty silver armchairs, matching the silver motifs adorning the room, Lady Brighthope sat, a look of acute irritation on her beautiful features.

Her brows snapped together as she caught sight of Kat and Marcus crossing the threshold. Marcus nodded to the man, who left the room and closed the door behind him.

"What do you want from me?" Lady Brighthope wasted no time in coming to the point once the man had left. "I've told you what I can."

"You have told us what you want us to know," Marcus responded as he came to a halt several feet from her. "No more games, Brighthope. What did that fellow Tremont have to do with the Chameleon attempting to assassinate Lord Newtown?"

"I do not know," Lady Brighthope declared

as she stood and threw her hands up into the air. "Truly I do not! All I know is that I heard his name being linked to Newtown for the house party this weekend." She looked at both Kat and Marcus, her eyes beseeching them to believe her. "Surely, you found something to link him."

"Not a thing," Marcus drawled.

"That's not my fault!"

"Who did you hear this information from?" Kat asked.

Lady Brighthope's eyes swung around to Kat; they were filled with fear. "You know I can't betray a client, but more than that…if this one finds out that I was snooping and overheard him, he will kill me, and I do mean literally."

Kat believed her. The woman obviously had to be a good actor in her profession, but the terror in her eyes was real. "Lady Brighthope, please, you must help us. You seem to be the only one who knows at least partially what is going on."

"We can assure your safety," Marcus added.

"Please!" Lady Brighthope scoffed. "You cannot even keep members of the peerage safe. Why would you even care about a lowly courtesan who sleeps with men for money?"

"If he says he will keep you safe, he will." Kat walked over and stood across from her.

"Like he kept his wife safe from the Chameleon?"

Kat saw Marcus's whole body stiffen.

Lady Brighthope turned and looked at Kat. "Did you know that she was stabbed to death in her bed, by her lover? That he"—she turned and nodded her head in Marcus's direction—"was too busy with his government position to even realize his wife was having an affair, and with a spy, no less? And then apparently when he found her dead, he shed no tears? Does that not concern you, that you have become attached to a man so cold and clinical? You can see why I would be somewhat dubious when he offers me his protection."

"Of course I know all of that," Kat replied. "But with the Great Game with Russia, naturally his attentions were elsewhere. An honorable woman would have understood that, instead of seeking solace elsewhere. The late countess did not deserve to have any tears shed over her, especially not from the man she betrayed."

Lady Brighthope seemed taken aback before she started laughing. "Oh, I do see why you two are attracted to each other. You're both as black and white as the other in your thoughts of right and wrong."

Kat raised her eyebrows. "I think you do not know either of us well enough to comment, Lady Brighthope."

"Possibly not. Though I am an excellent observer."

"That's what I am counting on when you assist us and tell us what you know. You do want vengeance on the Chameleon, do you not?"

A reluctant smile flittered across the corners of the woman's mouth. "You're a clever little cat indeed. The Chameleon must die, that is true. I suppose I should do my part to ensure that." The woman sank back into her chair and sighed. "Very well, I will assist you. But that is the only reason why. Otherwise, trust me. I never would have introduced myself to you, no matter how intriguingly attractive I find you."

"What the devil did you say?" Marcus spluttered, a look of shock on his face.

Lady Brighthope grinned at his reaction and Kat didn't quite know how to respond. It was not every day, after all, that the most sought-after courtesan in Europe professed her attraction to another woman. Well, it certainly was not in Kat's case.

"You heard me well enough." Lady Brighthope waved a dismissive hand toward him. "But I am expecting the full protection of the War Office." She looked over at Marcus at her pronouncement.

"You will have it," Sir Albert's voice echoed in the room, from the now open door to the library. The man shut the door behind him and briskly strode over to the three of them.

Marcus straightened from the bookcase. "Sir Albert? What are you doing back here? You were meant to stay in London with your guards."

"I can't hide in London when others are at risk," Sir Albert replied, as he bowed at Kaitlyn, before turning his attention on Lady Brighthope. "You must tell us what you know, madam. Several lives depend on it."

Lady Brighthope batted her eyelids at Sir Albert. "Including your own, Sir Albert?"

The man jerked backward a fraction, shock on his face. "I see you are well-informed, Lady Brighthope."

"One must be in my line of work, Sir Albert." She looked at him earnestly. "As you must be in yours. You are brave, for here you are, facing death and yet you do not flee."

Sir Albert puffed out his chest. "One can't be deterred by a mere threat, and besides I must ensure the War Office functions as it should."

"Of course you must," she agreed, looking up at him through her thick lashes. "And will you be able to ensure my safety?"

"It will be my privilege to personally guarantee your safety," Sir Albert intoned.

Kat rolled her eyes. The man had been wrapped around the woman's finger in five seconds flat.

"Please tell us what you know, dear lady," Sir Albert asked her.

She smacked her ruby red lips together and frowned. "Very well, if I must. The client I told

Lady Kaitlyn about earlier, the one with the list of names in his pocket. His name is Matthew Corkdale and I believe he works for the Chameleon. In fact, I think he's the Chameleon's most trusted right-hand man."

"Do any of you know him?" Sir Albert twisted around to ask Kat and Marcus.

Both shook their heads. The name was new to Kat.

"When he was at my residence the other evening," Lady Brighthope continued, "one of his servants delivered an urgent missive. I overheard him telling the servant to attend a Mr. Tremont immediately and give him a note. I sent one of my maids to follow his servant. She overheard the servant tell Mr. Tremont that he was to play his instrument with the orchestra at Lord Newtown's ball."

Kat and Marcus looked at each other. "The violin," they said simultaneously.

"Bloody hell, Mr. Tremont was a musician!" Marcus said. "And he was probably killed so the killer could take his place disguised as one of the orchestral musicians for the ball tonight. That's why his violin case was missing."

"We have to get back to the ball!" Kat lifted up her skirts and ran from the room.

"Stay with Brighthope," Marcus ordered Sir Albert as he followed close on Kat's heels.

Chapter Thirty-Three

Racing along the hallway to the ballroom ahead, Marcus and Kat careened through the doors into the crowded room, two of the War Office agents seeing them and rushing over. "Follow me," he told them, his eyes scanning the space until they landed on the small chamber orchestra at the far northern edge of the room.

He pushed past several of the guests, caring little for the words of affront coming from those he displaced. Stopping at the edge of the dance floor, Kat and the other two men pulled up beside him. "You two get Newtown and secure him well away from this room," he directed the men, who nodded before vanishing into the crowd.

Glancing down at Kat, Marcus was torn between wanting to demand she stay out of harm's way, but knowing full well she would do no such thing, and he was pragmatic enough to realize she could assist. He fought hard against the wave of fear that surfaced at the thought of her being placed in danger.

"I'm not staying put. You'd do best to not waste any time trying to convince me otherwise."

He sighed. "One of these days you will do as I tell you without argument."

"And one of these days you will give up such a ridiculous notion." She glanced over the field of faces.

"Very well, then, you take the right of the room and go around the dance floor to where the orchestra is and I shall take the left," he stated. "If the Chameleon has taken Mr. Tremont's place, he'll either be in the thick of the orchestra, or he may already be mingling amongst the guests."

Kat nodded and slipped off to the right. Marcus went to the left, but concurrently shook his head, wondering not for the first time if he was mad to let a lady take such risks. And not just any lady now, but his lady. As much as the very thought scared the hell out of him.

Because what if Kat ever betrayed him like Elizabeth had? He'd been able to handle Elizabeth's betrayal, but he had the horrible sensation he'd never recover if Kat betrayed him. Shaking his head free of his musings, he slowly came to a halt in front of where the orchestra was playing.

A ruckus sounded from behind him and Marcus swiveled around to see Lord Newtown standing near the refreshment table, refusing to go anywhere with the agent trying to usher him out the terrace doors.

He swore and strode over to them. "Goddamn it, Newtown, get out of here!" Marcus's voice was brooking no argument. "You've been told you're in danger."

Lord Newtown eyed him in vexation. "Good lord, Westwood! You know I am quite capable of defending myself. I have no intention of being run out of my own ball."

"This is no joke," Marcus said curtly. "You're on the Chameleon's assassination list. We think he is here tonight."

The man's face turned ashen and he nodded somewhat dazedly. "You don't say?"

"I do. Now is not the time to be heroic," Marcus admonished. "You need to leave and you need to do it right now."

From the corner of his eye, Marcus saw an object sailing through the air toward them. Everything slowed as he recognized that the object was a metal ball which had a burning wick in its center, and it was being lobbed directly at where they stood.

"Get down!" he roared, diving toward Lord Newtown and pushing him to the ground.

The sound of an explosion ripped through the assembly as the glass of the balcony doors behind them shattered outward, thousands of glass shards splaying onto the terrace.

Screams tore through the ballroom and the

music screeched to a halt. Pandemonium erupted as ladies and gentlemen fled in every direction.

Lifting his face, Marcus scanned the chaos, his ears ringing from the blast. His eyes searched for Kat through the mounting mayhem. He exhaled when he saw the glint of her red hair across the room as she dashed behind one of the many Greek statues positioned around the edges of the ballroom.

She was heading directly to the orchestra. Through the bodies still scrambling for the exit, Marcus saw the same blond man that killed Tremont hiding behind a trombone case at the back of the now abandoned orchestral equipment. He held a pistol aimed directly at Newtown and Marcus, but with all of the chaos, he was unable to get off a clear shot.

Marcus used the distraction to grab both the waistband of Newtown's trousers and his jacket collar. He heaved his arms back and threw Newtown bodily behind the refreshments table.

Without wasting a moment, he pivoted and dived in the other direction. The sound of several pistol shots reverberated around the space. He looked across and felt his heart stop.

Kat was grappling with the man and his pistol, minus the skirt of her gown.

Marcus sprang to his feet and made a mad dash across the ballroom, watching helplessly as

Kat fought the man, launching a spinning kick and knocking the pistol from the man's hand. The man used his other hand to pull out a knife, slashing at Kat.

A deep fury settled in the pit of his stomach when he saw the knife tear through the material of her gown and cut into the flesh of her arm.

Marcus bellowed and launched himself straight in the man's midsection, sending both of them crashing through to the terrace behind.

Landing on top of him on the stone floor, Marcus grabbed the man's wrist, which was still gripping the knife, and twisted it back as hard as he could. The man hollered as his fingers lost their purchase and the knife clattered to the ground.

Maintaining the pressure against the man's wrist, Marcus pressed one of his knees into the man's abdomen and used the other to crouch above him.

Twisting his wrist back even further, Marcus placed the hand into a wrist lock and bent the man's wrist back until a scream tore through him. "Who are you?" he demanded.

"You'll break my wrist," the man hollered as sweat trickled down his brow.

"I shall break a lot more of you if you don't start talking."

Marcus increased the pressure slightly, but the man only gritted his jaw against the pain.

"I will tell you nothing!" he spat out, bitter hatred emanating from the depths of his blue eyes.

Marcus dug his kneecap into the man's ribs. "Not the answer I'm after." He applied more pressure to the wrist lock.

A guttural cry tore from the man's throat as his wrist neared its breaking point. Marcus looked down into his eyes. "I will not ask again."

The man took in a hasty breath and a calm seemed to come over him. A smile twisted the corners of his mouth upwards. "Do your worst. The Chameleon will avenge me!"

A gunshot tore through the air and struck the stone plant pot a few feet from them, sending a cloud of soil into the air.

"Someone's shooting from the garden!" Kat took shelter behind a stone column to Marcus's left.

Another bullet hit the second plant pot, this one only fifty inches from where Marcus was hunkered over the man.

Grabbing the man, Marcus hurled him behind the other column and quickly followed, grasping the man's arm and twisting it behind the man's back. The man began fighting against him, but Marcus bent his arm backward, contrary to its natural flexion. The man screamed in agony but got the message and stopped moving. There was silence for a moment, followed by the sounds of rustling and breaking twigs.

"He's getting away!" Kat yelled as she darted out from behind the column and ran past them toward the landing.

"Get back here!" Marcus roared to her retreating trouser-clad backside as she jumped over the landing into the shrubs beneath, headed directly for where the shots had been fired.

"Goddamn it."

The man he was holding began laughing. Marcus used his free arm and grabbed a fistful of the man's hair. He pulled his head back and then slammed it straight into the column. The man slumped into unconsciousness. Marcus yanked off his bow tie and used it to tie the man's hands behind his back, then he lunged to his feet and sprinted after Kaitlyn.

The damn woman was chasing after a bloody assassin. If he did manage to convince her to marry him, having her as his wife was going to turn his hair white before their first anniversary.

Chapter Thirty-Four

Pushing past the low-hanging branches, Kat darted off the garden path and into the forest surrounding Lord Newtown's estate as she followed the route of the shooter. She could see his black great coat swirling about sixty feet ahead of her.

The branches slapped against her face and arms as she pushed past them farther into the depths of the trees, the bright moon slanting shafts of light where it could reach. She lost sight of him for a moment and stopped to listen.

A horse's nicker echoed along the night breeze, but the man's feet no longer thrashed through the underbrush.

Pulling out her dagger, Kat winced as the sound of steel sliding against the sheath was magnified sharply by the stillness of the forest.

Where was he?

She heard the loud crunch of footsteps running through the scrub once again off to her right. Racing to follow, she pushed her legs as hard as they could go, trying to catch him. His stride was long, and she watched as he easily jumped over a fallen log, his swirling, black coat gracefully following his leap. But then he ducked around to the right and she lost sight of him temporarily. Following the path he'd taken, she saw a clearing up ahead and hunkered behind a tree.

Craning her neck around the stump, she glanced across at the space. The full moon provided ample light for her to see a bay chestnut gelding tethered to a tree about thirty feet ahead with the man quickly untying its reins.

She gripped the hilt of her dagger nimbly and readied her wrist. Stepping half of her body free of the tree, Kat flung back her arm and let the dagger fly. It landed in the tree trunk a few inches from the man's head.

He drew back sharply with a slight gasp.

She retrieved her other dagger and had it aimed at him within seconds. "The first was a warning." Her voice was calm and seemingly loud in the small space. "The second will not be."

The man stilled for a moment before turning to face her.

It was Kat's turn to gasp. It was Nathaniel, dressed all in black, a rifle slung over his shoulder.

She shook her head. "You said you weren't the Chameleon." Her voice no longer sounded calm. "No. You can't be. I don't understand, I thought the man wrestling with Marcus was the Chameleon."

"No, he's not. Just one loyal follower whose purpose is finished." He held his hands up, palms open toward her.

"So you tried to kill him and Marcus?" She had to unclench her teeth and force herself to take a breath.

"Do you really think I tried to kill my own brother? You know me better than that."

"I used to think I did." But now she wasn't at all certain who the man in front of her was. "But you just shot at Marcus. What else am I to think but that you tried to kill him?"

"Damn it, Kat, there are bigger things at play here than you know." He took a step toward her. "And I wasn't trying to kill Marcus."

"Not another step!" she warned as she raised her dagger into a throwing position and aimed directly at his heart. "You know what I can do with this. What I should do with this."

"I do," he said, stopping in his tracks. "But you won't hurt me. We both know that to be the case."

She took in a deep breath. "Your arrogance will be your downfall, Nathaniel."

He smiled sadly at her. "It already has been. But I'm trying to remedy that." He turned back to the horse.

"I said stop!" she yelled as she strode farther into the clearing and stopped short as he finished loosening the rope and untethered the horse. "Don't make me do this."

He bowed his head briefly. "Kill me if you

must, but I need to make amends, Kat."

"Amends for what?"

"You were right, you see." His voice was no longer cocky, no longer arrogant, just deeply sad. "I was partly responsible for Victor's death...as well as so many others. I must fix my mistake."

"I can't let you go."

"You know my aim with a rifle is as good as yours with a dagger."

That stopped her short. What he said was true, he could hit a target practically blindfolded. "What does that have to do with anything?"

"I could have killed Marcus if I had wanted to. But I didn't. I missed on purpose, trying to separate him from grappling with Corkdale. I needed him away so I could shoot and kill Corkdale."

"Corkdale was the one he was wrestling with?"

Nathaniel nodded.

"Who is he to you then?"

"He's the Chameleon's ruthless right-hand man, and he would seek to kill you and Marcus." Nathaniel shrugged. "Newtown was just a diversion for Corkdale to draw you and Marcus out."

"Be that as it may, I still can't let you leave." She shook her head, refusing to allow his words to change her mind.

"Then you will have to kill me," he said. He stared at her for a moment before he turned and mounted his horse.

"Damn it, Nathaniel! Don't make me do this."

He looked at her. "I'm not the Chameleon, Kat. You must trust me. But I will kill the Chameleon. There's been too much death already. It has to stop, regardless of the promise I once made."

She stared into his eyes, the dark night concealing any true hint of emotion from their depths. She didn't know if he was or wasn't the Chameleon, but she did know it was Nathaniel. And that he was right, she couldn't kill him. She lowered her dagger and took in a deep breath.

He nodded to her before digging his heels into the horse's flanks and spurring him out of the clearing, off into the forest, away from Newtown's estate.

Kat closed her eyes for a second and swallowed. God help her, but she hoped she wouldn't come to regret her decision. Her heart sank at the thought.

"Nathaniel is alive?"

She spun around as the sound of Marcus's voice drifted from behind.

"And you already knew?" The betrayal on his face was jolting to see.

He had never looked at her with such an expression of utter distrust before.

"Were you ever going to tell me the truth?" Marcus's eyes tightened at the corners as he regarded her.

Kat opened her mouth to explain things but found herself closing it again equally as quick. How could she explain keeping the truth from him, especially when she knew in her heart he would never forgive her for deceiving him?

She felt a hysterical urge to laugh build inside of her. What else could she do now but tell him the truth? So, she told him, and she watched as with each word he pulled away from her. Not physically. No, he simply stood silent like a statue, but she could feel him withdrawing from her, any warmth fading as frost replaced it. "I'm sorry I didn't tell you sooner."

Marcus didn't reply for a minute, then it was as if he'd placed a shutter over his eyes as he stared past her. "We need to get back and question this man, Corkdale."

Taking a step toward him, she held out her hand. "Please, Marcus, don't be like this. I wanted to tell you from the start, but I promised him time to tell you himself."

"Don't," he all but growled at her. "Don't talk to me about it. I can't handle your treachery at the moment."

"Please don't be like this."

"Like this?" he roared. "I trusted you after I thought I would never trust another woman since Elizabeth's betrayal. It was a mistake to do so, and one I will not repeat." He turned away from hcr and strode down the path back to Newtown's residence.

It was in that moment that Kat felt more alone than she ever had in her entire life as the deep weight of knowledge settled in her heart. The knowledge that Marcus would never forgive her.

But then she got angry, furious even. She hadn't lied to him or been unfaithful to him or even been treacherous. She simply hadn't told him about Nathaniel. And because of that he was never going to forgive her? Unacceptable!

"Don't you dare liken me to Elizabeth!" she yelled as she strode after him. "I'm nothing like her."

He stopped and spun around. "She lied to me, just as you have, even after you gave me your word to tell the truth."

She marched up to him and pushed him in the chest. The man didn't budge an inch, but his scowl grew fierce. "I never lied to you. I simply didn't tell you about Nathaniel."

"There was nothing simple about keeping from me the fact that my brother is actually alive. How could you keep that from me, knowing I blame myself for his death? Knowing I grieve for him every day."

Her breath caught in her throat at the raw pain she saw reflected in his eyes. "I'm sorry I kept it from you. Deeply sorry. It's not something I wanted to do. I argued with Nathaniel about it, but he was adamant that you and your family would be in danger if you found out. That's why I promised him I wouldn't tell you, and that's why I didn't."

His jaw clenched tightly for a moment. "How long have you known?"

"Not long," Kat said. "He was waiting for me in the back gardens of my house, the night Sir William was attacked."

"The dagger used at Sir Williams... Was it Nathaniel who attacked him?"

"He says not."

"You don't believe him?"

"Honestly, I don't know." She bit her lip. "He's different now, Marcus. He's not the same Nathaniel I used to know. But I imagine anyone who spent two years as a prisoner in the Kremlin wouldn't be the same person they once were."

He exhaled sharply. "What happened?"

She told him everything Nathaniel had told her, and with each word she could see the pain intensify in his eyes.

"If I'd have known, I would have done everything to get him out of there. To save him." His words were raw, and Kat had to stop herself from reaching out and holding him.

Given how upset he was with her involvement, she doubted he'd welcome such an embrace. "As would I. But none of us knew."

"Why did he go to you and not me?" There was confusion and perhaps even a hint of an accusation in his glare.

"We trained for four years together, Marcus," Kat said. "We used to trust each other completely. Besides, he wanted to try to fix things himself without having his big brother ride in to save the day."

Marcus buried his hands in his hair. "A part of me is furious with you both, but then another part is beyond happy he's alive."

Hesitantly, she took a step over to him. "I know. It's how I felt when I found out."

"Then why didn't you tell me, Kat?" There was an almost pleading look in his eyes. "Why did you choose him instead of me?"

"It wasn't like that at all." How to make the stubborn man see reason? "You don't understand."

"Don't I?" He crossed his arms over his chest and glared at her. "What if Victor was the one who was alive and he approached me instead of you? Would you be fine with me keeping that knowledge from you? Especially when your main purpose at the moment is to avenge his death. Would you still trust me after I stayed silent?"

She raised her chin higher. "I'd be furious, too, but I'd be more upset with Victor for putting you in that position. And I certainly wouldn't have likened you to an unfaithful jezebel."

Marcus opened his mouth to say something

and then stopped. "Perhaps I was slightly hasty in labeling you a liar."

"You were," she said, the tightness at the thought he'd never forgive her easing greatly.

He paused and glanced beyond her. "I was jealous."

"Jealous? Why would you be jealous?"

"Because he came to you and not me. Because you kept his secret. Because I'm worried that you both still have feelings for each other... Romantic feelings."

"Romantic feelings?" A puzzlement filled her at his words. "Why would he and I have feelings for each other? We care for each other, or at least we used to. But I've never loved him romantically."

"If that's the case, why did you kiss him when you were younger?" His gaze returned to hers.

"How do you know that?" She could feel the mortification creeping up her face.

"Because he told me after the fact, years ago. He said he thought he was in love with you, but then you and Victor travelled to China on some mission for nearly a year, so that was the end of that. But now he's back. Do you care for him?"

The uncertainty in his voice had a slow smile creeping up at the corner of her lips. If he was worried about her caring for Nathaniel, then that meant that Marcus cared for her, at least a little. The thought was as surprising as it was welcome.

"Of course I care for him."

Marcus nodded slowly. "Of course you do."

"I care for him like a brother, you buffoon!" She placed her hands on her hips and stared him down. "You're the one I care about in an entirely non-brotherly way."

"You care for me?" His voice broke slightly on the last word.

"Do you really think I'd take you as my lover if I didn't?" she pertly questioned. "But don't go bandying that around. I have a reputation as the Ice Maiden to uphold."

"I wouldn't dream of it, my lady." A slow smile stretched across his face.

"Does this mean I'm forgiven?" she asked him offhandedly, but inside she was holding her breath waiting for his answer.

"Finding out that my brother is alive threw me, and I did react poorly." He stepped forward and picked up her hand. The touch sent such warmth through her entire body and her hand squeezed his in return. "It hurts me that he doesn't trust me enough to have come to me instead of you. And I took that frustration out on you. And for that, I am sorry. Do you forgive me for reacting so poorly?"

Reaching out, she took his other hand in her own and squeezed both of his hands. "I do. Though I didn't appreciate being likened to Elizabeth, your reaction to finding out the news was rather mild compared to what mine probably would have been, if the shoe was on the other foot."

"What would you have done?" he questioned, stroking the top of her knuckles with his thumbs.

"I daresay I would have likely already stabbed you."

He blinked for a moment and then threw back his head and laughed. "You bloody well would have, wouldn't you."

She arched an eyebrow at him. "It would have only been a flesh wound, of course, but yes I imagine I would have. Either that or kneed you in the nether regions again. You do know how I get when I am angry."

"That I do. I suppose we had better get back to question Corkdale. And after that, you know we're going to have to find my brother, because he's in well over his head in this mess."

"I know he is." Kat nodded. She just hoped he wasn't in too far that they couldn't pull him out.

Chapter Thirty-Five

A few minutes later, as Kat and Marcus hurried up the path to the house, she saw Lucas and Etta on the terrace, grave concern plastered across their faces.

"What's wrong?" Marcus asked as they strode up the stairs to join their friends. "Goddamn it!"

Kat glanced down to where he was staring. Corkdale was lying on the stone floor, a dagger through his heart. "What happened?"

"We thought you two would be able to answer that," Lucas replied. "I must admit that with your dagger skills, Lady Kaitlyn, I did assume this might have been your handiwork…"

Kat arched an eyebrow at the man. "I generally prefer not to stab a person in the heart. At least not until after I interrogate him." She crouched down beside the body. "Whoever did it knew what they were about." The blade had been plunged directly through the man's ribs, to perfectly pierce his heart. "It's too clean, though."

"What do you mean?" Etta asked, peering hesitantly down at the dead man.

"It's too clean a wound, meaning he didn't

struggle at all." Kat stood and glanced at Marcus. "He knew his killer."

Just then the doors to the terrace opened and out rushed Sir Albert with Lady Brighthope in tow.

"Lord Newtown is dead!" Sir Albert announced, an acute expression of dismay on the man's weathered face. "Appears he's not the only one," he added, catching sight of Corkdale's corpse.

Marcus's plethora of expletives filled the silent night and echoed Kat's own thoughts. They were always just a step behind, it seemed.

"How?" she asked. "Newtown was meant to be safe, being protected by men from the War Office."

"It looks like poison." Sir Albert dabbed at his forehead with a handkerchief. "Newtown was in the library, surrounded by our men, when he had some brandy, and a few minutes later he collapsed and died. I've sent for the police and reinforcements from London. Danbury is going to be most displeased. So, who is he? Please tell me it's the Chameleon."

Sir Albert pointed to the man lying on the floor, and beside him, Lady Brighthope gasped and grabbed ahold of Sir Albert's arm, all but collapsing on the spot.

"Oh dear," Sir Albert muttered, holding the lady up. "Are you all right, my lady?"

Both Marcus and Lucas rushed over to assist, each holding the lady up by one arm.

Lady Brighthope's eyes were glued to the dead man. "That is the client I was telling you about… Matthew Corkdale, the one I suspected to be working for the Chameleon."

Sir Albert approached the man and gasped himself. "Good Lord. That is Matthew Drysden. He's Danbury's personal secretary. I've met him on occasion at Danbury's residence… But what's he doing dead? Danbury is really going to have a conniption."

"Danbury was his employer? I have to leave, now." Lady Brighthope pushed away Lucas and Marcus, her terror giving her strength. "I always thought Danbury a fool, but if this man was his employee, Danbury could be the Chameleon…"

"What?" Sir Albert scoffed. "Danbury the Chameleon? No. Never." But then Sir Albert paused, and an expression of dawning horror crept up on his face. "Could he be? Could he have actually been playing us for fools the entire time?"

"I can't stay here," Lady Brighthope repeated, an almost trapped look in the lady's eyes. "Knowing Danbury is a great deal more involved than anyone suspected means I'm in grave danger. If he is the assassin, then he knows I've been assisting you. Which means I'm as good as dead if I don't disappear immediately."

"Danbury couldn't possibly be the Chameleon," Kat stated. "He's not that good an actor."

Brighthope looked up at her, fear swimming in their depths. "People wear many masks. You could be looking straight at someone and not truly see who they are, and though Danbury plays the fool often, there are some instances where I've seen brilliance in his gaze."

Kat had never seen such a thing. "Danbury does not have the brains nor the fortitude to be an assassin."

"Perhaps not, but he has the money to pay others to do such tasks if he had a mind to. He could have been sitting back for years, the whole resources of the War Office at his disposal, paying men to kill others in the name of the Chameleon. He could be paying someone right now." Brighthope seemed terrified at the thought. "But I certainly have no intention of staying and finding out if I am to be added to their number. Now, if you will all excuse me, I must pack and leave immediately."

"It's nearly three o'clock in the morning, Lady Brighthope," Marcus said, stepping forward and staring at the woman. "Wait until morning and travel then."

"Several of the men on that list are already dead," Lady Brighthope replied. "I'll have a far greater chance of staying alive on my own. Besides, there's plenty of moonlight tonight. No. I am most definitely leaving."

And with that, the lady turned on her heel and

strode through the doors back into the house, the skirts of her ruby red gown swishing in time with her gait.

"Should I send some men with her?" Sir Albert asked.

"No, let her go," Marcus answered. "She is probably safest on her own. After all, if Danbury is behind the assassinations, then we don't know who from the War Office can be trusted."

"Surely, he can't be the mastermind behind everything," Kat said. The thought rebelled against her intuition about the man.

"We need to talk to him," Marcus replied. "And we need to get you to a safe place, Sir Albert."

Sir Albert bristled. "I shall be fine. I've worked in this game for over thirty years now, and don't intend to go and cower in some corner just because my name is on some list. Your energy would be best spent discovering if Danbury is behind this, along with finding the two others on the list."

"Have you received any word on who Silas Morriset or Bellis Perennis are?" Kat asked him, knowing it was futile to fight with the man about his own safety.

"Bellis Perennis?" Etta exclaimed.

Kat glanced over to her friend. "Yes. Do you know her?"

A look of hesitancy crossed Etta's face. "Well, it's a name but it isn't… Bellis Perennis is actually the proper name of a daisy flower."

"A daisy?" Kat felt her heart slam in her throat as a sudden blinding sense of dread gripped her.

"It might not mean your aunt," Marcus said, immediately understanding her fear.

"Lady Montrose?" Sir Albert declared. "Surely not? Though she did assist your uncle, Lady Kaitlyn, in deciphering several missives around the time just before he was killed. I suppose it's possible she read something she shouldn't have. In fact, now that I think about it, Sir William even employed her to assist, and perhaps Bellis Perennis was her code name?"

"Sir William would have known her code name…" Kat's voice trailed off.

"And he said he'd never heard it before," Marcus added.

"I think we may have found our traitors. Both Danbury and Sir William," said Sir Albert.

"No. I will not believe Sir William is involved," Marcus growled. "At least not until I speak to him."

Sir Albert shrugged. "I shall send some men over to France to find him and then we will see. But perhaps the countess should be our main priority."

Suddenly, Kat's knees felt like they were made of soup. Without even thinking about it, she gripped ahold of Marcus's arm and he automatically pulled her against him, supporting her weight. She turned to stare at him. "Daisy is on the list. I can't let the Chameleon take her, too… I can't…"

"We won't let that happen," Marcus declared. "We will leave for London immediately." His head swiveled to Sir Albert and Lucas. "Lucas, you take Miss Merriweather and the duchess home, and then come to the Montrose residence. Sir Albert, take some men you trust completely and take Danbury into custody until we can sort out his involvement in all of this. Once Lady Kaitlyn and I secure the countess, then we will look at questioning Danbury. Are we all clear?"

Everyone nodded but all Kat could do was think about the last moment of Victor's life. But instead of his face, she kept seeing Daisy's in its place.

Oh God, please don't let her be too late again. Not again.

Chapter Thirty-Six

Marcus had been staring at Kat's pallor for the entire trip to London. He'd never seen her so quiet or so pale before. She'd always appeared fearless. Seeing her this vulnerable with the thought that she could also lose her aunt was gut wrenching, and at that moment there was nothing he wanted more than to kill the assassin for terrifying her. Justice be damned.

He still felt conflicted about her knowing Nathaniel was alive and not saying anything, even though he did understand why she'd done so. Thinking of Nathaniel and the fact that he was alive brought with it a bundle of emotions. Joy, relief, frustration, hurt… And the fact that his brother was immersed in the Chameleon's dealings up to his damn neck didn't help the situation one bit. Marcus would have to find him, and sooner rather than later, especially as he seemed to be on a quest for vengeance against those who'd set him up.

It was hard to imagine his carefree and fun-loving brother out for blood, but like Kat said, he had obviously changed. Marcus wondered if the brother he'd known and grown up with had died that night after all.

As the carriage pulled up at the curb of the Montrose residence, Kat didn't even wait for it to come to a full halt; she'd bolted out the door before Marcus even knew what she was about. He chased after her as she ran up the entrance steps, and nearly careened into her as she froze at the top, staring at the open front door.

She turned to him with eyes wide with an expression he'd never seen in them before. Fear. "Fenton never leaves the door open... It's always locked."

Marcus pulled out his pistol and glanced into the entrance hall. There were no servants about, which was ominous in itself. He heard the scrape of steel against leather and glanced at Kat. She'd drawn out her dagger and now instead of fear there was unbridled fury all but radiating from her every pore.

Straightening to her full height, she took in a deep breath. "If the assassin is still here, don't get in my way, Marcus." There was a flat coldness to her eyes.

"You're not a killer. And we need the Chameleon alive to vindicate Nathaniel."

"If the Chameleon has dared to hurt my family, I will kill him." She spun around and stepped over the threshold. "So, like I said, don't get in my way."

Stepping into the hallway, Marcus followed her, fighting his instinct to take the lead, knowing that this was her domain, and her family, and that for her own sanity, she needed to take charge. But he would get in her way if he needed to. She wasn't a cold-hearted killer and if she stepped into that territory, she would live with the regret of it always.

Without a sound, they both walked through the entrance and down the hall toward the back area of the house. The sound of people, both crying and talking, echoed down the corridor. Following the noise, Marcus saw a crowd of servants gathering around a doorway up ahead.

One of the footmen noticed them and stood to attention. "My lady! It's Fenton. He's been shot."

Kat broke into a run down the rest of the hall, and the crowd of servants parted for her and Marcus as they came to the door. Lying in the middle of the room was Kat's butler, bleeding from his chest.

"No, no, no," Kat cried, rushing into the room and over to Fenton's side, dropping her dagger on the floor. "Fetch a doctor! Hurry!" The men beside Fenton moved aside to allow Kat to be next to him and she took over pressing down on the cloth someone had already thought to push against his wound.

"A doctor is on the way, my lady," a maid murmured, tears streaming down the woman's face.

"What happened?" Marcus asked to the room

at large.

"There was a loud bang, my lord," one of the footmen answered, his eyes bright with tears, too. "We all came rushing in and found him like that. I fear we were too late."

"Where's Lady Montrose?" he asked.

"No one knows, sir." The man shook his head. "She and the young earl have disappeared."

• • •

Kat could barely see for the tears pooling in her eyes as she stared down at Fenton's pale face.

Her hands were already coated red with his blood as she pressed down on the cloth over his chest. Part of her knew it was too late, and she could feel his life slipping away from her. Just like Victor. "No. This isn't happening." Her voice broke on the last word.

God couldn't be so cruel as to take her family away from her again. Not Fenton. Not her rock. Not the man who used to sneak her sweets and biscuits when she was young. The one who would pick her up after a fall and dust her off. The one who was always so proud of her achievements and reserved his smile just for her.

"Fenton, please don't leave me." She leaned over him and whispered in his ear, her heart breaking into pieces, "Please don't go... Please, I need you." She raised her head, tears streaming down her face as she looked around the room at large. "Damn it! Don't just all stand there! Get a doctor here now." Her voice broke again on the last word, because she feared it was already too late. "Fenton, don't go. I can't do this without you. You promised Victor you would always look out for me. And you're always true to your word. So, you have to fight! Do you hear me? Fight, Fenton!"

"Kat." Marcus's voice sounded as if from a great distance away. "He's gone, Kat. You need to let him go."

"No! He can't be gone. Not Fenton," she yelled, shaking Marcus's hand from her shoulder. She couldn't believe that. She wouldn't. Fenton was too strong. He was always there for her. And she loved him like a grandfather but had never had a chance to tell him that. "Fenton, come back! Please come back to me..." Great heaving sobs wracked her body as she collapsed on his chest and hugged him like she never had before.

"I'm so sorry, Fenton." Her words were a blubbery mess, but part of her desperately hoped he could still hear her. "I failed you. I wasn't here to protect you and I should have been. I should have been protecting my family."

She lost track of how long she stayed holding him to her, her tears mingling with the crimson of his blood as she cried over him. Her heart had never felt so empty and so barren. She could have told Fenton anything, and he would have listened and offered council without criticism or censure. He was always there for her, like no one else had been. And now he was gone, taken from her in an instant. And he was never coming back. The thought was like someone had slashed through her heart, leaving her completely alone and so very empty.

But someone hadn't slashed through her heart; instead, they had shot Fenton in the chest. They'd taken him from her with a single bullet. "Who did this?" she yelled to the room at large.

Everyone was just a blur as she glanced up at the servants in the room, but they were all shaking their heads and murmuring *we don't know*. Well, someone had to know. Someone had gotten inside and shot Fenton. Black burning fury started to replace the desolation. It must have been the Chameleon.

"Kat?" Marcus said, gently shaking her, and she remembered that she wasn't so alone. But life was fragile, and Marcus could be so easily taken from her, too. She couldn't survive having her heart broken again. "Daisy and Samuel are missing."

His words were nearly the last nail in her coffin. But instead of succumbing to the crushing weight of grief, fury burned deep within her as everything became clear. She had to annihilate the Chameleon, piece by piece, until he felt the same pain she did.

She lifted her head and took one last look at Fenton. She bent down and kissed his weathered cheek and had to push down hard on the devastation threatening to spill out as her chest tightened in pain. "Rest easy, my dear friend. You'll always be in my heart. And now you can take care of Victor, who I'm sure has missed you greatly, as I will." She dashed away the further tears from her cheeks.

Gradually, the room and everyone within slowly came back into focus and she heard several maids crying behind her. Glancing at their stricken faces, she knew they felt Fenton's death keenly. He'd been a rock to the entire household, too, running a tight ship, but a very happy one. She stood up, catching sight of herself in the mantle mirror. She was covered in Fenton's blood and her eyes were glassy.

"I'm so sorry, Kat." Marcus's deep voice was like a balm to her soul, but it also terrified her how she was coming to need him. Especially as those she cared for always seemed to be taken from her. "Why don't you rest? I'll sort everything out here."

"I'll only rest after the Chameleon has suffered as I have." She took in several deep breaths and gathered herself, resisting the urge to bury herself in Marcus's arms. She had to be strong and she had to get through this. She would get through this. Fenton would expect no less of her. Even the thought of his name brought more tears to her eyes, but she ignored them. "Now what did you mean Sam and Daisy are missing?"

"Your staff tell me they haven't been seen since they heard the gunshot."

Everything inside of her felt unbearably tight and for a moment she just wanted to collapse and sink into the beckoning darkness, to a place where she couldn't feel anything. It all seemed too much. But she couldn't give up, that's not how she'd been raised.

"Brentley?" she called out to the underbutler who Fenton had been training and would take his place now. Oh God, even the thought of not calling out the name Fenton again had her gasping for breath. It felt so surreal. How could Fenton be gone?

Brentley stepped forward, his eyes bright with tears. "Yes, my lady?"

Seeing the man standing there, grief in his whole posture, gave her some strength. Fenton had been well-loved amongst the servants and he would want her to lead them in his absence. "Fenton trusted you to do his job if the need arose. I'll rely on you to do the same. Now more than ever we must pull together."

Breathe, Kat, just breathe, she kept reminding herself each time it felt like she was going to collapse.

The man stood tall. "I will not let you, or Mr. Fenton, down, my lady." His jaw was tight just like hers was. "You can count on that."

"I know it," she replied. "Now, we must find Lady Montrose and Samuel, then after they are safe, we can start questioning everyone about what happened to Fenton."

"Find me?" Daisy spoke from the doorway. "Why do you need to find me, I've just returned."

Kat had never been so relieved to see her aunt. Rushing up to her, she wrapped her arms around her in a fierce embrace. "Thank goodness you're safe."

"Why wouldn't I be safe?" Daisy said, pulling back from Kat, a slight frown marring her brows. It was rare for them to embrace. "What's wrong, Kaitlyn? You never cry." She looked beyond Kat and her eyes fell to Fenton. "Oh my goodness. What happened?"

"Fenton has been killed." The words came out effortlessly, but inside they echoed in her head like an avalanche. "Is Samuel with you, then?" Kat took in another deep breath. She could do this. She could. She had to.

"No. I was out paying some calls and I left him here." Daisy's eyes instantly tightened. "He is here, isn't he?" She asked her question to the room at large, her whole body starting to shake like a leaf in a strong breeze.

"No one has been able to find him since we heard the gunshot." Brentley spoke for the group. "I have men searching, but nothing yet. One of the maids saw him running across the lawns in the backyard shortly after the shot, and the back door was wide open, so we think he ran away scared, as he's done in the past. I've sent men outside looking for him."

"He's missing?" Daisy screamed, bending forward and gripping her waist. "Oh God, I can't breathe."

Marcus strode over and held on to Daisy's elbow. "Let's assist her across the hall," he said, guiding Daisy out of the room and into the room opposite.

Kat was loath to leave Fenton just lying there, but she nodded.

"Just breathe, Lady Montrose," Marcus soothed as he gently assisted Daisy onto the chaise longue in the next room. "Just breathe."

Kat sat beside Daisy and had to will herself not to break down, too. The thought of Samuel missing was nearly more than she could handle. But she couldn't break. She had to stay in control and think clearly, for them all. "It's all right, Daisy. He's most likely hiding somewhere in the garden, like he did on New Year's Day when they set off some firecrackers in Vauxhall Gardens, remember?"

Daisy closed her eyes and nodded.

"Can I have a word?" Marcus asked as he straightened and looked at Kat.

She nodded and followed him over to the doorway. "You're going, then?" She'd seen him dart a glance at the doorway.

"Do you think Samuel is safe?" he asked. "If you think he's in trouble, I'll join the men outside and try to find him."

She desperately hoped Sam was safe. "He's run away before, so I'm sure he is fine. Besides, he's not on the Chameleon's list, is he? Though neither was Fen—Fenton." Her voice nearly broke saying his name aloud. The pain like a hot lance stabbing through her insides.

"It's not your fault, Kat." Marcus lifted her chin up until she was looking at him.

"It is," she said, knocking his hand away. "I was told the Chameleon had taken an interest in me, but I didn't consider how that could place those I love in jeopardy. But I'll make amends for my mistake, if it's the last thing I do. The Chameleon will pay."

Marcus sighed. "Killing him isn't the way forward, Kat."

"It's the only way forward to protect my family." She crossed her arms over her chest. "But I need to find Samuel first and make certain he's safe."

"I can stay if you want me to and help find him."

"No. I'm fine." She straightened up and squared her shoulders. She had to be. Coming to rely on Marcus was dangerous, she could see that now. Later, when she was alone in her room, after everyone was safe, was when she could fall to pieces, but not here and not now. And not until after she caught the Chameleon. "Where are you going?"

"Lucas is waiting in the hall for me," Marcus replied. "He's received word that Silas Morriset is a law clerk of a Mr. Hendridge. If we can find Morriset, we can get him to talk and perhaps work out who is behind all of this."

"Hendridge? That's the solicitor we use."

Marcus's eyes narrowed. "That can't be a coincidence."

"I don't believe in coincidences," Kat said. "Perhaps I should come with you."

"You can if you want, but considering your aunt may well be on the Chameleon's list, do you feel safe leaving her?" Marcus asked. "And though it sounds like Samuel has just run off somewhere, I know you'll think of little else until he's found safe and sound."

"You're right." She nodded her head. Marcus's energy would be best spent on finding this Morriset, while Kat stayed and protected what was left of her family. What she should have done in the first place. "Go with Lucas and find Morriset, then hopefully we can unravel this mess and stop any more deaths. I'll stay here and protect Daisy and find Samuel."

"Are you going to tell her she's on the Chameleon's list?" Marcus nodded over to where Daisy was shivering on the chair.

"I don't know." And she really didn't. Her aunt was tough, and Kat rather suspected there were depths to Daisy she'd never seen, but most people tended to fall to pieces if they heard they were on an assassin's hit list.

"I'll get back here as soon as I can." Then, without warning, he leaned down and kissed her for everyone to see. It wasn't anything more than a quick press of his lips against hers, but it was tantamount to a declaration. "Stay safe, my love."

His words stopped her in her tracks as panic wrapped around her heart. Love? What they shared wasn't love. It couldn't be. It was simply attraction and mutual respect for each other's abilities. Love was too dangerous to feel. She'd loved Victor and Fenton and look where they were now. Dead.

"You too." The words felt too generic, but there was nothing else she could say right then. Nothing she felt safe saying. Kat didn't even want to think of what it would feel like if anything happened to Marcus.

Fenton's death had broken a piece of her heart. Marcus's death would burn it to ash, because she had a horrible feeling she'd done what she swore she wouldn't and had fallen in love with the man.

Chapter Thirty-Seven

The address given to them for where Silas Morriset was in hiding was a rundown tenement in the East End of London, consisting of buildings seemingly slapped together with some bricks and cement, without much attention to geometry.

"He must be scared to be living in a place like this," Lucas said as they both stood outside the building and assessed it.

"Hiding is more like it," Marcus remarked, catching sight of a young boy watching them from across the street. Marcus whistled him over.

"Aye, gov?" the lad asked, his eyes darting over Marcus's jacket and boots, an assessment in his gaze he hadn't quite yet learned to hide.

"Do you know the occupants living here?" Marcus nodded across to the building as he pulled out a gold coin, careful not to flash it about, but enough so the boy got a look.

The boy's jaw dropped but then his eyes narrowed in suspicion. "Some I do, some I don't."

"Silas Morriset. What can you tell me about him?" Often, the best information Marcus got was from the street urchins who were all too good at observing everything, for it was the only way for them to survive.

"Aye, I know him." The boy crossed his hands across his chest, though his eyes lit up in interest. "But it'll cost ya two of them coins if ya want me to talk."

"What a little mercenary," Lucas said.

Marcus merely laughed. "He's a capitalist, my friend. Nothing wrong with that in this day and age. All right, boy, you have a deal. Now tell me what you know."

The lad shrugged. "Not much. The man and 'is wife moved in a month or so ago. And the man can't hold 'is liquor none. Was telling all who could hear the other night how he was gonna be filthy rich soon and was expecting a big payment for him to stay silent 'bout some secrets he got on some rich toffs."

"Blackmail?" Lucas asked.

"Sounds like it. Anything else, boy?"

"Nah, that's it," the boy stated with a shrug.

Marcus grabbed two coins from his pocket and threw one then the other to the lad, who caught them deftly and pocketed them even quicker, before scuttling off.

"Come on, time to pay the man a visit." Marcus strode over to the wooden doorway that led into the block of apartments and pushed it open. A plethora of smells from excrement to burning fish assaulted his nostrils as he strode into the entrance area. The floor was threadbare, any semblance of carpet long since worn away, and the walls were dusted with mold and mildew.

"What a quaint place," Lucas said as he wrinkled his nose.

"Which room is it?" Marcus saw several wooden doors dotting both directions of the corridors, with a rickety wooden staircase at the far end of the hall.

"Number four," Lucas replied. "Around to the right, apparently, and thankfully on this level, because those stairs look like a bloody death trap."

"Clearly the blackmailing business isn't going so well for him thus far."

They walked down the hall, the rotting wood flooring creaking loudly with the two men's weight, until they came to a door that had a number four painted in the center of it. Pausing at the threshold, Marcus listened. There was silence, but then the sound of wailing started to emanate from inside.

Pulling out his pistol, Marcus slammed his foot into the door, which swung wide open to reveal a woman kneeling on the floor in the middle of the room, howling and holding a man to her chest. A man with a dagger protruding from his back.

"No, not my Silas. No. No. No. Please don't be dead," she kept saying as she rocked forward and backward, clutching desperately to the man, her blonde hair splattered with blood as tears streamed down her face.

Silas Morriset and his wife, Marcus guessed. Or rather, a dead Silas Morriset. Damn it, too late again.

"Are you hurt?" Marcus asked the woman, his eyes scanning the rather threadbare room that had a door leading off to the left.

The woman could only shake her head as she clutched Silas tight, her face all but buried in his chest. "He went that way, only a moment ago," she moaned, barely lifting her head from her husband as she pointed to the door. "He stabbed Silas, then left to the back garden." She collapsed on Silas and started crying again in earnest.

Marcus raced to the door and yanked it open, Lucas at his heels. They ran across the small back garden to where a gate was wide open. Sprinting through the gate they came to a back alley. He scanned in both directions, but the alley was empty. "Goddamn it!" Marcus kicked out his leg into the air and felt like smashing his fist in something. "Chasing our tails, once again."

Exhaling sharply, Lucas came to stand beside him. "We can keep looking. Maybe at the end of the alley we'll see something…"

They both knew the chances of finding a man who they didn't even know the description of was non-existent in the East End. The alley ran between two main thoroughfares, and the man would be long gone by now. "No. Perhaps, though, we can get a description of him from Morriset's wife, and possibly find some evidence."

Because if Morriset was in the business of blackmail, then hopefully he would have proof hidden somewhere in the apartment. They were close, Marcus could sense it; they just needed to catch a break.

Chapter Thirty-Eight

"Have you found him?" Kat asked Bentley as he entered the sitting room where she and Daisy were waiting for word on Samuel.

She'd wanted to go out herself and search for him, but leaving Daisy alone with the Chameleon still on the loose was too dangerous. When Marcus returned, she'd be able to go out, but considering he and Lucas had only just left about ten minutes ago, they'd most likely be a few hours yet.

"No, my lady. We're still looking for the young lord," Bentley replied. "But this was hand delivered for you, marked urgent."

He handed her an envelope.

"Thank you." She nodded to him as she turned over the envelope, while Bentley departed.

Her fingers froze on the parchment. Across the back of the envelope was a red wax seal with the letter *C* emblazoned in the middle. With a sense of dread, Kat flicked her finger under the seal and opened the note.

I have the boy.

If you don't want him joining his father,

bring Lady Montrose to the West India
South Docks overlooking Blackwell Reach,
in exactly thirty minutes from delivery of
this note. No games. No other people. No
one except you and Lady Montrose. If you
do not follow these instructions, I will cut
the boy's throat and throw him in the river.
You have my word. The clock is ticking.

Yours, the Chameleon.

For a minute, everything inside her froze. Her lungs seized up and she couldn't breathe. Stumbling over to the window, she opened the glass and had to draw in a shuddering breath. Not Samuel. She wanted to shout to the sky and curse everyone and everything.

Anger ripped through her fear, tearing away at it, until fury consumed her. She'd already lost Fenton today, she wasn't going to lose Samuel or Daisy, too.

"Kaitlyn, what's wrong?" Daisy had approached her from behind without Kat even knowing.

There was worry in Daisy's eyes as she stared at Kat, and for a moment Kat contemplated not telling her anything. If she told Daisy that Samuel had been taken, Daisy would panic, but then didn't the woman have a right to know her son had been taken? What was she to do? Kat couldn't actually take Daisy and give her to the Chameleon. That would be a death sentence. But then if she didn't take her with her, Samuel could be killed.

Never had it felt like such crushing decisions were upon her shoulders.

"Kaitlyn, what is it? You're worrying me."

It was then Kat realized the only thing she could do was tell Daisy the truth, for if their positions were reversed, it's what Kat would want Daisy to do. So, she quickly told Daisy everything. How Daisy was on the Chameleon's list of targets along with five or six others, and how the Chameleon was purporting to have Samuel.

It seemed as if Daisy was going to faint when she heard that, but then she seemed to pull herself together as she stared at Kat. "Why would I be the target of an assassin?"

"Sir Albert thinks it may be because you helped Victor translate some missives before his death, and may have inadvertently read something you shouldn't have, or you perhaps know something you don't even know you know. If that makes sense."

She nodded her head. "Yes, I did help Victor a great deal, though I never really paid attention to the contents of the correspondence, even though I was translating them. But, Kat, what about Samuel?" Daisy's voice shook when she mentioned her son's name. "Do you think the Chameleon has him? Perhaps it's just a bluff…"

It was possible the Chameleon was bluffing about having Samuel, but considering the Chameleon had obviously killed Fenton, he would have had ample opportunity to take Sam from the house, or from the grounds if what the maid had said, about seeing Sam running through them, was true. "Unfortunately, I must assume he has him, Daisy. To not do so would be folly."

Daisy's chin began to wobble, but she clamped down on her jaw and stayed silent for a moment as she wrestled for composure. "Then we best make our way to the docks mentioned in the note."

"I can't hand you over to the Chameleon, or take you anywhere near there." Did Daisy not understand? "He intends to kill you. And he most likely intends to kill me and Samuel to protect his identity. I need to work out a plan other than capitulation."

"There's no time," Daisy implored. "It will take us nearly thirty minutes to get to the docks. We have to leave now."

Daisy was right. "I'll go, but you will stay here. Bentley?" she called.

The door opened and Bentley marched in. "Yes, my lady?"

She walked over to him and pushed the note into his hands. "Give this to Lord Westwood when he returns, and have the carriage brought around immediately."

"Of course, my lady." He bowed and swiftly left the room.

"I'm coming with you." Daisy's voice was shaky, but there was a stubbornness in her bearing that Kat knew meant she'd not be deterred. "He's my son, Kaitlyn. I will do anything to protect him, including dying for him."

Kat believed her. Daisy had always been a protective mother, to the point of over protection, and the woman would do anything for Samuel.

But, damn it, she wasn't going to let it come to that. She wasn't losing more of her family today. And she was going to ensure the Chameleon never put someone else in this position again. "All right. Did Fen—Fenton teach you to use a pistol yet?"

Daisy reached into the pocket of her skirt and pulled out a small derringer. "Yes, and I've been carrying it on my person ever since."

"A good choice." Daisy was holding a double barrel Remington derringer, an effective little weapon at short range. Kat often carried one in her pocket, finding the two-barrel mechanism, allowing for two bullets, much more efficient that the single barrel Colt derringer. "Is it loaded?"

"Of course," Daisy scoffed. "Well, partially."

"Partially?"

"I used it for target practice the other day,

but Samuel's dog was distracting me while I was reloading it, so I only put in one bullet."

Kat pulled out a small leather pouch from her skirt and retrieved a point forty-one caliber bullet from inside. She took the weapon from Daisy and loaded the empty chamber then handed it back to Daisy. "Always keep a weapon fully loaded. Now, hide this in your pocket. It's time to go, but listen to me carefully and clearly, Daisy. You must do everything I tell you to. Samuel's life depends upon it."

"I understand." Daisy placed the gun in her pocket and nodded solemnly at Kat. "You've got to save him, Kat. You must. He's all I have."

To Kat, as well. She'd already lost too much of her family to risk losing her brother too.

Chapter Thirty-Nine

The carriage wheels clattered to a halt on the dirt road in front of the warehouse on the West Indian South Docks and Kat's eyes automatically surveyed the area, noting the empty buildings along the abandoned section of the wharf.

To her right was the warehouse and to her left the river, with the road etched between. Up ahead, beside the river, was a wooden dock that had definitely seen better days. It stretched perhaps a hundred feet into the water, though there were no boats docked, just a dilapidated wooden building at the dock's entrance.

The isolation, combined with the lack of workers, made the area a perfect place for an ambush, which was why Kat had dropped Daisy and their footman off a few blocks away, to keep her protected. Kat wasn't simply going to walk into a trap and bring the only bargaining chip she had with her. And though Daisy had been prepared to sacrifice herself for her son, Kat refused to allow her to.

It was a strategy certain to anger the Chameleon but would buy Kat some much-needed time to assess the situation and bargain with the man, which in turn would hopefully provide her with an opportunity to kill him first, before allowing him to further destroy everything else she held dear.

Pushing open the carriage door, Kat stepped onto the rough ground beneath, her black boots finding purchase, while her head darted right and then left, but there were no signs of anyone.

The chill breeze blowing across the Thames onto the land sent a swift shiver of apprehension along her spine. The day was turning dark as the grey clouds overhead travelled swiftly in from the west, bringing with them an ominous sign of an impending storm. A slight tickle of fear for Samuel began to creep into her throat again, and she had to push it down into the abyss with all her might. She had to stay focused. Sam's life depended on it.

Kat smacked the wood of the carriage door closed, and her driver drove the carriage away as she'd instructed him to, while she swiveled in a circle, her gaze taking in everything.

The place appeared abandoned, even though she'd made it there within the designated time period, but she still got the sense she was being watched. Her eyes drifted up to the roof of the two-story building across from her, and then back to the small building by the dock. If she were the Chameleon, she'd have positioned herself in one of the two buildings, with a direct view of where Kat was standing now.

In fact, she was counting on it.

The water of the river hummed in the background, as did some distant hammering, but there were no sounds within the immediate vicinity. Damn it, she was getting impatient to get this over with. Every further minute didn't assist Sam. "Well, I'm here, as directed," she yelled across the empty space, hoping to draw her nemesis out. Her eyes scanned over the windows of the warehouse, wishing to see a sign of something, or of someone. "Haven't you had enough of hiding? Don't you want to reveal yourself?"

"But I already have revealed myself to you," a soft and sultry voice said, carried along on the breeze to Kat's left. "You just didn't know it at the time."

Spinning around, Kat saw a woman with blonde hair step out from behind the building beside the dock and slowly walk toward her. There was a smile on the woman's blood red lips, which matched the red splatters staining some strands of the woman's hair. She came to a stop about fifteen feet from Kat. It took Kat a moment to see beyond the blonde hair, to recognize the woman who now stood in front of her.

"Lady Brighthope." A hollow sense of inevitability struck low in the pit of Kat's stomach, as things began to make an absurd sort of sense. "You're the Chameleon."

The woman who had bumped into Victor at the railway station before he was killed. The waiter at the theater who had been slight of stature. The fact that no man could be identified as the assassin. Everyone had assumed the assassin was male, Kat included. And considering people had always underestimated Kat herself because of her gender, she of all people should have known better than to make assumptions.

No wonder the Chameleon was called a ghost—no one had been looking for a woman.

"It's a pleasure to meet you properly, and allow you to see my true self." Brighthope curtsied, wearing trousers just like Kat's and seeming far too confident and in control than Kat would have liked her to be. "I thought you of all people would appreciate what I have accomplished, and how I have fooled everyone into thinking the Chameleon was a man. It's made things a great deal easier over the years. I managed to fool Westwood and Cantfield earlier today. It was thrilling as I thought they may have recognized me, even with the blonde wig, but they didn't. Men are so easy to fool, aren't they?" The woman pulled off the wig with a flourish.

"If you've hurt Marcus, I swear your death will be long and painful." Everything inside her rebelled at the possibility he could be hurt.

Brighthope lifted her dainty shoulders. "I

didn't harm him. He's not on my list and though he might be hunting me, he hasn't threatened me yet, so there's no need to kill him, for now. All he and Cantfield did was burst in on me only moments after I'd killed Mr. Morriset. I already had a plan in place in case I was interrupted, so I improvised, as I always do, and began wailing over the man's body, pretending to be his widow.

"They bought the act completely, and when they rushed out the back chasing the supposed assassin, I got away. It was all too easy, considering I'd very nearly been caught red-handed." She paused and smiled. "I did wish, though, that I could have stayed hidden somewhere and observed their faces when they realized they'd been fooled, but alas, I had this meeting of ours to attend."

"Where's Samuel?" Kat asked, relief flooding her that Marcus was safe.

"Your bluntness is something I've always admired," Brighthope replied with a slight laugh. "You should consider joining me. You'd make an excellent assassin. Not only do you have the skills, but just like me, no one would suspect you. It's the perfect profession for women trained as we have been. I could teach you everything I know."

"I intend to kill you, not join you."

"I know you do," Brighthope said, sounding delighted. "Why else do you think I revealed myself to you?"

"Why did you?"

"For too long I've been so bored with the world. Killing has become too easy for me, but then I became aware of you, and now I can't help but wonder which of us is better? I've never met an equal to me before, but perhaps I have with you, and I am intrigued."

"You kidnapped Samuel simply to see if you could best me?" Kat was sure the scorn she felt was apparent in her voice.

Brighthope shrugged daintily. "I also need to kill your aunt, of course, and that residence of yours is far too fortified to get into, so I needed you to bring her here, but I knew you'd need an incentive to come."

"You got into my residence earlier and murdered my butler, so it can't be all that fortified." The rage, the devastation, and the grief over Fenton's senseless death threatened to overwhelm her. Standing in front of her was the woman who'd taken both Victor and Fenton from her. In a few seconds, Kat could grab her dagger and fling it into the woman's heart and end her. And perhaps end the unrelenting ache of pain, too. But she'd promised Marcus she wouldn't. Not yet, anyhow.

"I wouldn't do that if I was you," Brighthope said, her eyes glancing down to where Kat's fingers inched closer to the dagger strapped to her leg. "I have a man watching from the building who is under strict instructions to slit the boy's throat if anything happens to me. In any event, I did not kill your butler."

The words were like a bucket of ice over Kat's head. "Yes, you did. You shot him, earlier today. A bullet to his chest."

"I've killed Danbury and Morriset today," Brighthope replied. "My schedule has been far too busy to add your butler to my list."

"I don't understand, you had to have killed him…" If it wasn't the Chameleon, who else could have killed Fenton?

"I didn't, I assure you. Though I did have a man, the one who took the boy, watching your residence earlier today." Her very posture and gaze seemed to radiate truthfulness. But she was a good actress, though Kat was inclined to believe her, because why would she lie? "Whoever killed your butler did me a favor by spooking the boy, sending him fleeing into the waiting arms of my man."

"Where's Samuel?" Kat asked, returning to the most important question.

Brighthope laughed. "There's that bluntness of yours again. I adore it." She whistled shrilly and a door to the warehouse on Kat's right creaked opened. A short and burly man appeared in the doorway, holding a pistol in one hand while his other clutched Samuel's upper arm like a vice.

It took nearly all of Kat's self-control to stop

herself from running over to him. "Are you all right, Sam?" she yelled across to him.

Samuel nodded his head, his eyes wide and skin pale, but there was a hint of determination in his stubborn little jaw which Kat took comfort in. Sam was a Montrose, and like all Montrose's, stubbornness and grit were built into his very core. And though obviously scared, he wasn't broken, either physically or mentally. Thank goodness.

"Now, disarm yourself carefully." Brighthope glanced at Kat's dagger and pistol strapped to her trousers. "And if you try anything, my man will kill the boy."

Slowly, Kat drew out both her daggers from their sheaths and threw them several feet behind her, cringing at the loss. Then she unholstered her pistol and tossed it toward the daggers. She felt naked without her weapons.

"Good. Now, I've kept my side of the bargain," Brighthope all but purred. "But it seems you haven't, my dear, for I do not see Lady Montrose with you. And that was the precondition to getting the boy back." Her head flicked over to Samuel and the man. "Take him back inside and wait for me in there."

The man stepped back into the space with Samuel and closed the door behind them.

"I'm disappointed you didn't heed my warning, for you know I do not bluff. I have a reputation I must maintain or else my name will not instill the fear or the financial reward it currently does. You were meant to bring her to me." There was a hard edge to the woman's words and Kat could tell she was angry. "Where is she?"

"Samuel is not on your list," Kat said. "Let him go. He's an innocent child."

"Then you should have bought your aunt with you."

"She's in the vicinity and when Samuel is safe she will attend here."

The woman arched a brow at Kat. "If I release the boy to you, there's no way you will risk your aunt. Although, perhaps you will, if you know the full truth."

Kat blinked as a tightness started to ball in her chest. "What do you mean, full truth?"

A slow smile split the woman's lips and she took a step closer to Kat, stopping short of arm's length. "Let me tell you a little secret regarding your uncle's death. Though it's true I killed him, and I would've done so regardless of getting paid to or not—"

"That's no secret." Kat narrowed her eyes at the woman. "My uncle was getting too close to discovering your true identity, wasn't he?"

The woman actually laughed. "He wasn't close at all. I wanted him dead because at the time I believed he was responsible for killing my sister,

Irena."

Irena? Nathaniel had been in love with a woman called Irena. "The bomb blast in Paris? When my uncle was hunting Nathaniel Black? That Irena?"

Brighthope's eyes tightened at the corners. "Yes. She was my younger sister who got caught up in this world of intrigue when she met Nathaniel Black and fell in love with him. I warned her against fleeing with him, after I'd assisted his superior in framing him as a traitor. But she didn't listen to me and ran off with him to Paris, where your uncle hunted them down at the War Office's request, and set the bomb that killed them both."

The woman took in a deep breath. "My beautiful baby sister was killed. Surely, you of all people can understand why I wanted to kill your uncle. That I had to avenge my sister, just as you want to avenge your uncle by killing me. It's the same, is it not?"

"No. It's not the same at all." The thought wound around in her head, trying to find traction but slipping into nothingness.

"It's exactly the same!" Brighthope hissed. "I wanted vengeance for my sister's death. You want vengeance for your uncle and intend to kill me to obtain it. How is that any different than me killing your uncle? Who is in the right? I was avenging my sister, and you are trying to avenge your uncle.

We're the same, you and I, as much as you might pretend otherwise. Your intention is to attain justice with my death, just as mine was, even though I was paid for it, too."

"We're nothing alike, you and I." Though Kat couldn't help but think that perhaps they were. Had she become so lost in her desire for vengeance? "Besides, my uncle wasn't responsible for planting the bomb that killed your sister. He would never have jeopardized innocent lives like that."

"I know that now," Brighthope conceded. "Turns out the one responsible was Lord Newtown who was carrying out orders at the behest of Sir Albert. But as you know I've taken care of Newtown, with your help, of course. You left me in his library, and I knew that's where Newtown would be sent for his safety after I ordered Matthew to create chaos at the ball. It was so easy to slip the poison into his decanter, which I knew he wouldn't resist having a drink from."

"Sir Albert is the traitor, not Sir William?"

"Yes. Who would have thought such a portly little man was the one selling secrets to the Russians, and framing Nathaniel Black for it. And now trying to frame Sir William. He's a dastardly little fellow who paid me to seduce Westwood's wife to retrieve the intelligence Westwood held in his safe regarding the Afghan border negotiations."

"You were the countess's lover?"

"The poor lady was so starved of affection from that cold fish, Westwood, it was all too easy to seduce her. In fact, I think she was rather thrilled with such an illicit liaison with another woman, having never been with a woman before. She was far too easy to manipulate and use to obtain access to the information Westwood was collating."

"Which you sold to the Russians?"

"Actually, Sir Albert hired me and then sold on that information to the Russians with my assistance. Though, of course, he didn't know he was hiring *me*, as he has no clue who the Chameleon is."

"And he was the one who arranged Victor's death?"

"He did. He is also the man now paying me to kill all those who present a threat to revealing the truth of his past. But don't worry." The Chameleon shrugged. "I've added him to my list, too. The fool has no idea who I am, or that Irena was my sister. He will pay for ordering the bomb that killed her. I shall have great fun killing him, which I would have done years ago if I'd known the truth."

"Why did Sir Albert frame Nathaniel? Surely, he would have known Westwood would never believe such a thing and hunt down those responsible for his brother's death."

"It was my suggestion to frame Nathaniel." The woman pressed her lips together. "He'd stolen my sister from me by convincing her to run away with him, so he had to pay, and what better way for a man than to have his honor destroyed. Which is what I shall do with Sir Albert's before killing him." She pulled out an envelope and tossed it at Kat's feet. "Evidence that proves Sir Albert's treachery and will exonerate Nathaniel Black."

Confusion rolled over her. "Why are you giving this to me?"

"Your friend's father owns a newspaper." The Chameleon smiled at her. "When she finds your body, she will ensure her father publishes it. It's rather salacious."

"You're confident things will go your way." She didn't know whether to admire the woman's confidence or deplore it.

"I am," she purred. "Because you'll be far too distracted by the truth to win against me."

"The truth?"

"Yes," Brighthope said. "Haven't you ever wondered *who* paid to have your uncle killed?"

"You said Sir Albert arranged it."

"He did, but he was only an intermediary, brokering the assassination." Brighthope's eyes were wide. "The one truly responsible for Victor Montrose's death was his dear wife."

Kat's whole world stilled. "Daisy?"

"Yes." There was a glance of perhaps compassion on the woman's face as she stared at Kat.

"Who else had the most to gain from his death?"

"No, that's not true. Daisy didn't pay to have him killed." Brighthope was toying with her, trying to get her to hand over Daisy so she could kill her. "You're a liar."

"Oh, I do regularly lie, that is true, but for what little it's worth, I promise you I'm not lying about your aunt." Brighthope paused. "I can see perhaps the truth is finally starting to penetrate your denials. Hand over your aunt and I will kill her for you, then justice will be served for your uncle. Both of us shall be happy."

"No, you're lying." She had to be lying. But in the recesses of Kat's heart it was all starting to make a sick sort of sense, and part of her was beginning to desperately fear that Brighthope might in fact be telling the truth. Surely, Daisy wouldn't have paid to have Victor killed?

"Don't believe me, then." Brighthope shifted her weight onto her back leg. "But it will be at your peril."

Suddenly, the woman sprung at her, drawing a knife from her pocket simultaneously and aiming it at Kat's throat. Pivoting backward, Kat blocked the woman's hand with her forearm, concurrently twisting and launching a spinning kick at the Chameleon's waist.

The woman anticipated the move and twisted to the side before spinning around with the knife held out in front of her. She grinned at Kat. "Oh, you are good. But I've had years more experience, my darling." She rushed at Kat, knife held steady.

Instead of pivoting away, Kat dove forward, slightly to the side, using the momentum of her legs to knock the woman's feet out from under her, sending Brighthope headfirst to the ground, her knife clattering to the side. Dust flew up around them as Kat jumped to her feet while Brighthope did a roll and came crouching up to stand.

The woman was fast and agile, and for the first time, Kat doubted her skills. Was she a fool to think she could beat a woman who'd been killing others for years? But with little time to think any other thoughts, the woman rushed at her again, launching into a front kick as she got close.

Kat blocked Brighthope's leg with her forearm and landed a swift counterstrike to the woman's ribs with her fist. Brighthope grunted, but elbowed Kat in the shoulder, knocking her slightly off balance.

For several minutes, they parried back and forth, striking and blocking each other's arms and legs. Both trained in Eastern fighting techniques, and both an equal match. They came perilously close to the dock edge and the water at one point, but Kat swiveled away, and they parried closer to the road, though kept straying back along the edge.

Kat's focus was on the woman in front of her

as sweat beaded on her forehead while she tried to outthink her with each step. Going on instinct, Kat let Brighthope's next kick connect with her legs and knock her to the ground. Brighthope immediately pounced on top of her, holding another knife she must have drawn from a hidden pocket or holster. Kat didn't flinch as Brighthope waved the blade in front of her.

"You are good." Brighthope panted heavily. "But I'm better."

Before Brighthope could blink, Kat flicked her hips up and threw Brighthope to the side, landing on top of her and grabbing the knife from the woman's hand.

She found herself holding the blade against the woman's throat. Revenge was hers. With the lightest twist of her wrist, she could have her vengeance against Victor's killer and end Brighthope here and now. She could kill the woman who'd already killed so many. She could finally protect her family and see justice done.

"Do it," Brighthope urged. "Kill me. I know you have it in you. I've seen death in your eyes."

For a minute, Kat fought with her inner demons. She'd longed, even dreamed of this moment. The thought of killing Victor's murderer had been a constant one in her mind ever since Victor's death, but now that the moment was here, she wasn't so certain anymore.

Yes, she had killed before, but that had been in self-defense. This would be murder.

"Do it!" Brighthope yelled. "You're just like me. Embrace the darkness inside you and become what you are meant to be."

It was then Kat knew to the depths of her being that though she may have killed in the past, and had intended to kill the Chameleon, she was not a killer. She wouldn't be brought down to Brighthope's level. "I am nothing like you. I *choose* to be nothing like you, and that is what makes us different." Slowly, she stood and stepped away from the assassin. "Marcus was right. Justice for you will be you spending the rest of your life in a cold, damp, dark cell, paying for the crimes you've committed. That will be a much greater punishment instead of a swift death. Now get up."

Brighthope got to her feet and grinned. "My man still has Samuel, darling girl. You might want to drop your dagger before his finger gets twitchy, thinking something may happen to me."

"Is he safe?" Kat glanced behind Brighthope to where Daisy now stood.

"He is. Our men are taking him home and will then return for us."

Brighthope swung her head around to Daisy and then back to Kat. "What did you do?"

Kat took in a deep breath. "While I occupied you with fighting, my coach driver and footman entered the warehouse and knocked out your man, saving Samuel. Daisy was waiting to give me word he was safe."

"You outwitted me?" There was shock pasted on the woman's face. "How did you even know beforehand I'd have him on site here, in the warehouse?"

"It's what I would have done. And though I might not have known your identity, I knew what the Chameleon would have done." Kat shrugged. "I anticipated you and distracted you to save my family."

"Well, aren't you clever. But how clever will you be dealing with your aunt?" The Chameleon grinned. "Are you going to let her get away with murder? Because though she may not have pulled the trigger, she did pay to have your uncle killed."

A shot rang out in the still air and Brighthope jolted forward, collapsing onto her front, a bullet hole in her back, blood slowly seeping from it.

Kat stared across at Daisy, who held a smoking pistol in her hands, which she now aimed directly at Kat.

Chapter Forty

Everything inside of Kat plummeted as a numbness stole through her entire body. "Brighthope was telling the truth, then? You paid to have Victor killed?"

"Victor was destroying the estate, and all but bankrupting us on his crusades for the government." Daisy's fingers clenched the weapon while she walked over to Kat, stepping around Brighthope's prone body. "Don't you understand that he was going to be our ruin? He was already trying to turn Samuel into a weapon like he did you. I wasn't going to let him do that. I couldn't let him risk my child as he risked you, and bankrupt Samuel out of his future inheritance. Surely, you understand? I had to protect Samuel. It was the only way to stop Victor."

Daisy came to a halt several feet from Kat, enough for her to be within easy aiming distance, but not enough for Kat to knock the weapon from her hands.

"Fenton. That was you, too, wasn't it?" Her voice was without feeling or inflection, as the full truth of the situation hit home. "The one bullet missing from your derringer… That was the bullet you used to kill Fenton."

"Fenton's death was entirely your fault. If you had stopped trying to chase the Chameleon as I had begged you to, over and over again, none of this would have happened. But you're so stubborn, just like Victor was," Daisy declared. "You simply wouldn't leave well enough alone, and you had to ask Fenton to look further into all of this, which he of course did, devoted to you as he was. He soon realized I was the one who paid for the assassin, which is why I had to kill him before he could warn you. And, thankfully, his shooting lessons came in very handy, as I suspected they would when I asked for them."

"You'd planned to kill Fenton all along?"

Daisy shook her head vehemently. "Not at all. I'd hoped you would listen to reason, but of course you didn't. I had to prepare myself to protect Samuel at all costs."

"How is killing Fenton or me, protecting Samuel?" Kat felt the numbness slowly lift as unadulterated fury began to edge up her throat. She wanted to claw Daisy's eyes out with her bare fingers.

"Samuel is the Earl of Montrose!" Daisy screamed. "He would be ruined if it was known I had his father killed."

"What a load of nonsense." Kat took a step toward her. "You aren't protecting Samuel."

"Stop right there!" Daisy stretched her arms out farther, the gun pointing at Kat. "Thanks to you I still have one bullet left in the second chamber."

Kat stopped her advance and focused all her rage into her voice. "You're protecting yourself, and pretending you're doing so for Samuel is what a coward would do. And a coward is exactly what you are! You'll burn in hell, Daisy, for your part in all of this, and I'll be glad for it."

"Don't you say that!" Daisy shrieked. "Don't you dare say that. I am protecting my son. God will forgive my transgressions."

"How could you have done this? Victor loved you."

"He never loved me!" There was bitterness in her words. "Victor was in love with your mother, Kaitlyn, he always was. He never loved me. He only ever had room to love your mother and his daughter, you."

"You know?"

"Of course I know. I stole the key to his safe when he was drunk on one of the anniversaries of your mother's death. He always used to drink himself silly on that night each year, though he always made sure to stay home in his bedroom. However, on one such occasion when he was passed out on his bed, I decided to take the key to his safe he always kept on him and see exactly what he kept in there."

"You read his letter to me."

"I did, though I never said anything to him, or anyone else. Could you imagine the scandal it would bring upon Samuel if it became known? And I assumed you'd probably also read the letter after he died, as I doubted he would have told you if he'd still been alive. You all but held the man up on a pedestal. I don't think he had the courage to knock himself off that, with the truth of your parentage. His brother must never have suspected, either, as he accepted you as his, and by all accounts doted on you. He would have been a much better father than Victor. He would have let you be the lady that you were supposed to be, instead of the weapon Victor made you into."

"Victor made sure I could protect myself." Kat had never felt such conflicting emotions before. On one hand, she wanted to kill Daisy. The woman had taken Victor and Fenton from her without thought or feeling. But Daisy had been part of her life for over a decade. And she was Samuel's mother. How could she kill her half brother's mother? Suddenly, she felt overpowered by sadness. "I loved you like an aunt, Daisy. You were family and I would've killed to protect you."

"Just as I'm killing to protect Samuel." Daisy took in a deep breath. "I am sorry, Kaitlyn, but now it really is impossible to let you live. I didn't want to do this. I had hoped that in seeking out Sir

Albert and having him arrange the death of Victor, that our troubles would stop. But then you had to keep chasing after Victor's killer. This is all your fault. Please know that. It was your choices that forced me into this position."

Kat exhaled harshly. "So Brighthope was telling the truth. Sir Albert was the one to arrange Victor's death? The traitor in the War Department."

"Yes. I realized he was the one selling secrets to the Russians after I translated a particular missive. Instead of telling Victor, I knew I could use the knowledge to obtain Sir Albert's cooperation in having Victor killed. Though I also knew that a man like Sir Albert would have no compulsion in having me killed too, especially as I was privy to such information about him."

"You always have been clever."

"I wrote everything down and left instructions with a solicitor that if anything was to ever happen to me, the information was to be sent to the relevant authorities and the press. It was my life insurance policy of sorts, which I made certain Sir Albert knew about, though, of course, I didn't tell him who or where my secret was being kept. Mr. Morriset must have used the information to try to blackmail Sir Albert, which is why Sir Albert sent the Chameleon after us all. The fool. And I'm glad the Chameleon got to Morriset. I just wish she'd also gotten to Sir Albert, too. Now it means

I'll have to kill him, though at least everyone will think the Chameleon did it, and no one will even bother to launch an investigation into his death."

"Well, before you go on this murdering rampage of yours, you might want to make sure that you cock the hammer of your derringer, first, Daisy. It won't fire otherwise."

And when Daisy glanced down at the pistol, as Kat knew she would, she rushed in toward her, and before Daisy could even register what she was about, Kat simultaneously wrenched the pistol from Daisy's hand and pushed her backward. As Daisy stumbled back a step, Kat twisted the pistol to point it at her aunt, her finger resting on the trigger.

Her eyes met Daisy's and all she could see was her aunt's betrayal flashing in their depths. Her gaze flicked down to her own finger, poised on the trigger and just itching to press backward, the ghosts of Fenton and Victor swimming in her vision.

"They trusted you, Daisy." Kat's jaw clenched as she could clearly see the lack of remorse on the woman's face. "We all did. You have to pay for taking them both from me. From Samuel, too."

"What? And you're going to make me pay? You're going to kill your half brother's mother?" There was scorn in her voice. "How would you ever explain that to Samuel? We both know you're not going to kill me, Kaitlyn."

"Do we, Daisy?" Kat's hand tightened on the pistol grip. "Because I'm not so sure about that. You paid to have my father killed. And then you murdered Fenton after he did *nothing* to you! You took them both away from me. It is because of you that I can never see them again. Never speak with them again. Never embrace them again. You went after my family."

"I've told you why I had to do that." There was a quiver in her voice, replacing the certainty that had been there a moment ago. "I was protecting Samuel. You can't take me from him."

"I can and I will." Kat took in a deep breath. "You deserve to die, Daisy. You truly do. You're the true monster in all of this. The Chameleon was just a pawn at the end of the day. I see that now."

"No wait, Kaitlyn! Please don't kill me. You mustn't. I beg you, please…"

As Kat stared into her aunt's eyes, eyes that were filled with terror, it was Samuel's face she saw reflected back at her. Even with the terrible things Daisy had done, she was family and Kat couldn't kill family. But she could make sure the woman rotted in a cold cell for the rest of her days. Slowly, she lowered her pistol. "You're right, Daisy. I can't kill you."

Relief flooded her aunt's eyes. "Thank you, Kaitlyn."

"Well, if you can't kill her, I will," a voice spoke

from behind Daisy.

Instantly, Daisy jerked forward, a grimace etched across her face. Almost in slow motion, Kat saw Brighthope crouching behind Daisy, ripping a dagger from Daisy's back as Daisy collapsed to the ground, blood pooling from her ribs. Brighthope launched herself at Kat, charging at her, holding a knife dripping with Daisy's blood in her hand.

Kat didn't hesitate. She pulled the trigger, her aim directed straight between Brighthope's eyes. The gun recoiled in her hand as the bullet penetrated Brighthope's skull, stopping her in her tracks, and flinging her backward to the ground, dead.

Glancing at the carnage that was both Daisy and Lady Brighthope's bodies, Kat collapsed to her knees and couldn't control the sobs that started emanating from a place deep inside her, a place she'd thought long buried after Victor's death, but had been unleashed earlier today with Fenton's death, and now with Daisy's.

Kat crawled over to Daisy, knowing that the deep crimson color of the blood gushing from her back meant the knife had hit an artery and that it would already be too late. Rolling Daisy over, Kat was confronted with the glassy stare of her aunt, and though she'd expected it, it still hit her hard and her breathing became shallow.

Daisy was dead.

And though Daisy was responsible for Victor

and Fenton's deaths, Kat felt the anguish over her death almost like a physical blow as her heart ached at the betrayal and the loss of a woman she'd considered family.

How would Kat explain this to Samuel? That she'd been unable to save his mother… That it was Daisy who'd been the one ultimately responsible for the death of his father? With a dawning of understanding, Kat began to comprehend the quandary Victor must have faced about whether to tell her the truth that he was her father. The fear of how she would react, knowing he was all too human after all and wasn't perfect as she'd believed him to be.

And now she was faced with the same decision about Daisy and what to tell Samuel. Glancing down at the alabaster face of her aunt, Kat was struck by the knowledge that Daisy really was dead. Her pale and lifeless body was just a shell of who she'd been only moments before, barren of any life or vitality that had made her who she was.

Daisy was gone. Fenton was gone. Victor was gone.

Kat was all alone now, left to look after Samuel. The thought hit her with such force that she collapsed over Daisy and held on to her, sobbing as she was wracked with the enormity of being so alone and so desperately missing those she'd lost. She wept and wept, her body heaving with the effort.

"Kat? Are you hurt?" It was Marcus's voice penetrating her awareness as if from a great distance, soothing her as nothing else could. Slowly, she raised her head, and saw him running to her. He crouched down and gently brushed his thumb over her cheeks, wiping away some of the tears still sweeping down her face. There was such concern in his eyes, that in that moment Kat understood she wasn't so alone.

Turning into his arms, she breathed in his strength and held onto him as if he were her lifeline from drowning. "No, I'm physically fine."

"You're going to be okay, my darling," he whispered into her hair. "I'm here for you. Everything is going to be all right."

Kat didn't know how long they sat like that, with her wrapped up in the cocoon of his arms, but she knew that she was going to be all right. She had to be, for herself and Samuel. Pulling back from his embrace, she raised her eyes to his.

"What happened?" he asked, his gaze glancing over first to Daisy's body and then to Brighthope's, as he helped her to her feet.

So, she told him everything, except the truth of her parentage. And as she was recounting what had happened, she realized with a sick sense of dread that Sir Albert was still a true threat.

"Yes, I found documents in Morriset's apartment authored by Daisy, confirming Sir

Albert's involvement. I need to find him," Marcus said, all but reading her mind. "I've sent Lucas for the police and he should return shortly. Once he arrives, do you wish to come with me or go to Samuel?"

"I'll go with you," she said, taking in one breath after another, trying to look anywhere than at Daisy.

"Are you certain, Kat?" Marcus asked, reaching out and brushing back a wisp of her hair. "After all you've been through today, no one would blame you for wanting to go home and be with Samuel."

The thought of returning home brought a knot of nausea with it. Walking through the halls, everywhere she'd turn she'd see shadows of Fenton and Daisy and her own lack of awareness of Daisy's betrayal. "I'll be fine. I need to see this through."

Chapter Forty-One

Sir Albert's townhouse overlooked Park Square in Marylebone, a neighborhood consisting of mostly upper-class inhabitants, with rather lofty terrace houses in a horseshoe formation surrounding the green park in the center.

But rather than approaching the residence from the front, Marcus had directed his carriage driver to drop him and Kat at the rear of the property, in the small laneway. Stepping down from the carriage, he glanced sideways at Kat as they proceeded to the back gate of the property.

Even though she said she'd be all right, he was still worried about her, having seen the devastation in her very being when he'd arrived at the docks. And though his first thought had been relief that she was alive, seeing her pain had nearly undone him. There'd always been such an inner strength and determination deep inside her that seeing her so despondent broke a little part of his heart.

And there was such heartbreak in her eyes, the entire carriage ride here. He didn't know how to comfort her. He couldn't imagine the hurt she must feel from her aunt's betrayal.

Not for the first time did he question whether he should have brought Kat with him. She'd endured so much pain today that he was worried about her. But perhaps she'd obtain some sense of closure and justice when they apprehended Sir Albert, and in doing so would prevent Nathaniel from doing something stupid, like killing the man, which Marcus believed was likely.

Even the thought of his brother cast a pang of regret within him. Why hadn't Nathaniel approached him? Told him he was alive? After three years of thinking he was dead, it was surreal to know the truth. His mother would be beyond thrilled, as would his sister.

Shaking away the bitter sense of betrayal and hurt, Marcus quietly lifted the latch on the gate and motioned for Kat to go ahead of him down the path leading to the back door. They paused on the threshold, listening for a moment. When he was satisfied the hallway beyond sounded free from movement, he twisted the handle and opened the door a notch. There were some stairs to his left, leading down to the kitchen below, but thankfully no servants seemed to be present in the hall.

He stepped inside, and then nodded for Kat to enter, too, before he silently closed the door behind them. He nodded to the right, down the corridor toward Sir Albert's study. If the man was home, that's the place he'd most likely be.

A few moments later, he paused in front of the door to Sir Albert's study and Kat followed suit. He could hear some slight murmuring through the oak. Unholstering his faithful Webley pistol, he felt the comforting weight of the weapon nestled against his palm. With his left hand, he twisted the knob and carefully opened the door but an inch.

"Do you really think killing me will exonerate you?" Sir Albert said.

"Perhaps not, but it will avenge Irena."

His brother's voice was unmistakable and for a moment Marcus felt such relief, having once thought he'd never hear the sound again.

Swinging the door wide, Marcus stepped into the room with Kat following. Sir Albert glanced up from where he sat behind his desk on the far side of the room, and then Nathaniel swung his head around to face them, his arm locked in front of him, holding a pistol steadily aimed at Sir Albert.

"Oh, thank goodness you're both here!" Sir Albert exclaimed upon seeing Marcus and Kat. "It seems your brother has been playing a dangerous game pretending to be dead, when in fact he's been working for the Russians. You must arrest him, immediately."

"You're a goddamn liar!" Nathaniel snarled, his eyes briefly returning to Sir Albert. "But you'll be a dead liar soon." He glanced back to Marcus and nodded his head. "It's good to see you, brother. Kat," he said. "But I do hope neither of you intend to try to stop me from ridding the world of this piece of vermin."

Kat had been right; Nathaniel had changed. Marcus could see that instantly.

Gone was the happy-go-lucky younger brother he'd grown up with, and in his place was an angry man, with a thirst for vengeance. And who could really blame him, when Sir Albert was the architect of so much misery in all of their lives over the past three years? Could justice really be obtained by arresting him?

"I haven't decided yet," Marcus told him, which was the truth. Though he believed in justice, he also knew that with the contacts Sir Albert had it was more than likely he'd escape at some point. Perhaps Kat was right—sometimes vengeance was necessary to obtain true justice.

"You worked out he was behind it all," Kat said to Nathaniel as she strolled closer to where he stood.

"I suspected, and now I'm certain," Nathaniel said.

"You're in league with the traitor, Lady Kaitlyn?" Sir Albert exclaimed. "Good God, Westwood, arrest them both!"

"Really?" Kat glanced over to Sir Albert. "That's how you're going to spin all this?"

"The game is up, Sir Albert," Marcus added,

raising his pistol until it also pointed at Sir Albert.

"You can't seriously think I had anything to do with any of this," Sir Albert said, his eyes narrowing upon them all. "Your brother is the traitor. For goodness sakes, he even faked his death over it. I expect you to do your duty, Westwood. You must arrest him."

Marcus turned to look at his brother, his pistol staying steady on Sir Albert. "You could have come to me, you know. Let me know you were alive." The words were out of his mouth before he could stop them. "I would have helped you."

Nathaniel's lips pressed together in a firm line. "That's why I didn't, Marcus. I'd already botched everything up royally. This mess was mine to clean up."

"It was both of ours," Marcus countered. "The Chameleon seduced Elizabeth to get the information I was holding in my safe. If I had paid better attention to what Elizabeth was up to, the information wouldn't have been stolen and given to Sir Albert to sell to the Russians in the first place. And then Sir Albert wouldn't have had to frame you as his scapegoat."

"What?" Sir Albert cried. "I'd never do such a thing. I'm on the Chameleon's assassination list! If I was guilty, I wouldn't be on there. You should be more worried about protecting me. Perhaps your brother is the Chameleon! Have you considered that?"

"The Chameleon is dead, Sir Albert," Kat said. "And she mentioned your involvement in everything before she died."

"She?" The word left Sir Albert's lips, absolute shock on his face, almost as if he were about to collapse.

"Yes, she. Natalia Brighthope was the assassin."

An unearthly silence filled the room at the pronouncement.

"The Chameleon was a female? I wouldn't have thought that possible…" He straightened in his chair and seemed to recover from his shock. "Surely, though, you don't believe the word of a woman like *that*?"

The man was good at playing the outraged innocent, Marcus would give him that.

"She was extremely convincing," Kat said as she pulled out her dagger and then tossed it in her hand, catching the hilt perfectly.

"She was nothing more than a lady of the night," Sir Albert continued. "No one would believe her. Don't you both see? It's perfect! She needed me dead to complete her target list, so she concocted such a tale." He waved his hands wildly about. "Telling you I was the culprit. Hoping, obviously, you'd both want to kill me after hearing such lies."

"That does make some sense," Marcus said.

Sir Albert puffed up. "Good, I'm glad you've seen reason. Now, would you both mind lowering your weapons, please."

None of them did as requested.

"Let me rephrase," Marcus said. "It would have made sense, except Lady Montrose also confirmed your involvement in everything before she died. How she discovered your perfidy when translating some missives for Victor, and rather than tell him what she'd found, she instead approached you to have Victor killed to keep her silence. Which you did, and I imagine if she hadn't told you that she'd written down all of your sins and had them in safekeeping with someone, to be released to the world at large if anything happened to her, I daresay you would have had the Chameleon kill her, too, straight after Montrose."

"Lady Montrose is dead?" Sir Albert said in a rush. "Well, then you have no proof."

Marcus walked over to Sir Albert's desk, his pistol staying steady on the man as he reached into his jacket pocket with his free hand and removed some papers. He flung Daisy's notes onto the table, far enough out of Sir Albert's reach, but enough so that he could see them. "We also found Silas Morriset, and he'd left Lady Montrose's detailed notes on your perfidy, Albert. Very detailed and incriminating notes. The woman was thorough."

The man's face blanched and his fingers gripped the edge of his desk until the knuckles were white. "You can't do this to me. I'm now the

Secretary of State of War, as Danbury is dead, so you will all drop your weapons and arrest him." He pointed over to Nathaniel. "Then leave my house!"

"No." There was no equivocation in Marcus's voice. "Like I said, the game is over, Sir Albert. There are others that know of this information. You can't keep pretending." Marcus prayed that the man would capitulate, especially before Kat took things into her own hands. He didn't like the glint of anger in her eyes as she stared at Sir Albert.

"That damn law clerk Morriset!" Sir Albert swore, banging his fist on the table, his jaw clenched. "He stole those notes and started blackmailing me! The fool. He is the one to blame for this whole mess."

It seemed Sir Albert was finally willing to concede his involvement. "You hired the Chameleon to find him and kill him, along with everyone else that had some involvement in the coverup?" Marcus asked.

"I had to." Sir Albert shrugged. "My men couldn't find Morriset, but I knew the Chameleon could. Thought I might as well tidy up everything while I was at it."

"Why, then, were you listed in the Chameleon's ledger that Fullbrink decoded?" That bit that had been puzzling Marcus. "Surely, you wouldn't have given your own name to the Chameleon?"

"Fullbrink came to see me first after decoding the thing, and I insisted he place my name on the list." Sir Albert slumped in his chair, defeat radiating from him. "I managed to convince him that if my name wasn't on there, then people might think I was behind the plot which would only serve to distract everyone and delay us from finding out who was really responsible."

"And Fullbrink believed you?"

"I'm convincing when I want to be." Sir Albert straightened in his seat and eyed Marcus in defiance.

"Why did you do it?" Kat asked the man, taking a step forward, now only a few feet away from the desk. "Why would you sell British intelligence to the Russians in the first place? How could you betray your country like that and blame Nathaniel in the process?" Kat's hand was steady on the hilt of her dagger as she stared at Sir Albert. "So many people died because of you."

"They had to die!"

"No, they didn't. They died so you could protect your secrets." Kat's eyes radiated absolute disgust.

"Why did you do it?" Nathaniel asked the man, taking a step forward. "Why did you blame me? Why did you bomb my apartment and kill Irena?" His hand was slightly shaky as his finger rested on the trigger of his pistol. "She died because of you."

"It wasn't my idea to blame you in the first place." Sir Albert stood and let out a cry of frustration. "Brighthope was my Russian contact and when it was suspected that an English agent was selling secrets to the Russians, she approached me suggesting I needed to find a scapegoat to brand as the traitor, otherwise Russia would not wish to continue paying me. Obviously, I had no idea she was the Chameleon then, or more recently, either. However, it was she who was the one to suggest you as a patsy. I guess she didn't like the fact that her sister had fallen in love with an Englishman, hence she was trying to get rid of you. She was protective of her sister. I was happy with the idea of deflecting any blame regarding my involvement with the Russians."

"So you ruined my life, and killed my love?" Nathaniel's hand gripped the pistol even tighter as he stared at Sir Albert, his arm trembling.

"The bomb was meant for you, not her," Sir Albert said as he sank back down in his chair. "You were the one supposed to die that day. Lucky for me, I laid the blame for the blast at Victor Montrose's feet. I daresay if Brighthope had known I was behind it, she would have killed me a long time ago."

"I'm glad she didn't know," Nathaniel replied. "Because that means I get the honor of sending you to hell."

"No, wait!" Sir Albert held up his hands, the buttons of his shirt straining with the movement. "There's no need to be hasty. If you kill me, you will be tried for murder, and no one will care about whether you were a traitor or not. You need me alive."

"Actually, Lady Brighthope kindly left a letter outlining your entire involvement with the Russians," Marcus said. "We don't need you alive at all to exonerate Nathaniel."

"Surely, you won't let me be killed in cold blood?" Sir Albert turned his attention to Marcus, his hands dropping into his lap. "You've always been a great believer in justice, Westwood. Don't falter now."

"Falter?" Marcus laughed. The audacity of the man was rather astonishing. "Do you think I'd lose any sleep if you died after all that you've done? Need I remind you, you orchestrated the death of my wife, sold intelligence to the Russians for which you framed my brother, then arranged for his death, organized the assassination of my mentor Victor Montrose, and goodness knows how many other people over the years, including several of the most recent assassinations I've been trying to stop. And yet you think I believe *you* deserve justice? I never took you for a dreamer, Sir Albert."

A wild-eyed desperation crossed Sir Albert's gaze, his attention darting between the three of them like a cornered animal. "You can't kill me in cold blood. None of you are murderers."

Marcus flicked his gaze to Kat and then Nathaniel. Both had been pushed to their limits, and though they needed closure, he didn't want them to kill in cold blood. Neither of them would forgive themselves. "He doesn't deserve a quick ending. It would be far more of a punishment to let him rot in prison for the rest of his miserable life."

"He has the contacts to escape a prison," Kat answered, her eyes steady on Sir Albert.

"She's right," Nathaniel added, his pistol still aiming at the man. "You know he does."

How could Marcus deny something that only moments ago had been his own thoughts on the matter? But before he could answer, from the corner of his eye Marcus saw Sir Albert's hand wrench a pistol out from under his desk. Everything slowed to a sickening, almost still-like quality, as Sir Albert's arm jerked up, his pistol outstretched and aiming straight at Kat.

"No!" Marcus yelled, instinctively aiming his own pistol at the man and pulling the trigger as he leaped in front of Kat, who threw her dagger. The explosion of shots reverberated throughout the room, bouncing off the walls and echoing loudly in Marcus's ears, as he and Kat tumbled to the ground.

For a moment he lay on top of her, both of them stunned.

Then he glanced to his side, toward Sir Albert. The man was sprawled back in his chair, his chest a bloody mess from both Nathaniel and Marcus's bullets, and Kat's dagger lodged in the man's right shoulder.

And in the end justice had been served, but he was glad to take the burden of taking the man's life instead of Kat having done so. As tough as she was, Marcus wanted to protect her with all that he had.

"Oh my God, Marcus, are you hurt?" Her hands frantically patted him across his back as she lay under him, seemingly searching for any bullet holes. "Please don't be hurt."

"I'm safe, my darling," he crooned in her ear, before pulling up on his elbows to look into her panic-stricken face. "Are you all right?"

"I'm fine." She nodded as they got to their feet. "You jumped in front of me?"

"Of course I did." His voice had become slightly hoarse all of a sudden as they now stood facing each other. "I'll always protect you."

"You could have been hurt or killed."

"I would die for you, Kaitlyn." It was the simple, unvarnished truth. The woman had infiltrated his heart, body, and soul, and he would give his life for her. He would give anything for her. If she would have him.

"Too many people have already died because

of me." Her voice was distant as she glanced over at Sir Albert. "I won't have you added to the list."

Nathaniel clearing his throat had them both whipping around to face him. "I hate to interrupt such a moment, but what do we do now?"

His brother had a point, of course. They had things to sort out here before he could sort out what the devil he and Kat were doing with each other. "Are you ready to come back from the dead?" Marcus asked him. "Because I know two ladies who would be desperate to see you again."

His brother closed his eyes and winced. "I don't know if I can face Mother and Isabelle, not after all that's happened."

"They'll understand."

"How could they? I didn't even attend father's funeral..." Nathaniel's voice trailed off.

"They will understand because I know first-hand what it's like to have mourned you only to have found out you're alive." Marcus approached Nathaniel and grabbed him in a bear hug. "It was the greatest gift I could have received."

Nathaniel returned the embrace. "I'm sorry for the pain I've put you all through."

Pulling away from him, Marcus kept his hands on his brother's upper arms and gave him a brief squeeze. "As I'm sorry for the pain you've suffered. But come, we'll sort this mess out, then we'll get Kat home. Tomorrow we can travel to the country and reveal the news to Mother and Isabelle."

Nathaniel nodded. "She doesn't seem like herself." He jerked his head over to where Kat was now standing by the far window, silently looking out across at the gardens.

Marcus quickly filled him in on the events of the day.

"I will miss him," Nathaniel said, referring to Fenton. "He loved her like a daughter. Like Victor never quite could."

"She'll feel the loss of Fenton always, I imagine," Marcus said. "Give me a moment with her."

Nathaniel nodded as Marcus walked across to where she stood.

She looked too still, almost like a statue, and he could feel the grief that was wrapped around her like a second skin.

Sensing his presence, she glanced at him. "It's finally over." There was neither joy nor upset in her voice.

"It is," Marcus said. "They can all rest in peace now."

"I hope so," Kat said, her voice devoid of emotion. "I thought I'd be more at peace when it was all over. Instead, I feel empty."

"Come on, let's get you home." He gently reached out and took her cold hand in his. "You've been through a lot today, and Samuel is going to need you."

And hopefully, if she was receptive, Marcus would be able to convince her of how much he needed her, too.

Chapter Forty-Two

It had been the most difficult day Kat had ever had to live through. A day she would go to bed hoping had all been a terrible nightmare, even though she knew it was shatteringly real.

Breaking the news to Sam that his mother was dead had very nearly broken Kat's heart, especially when his big green eyes had filled with tears and he'd launched into her arms and sobbed his little heart out. She'd held him tightly while he cried—while both of them cried, in fact. Both knowing the other was the only family they had left.

Sam had finally fallen asleep through sheer exhaustion from the exertion of crying, so Kat tucked him into his bed, vowing she would protect him with her life and do what she could to ensure he was also able to protect himself. Though she wouldn't be as rigid as Victor had been with her. Sam deserved to enjoy what little childhood he had left.

The thought of navigating life with just the two of them was daunting. And every time she'd even thought about it all evening, a horrid twisting sensation gripped her stomach and she felt sick with the thought of it. But they needed a fresh start. This house carried too many memories to be surrounded by, so soon after such grief. A trip to Europe or the Americas would help them to forget the pain.

Though each time she thought of traveling and leaving her friends, a knot formed in her stomach. And when she considered leaving Marcus, a sense of dread filled her. But what else could she do? He'd only mentioned marriage because he'd been worried about her falling pregnant, which she'd discovered a short time ago certainly wasn't the case.

Besides, she couldn't marry him, not with the scandal she could bring to his title if it were ever discovered she was Victor's daughter and not his niece. Marcus needed a countess who was not only free from scandal, but could actually be a wife and raise his children for him, a skill Kat had no idea if she possessed. The thought of being a mother terrified her. The only role model she'd ever had was Daisy, who turned out to be a murderer.

Fighting, strategy and organizing her informants, were basically the extent of Kat's abilities. And Marcus deserved so much more than that. He deserved a woman that would know how to look after him and run his household. A woman who didn't wear trousers, or scale balconies. He needed a countess of refinement and sophistication, not a woman who was secretly illegitimate with a penchant for causing scandals.

For a minute, she was mad with herself. She had to stop thinking of what could never be. And yes, the man might have captured her heart and made her feel things she never had. But that didn't mean she could throw caution to the wind and marry him. He'd end up hating her, if he knew the truth. And then hating her because she could never live up to being an ideal countess. And him hating her would be devastating, especially considering she was finally being truthful with herself and could acknowledge she'd fallen in love with the man.

How could she have let him worm his way into her heart, a place she was certain was frozen and impenetrable? But he had. Now she just had to work on pushing him away. Which was going to be difficult, especially as he was now waiting for her in the library, refusing to leave until she spoke with him.

Bracing herself, and putting on her most frosty of expressions, Kat made her way to the room. At the door, she stood there a moment as her eyes met his from across the space, to where he was standing beside the window.

"How is he?" Marcus asked, obviously referring to Samuel.

"Finally asleep." She walked into the room and went to stand by the hearth, as far from

Marcus as possible. "You didn't have to return. I know there's a lot to sort out with your brother's exoneration."

"I've already gotten Sir William onto all that, and he's ensuring Nathaniel will be fully cleared," he replied. "And I did have to return, as I will always be here for you."

"Don't say that, Marcus," she all but pleaded him.

He went to take a step toward her, but she held up her hand. "No. Please don't. I can't think clearly when you're too close to me…"

"That's a good thing, isn't it?" A soft smile spread across his lips. "And for what it's worth, I haven't been able to think clearly since meeting you. You've been in my thoughts like a constant spinning wheel. I wake up thinking about you. I go to bed thinking about you. Damn it, I think about you nearly every minute of the day."

"Stop. Please." She put her hand up to halt him. "Whatever this is between us can't keep going on. We can't keep having an illicit affair."

"I don't want to keep having an affair."

"You don't?" The words deflated her. "Well, that's good, then. We're in agreement."

"I want to marry you."

Her heart started to pound, but then she remembered why he was saying such a thing. "I'm not with child, Marcus. The reason you were going to break your vow to never marry again is gone, hence there's no reason to marry."

"But there's every reason." He walked across to her. "Now I'm going to lift my hand and place it under your chin, so don't try and defend yourself." He grinned while he did so, raising her chin until she was looking him fully in the eyes. "I can't imagine a world without you in my life. Marry me, Kat?" He smiled. "You see, I'm asking this time."

His words were a gentle plea and her heart twisted with them. But she couldn't marry him. "I've already told you I can't marry you. Please don't ask me again." She turned her back on him, unable to bear the close scrutiny of his all too penetrating eyes upon her for a moment longer. "Besides, I've decided that Samuel and I are going to travel overseas for a bit. I'm going to show him the world he's never been allowed to see."

"If you leave, then I will leave, too." Marcus shrugged. "I'll come with you."

"You can't leave," Kat replied. The thought was ludicrous. "You have estates to run."

He raised a brow. "I wouldn't be able to run my estates, because I'd be spending far too much time worried about what mischief you were getting up to."

Now it was Kat's turn to mimic his raised brow. "I don't need you to protect me, I can protect myself. And I don't get into mischief."

"I know you can protect yourself," he agreed, taking both of her hands in his. "But the truth is I love you, Kaitlyn. I love you so much that the thought of not seeing you every day for the rest of my life hurts me to my core."

"You can't love me!" Kat yelled. Didn't he understand how his words were piercing her heart just like a dagger would, if not more? "It is you who doesn't understand. I can never be a perfect countess for you. I know how to throw daggers, not dinner parties. Marriage between us would never work."

"That is nonsense," Marcus roared back. "I don't want a perfect countess. I had one of those and look how that worked out. I never want a god-damn perfect countess again. I want you, Kat. No one else but you. And if you won't have me, then I'll be alone for the rest of my life. Loving you and wishing you'd been more courageous with your heart to entrust it to me, as I'm willing to entrust my heart to you."

"I can't marry you."

"Of course you bloody well can," Marcus declared. "You're just scared and being stubborn about it."

"I'm protecting you."

"From what?"

"From the scandal of my birth." She inhaled a deep breath and before she lost her courage blurted out, "You wondered why I always call Victor by his name since he died, and not Uncle Victor? Well, it's because after his death I discovered Victor was my father, not my uncle. I'm illegitimate. Now do you see why I can't marry you?" Kat had thought she'd cried all her tears, but suddenly she felt like bawling, but she wouldn't do so in front of Marcus, not after revealing such a thing.

"I already knew that."

His words stopped her short. "*What*? But that's not possible… No one else except Daisy knew."

Marcus slowly took a step toward her. He reached over and picked up her hand. Kat let him, stunned into immobility with his pronouncement.

"One night, on the anniversary of your mother's death, about fourteen years ago, I went over to his residence and found him passed out in his study," Marcus said. "I helped him up to his room, and when I got him into his bed, he let slip that you were his daughter. He was lucid enough to mention he'd never told a soul before but drunk enough to tell me. So, yes, I know you're Victor Montrose's daughter, even though Society thinks you are his brother Edward's child."

Kat didn't know what to say. The fact that he'd known for literally years and had no qualms in asking her to marry him was somewhat incomprehensible. "Don't you understand what it means, though? If that's ever discovered, there will be a scandal. Your family could be ruined by it."

Marcus shrugged and grinned. "What's another scandal to add to my long list? My wife was an adulterer who was having an affair with a woman assassin, and my brother was labeled a traitor and only now is finally about to have his good name restored. So, really, even if anyone finds out you're Victor's daughter instead of his niece, I think that fact rather pales compared to the other scandals I've endured. Don't you?"

Goodness, she wanted to believe him. But everyone she had loved had been taken away from her. If she allowed herself to love Marcus like she wanted to, he'd surely be taken from her, too. "I can't do it, Marcus. I can't risk losing you, too. I'd be broken if I did. Who am I fooling? I'm already broken after today, as it is. But if I lost you, too, I wouldn't survive."

"Yes, you would, Kat. And you're not broken." He gently raised his hand to cup her cheek, and she let him, unable to resist feeling his palm against her skin one last time. "You are the strongest woman I know, mentally, emotionally and physically. You're hurting after all that has happened today, and that's human, and only to be expected.

"I love you, Kaitlyn Montrose. And I love that you can throw a dagger better than you can throw a dinner party. I want you for you. I don't want you to be anyone else, except my Kat. My bossy, stubborn, opinionated, headstrong woman who is one hell of a fighter and who I love more than I ever thought possible to love another person."

She briefly closed her eyes with his words. Life had taken so much from her, could she really trust it wouldn't take Marcus from her, too?

"You don't have to love me back," he continued. "The love I have for you is more than enough for a strong marriage, I know it. Please say you'll marry me. Don't leave me, Kat. I need you. Please be my wife. Make me the happiest man I will ever be…"

His voice broke slightly on his last few words and Kat felt her throat tighten with emotion. This man standing in front of her, baring his heart and soul, was a man she had fallen head over heels in love with. And considering he loved her for who she was and not what she could never be, filled her with a joy she never would have thought possible on such a day.

She did love him. And damn it, if there was anything she learned today, it was that life was short, and you never were promised another day. "I love you too, Marcus."

"You do?" He seemed full of tempered hope as his eyes scanned over her, like he was checking she had actually said the words.

"Yes, I do." She placed her own hand on top

of his which was still resting against her cheek and closed her eyes, reveling in his touch. Opening her eyes, she said, "But just so we're clear, you're also bossy, stubborn, opinionated and decidedly headstrong too. It is not just me."

"You forgot to mention I'm also a very good fighter, too." He laughed aloud but then stopped. "Does that mean you will marry me?"

For a minute, the thought of marriage sent a shiver of dread through her. How could she marry? She had no idea how to be a wife and do domestic duties. Daisy had always been the one to oversee such things in their household. How could she be a proper countess for him? But then, as he'd reminded her, he'd had a proper countess and that had turned out disastrously. Perhaps he didn't need a perfect countess. Perhaps what he needed was an improper one. The thought was intriguing.

She regarded him steadily and then she knew, without a doubt, that Marcus would cherish her always, and still allow her the freedom to be herself. This was a man she'd fallen in love with, who accepted her for who she was, daggers and all. This was a man she could spend the rest of her life with. This man was her love, her life, her future. "Yes, Marcus Black, God help you, I will marry you."

With a great big whoop of delight, he scooped her into his arms and spun her around in a circle before returning her to her feet. "I love you,

Kaitlyn Montrose, and I will love you for the rest of my days."

And with that declaration, his lips lowered to hers, gently sealing his pledge.

Epilogue

"We have to return to London!" Kat declared as she slammed her fist on the breakfast table.

Marcus glanced up from his paper and had to suppress a smile at the sight of his enraged wife sitting across the table from him, a letter in one hand, her other still balled into a fist on the table. "Trouble?" He glanced at the letter she was holding.

"When is there not trouble with the *Gazette*?" Her eyes narrowed as she flickered her gaze down to the note. "Etta tells me everything is under control, but I can tell she's simply saying that to placate me. There's a group of men making a concerted effort to unmask the writer of the *Gazette*. That means Etta is in danger and I must return to protect her."

He couldn't help but raise an eyebrow as he stared down to her belly. "My darling, I don't know if you've realized it, but you're not in any state to be protecting anyone right now, especially as Dr. Harrison has given you strict instruction to rest and relax in the country."

"Dr. Harrison is a quack," she declared. "I should've known he'd suggest the same thing with me as he did with Livie when she was pregnant. He obviously wants all of the pregnant ladies out of London!"

"I'm sure that's it," Marcus said, completely straight-faced.

It was a frequently debated topic in their household but considering Dr. Harrison was one of the queen's personal physicians, Marcus was willing to argue the point, especially as Kat considered any doctor who told her to rest in the last period of her confinement, a quack. Though, at least, the doctor was a proponent of still going for walks and keeping somewhat active, just not in the smog of London. The man seemed eminently reasonable to Marcus. "Darling, if you're worried about Etta, I'll send a note to Colver and he can get some of his men to protect her."

In the intervening months, after he and Kat had married by special license, Marcus had become good friends with Sebastian Colver, the notorious Bastard of Baker Street, and the husband to one of Kat's best friends, Lady Olivia. He and Marcus had rather hit it off, which had surprised them all.

Kat all but threw up her hands. "Colver's men can't blend in in the places Etta must attend to gather intelligence for the *Gazette*. She hangs about in ballrooms, not taverns."

Marcus had noticed that at nearly eight months pregnant, his wife was definitely getting more impatient about everything. And given patience had never been her strong suit in the first place, she was coming to resemble the Dragon Duchess more and more every day. Though he dared not tell her that; she still carried her daggers upon her person, after all.

A pregnant Kat was an unpredictable Kat and he loved her all the more for it. Even now just looking at her sitting there, a rosy flush on her cheeks, her belly swollen with his child, brought a rush of satisfaction and true happiness to him. He'd never so enjoyed being a husband before, as he enjoyed being Kat's husband. "Well, I'll get Lucas to keep an eye on her, then. Will that make you happy?"

"She can't stand the man, but yes he has the skills to protect her," she reluctantly conceded. "Though you'll have to warn him to behave himself around her, and bite his tongue. I don't want Etta's feelings hurt with his wit."

"Etta can hold her own around Lucas," Marcus felt he had to point out. "She gives as good as she gets."

Kat sighed. "Yes, I suppose she does. You'll also have to warn Lucas he'll need to attend all of the events she does and keep her safe, or he'll have me to answer to, or at least he will after I'm not so physically clumsy." She glanced down at her belly with the usual look of surprise at how big she was getting.

"Oh, and tell him to keep his hands to himself," Kat added. "If he so much as flirts with, let alone seduces and compromises my dear friend, I will make him a eunuch. And you know I'm serious with that threat."

"All too well, my darling. But you do know he can't stand her, either." Although, Marcus rather suspected that Etta and Lucas hating each other so much, perhaps was a disguise for an attraction neither of them wished to admit.

"He might not be able to stand her, but he's certainly attracted to her," Kat added. "I've seen how he looks at her, and her bosom, when he thinks no one is watching."

"That's rather observant of you."

"I'm always observant, Marcus Black!"

"In situations, yes you are. But when it comes to people and their emotions? Not usually." Marcus winced at the offended look on his wife's face.

"All right, my love." He held up a hand to placate her. "I will suitably warn Lucas that he will have you to deal with if he so much as hurts a hair on Etta's head or allows anyone else to. Acceptable? Now, can you please stop worrying about the situation? It will all be fine."

"Perhaps it will. But we should return to London to make certain Etta is safe."

"Kaitlyn Montrose, we are not going back to London." He must have said the same thing a thousand times since they'd arrived a fortnight ago. An idle lifestyle was not something that suited his wife at all, though she was reluctantly prepared to endure it to ensure the safety of their unborn child. At least most of the time.

"Morning!" Sam yelled in greeting as he raced into the room with D'Artagnan in tow. He skidded to a halt in front of the bacon and bread rolls and grabbed a handful. "Sorry, I can't stay," the boy apologized as he stuffed some food into his pockets. "Mr. Jenkins reckons the mare's going to birth her foal this morning." He grinned at them both. "Bit like you will be soon, Kat." The lad winked at her before scampering from the room. "Gotta get to the stables to help him." His voice echoed from the hallway as he dashed down the corridor.

"Well, at least Sam's loving the country," Marcus remarked as he took a sip of his coffee.

Sighing, she picked up her teacup and sipped. "He does, doesn't he? I don't know how he's my brother sometimes." Suddenly, Kat rubbed her belly. "Your son is kicking me soundly right now, clearly displeased about something. Perhaps he doesn't like being sequestered in the country with nothing to do, either…"

Marcus laughed. "If our child is kicking you and not enjoying the country, then our baby is a girl, and will be just like her mother."

"Would that be such a bad thing?" she pertly replied, her chin raised.

"Most definitely."

"What?" There was outrage in her voice as she threw a bread roll at him, which he caught deftly, noting the roaring fire in her eyes. God, the woman was bloody gorgeous when she was mad.

"It's a bad thing, because if she's even as half as beautiful as you, I'll have to follow her around with a rifle and warn off any would-be suitors."

Instantly, her ire vanished, and a smile spread over her gorgeous face. "Oh, my darling, you can be quite charming in amongst your goading. I do love you."

Marcus stood up and walked across to Kat. He crouched down next to her and kissed her cheek. "As I love you, my darling." He placed a protective hand on Kat's belly and was thrilled when his baby kicked underneath his hand from inside Kat's womb. "Yes, definitely a girl, who I will love with every part of me, as I love her most amazing mother."

"Oh, Marcus," Kat gushed. "I love you with every part of me, too. Even when you vex me so and refuse to take us back to London."

"I know, my darling. I feel the same way." Marcus leaned in and inhaled the fresh scent of her hair. She smelled of soap and roses, and so delicious he felt like scooping her up in his arms and striding with her to the bed. This woman had become his heart and soul, banishing away the dark memories of a horrendous marriage that had been Elizabeth's legacy to him for years.

Thank God they'd both found the courage to give love a chance.

Because with Kat by his side, he was home and finally at peace.

Author's Note

Dear readers,

I hope you enjoyed Kat and Marcus's story as much as I enjoyed writing it! I absolutely love the Victorian era, where inventions and technology abounded at such a rapid pace that they truly changed the landscape and direction of the era.

While researching this story there were some fascinating tidbits that I discovered, which I had to incorporate, and that I thought you might appreciate reading about in more detail.

One of those relatively simple yet remarkable inventions was the snap fastener or press stud, which were so important for Kat's detachable skirts. The modern snap fastener was first patented in 1885 by a German inventor, Heribert Bauer, for use in men's trousers. Once I read about Bauer's invention, which was patented in the same year that Kat's story was set, I knew I had to incorporate them into Kat's attire, giving her the ability to actually be able to use her legs in a fight. Hence, I used my dramatic license as an author to make Madame Arnout friends with the inventor Bauer, in order for her to be able to access the snap fasteners for Kat's special skirts!

The next interesting bit of research I wanted to incorporate was the fact that in the 1880s contraceptives became much more widely available, predominately because condoms were being made from rubber, which made them more cost effective and affordable to the masses. They also became widely available for sale in chemists and stores, which meant that Kat had access to purchase some (very important for such an independent woman who needed a way to embark upon an affair with Marcus, without risking pregnancy).

Isn't history fascinating! I especially love the Victorian era because that's truly where the Industrial Revolution boomed, and there were so many wonderful new inventions and technologies, that are so much fun to use in my stories.

Anyhow, hope you enjoyed a very quick read on some of my research, and stay tuned for Etta and Lucas's story, which is next up!

Happy reading! Love, Maddison xox